TRAVELS IN ICARIA

Utopianism and Communitarianism
Lyman Tower Sargent *and* Gregory Claeys

Etienne Cabet, from E. Cabet's *Voyage et Aventures de Lord Villiam Carisdall en Icarie* (Paris: Hippolyte Souverain, 1840). Reproduction courtesy of Archives and Special Collections, Western Illinois University.

TRAVELS IN ICARIA

Etienne Cabet

Translated by Leslie J. Roberts

With a Critical Introduction by Robert Sutton

Syracuse University Press

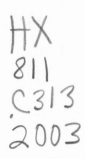

HX
811
.C313
2003

Library of Congress Cataloging-in-Publication Data

Cabet, Etienne, 1788–1856.
[Voyage en Icarie. English]
Travels in Icaria / Etienne Cabet ; translated by Leslie J. Roberts ;
with a critical introduction by Robert Sutton. — 1st ed.
p. cm. — (Utopianism and communitarianism)
ISBN 0-8156-3009-3 (pbk. : alk. paper)
1. Utopias. 2. Utopian socialism. 3. Icarian movement. I. Title.
II. Series.
HX811 .C313 2003
335'.02—dc21
2003012723

Manufactured in the United States of America

Contents

∾ Introduction

ROBERT SUTTON

Icarianism was France's last and largest flirtation with utopian socialism. In the 1840s, after the Fourierists, Saint-Simonians, and Babouvists had fizzled out, Etienne Cabet took up the crusade to create, in the words of Christopher H. Johnson, "a veritable worker's party." For a while, he was able to build one of that country's most popular utopian movements. But in 1847, following a series of setbacks and internal squabbles, he decided to emigrate to the United States. There, at five different locations between 1848 and 1898, he and his followers created one of America's longest-lived nonreligious communal experiments, a perfect society first described in his best-selling romantic novel *Voyage en Icarie* (Travels in Icaria).[1]

When the book appeared, the fifty-one-year-old Cabet had already earned a reputation as a radical republican member of the national legislature, a provocative editor of the newspaper *Le Populaire*, and a convicted felon. Born the son of a cooper in Dijon, he jumped into radical politics just after graduating from that city's law school in 1812. Because of his left-wing activities in the Côte-d'Or region, he was disbarred for one year. Soon afterward he moved to Paris and joined the Society of the Charbonnerie, a group led by Marie-Joseph Lafayette that pushed for the overthrow of the monarchy and the creation of a democratic republic. While running about the city by day on errands for the society, he found time to compose his first essay, *Exposé d'une révolution nécessaire dans le government de France* (Exposé of a necessary revolution in the government of France), which introduced some of the ideas he would later use in *Voyage en Icarie*.

In this pamphlet, Cabet called for the creation of a temporary dictator who would convene a national assembly to establish a democracy that would protect

---

1. Christopher H. Johnson, *Utopian Communism in France: Cabet and the Icarians, 1839–1851* (Ithaca: Cornell Univ. Press, 1974), 19. Robert P. Sutton, *Les Icariens: The Utopian Dream in Europe and America* (Urbana and Chicago: Univ. of Illinois Press, 1994), passim.

all citizens in "their liberty, their equality, [and] their property."[2] By the time he penned "Exposé," a crescendo of opposition was mounting against the Bourbon monarch, Charles X, and leading newspapers such as the *Patriote* and *National* demanded his abdication. Matters came to a head in the summer of 1830, when the Chamber of Deputies, backed by demonstrations in Paris and other major cities, deposed the king and replaced him with Louis Philippe, Duc d'Orléans.

When Lafayette and other members of the Charbonnerie came to power in the July Monarchy, as the new government was called, Cabet benefited from their largess. He was appointed procurer general of Corsica and on October 15, 1830, left Paris for Bastia, its capital. But he soon received the disturbing news that Louis Philippe had dismissed Lafayette as commander of the National Guard and had fired all other Charbonnerie from the government. Moreover, the king had instituted police surveillance of political organizations and threatened to begin censorship of radical newspapers. One fellow Charbonnier, Dupont de l'Eure, urged Cabet to return immediately to run for the Chamber of Deputies from his home district of Côte-d'Or. Cabet needed no encouragement to leave Corsica. On May 24, 1831, he boarded a steamboat at Bastia and headed for Dijon. With the help of the Charbonnerie, he won a majority of the district's 439 votes and in the fall of that year took his seat in the National Assembly.[3]

By this time, however, Louis Philippe was determined to suppress all opposition. He ordered the National Guard to crush an uprising of silk weavers in Lyons. In other cities, the police battled with demonstrators. When Cabet read about these outrages, he decided to write his own account of the July Monarchy, *Histoire de la révolution de 1830* (History of the revolution of 1830). It appeared in October 1832 and was an instant best-seller. Although he claimed that the book was objective, it actually was a vicious indictment of Louis Philippe. The king, he claimed, had abandoned the basic aims of the revolution—namely, to establish universal suffrage and to extend republicanism throughout Europe. More seriously, Louis had failed to alleviate the suffering of French workers, and Cabet now told the monarch what needed to be done to help them. The government must establish old age and health benefits, abolish all but luxury taxes, and institute a national system of free education.[4]

2. Etienne Cabet, "Exposé d'une révolution nécessaire dans le gouvernement de France," Archief Cabet, Manuscrits, International Instituut voor Sociale Geschiedenis, Amsterdam (hereafter IISG).

3. Johnson, *Utopian Communism*, 30–31.

4. Cabet, *Histoire de la révolution de 1830 et situation présente (sept. 1832) expliquées et éclairées par les révolutions de 1792, 1799, et 1804 et par la restauration* (Paris: A. Mie, 1832), passim.

Buoyed by public response to the book (the editor of *La Tribune*, for example, called it the "patriot's manual"), Cabet published four pamphlets in which he castigated suppression of the press and condemned "bloody and tyrannical" laws that allowed ordinary citizens to be tried by military courts. Then, in June 1834, he started his radical left-wing newspaper *Le Populaire*. In its pages, he demanded that universal suffrage be instituted immediately. Factory conditions must be improved. The people must push for their full political rights, not by violent demonstrations but "by discussion, by persuasion, by conviction, by the power of public opinion." Within a year, *Le Populaire* had more than twelve thousand subscribers.[5]

But in 1834 Cabet overstepped the boundaries of the law. In the January 12 issue, he stated that the king alone was to blame for all the oppression. He claimed that Louis was willing to have innocent Frenchmen killed to maintain power. A dangerous reactionary, Louis would "have French men shot, gunned down in the streets." The next month Cabet was arrested and arraigned before the Assize Court of the Seine. The tribunal ruled that Cabet's allegations constituted a violation of an 1819 statute that made it a felony to print anything that was an "affront to the king." The court consequently handed down the appropriate sentence: two years in prison, a 4,400 franc fine, and forfeiture of all voting and publishing rights for four years. Or, as was permitted under French law, he could choose the alternative of five years in exile. Cabet opted for exile.[6]

Arriving in London in May, he found comfortable lodging for himself, his wife, and infant daughter with Dr. Camille Berrière-Fontaine, a young physician and socialist. So accommodated, he walked every morning to the nearby British Museum, where, at his assigned desk in the Reading Room, he studied and pondered what had happened to France. By the winter of 1838, he had completed two manuscripts. The first, *Histoire populaire de la Révolution Française* (Popular history of the French Revolution), told the story of the revolution through the career of Maximilien Robespierre. He alone had brought true democracy to France and was responsible for its commitment to equality, universal public education, and freedom of religion. The Reign of Terror had been necessary to prevent the resurgence of the aristocracy. Robespierre was without ambition, a defender of democracy "against all the powers on earth, against the court,

---

5. Johnson, *Utopian Communism*, 37.

6. Cabet, *Faits préliminaires au procès devant la cour d'assises contre M. Cabet, député de la Côte-d'Or* (Paris: Rouanet, 1833), passim; *Poursuites du gouvernement contre M. Cabet* (Paris: Bureau du *Populaire*, 1834), 41–56; *Biographie de M. Cabet, ancien procureur général, ancien député. Directeur du "Populaire," et réponse aux ennemis du communisme* (Paris: Bureau du *Populaire*, 1846), 7.

against the nobility, against all the clergy, against all the aristocracy." Robespierre's ultimate goal was to abolish private property and to establish "the principle of brotherly love and equality, without exclusion." "When one looks at all the revolutions since 1789, all the corruption, all the treason," Cabet wrote, "is there no other remedy than the reordering of society?" But before this overhaul could begin, Robespierre was arrested and guillotined. Cabet described in his next book, *Voyage en Icarie*, what Robespierre had hoped to accomplish but failed to achieve.[7]

Cabet called this new social order *la communauté de biens*, or the "community of goods," and he described it in laborious detail in a novel of six hundred pages that drew upon history, political and utopian writers, and contemporary social critics. Although countless individuals, past and present, influenced his conception of utopia—he identified more than ninety authorities in chapters twelve and thirteen of the second part of the book—a few stand out: Thomas More, Louis Sébastien Mercier, and Robert Owen.

Cabet remembered that while reading More's *Utopia* for the first time in the British Museum, he had been "struck . . . in such a manner that after the first line I closed the book to plunge in deep thoughts that led me to the most complete and firm belief. . . . [I then] adopted my plan and started to write." He had suddenly realized that property was the cause of all political dissension and social misery and that the remedy, its complete eradication, must be "applied to an entire nation." Such utopian principles, Cabet wrote in *Voyage en Icarie*, "appear to us as the most advanced progress of human intelligence and the future destiny of the human family."[8] Consequently, his Icaria, like More's utopia, eliminated private property and money.

From the vast body of French fictional utopian literature, Cabet borrowed the ideas of Louis Sébastien Mercier, an obscure Bordeaux academic whose *L'An deux mille quatre cent quarante* (The year 2440) tells of a Parisian who goes to sleep, only to wake up years later in a utopia. Mercier describes a new, exciting Paris with promenades, public gardens, hospitals, theaters, libraries, and clean homes adorned with flowers. In the countryside lie productive farms where one hears the "songs of joy." The government, created by a revolution and led by "the heroism of one great man . . . a philosophic prince," is rational. France is

---

7. Cabet, *Histoire populaire de la Révolution Française, de 1789 à 1830, précédée d'une introduction contenant le précis de l'histoire des Français depuis leur origine jusqu'aux Etats Généraux*, 4 vols. (Paris: Pagnère, 1839–40), preface, 2: 539–40, 4: 91–127 and 633.

8. Cabet's remembrance of More's influence is found in *Toute la vérité au peuple ou réfutation d'un pamphlet calomniateur* (Paris: Prévot, 1842), 93. Cabet, *Voyage en Icarie* (Paris: Matlet, 1842), 480.

completely democratic because after the revolution the "philosophic prince" sees only to "the execution of the law." The nation is governed by a representative legislature, ruled by a simple majority, chosen every two years by voters in every province.[9]

Cabet also continually expressed his admiration for Robert Owen. Owen, in his weekly publication *New World Order* (published 1834 to 1845), had insisted that physical surroundings be improved in order to elevate man's moral character, that "permanent education" could increase happiness, and that total public control of property would promote the common good. Although Cabet rejected some of Owen's concepts, such as his "confidence in the goodness of sovereigns," he lifted the Welsh philanthropist's environmentalism almost intact for his own utopia. Fictional Icaria is a model of Owenite urban planning and hygiene; its system of universal education mirrors the plan in *New World Order*.[10]

It is interesting to note how little Cabet relied on French socialists. Although he briefly cited Charles Fourier and the Comte de Saint-Simon (Claude Henri Rouvroy) in the second part of the book, he thought both men had concocted a "defective community" because neither one advocated elimination of private property and money. He had no patience with Fourier's argument that the free play of human passions could create social harmony. And he openly rejected Saint-Simon's argument that a hierarchy of talent could lead men and women to utopia.

Cabet decided to publish his ideas as a romantic novel to avoid arrest for violating French press laws against seditious writings. Although there is little mystery about Cabet's choice of a literary format, debate persists about why he called his utopia Icaria. Some historians believe he had in mind Icarus, the mythical Greek youth who flew too close to the sun with wax wings and died. Cabet, though, never referred to this story. Historian Sylvester Piotrowski argued that Icaria referred to a slogan popular at the time of the French Revolution, *Ça ira*, or "it will succeed," but only circumstantial evidence supports this argument.

9. Louis Sébastien Mercier, *L'an deux mille quatre cent quarante* (Philadelphia: T. Dobson, 1795), 11, 84, 136, 262–64, 311–12, 316; Frank Manuel and Fritzie P. Manuel, eds., *French Utopias: An Anthology of Ideal Societies* (New York: Schocken, 1971), 7–16, 329–44.

10. Cabet, *Voyage en Icarie*, 518–20. Cabet's letter to Owen of August 15, 1847, indicates that they met frequently when in London. The letter and other relevant communication regarding the Peters Concession is in the Robert Owen Correspondence, Manchester Union Co-operative (microfilm in the Illinois Historical Survey, Univ. of Illinois, Champaign-Urbana); hereafter "Owen Correspondence." See also Owen to Cabet, August 10, 1851, published in *Le Populaire*, July 15, 1851.

The simplest explanation comes from Cabet himself. He told his readers that the people of his mythical country had adopted the name of Icaria out of veneration for their hero, the "immortal Icar," the "regenerator of the native land," who had established the republic in the glorious revolution of 1782.[11]

Voyage en Icarie

Cabet's novel recounts the journey of a young English nobleman, Lord William Carisdall, to an island nation located somewhere off the coast of East Africa. Through Carisdall and the people he meets, Cabet describes every detail of the "community of goods" created during the fifty years following a great revolution in 1782. Carisdall is at various times "amazed," "astonished," and "delighted" at what he sees. He strikes up a close friendship with his guide, Valmor, and soon falls in love with Valmor's fiancée, Dinaïse! The Icarian historian Dinaros explains to Carisdall how the nation was founded in 1782, when Prime Minister Lixdox and Queen Cloramide, the last of a series of evil tyrants, were deposed after a bloody fight. The revolutionaries chose their leader, "the good Icar," as temporary dictator, and under his benevolent rule they created "the republic and the community."[12] By the time of Icar's death in 1812, the nation named after him had become a democracy without property or money.

Icaria is divided politically into one hundred provinces, each subdivided into ten equal communes. A council elected by all the adult males governs every province. Every year the same electorate also chooses two thousand delegates for the National Assembly and an executive body (a president and a council) that enforces laws passed by the Assembly. There are, of course, no political parties. The Assembly decides all aspects of daily life: for example, food distribution, housing, work assignments, transportation, and education. If the people do not like a particular statute, they can call a referendum. The government, Dinaros concludes, is a pure democracy. "Everywhere here," he brags, "you will see equality and happiness".[13]

In the center of Icaria stands the majestic capital of Icara. This symmetrical city has gardens, wide perpendicular streets, promenades, public buildings, monuments, stadiums, theaters, and countless works of art. Icarians are obsessed

11. Sylvester A. Piotrowski, *Etienne Cabet and the "Voyage en Icarie": A Study in the History of Social Thought* (Washington, D.C.: Catholic Univ. Press, 1935), 76–77; Janis Clark Fotion, "Cabet and Icarian Communism" (Ph.D. diss., Univ. of Iowa, 1966), 118; Cabet, *Voyage en Icarie*, 308, 337–47.

12. Cabet, *Voyage en Icarie*, 40.

13. Ibid., 39.

with hygiene and locate their industries (factories and slaughterhouses) outside the city limits. The economy rests upon a highly mechanized system of workshops and farms that the workers themselves, women as well as men, both manage and operate. Conditions are ideal because machines have eliminated the dirt and drudgery of production. All work stops at one o'clock in the afternoon, and the rest of the day is free for leisure activities.

The farms are as efficient as the factories. Large family units raise crops with the latest in mechanization based on scientific information published in a national agricultural journal. Carisdall describes the idyllic Icarian farm, where land is geometrically arranged with acres set aside for grains, pasture, and orchards. As in the factory, cleanliness is the rule. He finds "everything clean . . . orderly . . . comfortable and elegant." Moreover, his Icarian guide and companion Valmor tells him that the harvests have increased a dozen times in the past fifty years. According to a plan adopted by the committees of the Assembly, the state distributes factory and farm products to each family every day on an extensive system of railroads, canals, and roads.[14]

No aspect of Icarian life fascinates Carisdall more than the system of education. The state provides free and equal facilities for both sexes from childhood through adult life. Its goal is not just to accumulate knowledge but to make each citizen a loyal member of the community. The curriculum is rigorous: agronomy, science, history, mathematics, literature, drawing, music. After completing this basic education at the age of eighteen (for males) or seventeen (for females), some young Icarians continue one to four more years of specialized training in a scientific, professional, or industrial pursuit; others enter on-the-job training in factories and farms. At all stages of education, the Icarians indoctrinate their youth with ideals of filial devotion, brotherly love, and honesty. They are given regular lectures on civic conduct that emphasize the duties and responsibilities of citizens and office holders. They are shown how to apply all knowledge to promote the highest standards of proper conduct in community politics, work, and play.[15]

Icarians love to play; in fact, they would rather play than work. Every afternoon, after the factories close, the state sponsors free entertainment. Thousands attend public shows, almost all with a strong political message, in large amphitheaters. In these same amphitheaters, they celebrate Icarian Independence Day (June 14, 1782). This annual commemoration of Icar's triumph over Lixdox and Cloramide brings out twenty thousand children, eighty thousand adults, a

14. Ibid., 145–65.
15. Ibid., 73–96, 126–27, 131–35.

marching band of six hundred drummers and ten thousand instruments that fills the air with "various tunes of victory and triumph." The show ends after dark with a fireworks display that fills the sky with "a thousand fires that burst into the air from all sides and cross each other in all directions, displaying a thousand colors and shapes." The finale is a balloon ascension of "a hundred balloons scattered five or six hundred feet above the city," eventually discharging "a great rain of stars and fires on the city."[16]

Icarians attend dances and concerts, go to the theater, and enjoy promenades and picnics. Carisdall witnesses one such dance, where he describes a panoply of dancing and waltzing couples as well as children and old folks. He marvels at how "finally everyone danced together, all ages and sexes, forming the most lively of spectacles." Their theatrical productions are more extravagant than their dances. Sixty plays are staged every year. The state sends tickets to each family, and if they want to see a different play than the one assigned by the government, they just exchange tickets with other families through a public bulletin board system. Of course, the productions are splendid. After seeing one, Eugene, a French visitor to Icaria, exclaims: "these beautiful outfits, these decorations: everything is magnificent." "The opera houses in London and Paris," he admits, "are no more beautiful than this one."[17]

Such pastimes are not considered frivolous distractions because a sober motif permeates all leisure activity. Carisdall is told that a committee of the National Assembly approves in advance all Icarian enjoyments and always chooses those activities that instill a patriotic and moral message. Dinaros emphasizes that they had wisely imposed on themselves three fundamental rules: "The first is that all our amusements must be sanctioned by the law or by the people. The second is that we may not seek the pleasurable until we have provided ourselves with that which is necessary and useful. The third is that we do not allow any pleasures other than those that every Icarian can enjoy equally."[18]

The Icarian family consists of a kin group of related people, as many as forty individuals. Valmor informs Carisdall that all adults must marry for life. Celibacy is looked upon with suspicion. Adultery, concubinage, and seduction are inexcusable. Even though marriage is extolled as sacred, divorce is easy to obtain so that the man and woman can remarry. Outside of the home, the sexes are usually separated, in factories for either women or men and in hospitals where women physicians attend only females and male doctors attend only males. Adult

16. Ibid., 266.
17. Ibid., 204, 222.
18. Ibid., 272.

women, although occupying important professions, have no political power and are required only to participate in the state-sponsored amusements with their husbands or families.[19]

The cohesive family ties and strict code of behavior between the sexes assure that public morality is evident everywhere in Icaria. Carisdall sees no prostitutes, no nude statues or paintings, and no graffiti. Icaria has no saloons and gambling houses. Tobacco, available only in pharmacies, is used only for medicinal purposes. Valmor says that crimes have disappeared because there are no motives to commit them. "What crimes do you imagine we could have today," he asks Carisdall, "when we have no money and when everyone has everything he or she could desire? Wouldn't you have to be mad to steal? And how could there be assassinations, fires, or poisoning," he continued, "when stealing is impossible? How could there even be suicides when everybody is happy?" Minor infractions of the rules happen from time to time, but such rare misdemeanors are punished by public ridicule or suspension of admission to the theater or spectacles.[20]

Icarian religion, like the family, reinforces the community's high moral standards. Icarians have no use for formal, organized religion with a required creed, priesthood, and liturgy; these institutions are condemned as pillars of the old tyranny. Valmor boasts that his countrymen have "replaced the expressions *god*, *divinity*, *religion*, *church*, and *priest* by new expressions that were so perfectly defined that they could not give rise to any ambiguity." Icarians practice a simple ethic: "Love your neighbor as yourself. Do not do any wrong to others that you would not want done to you. Do unto others all the good that you wish for yourself." Each Icarian gives thanks to the divinity "as he pleases within the confines of his own home." Children are taught religion only by talking about it with their family. At the age of seventeen, they are given what amounts to a course in the history and philosophy of past religions and are encouraged to adopt those opinions that suit their conscience. "Our religion," Valmor states, "is no more than a moral and philosophical system and has no other use than to lead men to love one another as brothers."[21]

The capital city of such an upstanding community is a model of later twentieth-century urban planning, of Lewis Mumfords's *"rus in urb,"* with its landscaping, foliage, gardens, and promenades. Cabet anticipated prefabricated construction. Icarians have incombustible fabrics and wood. Every home has indoor plumbing, with the sewage removed to a central sanitary processing plant.

19. Ibid., 113–14, 136, 139–43.
20. Ibid., 96.
21. Ibid., 169, 171.

Music is piped into the hospitals "by an invisible machine." All clothing is standardized and mass-produced by machines. The Icarians have a new energy source produced by *sorub* that would revolutionize railroad transportation. Cabet even anticipated astro-turf by having a stadium covered with a "soil" that "is perfectly level, composed of a wetted mastic that turns neither to mud nor dust."[22]

In *Voyage en Icarie*, Cabet describes a totally integrated community whose various parts reinforce each other. Its ordered and mechanized economy provide every citizen with the necessities of life. Its egalitarian education stimulates and sustains fundamental values of brotherly love and devotion to community. Leisure pastimes reinforce patriotism. Family mores create righteous citizens and eliminate crime. Religion, with its emphasis on individual application of the Golden Rule, unifies everyone in a bond of public virtue.

In fact, Cabet draws a picture of an eclectic, contradictory utopia. He never deals adequately with the question of what would happen to all those workers displaced by mechanization. Also, he merely assumes that Icaria's ever-growing economy will never result in useless surpluses. His workers, separated by sex, are unrealistically happy and content and are seemingly unaffected by boredom, lack of incentive, and overregimentation. He never reconciles his statements about sexual equality with what he labels the "natural differences" between men and women. For example, he claims that women are born with the same intellectual abilities as men and should be educated as equals. Marriage demands "equality between spouses, with the husband's voice merely carrying the most weight." The drudgery of housework is eliminated by state services such as those that provide daily food and laundered clothing. Yet Icarian women are second-class citizens. In fact, they are not citizens in the political sense of the word because they cannot vote or hold office. They are expected to continue doing all the household chores. Their education often leads to simple, assembly-line jobs in the workshops, where they have to maintain hours of total silence. They are encouraged to choose clothing that matches their hair color. They are forbidden to have any unsupervised conduct with men. They must choose marriage partners with whom they are compatible genetically.

In Icaria, both men and women surrender personal freedom in exchange for order and security. There is no freedom of the press because every provincial journal and the national newspaper are printed by the government. There is total censorship. Early in its history, the republic burned most books because the assembly judged them subversive and, in Valmor's words, not "the expression of

22. Ibid., 15, 112, 256.

our public opinion." Only one official history of the community, Dinaros informs Carisdall, has ever been written.[23]

Without realizing it, Cabet creates a paradox. He sketches a society of complete harmony, security, and fraternity where the Assembly and the executive department carry out the will of an educated electorate. Men and women are virtually equal socially and economically. Education is outstanding, cultural life varied and satisfying, religion undogmatic, and crime nonexistent. This same society, however, destroys individual choice by an oppressive "tyranny of the majority," in the words of Alexis de Tocqueville. In Icaria, citizens are, in fact, prohibited from thinking or acting as individuals and proscribed from expressing any self-interest.

Cabet published *Voyage en Icarie* in three parts in a two-volume first edition; subsequent editions combined the parts into a one-volume, six-hundred-page text. The first part recounts Carisdall's visit to Icaria. The second part spells out the history of Icaria and is weighted down with long verbatim quotations from ancient and contemporary writers who endorsed the idea of a community without property and money. The third part explains the philosophy of such a community and ends with the admonition that in order to understand the meaning of Icaria, the reader must re-read all three parts.

Because publishing all three parts would be prohibitively expensive, Syracuse University Press is publishing at this time only part one. There is important precedent for this decision. In 1970, the French publishing house of Anthropos reissued part one (in the original French) with a scholarly introduction for the same reason. In part one, Cabet displays best his inventiveness and forceful political rhetoric. The translation of part one of *Voyage en Icarie* will be of value to scholars as well as to a popular audience. A limited edition of a translation of the full work was published in 1985 and, although unavailable for purchase, can be obtained by interlibrary loan.

Icarianism in France

Cabet's exile ended in the spring of 1839, and that summer, after he returned to Paris, the first edition of the novel appeared as *Voyage et aventures de Lord William Carisdall en Icarie*. Rather than have his name on the title page as the author, Cabet had the page read that the book was "translated from the English version of Francis Adams by Theodore Dufruit, certified scholar of languages."

23. Ibid., 108, 197–98. Diana Marie Garno, "Gendered Utopia: Women in the Icarian Experience, 1840–48" (Ph.D. diss., Wayne State Univ., 1998), passim.

He was deeply concerned that the book might violate French press laws, and in the preface he claimed that it was only a "model" to get people thinking, a "travelogue," certainly not a call for political action. His precautions were unnecessary. As it turned out, the six-month probation required by the press laws passed without incident; thereafter, all subsequent editions were entitled *Voyage en Icarie*, and Cabet boldly listed himself as the author.

By 1840, France was gripped by rising hysteria over mounting labor violence. Communists had led strikes in Lyons, Belleville, and Rouen against layoffs, unsafe factory conditions, and soaring bread prices. In Paris that autumn, a communist attempted to assassinate Louis Philippe. In March 1841, the police raided a communist meeting in a Paris suburb. Shortly afterward, the government closed down the leading communist newspaper, *Le Travail*, in Lyons. By that summer, 137 men had been arrested and found guilty of sedition.[24]

Ironically, the fear of communism, with its attendant violence, worked in Cabet's favor because he alone among the communist writers in France condemned violence. Indeed, at the beginning of *Voyage en Icarie* he emphasizes that the community of goods was created by gradual, peaceful change after the tyrants were overthrown in only two days of fighting. Such a pitch was especially attractive to skilled artisans, who soon became the heart of the Icarian movement in France. These craftsmen abhorred the ignorant, unskilled laborers who were flocking to the communist rallies and marching in strikes, yet they hated the bourgeoisie and their cry for law and order at the expense of basic rights. Cabet gave these artisans an alternative to alliance with the violent communists or submission to the bourgeoisie-dominated authorities: the community of goods with its democracy, healthy environment, strong family structure, and ethic of brotherly love. In a word, at a time of a rising reaction against communism in France, Cabet, in *Voyage en Icarie*, rescued its essential message—the creation of a propertyless society—and made it respectable, at least for a while.

Early in 1841, Cabet resurrected *Le Populaire*, and its first issue on March 14 announced it as "the newspaper of social and political reorganization." He levied the same charge that had gotten him arrested seven years earlier: the government was ready to use force to crush both its opponents and civil liberty. France, Cabet wrote, had degenerated into "egotism and political indifference." He asked French men and women to "brave all obstacles" and praised them for their "good sense, justice, and . . . humanity." He called for the establishment of the community of goods "only by the power of public opinion, by the will of the nation, and by the rule of law." "Communists and reformists," he concluded, must

24. Johnson, *Utopian Communism*, 68–78.

"unite for our common defense. . . . Let us shun everyone who could alter our brotherly love; let us discuss our doctrines and principles, for . . . tolerance and moderation."[25]

The newspaper, always organized in two sections, quickly became one of the most widely read journals in the country. One section featured domestic problems and how Icarian ideas could solve them. The other half contained letters to the editor and accounts of governmental attacks on workers (such as police raids, mock trials, and violence against strikers). After describing such atrocities, Cabet repeated the same message: "None of this in Icaria!"

The pages of *Le Populaire* emphasized four basic themes: nationalism, feminism, a new feudalism, and the equation of Icarianism with Christianity. Cabet argued that France should lead the fight against the reactionary governments of Europe just as it had done in 1794. Failing to carry the flag of republicanism on the continent, he said, was a national disgrace. He claimed that working women were degraded and their innate beauty destroyed, that wives were considered a form of property with few or no legal rights. He wrote that France was ruled by the "lords of wealth" who now controlled the Chamber of Deputies and enacted laws that benefited only their interests. The consequences were such evils as the creation of monopolies, the suppression of unions, and the destruction of the free press. He claimed that the community of goods and Christianity were one and the same. Christ was the "great communist" who condemned private property and wealth. When Christ referred to the kingdom of God on earth, he meant a community without property or money. He wanted the establishment of "the equality and fraternity of men, the freeing of women, the abolition of opulence and misery . . . the creation of the community of goods."[26]

Cabet's language in *Le Populaire* was as flowery as that of *Voyage en Icarie*. Workers were "squeezed like grapes." The factory was a "battlefield." The new feudal lords "trampled upon honest workers and devoured them." The prevailing "torrent" of free competition was a war of "the strong against the weak" that resulted in unemployment, long hours, and low wages. The nation was disintegrating into anarchy and was held together only by the power of the entrenched elite. To avoid a final calamity, French men and women had to organize into a political party and overhaul the country from top to bottom by eliminating all private property.

In September 1841, Cabet published *Ma ligne droite, ou le vrai chemin du salut*

25. *Le Populaire*, Mar. 14, 1841.
26. Ibid., Sept. 11, 1842.

pour le peuple (My straight line, or the true path of salvation for the people). In this pamphlet, he denounced violence as "useless" because it gave the government an excuse for "pillages, murders, searches, arrests, and seizures." The people had to disband secret societies and stay away from demonstrations. The best strategy for them to follow, he advised, was to practice "civil courage," to become aware of their rights, and to use them when arrested. Only by such informed passive resistance and forbearance could the people fight governmental repression.[27]

To back up such propaganda, Cabet organized Icarian chapters in all major cities, linked to his headquarters in Paris at the office of *Le Populaire*. Lyon became the largest center of Icarianism in the provinces, with 553 followers led by a factory foreman named Champius. At Reims, a salesman named Charles Chameroy, aided by a weaver named Eugene Butot, recruited 443 signatures. The tailor Pedron at Nantes signed up 98 Icarians. At Tours, the physician Desmoulins listed 150 supporters. At Marseilles, a shoemaker's tools salesman named Coignard claimed 115 converts. And so it went in thirty-three cities.

At the capital, Cabet kept the financial records and edited *Le Populaire*. Around him, three assistants—the Polish mystic Louis Krolikowski, the tailor Firman Favard, and the cabinetmaker Jean Pierre Beluze—maintained regular communication with the chapter leaders, called *correspondants*, who received and distributed *Le Populaire*, collected donations from chapter members, and organized meetings. By 1845, Cabet claimed a following of about 100,000 men and women, or *communistes Icariens*, in seventy-nine of the nation's one hundred departments. Professor Christopher Johnson has rightly observed that by then "Icarian communism had come to France."[28]

The typical Icarian was a literate married craftsman (his wife could join, too, but there were few single women in the movement) between the ages of thirty and fifty with a penchant for altruism and moralism. Icarians denounced violence and turned to Cabet's ideas as the only solution to the struggle between the riotous, illiterate day worker and the repressive bourgeoisie-dominated July Monarchy. The day laborer had no patience with Cabet's lofty intellectuality and high-minded appeals to brotherly love and the salvation of mankind. Middle-class shopkeepers and businessmen, always respectable, saw no difference between the *communistes Icariens* and the violent riffraff of the labor strikes: both groups wanted to destroy private property, the foundation of society.[29]

27. Cabet, *Ma ligne droite, ou le vrai chemin du salut pour le peuple* (Paris: Prévot, 1841), 17.
28. Johnson, *Utopian Communism*, 108, 185–206, quotation on 144.
29. Ibid., 153–57.

The skilled artisans who became Icarians lived in cities where the factory system was fast replacing the traditional backyard craft shop with its masters and apprentices whose families had often done the same work for generations. Now these proud workers saw all around them large shops with more than twenty employees, all turning out standardized products on an assembly line. They saw a future where they soon would be nothing more than hirelings of a bourgeoisie entrepreneur.

In letters to *Le Populaire*, these craftsmen vented their frustrations. They lamented their exploitation by "mercantile selfishness." The "egotistical bourgeoisie" violated all their rights. They wrote of "the haunting reality of an intolerable world." Professor Jacques Rancière's 1985 investigation into the Icarian temperament discovered an obsessive melancholy colored by misery and despair. France would never change. A Nantes Icarian wrote that "death is preferable to life in the wretched society of today." Another Icarian from Périgueux told Cabet that even material things did not matter because they were only "ornaments" and that life was not worth living.[30]

Yet this same Périgueux Icarian confided that as soon as he read *Voyage en Icarie*, his courage revived: now the promise of Icaria "gives us certainty of a better future." Turgard, a Parisian maker of artificial flowers, rejoiced that he saw in Cabet's utopia "paradise on earth, men living as brothers, each sharing with the other according to need and capability, equality, unity, community—in short, one for all and all for one." Emile Vallet, a Le Mans shoemaker read *Voyage en Icarie* and told Cabet that "the theory was beautiful" and that his own family was committed to creating "a society where reason and conscience would rule. . . . Without king or priest. . . . No poor, no rich. No tyranny, no oppression. A paradise on earth."[31] The wife of a Lyon Icarian said that Cabet's ideas had made her husband withdraw from dangerous secret societies that had exposed him to arrest. Now "we no longer fear those dreadful searches," she wrote. She could go with her husband to open Icarian meetings and "discuss things together." Another woman from Angou flatly proclaimed, "What happy women are the women of Icaria!"[32]

In 1846, Cabet published his next book, *Le vrai Christianisme suivant Jésus-Christ* (The true Christianity according to Jesus Christ). In this lengthy historical

30. *Le Populaire*, June 6, 1848; Jacques Rancière, *The Night of Labor: The Workers' Dream in Nineteenth-Century France*, translated by John Drury (Philadelphia: Temple Univ. Press, 1989), 361.

31. *Le Populaire*, June 6, 1841; Turgard to Cabet, 8 Feb. 1841, Papiers Cabet, Bibliothèque historique de la Ville de Paris (hereafter BHVP).

32. *Le Populaire*, Nov. 13, 1842, Oct. 31, 1846, Sept. 5, 1847.

narrative of Jesus, the apostles, and the early Church Fathers, Cabet tried to prove that "communism is Christianity." Both emphasize brotherly love because in both "all men are brothers . . . and only form one family." Both insist upon pacifism. Both stress "the community" and the "general, social, and common interest." "It is an evident and a manifest fact," he wrote, "that *Christianity* for the Apostles, for the first Christians, for the fathers of the church, was *communism*. . . . Yes, Jesus Christ was a communist!" Moreover, Christ, in preaching salvation, meant "an earthly kingdom of God." Icaria, the community of goods, "realizes this terrestrial paradise and [its] possible perfections; it is above all the communist who ought to admire, love, and invoke Jesus Christ and his doctrine."[33]

At that point, Icarianism began to change from a political movement into a messianic crusade. By the time Cabet wrote *Le vrai Christianisme*, he had profoundly altered his thinking. In *Voyage en Icarie*, Christian morality, or the Golden Rule, was just one part of his vision. He now reorganized his plan of a secular utopia to comply with Christian eschatology. As a result, almost immediately after the appearance of *Le vrai Christianisme* some of his followers elevated him from a political leader to savior of humankind. Other Icarians applauded his compassion for the oppressed, his Christ-like dedication to exposing hypocrisy. An undated letter to the Paris office signed by "Encontre" is typical of the correspondence that began pouring into *Le Populaire*. After lofty praise of Cabet's greatness, Encontre ends: "Hail to Citizen Cabet, who has understood the sublime mission! Hail to the apostle of eternal truths! Hail to the stringent supporter of democracy! Hail to the father of the worker! Hail to the continuer of *true Christianity!* Hail to the creator of blessed Icaria! Hail to the champion of justice, to the defender of the rights of men, to the hero of brotherly love! Hail to Citizen Cabet."[34] Less than a year after the publication of *Le vrai Christianisme*, Cabet called his Icarians to follow him to an earthly paradise at the edge of civilization, along the Trinity River in Texas.

The decision to emigrate was not an impulsive one, however. As early as March 1843, Cabet had expressed a hope to build a "small community" in America someday. In another letter to the Democratic Society of London, he said that it would have to be a "small community," a "place where everyone could join hands." It would contain "elite men . . . superior in their ability . . . character . . . devotion," who would be able to obtain "all the *necessary funds*." In a letter to Dr. Berrière-Fontaine the next year, he again mentioned a "great project" and prom-

33. Cabet, *Le vrai Christianisme suivant Jésus-Christ* (Paris: Bureau du *Populaire*, 1846), 160, 165–96, 234–50, 267, 386, 622, 627–29, 619–20.

34. Encontre au citoyen Cabet, n.d., Papiers Cabet, BHVP.

ised to provide details later. But there is no doubt that the reaction to *Le vrai Christianisme* was the key factor in his final decision because that response convinced him that he was, in the words of one letter printed in the *Le Populaire*, "the living martyr to the cause of the brotherhood of man." Small wonder that in August 1846 Cabet claimed that "Only communism can say: I am the resurrection and the life."[35]

Cabet's altered self-image as a martyr to the cause of humanity coincided with new problems within chapters of the Icarian movement. In the fall of 1846, the country was hit by a severe depression brought on by the failure of the wheat harvest. The price of bread soared to unprecedented levels, and inflation set in on all fronts. Unemployment rose and bread riots multiplied. Ignoring Cabet's teaching, Icarians became frequent participants in the violence. Many artisans, the backbone of Icarianism, became infected with "an attitude of desperation," in the words of Christopher Johnson. Some of them, such as Louis Desmoulins, the head of the Tours chapter, told Cabet to abandon his pacifism, to join with the militant communists, and to make all workers a force for change in France. He also told Cabet that some rank-and-file members were deeply frustrated with his timidity and that other Icarians were coming to believe that he was "the sole obstacle that prevents the Communist Party" from taking control of the government.[36]

Then in the spring of 1847, compounding internal dissension, the authorities cracked down. The prefect of the Paris police ordered surveillance of editors who exacerbated the growing unrest. Cabet learned that the minister of the interior, Count Tanneguy Duchatel, had decided that *Le Populaire* was a dangerous newspaper that inflamed "popular passions" and that its editor should be arrested. At the same time, Cabet heard of Icarians being harassed in the provinces. In Mirecourt and Toulon, his followers were dismissed from their jobs; at Nantes, the police tried unsuccessfully to arrest Icarians for nailing up communist posters.[37]

On March 19, Cabet brought up the emigration scheme once more in a letter to Berrière-Fontaine. He boasted that he was confident that "a thousand workers of all sorts . . . the elite of the people, would follow me there." He asked

35. *Le Populaire*, Feb. 26, Mar. 26, May 26, June 27, Aug. 28, 1846. "Cabet to the French Democratic Society of London," 1843, Archief Cabet, IISG; Cabet to Camille Berrière-Fontaine, Apr. 7, 1844, Cabet Collection, Southern Illinois Univ.-Edwardsville, folder 2, no. 29 (hereafter SIUE).

36. Johnson, *Utopian Communism*, 235–37; Desmoulins to Cabet, Nov. 26, 1846, Papiers Cabet, BHVP.

37. Johnson, *Utopian Communism*, 237–38.

Berrière-Fontaine what he thought of the idea. Berrière-Fontaine told him: "Don't say anything more about colonies." On April 20, Cabet again wrote to say that he was going to America. Emigration was "the only means to avoid persecution." Berrière-Fontaine wrote back in desperation: colonization was a waste of time; it would succeed only on a very small scale and would have no effect "on the vices of the current social order." But his advice came too late. The combined pressures of internal discontent among Icarians, harassment of loyal disciples throughout France, and the imminent threat of arrest intensified Cabet's messianic zeal. On May 9, 1847, he announced in bold type on the front page of *Le Populaire: "Allons en Icarie!"* (Let's go to Icaria!)[38]

But Cabet had no idea where to go or how to get there. He immediately turned to Robert Owen, whom he had met while in London, hoping that he might have some idea of how to plan an Icarian community in America. He asked a mutual friend, T. W. Thorton, an English Owenite then in Paris, to contact Owen about a meeting. He also wrote to Charles Sully, a young French Icarian living in London, and told him to get in touch with the Welsh philanthropist. Through the efforts of these two men, a September meeting was arranged with Owen in London.[39]

Cabet arrived in London on September 9 and went to see Owen the following morning. Owen told Cabet of a golden opportunity to acquire free land in Texas through a scheme already suggested to him earlier that year by William Snelling Peters, agent for a large Texas land company. Peters had proposed that Owen himself plant a colony along the Trinity River because of the area's "astonishing productivity . . . and temperate, bountiful, healthy climate." Although Owen told Peters he was no longer interested in colonization, he passed on to Cabet the essentials of the Peters plan. If the Icarians could come up with one thousand colonists, they would be given 3,000 acres of free land along the banks of the Trinity River. They had only to establish homesteads on the land by July 1, 1848. There was one curious stipulation, though. The land allocated in the "Pe-

38. *Le Populaire*, May 9, 1847.

39. Ibid., Apr. 20, May 30, Sept. 26, Nov. 28, 1847. Cabet to Berrière-Fontaine, Mar. 19, 1847, Cabet Collection, SIUE, folder 2, no. 29. Berrière-Fontaine told Cabet that there was little support in London for emigration. See Berrière-Fontaine to Cabet, Apr. 27, 1847, Papiers Cabet, BHVP. The story of the dealings with William Snelling Peters is in the letters of Charles Sully to Robert Owen, Aug. 17, 1847; T. W. Thorton to Owen, Jan. 25, July 5, 1847; W. S. Peters to Owen, Mar. 5, June 7, 1847: Owen Correspondence, nos. 1445, 1447, 1457, 1472. The best account of the Texas land company is in Seymour Connor, *The Peters Colony of Texas: A History and Biographical Sketches of the Early Settlers* (Austin: Texas State Historical Association, 1959).

ters Concession," as Cabet would hereafter call the deal, was in *alternate* half sections of 320 acres. The other contiguous tracts were reserved for the Peters Company and the state of Texas to sell later on. In other words, the concession was a checkerboard where an integrated Icaria that Cabet had planned could not possibly be created.[40]

Cabet nevertheless accepted the Concession, returned to Paris, and announced in *Le Populaire: "C'est au Texas!"* (It's in Texas!). He said he would send Sully to America to organize the expedition. He would establish admissions committees in the cities to recruit emigrants and to collect the registration fee of 600 francs for each person going to America. There would be an Icarian uniform and an anthem. The First Advance Guard of the "Soldiers of Humanity" would leave for Texas in a matter of months. Cabet never mentioned the checkerboard land survey.[41] He put out a pamphlet called *Prospectus: Grande émigration au Texas, en Amérique, pour réaliser la communauté d'Icarie* (Prospectus: Great emigration to Texas in America in order to implement the Icarian community), in which he claimed that he had contracted for a million acres of "salubrious, fertile" land along the Trinity River, made up of "woods and prairies, well watered, whose climate resembles that of Italy." The site was accessible by a pleasant steamboat trip from New Orleans on the Mississippi and Red Rivers and by a short overland trip on "the national road of Bonham" to the Peters tract.[42]

Most Icarians wanted nothing to do with Cabet's Texas venture. Subscriptions to *Le Populaire* dropped by 30 percent. Twenty-eight of the ninety-four Icarians in Nantes signed a letter that told Cabet to fight out the course of humanity in France. A majority of the members of the Lyons chapter said the same thing and added that they had no desire to flee France as "fugitives." Some Icarians complained that although they might consider going to America, the 600 francs per person emigration fee was far out of reach for the unskilled or apprentice worker whose average weekly pay was about only 12 francs. "The doors of Icaria," one Parisian complained, "are forever closed to us." Cabet ignored these

40. T. W. Thornton to Owen, Aug. 6, 1847; Charles Sully to Owen, Aug. 14, 1847; Cabet to Owen, Aug. 18, 1847; W. S. Peters to Owen, July 9, 1847: Owen Correspondence, nos. 1497, 1502, 1503, 1534.

41. *Le Populaire*, Nov. 14, 1847; Jules Prudhommeaux, *Icarie et son fondateur Etienne Cabet* (Paris: Edouard Cornély et Cie, 1907), 203–15, 219–23. Cabet to Berrière-Fontaine, Jan. 20, Jan. 25, Feb. 6, Feb. 21, 1848, Cabet Collection, SIUE, folder 2, no. 29.

42. Cabet, *Prospectus: Grande émigration au Texas, en Amérique, pour réaliser la communauté d'Icarie* (Paris: Bureau du *Populaire*, 1848). W. S. Peters discusses *Prospectus* in a letter to Robert Owen, Nov. 2, 1847, Owen Correspondence, no. 1529.

protests and stated in *Le Populaire* that there was enthusiastic response to the Texas emigration among the "majority" of Icarians.[43]

On September 18, 1847, immediately after the meeting with Owen, Cabet published *Contrat social*, in which he laid out the rules for the Texas Icaria. He would be the temporary dictator of the community and would have all power "that was indicated in *Voyage en Icarie* and all that would continue to be outlined in an Icarian program." He alone would approve new members, control finances, make all purchases, and administer the daily economic life of the community. He would have "all moral responsibility." After the temporary transition period was over and community life had stabilized, he would call for elections and establish democracy. *Contrat social* only alienated more Icarians. Jean Baptiste Millère, a Bordeaux lawyer, called the plan "degenerate" and accused Cabet of trying to create an absolute monarchy worse than any seen in the Old Order. An "old patriot" from Toulouse told Cabet that he wanted nothing to do with such despotism.[44]

Cabet was impervious to these criticisms. By the end of January 1848, he had organized the First Advance Guard of sixty-nine men. He appointed Adolphe Gouhenant, a forty-three-year-old Toulouse sign painter and leader of that city's Icarian chapter, as head of the Guard. On January 3, they left Paris by train for Le Havre. On the morning of February 3, the "great departure" was ready. The Guard, dressed in black velour tunics and gray felt caps, huddled on the wharf. Bystanders gathered to observe the spectacle.

Cabet stood before the departees and bellowed: "Are you loyal adherents . . . to the *contrat social?*"

"Yes!"

"Are you sincerely devoted to the cause of communism?"

"Yes!"

"Are you willing to endure hardship for the benefit of humanity?"

"Yes!"

In silent procession, they marched aboard the ship *Rome* and assembled on the stern deck. As the boat slipped out to sea, they bellowed the couplets of their new anthem, "Chant du départ Icarien" (Song of departure), to the tune of a traditional song from the French Revolution.

43. Cabet, *Réalisation d'Icarie, grande émigration en Amérique* (Paris: Bureau du *Populaire*, 1849–50), 6: 262. *Le Populaire*, Apr. 11, July 4, July 15, Aug. 20, Oct. 10, Oct. 31, Nov. 18, 1847. See also F. Le Chapt to Cabet, May 27, 1847, Papiers Cabet, BHVP.

44. *Le Populaire*, Sept. 19, Nov. 28, 1847.

Arise, workers bent down in the dust,
The hour of awakening has sounded.
On the American shores,
See the flag of the Holy community waving.
No more vice, no more suffering,
No more crime, no more pain.
Hallowed Equality advances.
Proletariat, dry your tears.
Let us go to found in Icaria,
Soldiers of Brotherly Love,
Let us go to found in Icaria,
The happiness of Humanity![45]

After the ship dropped out of sight, Cabet forgot about the Advance Guard and returned to Paris to join the political turmoil leading up to the revolution of 1848. On February 24, the Chamber of Deputies deposed Louis Philippe and proclaimed the Second Republic. On February 25, Cabet issued his *Manifeste aux communistes Icariens* (Manifesto to Icarian communists). He demanded freedom of the press and universal education. He denounced violence because "all Frenchmen are brothers." Then, in an amazing about face, he proclaimed that there must be protection of private property! He said that because not enough Icarians were willing to go to America, he would dismantle the emigration organization. The next month he published *Bien et mal, danger et salut après la révolution de février 1848* (Good and evil, danger and salvation after the revolution of February 1848). He again stated that the government must grant freedom of the press and universal suffrage, and it must admit workers into the officer corps of the National Guard.[46]

That April, another hysterical reaction to communism swept Paris and other cities. Posters denounced all communists as the "true enemies" and "the most dangerous enemies of the republic." Cabet could not escape his past

45. A letter from A. Bertrand to Cabet of Aug. 15, 1847, has the words of the "Chant du premier départ"; Cabet Collection, SIUE, folder 8, no. 11. See Prudhommeaux, *Icarie*, 218, for the text of the song. Cabet, "Adresse de la 1ère avant-garde," in *Opinions et sentiments publiquement exprimés concernant le fondateur d'Icarie* (Paris: 3 rue Baillet, 1856), 13–14. For a reaction by one of the members of the First Advance Guard to the departure, see Pierre Grillas to Rose Grillas, Jan. 28, 1848, Grillas Papers, Center for Icarian Studies, Western Illinois University, Macombe (hereafter CIS).

46. Cabet, *Bien et mal, danger et salut après la révolution de février 1848* (Paris: Bureau du Populaire, 1848).

overnight. The cry arose: "Down with the communists! Death to Cabet!" Icarians were branded as incendiaries and plunderers in a backlash of blind fury against communism. Cabet's friend Thorton observed that escape was now the only alternative. He was right. On the night of April 16, a mob gathered in front of Cabet's house screaming for his arrest. They yelled that he had plotted to assassinate the leaders of the republic. He would start a reign of terror. He wanted to hold all property and all French women in common! Faced with such venom, Cabet announced a week later that he was "going to resume the march of our emigration . . . we will emigrate to the United States." Still, he could not resist the temptation to enter his name in the June elections to the Chamber of Deputies. He lost.[47]

Over the rest of the summer and autumn, Cabet tried to resuscitate the emigration, but it was hopeless. At Périgueux, only sixteen Icarians signed up, and their leader confessed that the movement had been "crushed." At Nantes, Cabet was able to recruit just ten men. Still, in *Le Populaire* he praised the Advance Guard for their devotion and courage. He said that the 3,000 acres would be ideal for the community of goods. He reprinted letters from Gouhenant about the encouraging developments in Texas and announced the dispatch of other Advance Guards. On December 3, 1848, without his wife or daughter, he left Paris bound for Le Havre and New Orleans.[48]

Icarianism in America

A little more than eight months earlier, on March 27, 1848, the First Advance Guard had landed in New Orleans. Within a week after their arrival, Charles Sully, who had come to the city in December 1847 as Cabet's agent, told Gouhenant the grim facts. He said that they could not reach the Peters Concession by steamboat as Cabet had promised. Instead, they would have to disembark at Shreveport, three hundred miles from the site, and head overland across unmapped terrain toward the Trinity River. The Bonham highway that Cabet had mentioned was a footpath. But not all the news was so discouraging. Sully had been able to borrow $4,000 at 10 percent interest from John Beckwell, a Titus

47. Léopold Domart to Cabet, Mar. 22, 1848; Vigner to Cabet, Apr. 10, 1848; Marie Esnault to Cabet, May 2, 1848; Forestier to Cabet, Mar. 26, 1848: Papiers Cabet, BHVP. *Le Populaire*, May 22, May 28, 1848. Cabet, *Société fraternelle centrale.—Discours du citoyen Cabet, 10ème discours, mai 1848. Exposé rapide sur la doctrine et la marche du communisme icarien* (Paris: Bureau du *Populaire*, 1848).
48. Autun Laty to Cabet, May 2, May 4, 1848; Paquet to Cabet, June 19, 1848: Papiers Cabet, BHVP. *Le Populaire*, May 22, May 28, 1848.

County businessman, with the 3,000 acres as collateral. He had purchased a small farm at Sulphur Prairie, a small settlement between Shreveport and the tract. After meeting with Gouhenant, Sully left New Orleans to get ready for the Advance Guard at the Sulphur Prairie stopover.[49]

In mid-March, Gouhenant led the "soldiers of humanity," with their heavy luggage, up the Mississippi River aboard a steamboat to Shreveport. There they divided into two units and loaded the supplies onto two ox-drawn wagons. One contingent set out to meet Sully at Sulphur Prairie. Gouhenant ordered the second group to stay in Shreveport and build shelters for the next Advance Guards and the other immigrants expected to arrive during the following months.

On April 8, the first group of twenty-five men headed west on the Bonham trail. A few days out the wagon broke down. They had to wade through swamps and neck-high prairie grass and sleep on damp ground under the stars. They ran out of food. In the meantime, some of the second unit—fourteen men with a second wagon—left Shreveport. In the words of one survivor, they tramped through "a country where ten to fifteen leagues [passed] without our coming across any dwelling." Eleven days later they overtook the beleaguered first party, and together thirty-nine men slogged on toward Sulphur Prairie. Late in the afternoon of April 21, the cluster of exhausted Icarians hobbled into the settlement, where they found Sully, bedridden from dysentery.

He told them that the situation was hopeless. They would never be able to meet the terms of the agreement—that is, to establish homesteads on 3,000 acres within two months in order to get title to the land. He calculated that even if, with heroic effort, they established homesteads on some of the half sections, they would still have to purchase the rest of the land at one dollar an acre. He advised them to remain at the outpost until the rest of the men arrived from Shreveport and then decide what should be done.

Gouhenant was determined not to be faint-hearted. They were going to create a community, he said, for the salvation of humanity! Push out for Icaria! They did. On June 27, they arrived at the Peters tract on the Elk fork of the Trinity River near the junction of the Denton and Olliver Creeks. Sully had been right. By the July 1 deadline, they were able to put up only a few log cabins and a log re-

49. "Correspondence et documents divers concernant les communautés icariennes au Texas, 1847–1848," Etienne Cabet Papiers (18148–18153), Bibliothèque Nationale, Département des manuscrits. The letter of Lévy of Reims to his family of June 2, 1848, and printed in *L'observateur,* Dec. 4, 1880, describes the expedition to the Peters Concession. See also Alexis Armel Marchand's letter to his brother, reprinted in the same newspaper in January 1881. Jules Prudent to Jean Pierre Beluze, Oct. 1, 1849, describes the Texas disaster.

fectory, start work on a mill and bakehouse, and plant crops on just thirty-two half sections. They boasted: "Icaria is founded!"[50]

But in August swarms of mosquitoes descended on the men, and malaria swept the settlement. Cholera struck. Four men died. Their physician, driven insane by the stress, deserted. When the rest of the men arrived from Shreveport, they were flabbergasted. Their leader, Pierre Joseph Favard, decided on the spot that they would have to abandon the site. He explained the desperate situation in a letter to Cabet that arrived in Paris in November 1848. The dejected men headed back. During the next four weeks, one by one, the half-starved, debilitated utopians trickled into Shreveport. Four men never made it. In October, the survivors boarded a steamboat and returned to New Orleans.[51]

By the time the remnants of the Advance Guard docked at New Orleans, 480 Icarians were living there in two buildings on St. Ferdinand Street. In cramped quarters, without leadership from Cabet, who was then still in Paris, dissension surfaced. Some wanted to forget the whole idea and return to France; some simply left the community to find work for themselves in the city; still others hoped to hold out until Cabet came over to take charge. But the ghastly accounts of the Advance Guard demoralized the community, and by the time of Cabet's arrival there on January 19, 1849, the colony was split in half. The 218 "dissidents," as Cabet labeled them, wanted to have him arrested for fraud, to dissolve the common treasury of 86,000 francs, and to go back to France. Some 280 loyalists, on the other hand, pledged their eternal devotion to "Papa" Cabet, a "venerated messiah," and to his goal of creating a "paradise on earth." Standing before the assembled émigrés, Cabet promised that in two days he would convene a general meeting, where they would decide what to do. On January 21, he opened the discussion by stating that he would abandon Icaria if that was what the majority voted to do. A slim majority, 280 men and women, chose to stay on and try again. The 218 Icarians who wanted out were reimbursed their 600 franc admission fee, set sail for France, and sued Cabet for swindling.

Huddled in their apartments, the loyalists waited for the report of a special reconnaissance commission, led by the German railroad engineer Jean Jacques Witzig, that had left New Orleans on December 31, 1848, to see what other sites might be found along the Mississippi River. On February 5, 1849, the commission returned with encouraging news. They had located an abandoned city about

50. *Le Populaire*, July 11, Aug. 20, Oct. 1, 1848. Prudhommeaux, *Icarie*, 229 n. 1.

51. *Le Populaire*, July 11, Nov. 12, and Dec. 3, 1848, July 1, 1849; *L'observateur*, Aug. 1880; *Northern Standard* (Clarksville, Tex.), Jan. 20, 1849; *Colonie Icarienne*, Aug. 2, 1854; Jane Dupree Begos, " 'Icaria,' a Footnote to the Peters Colony," *Communal Societies* 6 (1986): 84–91.

one hundred miles above St. Louis, called Nauvoo, that would prove ideal for the building of Icaria. It was once, Witzig said, a town of more than twelve thousand citizens built by the Mormons, but had been abandoned in 1846 after the death of their prophet, Joseph Smith. It contained homes, workshops, farmsteads—all deserted. And, most significant, it was reachable directly by steamboat. Two weeks later the Icarians voted to move to Nauvoo, and on February 28 the 142 men, 74 women, and 64 children boarded a steamboat for Icaria.[52]

At nine o'clock in the morning of March 15, they docked at the Nauvoo wharf, unloaded their luggage, and followed Cabet to the northern bluffs, the Temple Square, that overlooked the city. Here they found rooms in Mormon buildings Witzig had rented. The next day Cabet met with the Mormon agents left behind to settle matters with any potential buyers and informed them that he wanted only the Square and some adjacent farms. They agreed upon a price: $3,000 for the Square, including the remains of the granite temple, and some contiguous properties on the west and south. He leased four farms for a total of 2,000 acres, 400 of which were already cultivated.

Almost overnight Icaria appeared, a miniature model of the community of goods described in the book. The settlers built a school house, two infirmaries, a pharmacy, a refectory (that included the dining hall, theater, library, tailor shop, and living quarters), a wash house, laundry room, and workshops on either side of the Square. They erected barns and stables and purchased a saw and flour mill and a distillery, both located on the river bank. Cabet assigned jobs according to sex. He put men in the workshops as tailors, wheelwrights, shoemakers, tanners, butchers, and so on, and on the farms as field hands. The women were assigned to work as cooks, washwomen, seamstresses, ironers, and teachers. He opened retail shops in Keokuk and St. Louis, where the Icarians sold flour and whiskey. They crafted a constitution that created a "democratic republic" with a president (elected annually), a secretary, and a board of directors (elected every six months) that was to administer finances and food, lodging and clothing, education and health, industry and agriculture. The General Assembly, in which women could vote only on special issues, met every Saturday. It exercised all legislative and judicial power and determined who would be admitted to the community. By the summer of 1851, Icaria numbered 365 members.[53]

52. *Le Populaire*, Jan. 21, Feb. 18, Apr. 15, July 1, 1849; *Daily Orleanian* (New Orleans), Jan. 27, 1849; *Louisiana Courier*, Nov. 28, 1848, Apr. 16, 1849; "Rapport de Durond et Witzig," Cabet Collection, SIUE, folder 8, no. 16; Cabet, *Icarie* (Paris: Bureau du *Populaire*, 1849), 4–11.

53. Hancock County, Ill., Deeds, 1849, 562, 2909; *Le Populaire*, May 20, July 1, Oct. 7, 1849; Job [Fredrich Olinet], *Voyage d'un autunois en Icarie à la suite de Cabet* (Autun, France: Dejussieu,

Every work day began at six o'clock with a bugler sounding reveille. After the men downed a shot of whiskey, all Icarians reported to their assigned tasks. At eight o'clock, they convened in the refectory for breakfast, where they sat in family units. An hour later work resumed. After a brief respite for lunch, they worked until suppertime, at six. Cabet constantly, almost obsessively, rotated the men's jobs. For example, one Icarian remembered that in just three month's time he was assigned to work in the garden and the mill, as well as to clean streets, lay bricks, repair the gutters, plant corn, and pitch hay—a routine he described as "exhausting, disgusting, and unproductive." The women, though, stayed anchored in the kitchen, dining hall, laundry and tailor shops, and the school.[54]

By July 1855, the community had 469 men, women, and children living on or near the Square and a vigorous cultural and intellectual life. Their orchestra of thirty-six musicians gave regular Sunday afternoon concerts of popular French tunes and Icarian hymns such as "Song of the Transporters" or "Hymn of Harmony." These concerts became so popular with Americans that Cabet had to set "rules of order." The refectory could not handle the large crowds, he said, so each person had to have a ticket in advance. Parents must accompany their children, and decorum must prevail. "It is understood," he wrote, "that admittance is allowed only under the condition that nobody will . . . make any noise or cause any disorder."[55]

The orchestra also accompanied theatrical productions. About once a month, a new play was staged in the main room of the refectory, and outsiders were admitted with tickets. One visitor recorded that at the time of the performances "the stage is located at the end of the dining hall. . . . Benches used for the meals are placed in such a ways that everyone can see very well." He continued, "I attended the performance of *The Salamander, The Hundred Piques, The Miser's Daughter,* and I myself was a member of the cast in *The Fisherman's Daughter.*"

1898), 107–9; A. Holinski, "Cabet et les Icariens," *La Revue Socialiste* (1891): 539–50; (1892): 40–49, 201–4, 315–21, 449–56; (1893): 296–307; Cabet, *Colonie icarienne aux Etats-Unis d'Amérique. Sa constitution, ses lois, sa situation matérielle et morale après le premier semestre de 1855* (Paris: 3 rue Baillet, 1856), 136–36; "Assemblée des Citoyens à Nauvoo, l'établissement des Icariens," Cabet Collection, SIUE, folder 8, no. 15.

54. A detailed description of the Nauvoo Icaria is in Elizabeth Ann Rogers, "Housing and Family Life of the Icarian Colonies" (M.A. thesis, Univ. of Iowa, 1973); Fernand Rude, Voyage en Icarie: *Deux ouvriers viennois aux Etats-Unis en 1855* (Paris: Presses universitaires de France, 1955), 149–51, 257–66; Cabet, *Colonie icarienne aux Etats-Unis,* 114–23, 147.

55. *Colonie Icarienne,* Sept. 27, 1854; *Center for Icarian Studies Newsletter* (spring 1982), 7; Rude, Voyage en Icarie: *Deux ouvriers,* 46; Cabet, *Colonie icarienne aux Etats-Unis,* 160; "Icarian Concerts," Archief Cabet, IISG.

The Icarians loved their excursions, called promenades in Cabet's novel, along the Mississippi River. Pierre Bourg, secretary of the colony, lovingly recounted a pastoral outing during the summer of 1850.

> Our venerable and venerated patriarch walked with a joyous air in the middle of our whole ensemble [of two hundred people], which had the appearance of a large and happy family. A magnificent sky, pure, fresh air, trees, flowers, fruits unknown to us, the prairie, the valleys, the forests: all of this luxury of light, of vegetation, of the vigorous American greenery intensified, doubled, our holiday feeling. Having picked a grove of trees in the woods situated along the river, we had our dinner set out on the grass, in a glen, next to a brook under a tent of foliage; and then . . . our orchestra played some quadrilles and waltzes, which caused us to sing and pirouette like the mythological hosts of the ancient forest. . . . Finally, at sundown, very tired but happy, we returned to the communal building.[56]

The colony published a biweekly French-language newspaper, edited by Cabet, called *Colonie Icarienne*, up to 1854, when it became *Revue Icarienne*. Cabet printed letters from Icarians in Europe, the community's laws and regulations, essays on brotherly love and equality, and accounts of daily life in the community. In the same building that housed the print shop, they stored a four-thousand-volume library, the largest in the state. The books, mainly on history, biography, and the applied sciences, were loaned out to individuals, both Icarians and Americans, for as long as they wished to keep them. On Sundays, they gathered in a fellowship called the *cours icarien* (Icarian school). Led by Cabet, they discussed Icarian ideals and principles or heard "Papa" read from his book *Le vrai Christianisme.*[57]

In the pages of the *Colonie Icarienne*, Cabet boasted of Icarian education. At Nauvoo, children of four years and older were boarded in a limestone two-story schoolhouse at the southwest corner of the Square. Girls were taught on one side of the first floor and boys on the other, with the same plan of segregation applied in the sleeping quarters on the second floor. Of course, they always had meals with their families, and on weekends they stayed with their parents. The four-

---

56. *Le Populaire*, Dec. 2, 1849; Robert P. Sutton, "Utopian Fraternity: Ideal and Reality in Icarian Recreation," *Western Illinois Regional Studies* (spring 1983): 23–38; P. Bourg and E. Cabet, "Célébration en Icarie de l'anniversaire du 3 fév. 1850," Cabet Collection, SIUE, folder 9, no 5.

57. Cabet, *Colonie icarienne aux Etats-Unis*, 159–61; Rude, Voyage en Icarie: *Deux ouvriers*, 46; Emile Vallet, *Communism: History of the Experiment at Nauvoo of the Icarian Settlement* (Nauvoo, Ill.: n.p., 1917), 19.

year-old children were taught to read and write in French and English. From age five to sixteen, they were drilled in grammar, arithmetic, geometry, history, geography, science, drawing, music, and hygiene. Emile Vallet, who lived at Icaria as a teenager, remembered the strict discipline that prevailed in the school. There was a special "punishment room," he wrote, where "three of the older boys were taught separately from the others ... by a special teacher, having shown an uncontrollable disposition and being considered a dangerous example." Cabet personally took charge of the moral lessons and instructed the children to "do unto others as we wish others to do to us." He taught them to "protect, live, and work for the feeble, the sick; to forgive; to turn the other cheek when smitten on the one; to be kind, one to another; to love and respect your parents and everybody in general."[58]

But all was not well in this bucolic utopia. The socialist writer A. Holinski visited the community in 1855 and later remembered that the Icarians were "dispersed in little groups ... not talking too much. . . . Their faces," he wrote, "were inert and did not reflect any internal gaiety." The women and men sat apart from each other in silence, "with melancholy and pale faces." Bickering and dissension apparently were there from the beginning. Some members griped about the monotony of the food, and others complained about the "bureaucratic formalities" required in the workshops. More serious, though, was the charge that Cabet had instituted a spying operation. In April 1850, sixteen Icarians signed a protest in which they charged him with "suppression of liberties" and "censoring of private letters of domestic communications." The following winter, twenty Icarians departed because, they said, of Cabet's "spying and treachery."[59]

Such unrest might have been contained if Cabet had not been called back to France to answer charges in court brought against him by the New Orleans dissidents. These "blind accusers," as he called them, had filed a complaint on September 29, 1849, in the Commercial Court in Paris, alleging that he had deceived them in the Texas enterprise. They claimed that he had stolen their donations and personal property. If found guilty, he could be sentenced to two years in prison and fined. He tried unsuccessfully to have lawyers plead his case but de-

58. Vallet, *Communism*, 18–19; Homer Brown to Cabet, Dec. 14, 1855, Illinois State Historical Library, Springfield.

59. Cabet, *Colonie icarienne, réforme icarienne du 21 novembre 1853* (Paris: 3 rue Baillet, 1853), 122; Cabet, *Lettre sur la réforme icarienne du 21 novembre 1853. Réponse du citoyen Cabet à quelques objections sur cette réforme* (Paris: 3 rue Baillet, 1854), 13; Prudhommeaux, *Icarie*, 313; Cabet, *Colonie icarienne aux Etats-Unis*, 189–90; Prudent to Beluze, Apr. 20, 1852, in Cabet, *Opinions et sentiments*, 29.

cided that he personally had to clear his name. On July 19, 1851, he argued his case before the tribunal for three hours. The court, impressed with the facts, handed down a verdict of not guilty. He delayed returning to Nauvoo for almost a year while he dabbled in French politics, made some organizational changes at the office of *Le Populaire*, and gave his son-in-law Jean Pierre Beluze full authority over fund-raising and recruitment. Finally, on July 20, 1852, he arrived back in Icaria.[60]

Cabet was thunderstruck at what had happened while he was gone. "During his absence," historian Sylvester Piotrowski observed, "the Icarians conducted themselves as schoolboys on a holiday." Cabet told Beluze that he "found a great relaxation in the execution of our rules and a great many small disorders resulting from allowances and concessions that my absence had made almost inevitable." He specifically lamented that the Icarian principle of equality had been replaced by vanity and selfishness. New arrivals were hoarding their personal possessions. The women wore make-up. Production in the workshops had fallen off drastically. He concluded that "it was time to put a stop to it."[61]

And so he did. In October 1853, he had the General Assembly, with women voting, adopt his Forty-Eight Articles. The new rules required that all new members display full knowledge of all of Cabet's publications. Everyone had to take a vow to respect equality, liberty, and brotherly love; surrender all private property; and abjure tobacco and alcohol. They had to maintain silence in the workshops. There would be no more grumbling about the food. No more hunting or fishing for pleasure. Finally, every Icarian had to accept the new regulations "without criticism and without grumbling."[62]

The articles caused a rebellion. The opposition, led by Jean Baptiste Gérard and Alexis Armel Marchand, both community officers, charged that Cabet was trying to become a dictator. Cabet was furious at such insolence and, in Vallet's words, "became raving mad." Soon the utopia degenerated into a name-calling melee. The opposition, calling itself "the Majority," charged that Cabet, in ca-

60. Cabet, "Protestation du cit. Cabet contre la 2ème condemnation par défaut," May or June 1850, and "Au président de la cour d'appel de Paris, chambre correctionnelle," Paris, Apr. 17, 1851, Cabet Collection, SIUE, folder 3, nos. 3, 4, 7, 8; "Départ du cit. Cabet," May 17, 1851, Cabet Collection, SIUE, folder 7, no. 13; *Colonie icarienne aux Etats-Unis*, 20. "Les Icariens de Nauvoo du citoyen Cabet," SIUE, folder 7, no. 7. *Le Populaire*, Apr. 7, 1850, June 27, 1851. Jean Pierre Beluze, "Nouvelle victoire du cit. Cabet," Cabet Collection, SIUE, folder 9, no. 19; Thomas Teakle, "History and Constitution of the Icarian Community," *Iowa Journal of History and Politics* (Apr. 1917), 231.

61. Piotrowski, *Etienne Cabet*, 135; Cabet to Beluze, Jan. 11, 1853, Cabet Collection, SIUE, folder 5, no. 1.

62. Prudhommeaux, *Icarie*, 348–61.

hoots with Beluze, had siphoned off funds for the support of his wife and daughter still living in Paris. He had brought the community to the brink of bankruptcy. The articles, especially silence in the workshops and prohibition of hunting and fishing, were outrageous violations of the spirit of toleration and brotherly love. Cabet was incompetent as an administrator, a haughty, aloof tyrant! Because this group did indeed have a majority of the adult males' votes in the General Assembly, they passed a resolution that denied Cabet and his followers access to the refectory and supplies.[63]

Cabet's supporters, the "Cabetists", counterattacked. "Papa," they said, was a self-sacrificing leader devoted to the cause of Icaria. Cabet claimed that he alone had authority to rule in Icaria, "to carry the flag of the community," and "to guarantee and consolidate the Icarian way." He demanded a constitutional amendment to give him a presidential term of four years instead of one. The Cabetists paraded in front of the refectory, carrying empty buckets and waving wooden poles topped by pieces of bread. Emile Vallet remembered that Cabet, observing the spectacle from the window of his apartment just across the street, "encouraged them and laughed at their doings." Then the Majority, led by Gérard and Marchand, marched around the refectory singing "La Marseillaise." The Cabetists stormed the refectory, where some of them attacked Gérard and tried to strangle him to death. Cabet moved to another house about a ten-minute walk from the Square and set up a personal bodyguard who stood vigil day and night. When the Majority took over the school and ousted all the Cabetists, Cabet sent a Madame Raynaud riding pell-mell into the Square in a horse-drawn wagon and yelling, "Rise up! Rise up!" The children screamed bloody murder. Icarians from both camps rushed to the building.[64]

That was enough. The Americans called the sheriff. He restored calm and told the mayor of Nauvoo what had happened. The mayor told Cabet to get out of town. In October 1856, the Majority formally expelled the Cabetists and adopted *The Fourth Address of the Faithful Icarians of Nauvoo to Icarians of All Nations.* Here they stated that Cabet had lied and deliberately tried to destroy the community by ordering his people not to work in the shops and fields. He had

63. Henry King, "M. Cabet and the Icarians," *The Lakeside Monthly* (Oct. 1871), 296; Cabet, *Colonie icarienne aux Etats-Unis*, 208–24; Cabet, *Guerre de l'opposition contre le citoyen Cabet, fondateur d'Icarie* (Paris: 3 rue Baillet, 1856), 5–13.

64. Cabet, *Colonie icarienne aux Etats-Unis*, 222–30, and *Guerre de l'opposition*, 38–64; "Proposition of M. Cabet as it was read to the General Assembly on the 16th of December, 1855," signed Jean Baptiste Gérard, Iowa State Historical Library Collection, CIS, box 5, folder 3; King, "M. Cabet," 296; Jean Pierre Beluze, *Lettre sur la colonie icarienne par un Icarien* (Paris: 3 rue Baillet, 1856), 30–34.

brought financial disaster to the colony. He had refused to obey the decisions of the Assembly. He had "used all the resources of trickery, hypocrisy, and lies to achieve his goal: the annihilation of the community." Cabet counterattacked. In his *Declaration of Rights,* he demanded that the Majority name him president for four years with power to appoint all officers and committees "with or without the confirmation of the General Assembly." He would control all finances, assign all jobs, run the school, conduct the *cours icarien,* and publish the newspaper. All Icarians must "practice religiously . . . good manners, temperance, solicitude, order, economy, organization, discipline, and solidarity." Whiskey and tobacco were forbidden. Seventy-one men and forty-four women signed a loyalty statement accepting all of Cabet's demands. They said that Cabet would be "always for us the *Founder of Icaria.*" They said that he had never deviated "from his democratic and Icarian principles," and with "confidence without limits" they would follow him "to continue the true Icaria." In October, they packed up and left Nauvoo.[65]

On the morning of October 20, just before he departed, Cabet penned his valedictory. His "oppressors" had worked their mischief, and tyranny had prevailed in a "civil war." The Majority had inflicted "inhuman barbarity" on the Cabetists by denying the necessities of life and condemning them to "die from hunger and the cold" while they themselves lived in "abundance and profusion, in drunkenness and vice." These "abominable ingrates" had convinced him "that the spirit of revolution and factionalism coexists with the spirit of the reformer, that sensualism and materialism coexist with the spirit of order and economy, finally that the spirit of egotism coexists with the spirit of devotion and brotherly love." Nevertheless, he was still "indissolubly attached" to the cause of humanity. He would begin another recruitment in France and told his supporters to embrace it "with devotion." "Hope, therefore," he proclaimed, for "trust and fraternal devotion."[66]

Cabet led his 179 followers to St. Louis, where, for the third time, he started to build Icaria. But on November 7, 1856, he suffered a stroke and died the next day. After a week of mourning, the Cabetists, led by the young lawyer named Benjamin Mercadier, led a cortege to the Old Picker Cemetery, where they interred the casket. For a while, the Cabetists rented three buildings in New Bremen, a German section of the city. But these structures were a mile apart from

65. *Revue Icarienne,* Oct. 2, 1856; Cabet, *Colonie icarienne aux Etats-Unis,* 72; Cabet, *Départ de Nauvoo du fondateur d'Icarie avec les vrais Icariens* (Paris: 3 rue Baillet, 1856).

66. Cabet, "Adresse du citoyen Cabet aux Icariens en France sur la séparation et le départ pour St. Louis," in *Départ de Nauvoo,* 20–21.

each other, so Mercadier decided to relocate the community to Cheltenham, a 1,000-acre tract that he had purchased in the fall of 1857 adjacent to the Pacific Railroad about six miles west of the city. Cheltenham was charming enough, with a glen traversed by the River des Pères, but the financial arrangements proved disastrous. With no money to buy the property, Mercadier arranged with a St. Louis banker to assume a mortgage of $25,000, at 6 percent interest, payable in ten annual installments. Communal income could barely cover expenses, however, and the commitment proved impossible to meet. Within four years, the colony was in bankruptcy. However, for a short time, the Icarians at Cheltenham managed to re-create some of the life they had known at the Nauvoo utopia.[67]

They ate together in the largest building, a stone house that served as living quarters. Here they celebrated the February 3 anniversary of the departure of the First Advance Guard from Le Havre, regarded as the birthday of what they called the "Icarian Nation." At the evening festivities, a small band played "La Marseillaise" and other songs. To the accompaniment of the band, everyone sang the "Song of Departure." On Sunday afternoons, as in Nauvoo, they enjoyed more concerts and, as before, joined in the *cours icarien*. Mercadier insisted that everyone "participate with . . . heart and spirit" because, he said, the *cours* reinforced love of the community. Mercadier preached that they must be sober and temperate, engage in useful work, and be fraternal. The women, he warned, must do without "those items that are particular to the facial care and coquetry that the community cannot supply." After the sermon each adult read aloud parts of *Le vrai Christianisme* as the book was passed around the group. In closing, the band played Icarian hymns "to make the *cours* enjoyable," in Mercadier's words. Then he admonished: "We have only to continue in the path which we follow and the Icarian cause will provide all the benefits that we expect of it."[68]

He was wrong. Cheltenham was in serious danger both physically and financially. Almost every family was struck with what Mercadier described as a "veritable epidemic" of dysentery and fever from the stagnant water of the River des Pères, actually a run-off sewer for nearby homes, whose swamps were a breeding ground for mosquitoes. Without an infirmary or adequate medicine, chronic illness was rampant. Between October 23, 1858, and February 3, 1859, for exam-

67. Jean Pierre Beluze, *Mort du fondateur d'Icarie* (Paris: 3 rue Baillet, 1856), passim; Robert P. Sutton, " 'Earthly Paradise': The Icarian Experiment in St. Louis," *Gateway Heritage: Quarterly Magazine of the Missouri Historical Society* (spring 1992), 51–53.

68. Boris Blick and H. Roger Grant, "French Icarians in St. Louis," *Missouri Historical Society Bulletin* (Oct. 1973): 3–28.

ple, the colonists lost 1,500 workdays because of illness. By then, their financial health was just as fragile. The total income for 1859 amounted to about $7,500, and expenses, not including the mortgage payment due that month, tallied more than $7,000. To make matters worse, a fight over revision of their constitution that year had resulted in the exodus of forty-four Icarians and reduced the community to only ninety-three adults.[69]

Mercadier told them that if they were to survive, they would have to change into a Fourierist phalanx and concentrate on making products "on a large scale" that could be sold for a profit in St. Louis. Icarians had to become capitalists! They had to learn "how to make contracts, . . .to buy at the lowest price and sell at the highest." They must become "familiar with the commodities and raw materials provided by the markets of New York, England, France, Paris, Rio de Janeiro, Buenos Aires, etc." But it was too late. The wolf was at the door. The St. Louis bank foreclosed on the mortgage. In January 1864, eight men, seven women, and a few children were all that remained of the utopia. Arsène Sauva, their new president, locked the gate and turned the keys over to banker Thomas Allen.[70]

Back at Nauvoo, the Majority fell upon hard times. Albert Shaw, who in 1884 published the first account of the American Icarians, observed that "their industries were no longer a source of profit; creditors pressed their claims." Consequently, they voted to relocate to new federal lands just opened for sale in southwestern Iowa. They chose Alexis Armel Marchand as president, inventoried their assets, and in January 1858 dispatched the first contingent of Icarians west to Adams County, Iowa, in canvas-covered wagons. They chose Gérard as trustee to remain behind and dispose of their property, estimated by their figures to be worth $60,000. But at public auction they realized only one-third of what they had expected.[71]

With part of this money as collateral, they borrowed enough money to put up a down payment for title to 3,100 acres near Corning, the new county seat of

69. Sutton, " 'Earthly Paradise,' " 56–57; Jean Pierre Beluze, *Lettres icariennes à mon ami Eugène*, 2 vols. (Paris: 3 rue Baillet, 1859–62), 1: 341–43; Joseph Loiseau to Beluze, June 4, 1860, Cabet Collection, SIUE, folder 12, no. 49; Prudhommeaux, *Icarie*, 452 n. 2.

70. Sutton, " 'Earthly Paradise,' " 54–56; Blick and Grant, "French Icarians," 19, 22.

71. Albert Shaw, *Icaria, a Chapter in the History of Communism* (New York: G. P. Putnam, 1884), 77, 159–60; H. Roger Grant, "Icarians and American Utopianism," *Illinois Quarterly* (Feb. 1972), 13; Cabet, *Colonie icarienne aux Etats-Unis*, 163–65; Rogers, "Housing and Family Life," 58; Prudhommeaux, *Icarie*, 319 n. 1, 481–82; André Prévos, "A History of the French in Iowa" (Ph.D. diss., Univ. of Iowa, 1981), 239; Paul S. Gauthier, *"Quest for Utopia": The Icarians of Adams County, Iowa* (Corning, Iowa: Gauthier, 1992), 56–58.

Adams County. Within a year, they had 366 acres under cultivation and had purchased horses, cattle, oxen, sheep, and pigs. They had started to build a saw- and flour mill on the banks of the Nodaway River that bisected their land. With the only markets located at St. Joseph, Missouri, a month-long journey of one hundred miles over roadless prairie and forests, their debts by 1862 soared to $17,561. The Civil War saved the colony when, in early 1863, Union troops between the Des Moines and Missouri Rivers began to stop there for supplies. Soon federal agents came up from St. Joseph and paid top prices for the colonists' wool. By 1865, the Icarians had enough cash to pay off all debts, and two years later they had reduced their mortgage principle from $3,875 to $800.[72]

But a different sort of utopia took shape on the Iowa prairie than the one Cabet had created in Illinois. For all intents and purposes, it was an agricultural commune in which most men worked in the fields and the women carried out simple daily chores of sewing, cooking, and doing the laundry. Their constitution allowed only a weak president whose main responsibility was to represent the community to the outside world. Their directors were "elected to execute the decisions of the General Assembly and have no other power." They lived not in communal apartments, but as families in neat frame houses arranged on the east and north sides of the communal village. Unlike Nauvoo, where Cabet had prohibited informal contact with the Americans, children went to a public school within walking distance of the colony, and the young people at Corning regularly interacted with their neighbors. Marie Marchand Ross, who was born in the community and later published her reminiscences as *Child of Icaria*, wrote that because there "were so few young people in the colony . . . they began associating more and more with the outside world. . . . There was much visiting back and forth and even staying with friends over weekends without troubling to ask the Assembly's permission." Often they invited Americans to visit, and "on weekend evenings together at the common dining hall they sang, played games, or danced."[73]

72. Marie Marchand Ross, *Child of Icaria* (New York: City Printing, 1938), 7; Rogers, "Housing and Family Life," 62; "Minutes of proceedings of the Icarian Community translated from the French language into the English; to wit: Book Exhibit 1, November 1, 1860; U. Blanche, Director," A. Gauvain, Secretary, to Cher ami, July 10, July 30, 1860, Univ. of Nebraska-Omaha Institute for Icarian Investigations Collection, CIS, box 1, folders 1 and 2; "Statement of Revenue of Agriculture Since 1860," Iowa Historical Library Collection, CIS, box 5, folder 1; Shaw, *Icaria*, 81–82; *The Communist*, July 1867; Gauthier, *"Quest for Utopia,"* 59–60.

73. Shaw, *Icaria*, 116–17; William Alfred Hinds, "Icarian Community," in *American Communities and Co-operative Colonies* (Chicago: H. Kerr, 1900), 382–88; Ross, *Child of Icaria*, 25–26, 122, 125, 127.

Some of the essentials of the Icarians' earlier life, however, were retained even on the Iowa frontier. They had a refectory whose main floor doubled as a theater and dance hall and whose second story served as a library and recreation room with a billiard table. The *cours icarien* reappeared after the Civil War, when Arsène Sauva arrived from Cheltenham. Every Sunday afternoon Sauva read from Cabet's writings and then led the community in songs. Sometimes the adults lectured on brotherly love, equality, and other lofty principles. Others told newcomers about past events in Texas or Nauvoo. They enjoyed picnics where, as Marie Ross wrote, "nearly all the colony folks would go in several big wagons." Just as before, they walked to a shady spot by the Nodaway River to enjoy a picnic of fried fish, potatoes, flapjacks, pies, cakes, lemonade, and coffee. The children would play on rope swings that the men had strung for the occasion or would play hide-and-seek. At the end of one afternoon, Ross recalled, "the horn was blown again to warn everyone that it was time to go home, and all who had wandered away came to the camp as fast as they could." The walk back to the village was enlivened by songs and laughter. They celebrated special holidays, such as the February 3 anniversary of the first departure, with a banquet in the refectory, all bedecked with garlands. After the meal, they turned the floor into a makeshift theater and, seated on benches placed in front of a small stage, enjoyed a play chosen for the event. Then they finished the evening by dancing to the music of their orchestra.[74]

By the mid-1870s, this congenial ambience evaporated because of a growing hostility between the original Icarians who had come out from Nauvoo and younger, new arrivals from France who called themselves the Progressives. The latter were enthusiastic communists, many of whom had participated in the 1871 Paris Commune insurrection. They were appalled at the complacency of a rural commune that, in their eyes, had abandoned the high goal of Icaria's serving as a beacon light for oppressed humankind. The father of the Progressives, Jules Leroux, sarcastically remarked that the older Icarians were little more that "small farmers . . . associates in growing pigs, sheep, legumes, vines, and cereal," who stayed together only for the goal of "mutual assistance in self-confidence and in shearing." Led by Emile Peron, the Progressives tried in vain to revitalize the *cours icarien*, which they thought had degenerated into a boring ritual of recitations. They wanted to discuss important social and economic issues such as the evils of capitalism, the oppression of monopolies, the inequality of

74. Ross, *Child of Icaria*, 13–14, 28–30; Prévos, "A History," 280 n. 58.

mankind—not listen to Cabet's homilies. They wanted to give the Icarian women a vote in the General Assembly![75]

Marchand and the other Nauvoo Icarians, otherwise known as the Conservatives, could not comprehend what the Progressives were saying. To survive, Icaria must keep its priorities straight. The crops had to be planted and harvested, and livestock taken care of; flour had to be ground in the mill, and lumber sawed and sold to the Americans. The Progressives, faced with such intransigence from the older Icarians, brought matters to a head. Peron, in September 1877, announced that they were withdrawing because the Old Guard would never compromise on such matters as reforming the *cours icarien* or enfranchising the women. Effective immediately, he said, the Progressives would refuse to do any communal work. They exited the meeting in silence.[76]

At the October 6 meeting of the General Assembly, the Progressives moved to dissolve the community into two colonies, each with separate villages. Seeing that there was no alternative, the Conservatives agreed to create a committee of three men from each side to make the arrangements for the division. The commission got nowhere because neither side would cooperate. So in November the Progressives took the matter to the Adams County Circuit Court. The judge suggested arbitration by a court-appointed board of men. Neither side accepted the idea. The judge then ordered a jury trial for August 1878.

Here the two sides, with lawyers representing them, presented their arguments. On August 16, the jury decided that because the community had violated the Iowa state charter (which designated the community only as an "agricultural society") by operating a sawmill and selling wool for profit, it should be dissolved. The judge declared the charter void and named three American trustees to distribute all assets among the members. So ended, as William Alfred Hinds, a contemporary, wrote in 1908, "one of the saddest phases of the Icarian strife . . . [which] sundered ties that should have grown stronger with each succeeding year."[77]

A year later, after the two factions had divided the assets and agreed to live in

75. Jean Baptiste Gérard, *Quelques vérités sur la dernière crise icarienne* (Corning, Iowa: n.p., 1880), 21; Arsène Sauva, *La crise icarienne 1877–1878* (Corning, Iowa: Icarie, 1878), 2–5; *L'Etoile du Kansas et de Iowa*, June 23, 1877, Sept. 1, 1877, Apr. 1, 1880, May 1, 1880.

76. Emile Péron, "Project of Contract 26 Sept. 1877," Iowa Historical Library Collection, CIS, box 3, folder 1.

77. Sauva, *La crise icarienne*, 7–10; Hinds, *American Communities*, 370–79. Court proceedings are in the land records, Adams County, Iowa, abstracts nos. 2827, 3876, 3894, Gauthier Collection, CIS, folders 1 and 2, and in *State of Iowa v. Icarian Community*, Univ. of Nebraska-Omaha, Institute for Icarian Investigations Collection, CIS, box 3, folder 1.

separate locations as two different Icarias, the Progressives adopted their own constitution and new name, Jeune Icarie, or Young Icaria. There was to be no president or board of directors. The Assembly, in which the women now were voting members, had authority over all community matters, and each year it chose four people, called delegates, to administer its decisions. Everyone had to surrender their property, however. For a while, the colony prospered. Five new families joined, bringing total membership by 1880 up to seventy-two Icarians. They published their own newspaper, called *La Jeune Icarie*. Having received the original village as part of the settlement, they immediately made improvements by expanding the refectory into a building where they gave concerts, held dances, and performed plays.

But the community soon unraveled. The problem was threefold. First, the Young Icarians came from divergent backgrounds and joined the colony with different expectations. Second, because of their constitution, they were leaderless. Historian Albert Shaw, who saw events in Young Icaria firsthand, commented: "There were too many clever men, and no one with a gift of leadership sufficient to assimilate and unify the group." Third, most of the men hated farmwork and wanted to ply their crafts as barbers, house painters, or shoemakers. When they realized that they would *have to* plant, weed, and harvest to keep the community solvent, they quit.[78]

Armand Dehay, one of the disgruntled barbers, investigated the possibility of relocating the colony in California, where they might be able to establish an economic basis for Icaria other than farming. In 1881, he traveled to San Francisco, where his brother lived, and became convinced that if Icaria were near the city, they would find a profitable market for wine and dairy products. He wrote to his colleagues in Corning. In April, three families joined Dehay to locate a site for the relocation. After exploring various options, they decided on an 885-acre ranch near the town of Cloverdale, some eighty miles north of San Francisco. With their approximately 1,500 acres of Iowa land as collateral, they secured a mortgage of $15,000 for the property. Over the next two years, those Young Icarians who wanted to emigrate joined the others, and early in 1883 they adopted a formal charter, the Contract and Articles of Agreement, that named their community Icaria Speranza, or Icaria of Hope, and deposited it in the Santa Rosa County courthouse.[79]

78. *La Jeune Icarie*, Dec. 31, 1880; Prudhommeaux, *Icarie*, 572.

79. Robert V. Hine, *California's Utopian Colonies* (Berkeley and Los Angeles: Univ. of California Press, 1983), 58, 64–67; Prudhommeaux, *Icarie*, 572–73; *L'Etoile des pauvres et des souffrants*, Dec. 1, 1881.

Icaria Speranza included only twenty-four adults, so, despite their high expectations, the colony was doomed to failure from the start. Their Iowa land
never brought the $8.00 per acre they had expected. Morever, they never estab-
lished a market in San Francisco and, instead, tried to sustain the community by
retail outlets in the small town of Cloverdale; these efforts collapsed within a
year. To make matters worse, their admissions requirements to the community
were so high that its maximum number of members reached only fifty-two men,
women, and children. For instance, every new member had to have read most of
Cabet's publications, all of which were in French. Every applicant "should suffi-
ciently know the French language to speak it and read it fluently." He or she also
had to go through a one-year probation period. Every Icarian had to live on the
ranch, and any person who "sojourned for more than three consecutive days"
would be asked to leave permanently. The end was already in sight when the
Conservatives in Iowa sued the Young Icarians for not fully implementing the
terms of the separation order. In August 1886, the judge of the Adams County
Circuit Court agreed with the complainants, dissolved Icaria Speranza, and ordered a sheriff's sale of its remaining Iowa assets to satisfy the demands of the
Conservatives.[80]

The Conservatives, led by Marchand, had relocated in 1878 about a mile
east of the Corning village and started the "New Icarian Community of Adams
County." Their constitution created a replica of the first community, with a
president and directors. Women still could not vote except on specific matters
such as admissions and constitutional revisions. To avoid a recurrence of the
squabbles and acrimony, the document stipulated that everyone "obey the Directors and execute the work that will be assigned to them." If a person "re-
volted against" the officers or "tried to set up an isolated party," he or she could
be expelled.

New Icaria physically resembled the old one. The members built a refectory,
eight frame houses, and workshops for a blacksmith and carpenter. They
survived as a communal farm. Gradually, though, all semblance of the earlier cultural and intellectual life disappeared. They seldom used the one-thousand-
volume library and never revived the *cours icarien*. Although they continued to
publish a newspaper in Marchand's home, called the *Revue Icarienne*, it soon became a bland accounting of weather, crops, visitors, and birthdays. Now the Icar-

80. Lorraine Berry, "Biographical Sketch of Armand Dehay," *Center for Icarian Studies Newsletter* (spring 1984), 4–5; Hine, *California's Utopian Colonies*, 63–65, 71; Shaw, *Icaria*, 204–16; *L'Etoile des
pauvres et des souffrants*, Feb. 1, May 1, Aug. 1, Dec. 1, 1881; *Revue Icarienne*, July-Aug. 1886, June
1887.

ians only occasionally went for a picnic on the Nodaway River or came together in the refectory after dinner to sing Icarian songs.[81]

During the 1880s, the community atrophied. One by one, as the *Revue Icarienne* reported, members left New Icaria. When Marie Ross visited there in the early 1890s for the last time, she was heartsick. "The community really did not exist any more," she confided; "there were only a few people left and most of them very old and not able to do the heavy work of the farm." So it was that in mid-February 1895 the eight surviving members of New Icaria gathered together around one of the round tables in the center of the vacant refectory. Here, with Marchand presiding, this last "General Assembly of New Icaria" voted unanimously to dissolve the community. They drew up a list of sixteen individuals who would be eligible to receive a portion of their estimated $16,000 in assets. It took three years to work out in court the details of the dissolution, but finally, on October 22, 1898, Judge M. Towner signed the order that legally vacated their charter.[82]

H. Roger Grant has called the Icarian communal experiments "the quintessence of nineteenth-century American utopianism," an embodiment of the vision of America as the "place where the ideal society could be successfully created."[83] There is little doubt that these experiments collectively represent the most enduring, if not the most persistent, commitment to nonreligious communalism in the United States. The Icarians lasted fifty years, much longer than the average fifteen-year life span of other nineteenth-century nonreligious communities. Moreover, their extraordinary level of cultural and intellectual activity far surpassed other such societies. At Nauvoo, they collected the largest library in Illinois. The *cours icarien* tried, and often succeeded, in maintaining a high level of discussion on ethics, social issues, and current events. Their concerts and theatrical productions impressed every visitor with their variety and quality. At Nauvoo, the Icarian emphasis on a rigorous academic education was unmatched by any other American community.

Still, the Icarians were plagued with problems that appeared even before they started their community—in Cabet's description of the community of

81. Ross, *Child of Icaria*, chaps. 26, 32; Shaw, *Icaria*, 115–20; Rogers, "Housing and Family Life," 93–95, 165–69; *Revue Icarienne*, Mar. and Sept. 1879, Feb. 1888.

82. Ross, *Child of Icaria*, 130–33, 142; Martha Browning Smith, "The Story of Icaria," *Annals of Iowa* (summer 1965), 48; Hinds, *American Communities*, 352; Shaw, *Icaria*, 162; Prudhommeaux, *Icarie*, 601–2; *Revue Icarienne*, Apr. 1884, Feb. 1888; *Adams County Union Republican*, Oct. 27, 1898.

83. Grant, "Icarians," 13.

goods. His perfect society in *Voyage en Icarie* was simply irrelevant to the American environment where all but one colony was established. He described essentially an urban utopia, with its population concentrated in cities and satellite towns supported only in part by scientific farming. Except for Cheltenham, the Icarians were faced with building a self-sustaining community based on agriculture and modest home industry. Moreover, they had no real commitment to hard work; it was a means to the higher ends of concerts, discussion, play acting, dances, and picnics. Only one of the colonies, the Corning Icaria, was economically viable. As one student of Icarianism has put it: "the issue of how to get work done without resorting to coercion" was never solved. "The commitment to human improvement, the *élan vital* of Icarian communism," he wrote, "was incapable of resolving the fundamental problems of community production and political life."[84] All the Icarians were to a degree xenophobic. They envisioned a *French* utopia and put up a language barrier that discouraged American applicants, a quirk that became more severe at Icaria Speranza.

In addition, the problem of leadership constantly plagued them. In the novel, the benevolent dictator Icar is just that, a high-minded patriot uninterested in personal power. But in the real Icarias, the presidents became dictatorial. Cabet was arbitrary and unreasonable when his authority was challenged; he was also the only communal leader expelled by a majority of his followers. Mercadier was equally high-handed. Marchand, although more benign in his personal dealings with his fellow Icarians, nevertheless stubbornly resisted the Progressives' attempts to bring about change. Both Young Icaria and Icaria Speranza were, for different reasons, deprived of effective leadership.

A more insidious condition undermined community stability. Despite the Icarians' apparent determination to remain separate from American society, they were never far from the pressures and influences of ordinary American life, except for the early days at Corning. Let us take Nauvoo as an example. Most studies of this utopia give the impression that the Icarians built their community in a deserted city abandoned by the Mormons a few years earlier. But the census data for 1850 show that the town had 1,131 inhabitants, of whom only 281 were Icarians. In 1855, they still formed just 25.3 percent of the residents. In other words, they were a minority surrounded by Americans who *lived with* their families in homes, *dressed* as they pleased, *ate meals* when they felt like it, *spent money* earned from their labor—all without the slightest concern about the impact of their actions on the brotherhood of mankind. At Cheltenham, the Icarians were forced

84. Robert D. Bush, "Communism, Community, and Charisma: The Crisis in Icaria at Nauvoo," *The Old Northwest* (Dec. 1977), 416, 420.

to try to adapt to the economic realities of St. Louis, but were unsuccessful in the attempt. At Corning, they became farmers, just like their neighbors, and regularly exchanged visits with them. The fact that more people left the communities than stayed suggests that the temptations of American life proved too much to resist for all but a small, steadily diminishing cadre. Most Icarians, beset with all the problems facing their particular community and constantly observing the advantages of what America had to offer, decided that the expectations of the author of *Voyage en Icarie* were too unrealistic. Still, some Icarians' stubborn refusal to abandon the dream of an ideal community of goods in the face of repeated frustrations and failures draws both interest and admiration today.

Bibliography

Begos, Jane Dupree. " 'Icaria,' a Footnote to the Peters Colony." *Communal Societies* 6 (1986): 84–91.

Beluze, Jean Pierre. *Lettres icariennes à mon ami Eugène.* 2 vols. Paris: 3 rue Baillet, 1859–62.

———. *Lettre sur la colonie icarienne par un Icarien.* Paris: 3 rue Baillet, 1856.

———. *Mort du fondateur d'Icarie.* Paris: 3 rue Baillet, 1856.

Berry, Lorraine. "Biographical Sketch of Armand Dehay." *Center for Icarian Studies Newsletter* (spring 1984): 4–5.

Blick, Boris, and H. Roger Grant. "French Icarians in St. Louis." *Missouri Historical Society Bulletin* (Oct. 1973): 3–28.

Bush, Robert D. "Communism, Community, and Charisma: The Crisis in Icaria at Nauvoo." *The Old Northwest* (Dec. 1977): 409–428.

Cabet, Etienne. *Bien et mal, danger et salut après la révolution de février 1848.* Paris: Bureau du *Populaire*, 1848.

———. *Biographie de M. Cabet, ancien procureur général, ancien député, Directeur du "Populaire," et réponse aux ennemis du communisme.* Paris: Bureau du *Populaire*, 1846.

———. *Colonie icarienne aux Etats-Unis d'Amérique. Sa constitution, ses lois, sa situation matérielle et morale après le premier semestre de 1855.* Paris: 3 rue Baillet, 1856.

———. *Colonie icarienne, réforme icarienne du 21 novembre 1853.* Paris: 3 rue Baillet, 1853.

———. *Départ de Nauvoo du fondateur d'Icarie avec les vrais Icariens.* Paris: 3 rue Baillet, 1856.

———. *Faits préliminaires au procès devant la cour d'assises contre M. Cabet, député de la Côte-d'Or.* Paris: Rouanet, 1833.

———. *Guerre de l'opposition contre le citoyen Cabet, fondateur d'Icarie.* Paris: 3 rue Baillet, 1856.

———. *Histoire de la révolution de 1830 et situation présente (sept. 1832) expliquées et éclairées par les révolutions de 1792, 1799, et 1804 et par la restauration.* Paris: A. Mie, 1832.

———. *Histoire populaire de la Révolution Française, de 1789 à 1830, précédée d'une introduction contenant le précis de l'histoire des Français depuis leur origine jusqu'aux Etats Généraux.* 4 vols. Paris: Pagnère, 1839–40.

———. *Icarie*. Paris: Bureau du *Populaire*, 1849.

———. *Lettre sur la réforme icarienne du 21 novembre 1853. Réponse du citoyen Cabet à quelques objections sur cette réforme*. Paris: 3 rue Baillet, 1854.

———. *Ma ligne droite, ou le vrai chemin du salut pour le peuple*. Paris: Prévot, 1841.

———. *Opinions et sentiments publiquement exprimés concernant le fondateur d'Icarie*. Paris: 3 rue Baillet, 1856.

———. *Poursuites du gouvernement contre M. Cabet*. Paris: Bureau du *Populaire*, 1834.

———. *Prospectus: Grande émigration au Texas, en Amérique, pour réaliser la communauté d'Icarie*. Paris: Bureau du *Populaire*, 1848.

———. *Réalisation d'Icarie, grande émigration en Amérique*. Paris: Bureau du *Populaire*, 1849–50.

———. *Société fraternelle centrale.—Discours du citoyen Cabet, 10ème discours, mai 1848. Exposé rapide sur la doctrine et la marche du communisme icarien*. Paris: Bureau du *Populaire*, 1848.

———. *Toute la vérité au peuple ou réfutation d'un pamphlet calomniateur*. Paris: Prévot, 1842.

———. *Voyage en Icarie*. Paris: Matlet, 1842.

———. *Le vrai Christianisme suivant Jésus-Christ*. Paris: Bureau du *Populaire*, 1846.

Connor, Seymour. *The Peters Colony of Texas: A History and Biographical Sketches of the Early Settlers*. Austin: Texas State Historical Association, 1959.

Desroche, Henri. Préface. En *Voyage en Icarie*, par Etienne Cabet. 1848. Reprint, Paris: Editions Anthropos, 1970.

Fotion, Janis Clark. "Cabet and Icarian Communism." Ph.D. diss., Univ. of Iowa, 1966.

Garno, Diana Marie. "Gendered Utopia: Women in the Icarian Experience, 1840–48." Ph.D. diss., Wayne State Univ., 1998.

Gauthier, Paul S. *"Quest for Utopia": The Icarians of Adams County, Iowa*. Corning, Iowa: Gauthier, 1992.

Gérard, J. B. *Quelques vérités sur la dernière crise icarienne*. Corning, Iowa: n.p., 1880.

Grant, H. Roger. "Icarians and American Utopianism." *Illinois Quarterly* (Feb. 1972): 5–15.

Hinds, William Alfred. *American Communities and Co-operative Colonies*. Chicago: H. Kerr, 1900.

Hine, Robert V. *California's Utopian Colonies*. Berkeley and Los Angeles: Univ. of California Press, 1983.

Holinski, A. "Cabet et les Icariens." *La Revue Socialiste* (1891): 539–50; (1892): 40–49, 201–4, 315–21, 449–56; (1893): 296–307.

Job [Fredrich Olinet]. *Voyage d'un autunois en Icarie à la suite de Cabet*. Autun, France: Dejussieu, 1898.

Johnson, Christopher H. *Utopian Communism in France: Cabet and the Icarians, 1839–1851*. Ithaca: Cornell Univ. Press, 1974.

King, Henry. "M. Cabet and the Icarians." *The Lakeside Monthly* (Oct. 1871): 289–98.

Manuel, Frank, and Fritzie P. Manuel, eds. *French Utopias: An Anthology of Ideal Societies*. New York: Schocken, 1971.

Mercier, Louis Sébastien. *L'an deux mille quatre cent quarante*. Philadelphia: T. Dobson, 1795.

Piotrowski, Sylvester A. *Etienne Cabet and the "Voyage en Icarie": A Study in the History of Social Thought*. Washington, D.C.: Catholic Univ. Press, 1935.

Prévos, André. "A History of the French in Iowa." Ph.D. diss., Univ. of Iowa, 1981.

Prudhommeaux, Jules. *Icarie et son fondateur Etienne Cabet*. Paris: Edouard Cornély et Cie, 1907.

Rancière, Jacques. *The Night of Labor: The Workers' Dream in Nineteenth-Century France*. Translated by John Drury. Philadelphia: Temple Univ. Press, 1989.

Rogers, Elizabeth Ann. "Housing and Family Life of the Icarian Colonies." M.A. thesis, Univ. of Iowa, 1973.

Ross, Marie Marchand. *Child of Icaria*. New York: City Printing, 1938.

Rude, Fernand. Voyage en Icarie: *Deux ouvriers viennois aux Etats-Unis en 1855*. Paris: Presses universitaires de France, 1955.

Sauva, Arsène. *La crise icarienne 1877–1878*. Corning, Iowa: Icarie, 1878.

Shaw, Albert. *Icaria, a Chapter in the History of Communism*. New York: G. P. Putnam, 1884.

Smith, Martha Browning. "The Story of Icaria." *Annals of Iowa* (summer 1965): 36–64.

Sutton, Robert P. " 'Earthly Paradise': The Icarian Experiment in St. Louis." *Gateway Heritage: Quarterly Magazine of the Missouri Historical Society—St. Louis* (spring 1992): 48–59.

———. *Les Icariens: The Utopian Dream in Europe and America*. Urbana and Chicago: Univ. of Illinois Press, 1994.

———. "Utopian Fraternity: Ideal and Reality in Icarian Recreation." *Western Illinois Regional Studies* (spring 1983): 23–38.

Teakle, Thomas. "History and Constitution of the Icarian Community." *Iowa Journal of History and Politics* (April 1917): 214–86.

Vallet, Emile. *Communism: History of the Experiment at Nauvoo of the Icarian Settlement*. Nauvoo, Ill.: n.p., 1917.

ᴄᴧᴏ Translator's Note

LESLIE J. ROBERTS

My goal as translator was to render Etienne Cabet's style and message as accurately and faithfully as possible. After a brief overview here of Cabet's style, I highlight a few of the problems that emerged in the translation of this particular work.

Cabet was a child of the eighteenth-century French Enlightenment, firmly grounded in the writings of the *philosophes*, in particular Montesquieu, Voltaire, and Rousseau. Voltaire's influence is apparent in the chapters on religion, and Rousseau's in the romanticizing of nature and women; the prose style in which the latter wrote about these subjects is strongly echoed in the novel. Another genre of literature—British and French sentimental adventure novels of the period—provided the fictional framework and intrigue: the travels and romances of Lord William Carisdall. Cabet may have read and been influenced by Charles Dickens and Victor Hugo, who adhered to the cult of womanhood that pervaded pre-Victorian society. Cabet's heroines, like those of Dickens and Hugo, are pure, yet they are capable of a monogamous passion so intense that the fear of not consummating it brings on a psychosomatic illness. Once Icarian women do marry, they are perfect lovers to their husbands and devoted mothers to their children.

Cabet intended to popularize his social theory by polemic and propaganda—to exert a direct influence on manners and morals by decrying the corrupt and abusive political systems in France and England. He dressed his social theories in the form of a novel in order to make them palatable to a wide audience, women as well as men, while targeting the skilled artisan class.

Cabet's style reflects his social class, his professional identity as a lawyer and politician, and the breadth of his reading in political science, history, philosophy, and religion. Most passages are written in the same elevated, formal rhetorical register as his theoretical and historical writings. This is Cabet's public voice, the one he used in the National Assembly.

Cabet used only words that were in standard usage: no swear words and not a word in bad taste. In fact, he used no popular language at all: no colloquialisms, no slang, no regionalisms, and no idiosyncratic speech patterns. As befits a rhetorical style, his sentences are long. Endless strands of main, subordinate, and relative clauses are joined by semicolons. The same short rhetorical phrase begins three or more consecutive sentences, and both conjunctions and relative pronouns abound.

Following the eighteenth-century neoclassical model, Cabet's metaphorical language borrows heavily from Greek and Roman mythology. Another set of images contains references to biblical characters and subliminally reinforces a vision of Icaria as the new Palestine, where Icar, an amalgam of Jesus Christ and Cabet, of humble carpenter and patriarch, benevolently led his flock to transform the country into a new and improved Eden. Cabet's tone and his intense identification with nature, however, are that of the Rousseauian romantic.

Eugene is the author's principal mouthpiece. A politician like Cabet, he was exiled from France after the July revolution. He decries the abuses of the current French social system and mocks the British for their false claims to representative government, their foppish royalty, their idiotic Sunday laws forbidding drinking, and their hypocritical prudery in action and word (as he explains it, British high-society dames think nothing of stepping over the cadavers of a mother and child who have frozen to death near the gate of a stately home, but blush if you say "chicken thigh" in front of them). Cabet was on home ground in politics and philosophy. Characters such as Valmor's grandfather make fiery speeches to the National Assembly denouncing the immorality and brutality of French representatives and the behavior of British members of parliament.

Carisdall copies into his journal chapter-length letters from Eugene to his brother in France. Male and female Icarians describe community customs, lifestyle, and history in interchangeable passages that often go on for twenty pages or more. The diction of all these characters—be they British, French, or Icarian; aristocrat, revolutionary, or worker—is virtually identical, whether they are speaking or writing journal entries or letters. They use either an elevated register or switch to the language of serial romance, the 1830s equivalent of soap opera, to communicate the elations and disappointments of their budding adolescent passions.

Why did Cabet choose to have all characters speak the same way and why in this particular way? Perhaps he was incapable of creating differentiated characters or was not interested enough in his characters to bring them or their story to life. There is, however, another possible explanation. Cabet postulated a society where there are no social classes, no distinctions, no hierarchy. Every member of the society receives the same general education; all persons of working age work, and all occupations are valued; each person has the same amount and quality of living space, furniture, clothing, food, and amusements. It would follow that all members of Icarian society would speak in the same register. It was therefore incumbent upon Cabet to choose a register that best reflected his communitarian ideal.

Like other utopians, Cabet had the Icarians create an egalitarian language. A panel of experts developed it in committee by studying all existent languages and constructing from them a perfect, rational phonetic language based on a brief set of rules. There are no irregularities in grammar or spelling. All syllables are equal and coexist in perfect harmony. The desire to invent a new language for a transformed or regenerated society stems from the premise that language creates social reality. However, Cabet did not go beyond designing the barest skeleton of a language. The rare neologisms are words designating new jobs or inventions. For example, the caretaker on a boat is a *tegar*. Two new types of carriages are *staramoli* and *staragomi*. At one point, Icarian beauty Corilla says to Lord William, "We must 'dearistocratize' you!"

Paradoxically, Cabet did not dearistocratize his own vocabulary and register. In fact, he showed himself to be bourgeois and even elitist in his choice of main characters and narrative voice. The Icarians we meet have unusual brilliance, beauty, or musical talents. Although they all are workers or artisans, their oral and written diction and vocabulary contain no elements of the demotic. There are no colloquialisms, no words from the trades, no local color of any kind. Every Icarian now enjoys gourmet food, elegant clothing, horseback riding, and leisure time. All women are charming, witty, and elegant, even in their work uniforms. All men are handsome, healthy protectors of women's virtue.

Why does Cabet clothe his Icarians in the language, appearance, and tastes of the upper middle class or the aristocracy? There was precedent for this choice in earlier utopian writings. In the Eldorado section of *Candide*, Voltaire's utopians enjoy a luxurious lifestyle. Cabet's choice also may have been based on his intended readership. Members of the artisan class or lower bourgeoisie aspired to and imitated the manners and lifestyle of the class above them. In France and England, this imitation took the form of their having lace curtains, period furniture, meticulous gardens, and houses. An artisan-class woman would have been attracted to the idealized Icarian husband and lover. She wanted to believe in the possibility of a society where she could choose her mate freely after getting to know him, with the consent and encouragement of enlightened parents. She craved a husband who would be passionately attached to her while respecting her for being well educated and skilled at her profession. She longed for a world where seduction and rape, crimes as heinous as murder, were unheard of. It probably pleased her that in Icaria it would be illegal for her husband to go out with his cronies or with another woman.

What was Cabet's message to potential members of the community of goods? "In the new Eden, you will have every possession and activity now enjoyed only by the rich, but you must work for community *now*." This message was reinforced both consciously and subliminally by the language in which it was communicated.

Least palatable to modern taste are the sections of sentimental melodrama and exaggerated political zeal. They include a summary of scenes from a political play, *The Gunpowder Plot*, and a lengthy description of the annual festival when the entire population reenacts the Icarian revolution. The characters' names are a garbled mixture of Greek, Italian, and French, and are out of sync with the pure, simple Icarian language. My favorites among the women's names are Dinaïse and Cloramide, and among the men's, Miguf, Kalar, Dinaros, and, above all, Lixdox.

Cabet's proselytizing fervor caused him to exaggerate and to equate quantity with strength or quality. Lord Carisdall is propelled into rapturous amazement by millions of voices raised in revolutionary song. His starry-eyed description of a millinery factory where thousands of charming, attractive, joyful women sing hymns praising Icar even while repeating the same mindless assembly-line task each day of their working lives is more disconcerting than amusing.

The long sections on Icarian history are replete with melodrama. Morally good people exhibit every sterling quality, and evil manifests itself in grotesque physical deformities and heinous acts. Villainous Lixdox, brother of the dethroned king, is "little, ugly, one-eyed, and hunchbacked . . . treacherous and deceitful . . . ambitious and tyrannical." A look at the portrait of the brave Icar provides insight into what Cabet thought about himself and his role in the world; indeed, many of the incidents in Icar's fictional biography come directly from Cabet's own past. For example, "Love of humanity was Icar's ruling passion. . . . Philosophy books were his favorites. . . . He invoked unceasingly the name and words of Jesus Christ in favor of equality, fraternity, and even of communal ownership of property. . . . Like the early Christians, he was accused of conspiracy and of advocating regicide and civil war. Like them, he was called an anarchist, a drinker of blood, and an enemy of the people and of humanity." Cabet turned melodrama into farce by subjecting Icar to every possible twist of fate.

I have tried to remove obstacles to the modern reader's understanding and enjoyment while representing Cabet's style, diction, and tone accurately. The only significant alterations I made were in orthography, punctuation, and sentence and paragraph length.

Cabet's orthography showed the same lack of precision that resulted in an overabundance of melodramatic elements. Indiscriminate capitalizations and italics distracted rather than aided the reader. Because contemporary authors use neither of these devices, and key phrases are perfectly clear without them, I decided to omit them. This translation is therefore a modern reader's edition.

Cabet was also prone to an overzealous use of the semicolon. He strung together any number of clauses (often six or seven), both independent and dependent, with a similar number of semicolons. Replicating these serpentine utterances in English sometimes proved impossible and was stylistically unsound. I chose to transform some of them into groups of shorter sentences, while retaining others to preserve the novel's tone. I also modified slightly some of the rhetorical repetitions of single words or short phrases that did not work in English. I changed punctuation for dialogues from the French dash to English quotation marks. I also reduced double and triple exclamation points (!!!) to a manageable number. In contrast to the unwieldy sentences, paragraphs were unusually short for no apparent reason, so I modified paragraph length to coincide with transitions in content.

When making choices about the translation of specific words or expressions, I researched the corresponding 1830s British constructions and vocabulary. The narrator is, after all, British, and Cabet wrote the novel while seated at a desk in the British Museum. *La communauté des biens*, for example, became *community of goods* rather than *communal ownership of goods*. I used British turns of phrase such as "I took my leave" and "We went to fetch him" when appropriate. To render the formal register faithfully (*vous* is used rather than *tu*, with no substandard language), I used few colloquial English expressions and few contractions. *Do you not* seemed to convey Cabet's diction more accurately than *don't you*, and *cannot* more than *can't*. In a few cases, however, contractions seemed appropriate.

The usual dilemmas inherent in translating a gendered language into a non-gendered one presented themselves. In French, for example, *the people* is masculine singular; *republic* is feminine singular. Gender attribution personifies and personalizes these collective nouns to some extent. In English, however, *people* is plural, and so the appropriate pronoun is *they*; similarly, the republic is referred to as *it* in conventional English.

I made some vocabulary choices based on a subjective judgment of which English word conveys the intended meaning most accurately. For example, I chose to translate the oft-repeated phrase "le nécessaire, l'utile, et l'agréable" as "the necessary, the useful, and the pleasant," when I could have chosen "the essential, the utilitarian, and the pleasing." The word *opinions* in "opinions religieuses" could be translated as *beliefs*, *viewpoints*, or *opinions*. I chose to vary the translation according to which of these meanings Cabet seemed to imply in specific instances.

My most difficult task was to control an impulse to "improve" the original by making the language more precise or accurate. Two examples of imprecision are Cabet's use of the words *citoyenne* and *charmant*. Although Icarian women are not actually citizens and have no voice in political decisions, Cabet often refers to them as *citoyennes*, using the feminine form of the noun. *Female citizens* was the only accurate translation of this inaccurate word. In passages where Cabet used the word *charmant* five times in two sentences to describe Icarian women, children, workshops, sunsets, and just about everything else, it was a struggle not to remove a few instances of that adjective, which, through overuse, had lost its charm.

Judged by a universal standard, *Travels in Icaria* is not a great work of art. The factual content of its detailed descriptions of Icaria is of far greater interest than the fictional frame in which it is set. Cabet's style is neither innovative nor uniformly effective, and the formal, rhetorical nineteenth-century vocabulary and syntax do not resonate with a contemporary audience. In many forceful and moving sections, however, Cabet's style is well suited to his subject: the chapters on religion and education, the lines of condemnation of specific abuses of French and British society, and the passages that echo Cabet's own battles, hardships, and exile. What is both inspirational and poignant today, given the fact that Western civilization is not much farther along the path to enlightenment than it was in 1839, is Cabet's unshakeable idealism, his certainty that a community founded on equality, responsibility, participation, and justice for all was realizable then and there. Etienne Cabet would be pleased that a translation in English of part one of his utopian novel is available to a wide audience.

Evansville, Indiana   Leslie J. Roberts
May 2003

๑ Preface to the Second Edition, 1842

When we consider the riches that benevolent nature has bestowed on the human race, and the intelligence or reason she has given man so that it may serve him as instrument and guide, it is impossible to accept that man's destiny is to be unhappy on earth; and when we consider that man is essentially sociable, and consequently sympathetic and affectionate, it is equally impossible to accept that he is naturally evil.

However, in all eras and in all countries, history shows us only disturbance and disorder, vice and crime, war and revolution, torture and massacres, catastrophes and calamities. But if these vices and misfortunes are not the effect of nature's will, then we must look elsewhere for the cause. Can that cause not be found in the bad organization of society? And is the fundamental vice of that organization not inequality, which serves as its base?

There is no other question as worthy of exciting universal interest, for if it could be proven that the sufferings of humanity were an immutable sentence of fate, its remedy could be found only in resignation and patience. If, on the contrary, the evil is merely the consequence of bad social organization, and in particular of inequality, we should not waste one moment, but should work to erase that evil by erasing its cause and by substituting equality for inequality.

As for ourselves, the more we study history, the more we are deeply convinced that inequality is the generative cause of poverty and opulence, of all the vices that stem from the one and the other, of cupidity and ambition, of jealousy and hatred, of strife and wars of all kinds, in short, of all the evils that overwhelm individuals and nations.

And our conviction becomes unshakeable when we see almost all the philosophers and all the sages proclaim equality; when we see Jesus Christ, author of a great reform, founder of a new religion, worshiped as a god, proclaim fraternity as the way to save the human race; when we see all the fathers of the church, all the Christians of the early centuries, the Reformation and its innumerable partisans, the Philosophic movement of the eighteenth century, the American Revolution, the French Revolution, and universal progress proclaim equality and fraternity of men and of nations.

Today, therefore, the doctrine of equality and fraternity, or of democracy, is the intellectual heritage of humanity; the fulfillment of this doctrine is the goal of all efforts, struggles, and combats on this earth.

But when one seriously and passionately delves into the question of how society could be organized into a democracy—that is, on a foundation of equality and fraternity—one comes to recognize that this organization requires and must involve communal ownership of goods.

And we hasten to add that this community was also proclaimed by Jesus Christ, by all his apostles and disciples, by all the fathers of the church and all the Christians of the early centuries, by the Reformation and its sectarians, and by the philosophers who are the light and the pride of the human race.

All of them, and Jesus Christ first of all, recognize and proclaim that the Community, based on education and on the public or common good, constituting a general and mutual insurance against all accidents and misfortunes, guaranteeing to each person food, clothing, shelter, the opportunity to marry and raise a family, conditional only upon moderate work, is the only system of social organization that can bring into being equality and fraternity, prevent cupidity and ambition, wipe out rivalries and antagonisms, destroy jealousies and hatreds, render vice and crime almost impossible, assure harmony and peace, and finally bring happiness to a regenerated humanity.

But for a long time the self-serving and blind adversaries of community, although recognizing the marvels that it would engender, have succeeded in establishing this judgment: that it is impossible, that it is merely a beautiful dream, a magnificent chimera.

Is or is not community realizable and possible? That is the question. The study in depth of this question has profoundly convinced us that the community can easily be established as soon as a nation and its government choose to adopt it. We are also convinced that the progress of industry makes the establishment of community easier today than ever before; that the current and limitless productive power by means of steam and machines can assure equality of abundance; and that no other system is more favorable to the perfection of the fine arts and all the reasonable pleasures of civilization. It is to render this truth in palpable form that we have written *Travels in Icaria.*

In Part One, we tell, we describe, we show a great nation organized into a community; we show it in action in all of its diverse scenes. We guide our readers through its cities, countryside, villages, and farms; on its roads, railroads, canals, and rivers; in its stagecoaches and omnibuses; into its workshops, schools, hospitals, museums, public buildings, theaters, games, festivals, amusements, and political assemblies. We set forth the organization of food, clothing, shelter, furnishings, marriage, family, education, medicine, work, industry, agriculture, fine arts, and colonies. We tell of the abundance and riches, the elegance and magnificence, the order and unity, the harmony and fraternity, the virtue and happiness that are the inevitable result of community.

Moreover, the community, like the monarchy, like the republic, like a senate, is open to an infinite variety of organizations, with or without cities, for example; and we do not presume to believe that we have found, on our first attempt, the most perfect system for organizing a great community. We wish only to present an example, to suggest the possibility and utility of the communitarian system. The race is on. Let others set forth better organizational schemes, better models! And moreover, the nation will certainly learn to correct and perfect the system, just as later generations will know how to modify and perfect it even more.

As for the details of the organization, many are applicable to a simple democracy as well as to the community, and we would like to think that they might be of some practical use at this very moment. We have assumed that the political organization of Icaria was the republic: but we mean *republic* in the largest sense of the word (*res publica*, the public thing), the meaning ascribed to it by Plato, Bodin, and Rousseau, who classified as a republic any state or society governed or administered in the public interest, whatever the form of government: simple or multiple, hereditary or elective. A monarchy that is truly representative, democratic, and popular is a thousand times preferable to a republic of the aristocracy; and community is no more impossible with a constitutional monarch than with a republican president.

In Part Two, we show how the community can be founded, how a great and old nation can be transformed into community. We are sincerely and personally convinced that this transformation cannot take place in an instant, as a result of violence and constraint, and that it can be only gradual and progressive, the result of persuasion, conviction, public opinion, and the national will. We set forth a transitional regime, which is nothing more than a democracy that adopts the principle of community and applies immediately all that can be so applied, thus preparing the progressive achievement of the rest, fashioning a first generation for the community, enriching the poor without depriving the rich, respecting the acquired rights and habits of the present generation, but abolishing poverty without delay, guaranteeing work and life to all, giving happiness to the masses through work. Also in Part Two, we discuss the theory and doctrine of community, while refuting all objections; we present the historical panorama of the progress of democracy, and we review the opinions of the most famous philosophers concerning equality and community.

Part Three contains the summation of the principles of the communal system.

In the form of a novel, *Travels in Icaria* is, in fact, a veritable treatise of morality, philosophy, and political and social economy—the fruit of long work, of immense research, and of constant meditation. In order to know it well, it is not enough to read it; it must be reread, reread often, and studied.

We cannot flatter ourselves that we have made no errors; but our conscience consoles us with the truth that our work is inspired by the purest and most passionate love of humanity.

Already saturated with calumnies and affronts, we need courage to confront the hatred of opposing groups, and, perhaps, persecution. But noble and glorious examples have taught us that a man who is inflamed and moved to action by devotion to saving his brothers must sacrifice everything for his beliefs; and no matter what the sacrifice may be, we are ready to accept it in order to render, everywhere and forever, a solemn homage to the excellence and benefits of the doctrine of community.

Cabet, February 1842

TRAVELS IN ICARIA

❧

PART ONE

Voyage. Narrative. Description.

1 Purpose of the Voyage and Departure

The reader will forgive me, I hope, if I think it necessary to begin with a short explanation of the circumstances that led me to publish the story of a trip made by another man.

I met Lord W. Carisdall in Paris, at the home of General Lafayette; and you will understand the pleasure I felt in 1834 when I found him in London if, careful not to wound his modesty, I speak of the traits of his spirit and his heart. I could say, without meaning to offend him, that he is one of the wealthiest lords in the three kingdoms and one of the handsomest men that I have ever seen, with the most pleasing countenance that I have ever known, because he draws no glory from these favors of chance; but I will not speak of the scope of his knowledge, or of his noble character, or of the gentility of his manners. I will merely say that, deprived of his father and mother in childhood, he spent his whole youth traveling. His passion was the study not of frivolous things, but of all those matters that are of interest to humanity.

He used to repeat often, sadly, that he had found man to be unhappy all over the earth, even in those places where nature seemed to combine everything for his happiness; he bemoaned the vices of social organization in England as elsewhere. However, he believed that an aristocratic monarchy, like the one in his country, was still the form of government and society best suited to the human race.

One day, when he came to tell me his plan to marry Miss Henriet, one of the richest and most beautiful heiresses in England, he noticed on my table a volume whose binding was as strange as it was beautiful and which a traveler recently returned from Icaria had given to me.

"What is this book?" he asked, picking it up to examine it. "What beautiful paper! What superb print! You say it's a grammar book?"

"Yes, a grammar and a dictionary," I replied, "and this should make you happy! You often complain about the obstacle to the progress of enlightenment

3

created by the multiplicity and imperfection of languages. Well now. Here is a perfectly rational, regular, simple language that is written as it is spoken and is pronounced as it is written; whose rules are very few in number and without exception; all of whose words, composed in a regular fashion from a small number of roots, have a perfectly defined meaning; whose grammar and dictionary are so simple that they are contained in this slim volume; and the study of which is so easy that the average person can learn it in four or five months."

"You don't say! This would be, in short, the universal language I have longed for!"

"Yes. I am certain that every nation will adopt it sooner or later, either to replace its own or to use it concurrently, and that this Icarian language will one day be the language of all the earth."

"But where is this country of Icaria? I have never heard of it."

"I am not surprised. It is a country as yet unknown and that has just been discovered recently. It is a sort of New World."

"And what does your friend have to say about it?"

"Oh! My friend talks about it like a man driven mad by enthusiasm. If he is to be believed, it is a country as populous as England and France together, although scarcely as big as one of them. According to him, it is a country of marvels and wonders. The roads, rivers, and canals are magnificent, the countryside delightful, the gardens enchanting, the dwellings exquisite, the villages charming and the cities superb, with public buildings reminiscent of those of Rome and Athens, Egypt and Babylonia, India and China. According to him, its industry surpasses that of England, and its arts are superior to those of France. Nowhere else will you see such immense machines; the people travel in hot-air balloons; and the aerial displays that take place there outshine the most brilliant earthbound celebrations. Trees, fruit, flowers, and animals of all species: everything there is worthy of admiration. All the children are charming, the men vigorous and handsome, the women enchanting and divine. According to him, all the social and political institutions bear the hallmark of reason, justice, and wisdom. Crime is unknown there. Everyone lives in peace, pleasure, joy, and happiness. In a word, Icaria is truly a second promised land, an Eden, an Elysium, a new earthly paradise."

"Or your friend is a true visionary," Milord said.

"That is possible, and I fear it may be the case. He is, however, reputed to be a philosopher and scholar. Moreover, this grammar book, with its perfect binding, paper, and print, and the Icarian language in particular—do they not constitute a first marvel that may foretell others?"

"That is true! This language amazes me and thrills me. Might you lend me the grammar book for a few days?"

"Certainly. You may take it with you."

And he took leave of me with an expression that was both dreamy and eager. I went to see him a few days later.

"Well then," he said when he saw me, "would you like to take a trip? As for me, I am leaving!"

"And where are you going?"

"What? You cannot guess? To Icaria."

"To Icaria! You must be joking!"

"No, I am really going! It will take me four months to get there, four to tour the country, and four to get back. A year from now, I will come and tell you what I have seen."

"But what about your marriage?"

"My betrothed is not yet fifteen years of age, and I am scarcely twenty-two. She has not yet come out, and I have not yet completed my studies. We have never met. Absence and this portrait that I am taking along will make me desire the original even more. Besides, I am burning with desire to visit Icaria. You may laugh at me, but I am feverish with the thought of it! I want to see a perfect society, a nation that is totally happy. And in a year I will come back to get married."

"I am truly sorry that my friend has already gone back to France. But I will write to ask him the details of his trip so that they may guide you in yours."

"Not at all! That is unnecessary. Thank you anyway. I do not wish to learn any more about it. I would even like to forget all that you have told me. I want to savor fully the pleasure of surprise. My passport, two or three thousand guineas in my purse, my faithful manservant John, and the Icarian grammar book that I am stealing from you; that is all I need. As I already know seven other languages, it will be easy for me to learn this one during the trip."

"And if I hear anyone calling you odd or eccentric?"

"You mean mad, do you not?"

"Yes, mad!"

"Well then, you may chime in, if you wish. I will have the last laugh if I have the pleasure of encountering a people that resembles the human race as I would like to see it."

"You will keep a journal of your trip?"

"I certainly will."

He had returned by last June (1837), even more excited about Icaria than my friend whom he had called a visionary. He was, however, ill, consumed by grief, heartbroken, and near death. I found his journal (he had kept his word) so interesting and his adventures so touching that I encouraged him to publish it. He consented; but as he was suffering too much to work on it himself, he left me his manuscript, making me responsible for any deletions I felt advisable, and even asking me to correct the faults in style that haste in writing had multiplied. I decided to omit, in fact, some details, which will probably appear later; but I was careful to make no corrections, preferring to retain some errors rather than change the original narrative. The young and noble traveler himself will recount his adventures and his trip, his pleasures and his sorrows.

2 Arrival in Icaria

I left London on December 22, 1835, and I arrived on April 24, with my faithful traveling companion, my man John, at the port of Camiris, on the east coast of the country of the Marvols, separated from Icaria by an arm of the sea that takes six hours to cross.

I will not dwell on the thousand misadventures that befell me during the trip. Robbed in almost all the inns; almost poisoned in others; persecuted by the police or the authorities; annoyed and outraged by the customs officers; arrested and imprisoned for several days for having reacted to the insolence of a customs officer; often almost finished off along with the carriage on appalling roads; miraculously saved at the brink of a precipice over which a wretched driver blinded with drink was hurling us; almost buried in the snow and then in the sand; attacked three times by brigands; wounded while sitting between two passengers who were killed alongside me: all these experiences only made me feel even more strongly inexpressible happiness when the end of my voyage was at last in sight.

My happiness increased when, meeting some Icarians there, I became certain that I could understand and speak the Icarian language, which had been the single focus of my study throughout the trip. I was even more pleased when I learned that foreigners who did not speak the language were not admitted to Icaria, and that they were obliged to stay for several months in Camiris to learn it.

I soon found out that the Marvols were allies of the Icarians; that Camiris was almost an Icarian city; that an Icarian vessel was supposed to leave the next day for Tyrama, in Icaria; that first of all, you had to contact the Icarian consul, whose offices were near the embarkation dock; and that this functionary was always available to foreigners. I went right away to the consulate and was admitted immediately. The consul received me with genuine warmth and had me sit down next to him.

"If your goal," he said, "is to buy merchandise, do not go to Icaria, as we sell nothing. If, however, you are motivated solely by curiosity, you may continue. Your trip will be filled with pleasure."

"They sell nothing. They buy nothing," I repeated to myself in amazement. I told him the reason for my trip while handing him my passport.

"So you are curious to see our country, Milord?" he said after perusing my documents.

"Yes. I want to see if you are as perfectly organized and as happy as I have heard. I want to study and to learn about your country."

"Excellent! My fellow citizens are delighted to welcome foreigners, above all influential persons who come here to learn the means to happiness in order to take this knowledge back to their countries. You may travel through and visit all of Icaria. Everywhere you go, the Icarian people, considering you their guest and their friend, will be eager to show you their country.

"I must, however, in your own interest and that of my fellow citizens, point out to you the conditions of your admission to our country. You will pledge to abide by our laws and our customs, set forth in detail in the *Visitors' Guide to Icaria*, which was given to you at your hotel. You will promise above all to treat with inviolable respect our girls and women. If by chance these conditions are not acceptable to you, do not proceed any further."

After I had declared that I would obey all these rules, he asked me how much time I planned to spend in Icaria. When I answered that I hoped to spend four months there, he said that my passport was ready and instructed me to deposit in the bank two hundred guineas for myself and the same amount for my companion, the fee being determined by the length of one's stay. Despite the consul's politeness, I still thought that two hundred guineas was a great deal of money for a passport; and fearing that, if all the prices were equally high, my purse, as ample as it was, would not suffice for my other expenses, I ventured to ask him for some additional information.

"How much will I have to pay for my passage?" I asked him.

"Nothing," he replied.

"How much will the carriage cost that will take me to the capital?"

"Nothing."

"What, nothing?"

"Yes, nothing. The two hundred guineas that you deposit constitute payment in full for all your expenses during the four-month period. You may go anywhere, and wherever you go, you will have the best seats in public conveyances, without ever paying a penny. You will find, at each stop, a Foreigners' Hotel, where you will be lodged and fed, where your laundry will be done, where you will even be given clothing if necessary, without ever having to pay anything in return. You will likewise be admitted without cost to all public establishments and theatrical productions. In short, the nation, which receives your two hundred guineas, undertakes to provide you with everything, as it does for its own citizens.

"And because selling," he continued, "is unknown among us, it follows that you will find nothing to buy. Because individuals have been forbidden to use money ever since the good ICAR saved us from that plague, you are going to deposit for safekeeping all the remaining money you have with you."

"What? All the rest of my money?"

"Have no fear. This deposit will be returned to you at the frontier you choose for your departure."

I had not yet gotten over my amazement at all these unusual novelties when, the next day, toward six o'clock in the morning, we boarded an enormous and magnificent steamboat. I noted with pleasure that you entered the vessel directly. The women were not obliged to begin by boarding little rowboats that cause them greater trepidation, put them in greater danger, and often do them more damage than anything else during the remainder of the trip. I was amazed and delighted to find a steamboat as beautiful as our most superb English boats and even the finest American ones. Although its staterooms were not fitted with mahogany, but with a native wood that looked like the most beautiful marble, the boat seemed to me more elegant and certainly more comfortable and pleasant for the travelers.

A Pagilois who had never seen a steamboat before could not stop exclaiming about the richness and beauty of the two drawing rooms, the dazzling carpets, mirrors, gilt, and flowers, and the profusion of charming pieces of furniture, including a piano and many other musical instruments. The Pagilois raced to and fro, up and down, and went into raptures like a madman when he saw people reading, writing, playing games, and making music in this floating palace, and particularly when he watched the boat majestically breaking the waves without oarsmen, sails, or wind, on a motionless sea.

As for myself, I was most impressed by all the precautions taken to guard the travelers not only from cold and heat, sun and rain, but also from all the dangers and inconveniences of the trip. Not only was there a long, wide deck, perfectly clean and flat, furnished with elegant seats, where everyone could stroll or sit and enjoy the magnificent spectacle of the sea while breathing fresh air under a canopy; not only were there two superb drawing rooms, where each person could warm himself by a good fire; but every person had his own room, which contained a comfortable bed and all the other furnishings one might need.

The Icarian consul had even gone to the trouble of having printed and distributed to each traveler, in his hotel, a *Guide for the Sea Traveler*, which told what each person, according to his or her sex or age, should do to prevent or diminish seasickness. Perusing that little book, with its attractive format, I was pleased to see that the Icarian government had set up a competition among doctors and had offered a great reward to the person who would discover the means of preventing that wretched seasickness. I noted with even greater pleasure that they had succeeded in rendering it almost nonexistent.

Right after embarkation and before departure, the captain of the ship, called *tegar* (the caretaker), assembled us and told us that we should put aside all anxiety, for the ship, the sailors, and the workers were excellent, and every imaginable precaution had been taken to make a shipwreck, a steam explosion, a fire, or any sort of accident impossible. I found these reassurances repeated in my little *Guide for the Sea Traveler*, and I read with pleasure that the captains, pilots, and sailors were not authorized to work until they had passed exams at the conclusion of an excellent practical and theoretical education. The workers in charge of the steam engine were also mechanics with training, experience, and proven skill and wisdom. I was also happy to read that, before departure, the caretaker, himself a very skilled man, always inspects the whole ship, in particular the engine room, and that he writes an official report stating that no accident is possible. The admiration I felt for all this solicitude and concern for the safety of the passengers increased even more when I learned that, as in the case of seasickness, the government of Icaria had set up a competition and given a great reward to the person who presented the best design in all respects for a steamboat. This made me examine with greater attention and pleasure two bronze statues I had barely noticed before of the creators of the two winning entries in the competitions, along with the names of the creators of the ten next-best entries. Now I understood how the ship was able to offer such perfection to its passengers; this became even clearer to me when I saw an enormous, superb book set aside for the observations and ideas of each passenger about the further improvement of the ship.

Toward eight o'clock, when we had completed a third of the passage, we all ate together in the lounge. Although the meal was noteworthy for the elegance of everything placed on the table, I found all my attention taken up by the Pagilois, who could not believe that the glasses and bottles were not moving about, and whose gestures and exclamations amused everyone a great deal. Shortly after nine, the wind came up suddenly from the direction of Icaria, and we found ourselves in the midst of a violent storm, which permitted me to admire once more the care shown the passengers. Everything was set up to avoid whatever might cause alarm. All the objects were placed and secured so that nothing rolled or caused disorder or noise.

While the captain and his sailors were busy navigating, the assistant caretaker was busy reassuring the passengers. He told us that his government was a thousand times more concerned with people than with merchandise; that the safety of the passengers was the principal object of its concern; that it reserved its best ships to carry people; that shipwrecks were almost impossible with ships of this type; and that there hadn't been one for ten years, although there were frequently storms as violent as this one. Thus, no one was afraid. As I know of nothing more beautiful than a storm at sea, I stayed on deck, where I enjoyed contemplating the waves, green or white with foam and bellowing, advancing on us like mountains ready to engulf us, and which, passing under the ship and raising it, seemed to pull us to the bottom of the black abyss, where we could see only water, and then to raise us high in the sky, where we could see only dark clouds.

Noticing several big boats, which seemed to be watching us, I asked the captain if they were customs boats.

"Customs!" he said in amazement. "We haven't had any Customs for fifty years. The good ICAR destroyed that den of thieves, more ruthless than pirates and storms. Those boats that you see are lifeboats that come out during storms to lead or aid other boats that are in danger. Now they are departing, as the storm is starting to let up."

Soon afterward, we spied the coast of Icaria and then the city of Tyrama, whose port we immediately entered. I hardly had time to take note of the shore, the houses, and the vessels. Our boat stopped at the end of a long, wide iron pier, suspended over the ocean like Brighton Bridge, built for the express purpose of making disembarking as easy as possible and acting as a promenade. A magnificent staircase, which we stepped onto right from the boat, took us up on the pier. At the end of the pier, a gigantic gate, topped by a colossal statue, had the following words inscribed in enormous letters: *The Icarian Nation is brother to all other Nations.*

The assistant caretaker, who had told us what we would be required to do upon arrival, led us all to the Foreigners' Hotel, situated right near the great gate, on the site of the old customs house. Our baggage arrived almost at the same time we did, without our having to deal with it or to pay any money to anyone.

Men who seemed more like masters than servants led us with great civility to separate suites that were identical, elegant, and clean, and fitted with everything a traveler might need. There were even baths at the hotel. Every room had a framed notice telling the foreigner everything he needed to know and informing him that he would find, in one particular room, road maps, street maps, books, and all other information he might require. Soon afterward, we were served an excellent meal, during which a venerable magistrate came to welcome us in the name of the Icarian people and sat with us to talk about his country and to tell us about our upcoming trip. He seemed delighted to have an English lord visiting Icaria.

"Since you have come to study our country," he said to me after dinner, "I suggest that you go immediately to the capital by taking the carriage that leaves here this evening at five because your traveling companion will be a charming young man, the son of one of my friends, who will be pleased to serve as your cicerone. As you have a three-hour wait, I will provide you with a guide if you would like a brief tour of our city."

I had not yet gotten over my surprise and was still telling the obliging magistrate how touched I was by his warm welcome, when the guide arrived and we went out to take a quick tour of a few districts of the city. Tyrama appeared to be a new city, symmetrical in design. All the streets I walked down were straight, wide, and perfectly clean. They were lined with sidewalks, or, rather, columned porticos. All the houses I saw were charming. They were all four stories high, graced with elegant handrails, doors, and windows, and painted in various glazed colors. All the buildings on each street were the same, but the streets were different. I almost felt as if I had been transported to the beautiful streets of Rivoli and Castiglione in Paris, or to the handsome neighborhood of Regent's Park in London, but I found this district of Tyrama even more beautiful. In addition, one of my traveling companions was going into raptures at every step over the elegance of the houses, the beauty of the streets, the charm of the fountains and the squares, and the magnificence of the palaces and public buildings. The gardens, which also serve as public promenades, seemed particularly charming to me. I must admit that, from the little I saw, I felt that this was the most beautiful of all the cities I knew. I was truly dazzled by everything I was seeing in this country of Icaria.

When our guide told us it was time to end our tour, we wended our way back through the streams of a population that gave all appearance of wealth and happiness. I reached the carriage, vexed that I could offer no token of my thanks to the persons whose warm politeness had charmed me.

3 Arrival in Icara

The sight of the carriage, called a *staramoli* (a passenger cart), harnessed to six horses, gave me great pleasure, for it reminded me of the handsome "stage-coaches" and horses of my dear country. The steeds resembled our most handsome English horses. They were spirited yet docile, well brushed and shining, and were barely covered by an elegant, light harness. The carriage, as handsome as the English ones, was as light, although bigger, because it holds only the passengers and their small cases. It seemed perfect in all matters pertaining to the safety of the passengers. I noticed, with as much pleasure as amazement, innumerable small precautions to protect against the cold, particularly on the feet, and against fatigue and accidents.

The young Icarian the magistrate had told me about came over to offer his services most graciously. I willingly accepted, thanking him for his kindness.

"It is beautiful weather," he said. "I suggest we sit up on the highest seat so that we can see the countryside better." We sat on the front bench, facing the road; and the horses, after being led slowly through the city, soon raced forward to the sound of a trumpet playing a military fanfare. I could not help admiring the beauty, the spirit, the appearance, and the movements of the superb steeds who carried us away, flying so fast that we hardly had time to make out the multitude of objects that passed before our eyes.

Although I am used to the carefully cultivated fields and beautiful countryside of England, I could not help crying out in admiration when I saw the perfection of Icarian cultivation and the striking beauty of the countryside, every inch of which was planted, covered with new crops, vines, meadows, flowering trees, shrubbery, forests that seemed planted to give pleasure to the eye, farms, villages, mountains and hills, beasts of burden and laborers. Nor could I stop admiring the road, which was as or even more beautiful than our English roads, as flat and smooth as a path. It was lined with sidewalks for pedestrians, bordered by flowering trees, and dotted with charming farms and villages. It intersected frequently with bridges and rivers or canals and was filled with carriages and horses going in many directions. It seemed like one long, unending street in an endless city, or perhaps one long and magnificent promenade in the midst of an immense and magnificent garden.

I soon got acquainted with my young cicerone, who was overcome with joy when he learned my identity and the purpose of my journey.

"You seem," he said, "to be examining our carriage very carefully."

"Above all," I replied, "I was admiring with what care everything is set up for the comfort of the travelers."

"Ah!" he said. "Our good ICAR has engraved on our minds, through education and government, the principle that we must seek, in everything, the useful and the pleasing, but that we must always begin with the necessary."

"You are truly a nation of civilized men!"

"We try to be worthy of that title."

"Would you be kind enough," I said to him, "to explain something that has been troubling me. Your consul told me that you are forbidden to use money. How do you pay for your seat in this carriage?"

"I don't."

"And the other passengers?"

"They don't either."

"What do you mean?"

"The carriage belongs to our noble sovereign."

"And the horses?"

"To our all-powerful sovereign."

"And all the public carriages and all their horses?"

"To our wealthy sovereign."

"And your sovereign transports all the citizens without charge?"

"Yes."

"But . . ."

"I will explain all this to you shortly." As he was saying these words, the carriage stopped for two women who had been waiting for it. Judging from the respectful eagerness with which every man offered them his seat or helped them up, you might have guessed that they were women of noble rank.

"Do you know these women?" I said to my companion.

"Not at all," he said. "They are probably the wife and daughter of one of the local farmers, but we are in the habit of respecting and helping all our female compatriots as if they were our mothers, our wives, our sisters, or our daughters. Does this custom shock you?"

"On the contrary." And I was telling the truth, for his answer, which had at first astounded me, filled me with admiration for a people capable of such a sentiment. In turn, Valmor—for that was his name—asked me many questions about England, repeating constantly that he was delighted that a lord had come with the express purpose of visiting his country of Icaria. He told me that he was twenty-two, he was studying to be a priest, and he lived in the capital with his parents. All his family members, twenty-six in number, lived together in the same dwelling. It took some effort for me to find out (because he was so modest and reserved) that his father was a chief magistrate, and that Corilla, his older sister, was one of the most beautiful girls of the country. Everything he told me about his family members made me very anxious to meet them.

At nightfall, we had to cross a chain of rather high mountains, but the magnificent full moon allowed us to see a multitude of picturesque sights. What I admired most, yet again, was the road, which was always clearly marked. It was almost always very gradual in slope. Consequently, we kept going at full gallop even at the steepest points, with two, four, or six lively horses, added to the original six, smoothing out all difficulties. And I admired, once more, the precautions taken everywhere to make all sorts of accidents impossible. We were able to descend quite a steep mountain, by the banks of a raging stream and a frightening precipice, at a gallop because there was a parapet placed on either side of the road, and because the lock on the brakes was so good that it was no more difficult for the horses to pull the carriage down than to pull it up the slope. Valmor kept pointing out to me with what concern his benevolent sovereign had seen to the safety of the traveler, while I remembered with pain and fright the innumerable accidents that happen elsewhere owing to the negligence of the government.

"These precautions," he told me with visible satisfaction, "are taken everywhere by our good sovereign, on the roads and rivers as well as on all the streets, because the safety of the people is, in her eyes, a goal of primary necessity. Everywhere, the sovereign causes rocky precipices to be destroyed or pushed back or sees to it that all necessary barriers are put up to keep vehicles from crashing over them; for our sovereign feels it would be foolish, even criminally negligent, not to build whatever works are necessary on bridges, wherever a fall might be possible."

After passing through many villages and five or six cities, without stopping anywhere (because the horses were unhitched and harnessed so quickly), and without meeting up with gates, barriers, or intruders, we stopped for supper in a Travelers' Hotel similar to the one at Tyrama.

"How did you pay for your supper?" I asked Valmor.

"I didn't pay for it."

"Does this hotel also belong to your sovereign, like the carriages and the horses?"

"Yes."

"It is your sovereign who feeds and transports her subjects?"

"Yes."

"But . . ."

"Patience! I will explain everything that amazes you."

Descending onto the plain, we entered a road lined with artificial grooves, some made of iron and others of stone, in which the carriage flew as if it were on rails. Soon afterward, we reached a great railroad, whose steam power carried us along at the speed of wind or lightning. I was not particularly surprised to see this railroad cut through a mountain and then hang suspended over a valley because I had seen similar wonders in England; but I was quite amazed to see the road set at different levels like a canal, with powerful machines raising and lowering the cars, just as locks raise and lower boats.

"Do you have many of these railroads?" I asked Valmor.

"We have twelve great ones that cross the country in all directions and a multitude of small ones that connect with the principal lines. It seems, however, that a chemical agent has just been discovered that is stronger than steam and is produced from *sorub*, a raw material more plentiful than coal. This will cause a revolution in the industry and will allow us to increase the railroads even more. We also have a great number of canals, and almost all of our rivers are connected to canals. In less than an hour, we will be traveling on one of our most beautiful rivers."

The sky had just become light when we arrived at Camira, situated on a wide river covered with steamboats, some for transporting passengers and others for merchandise. The railroad had taken us right up to the boat, so I was not able to see the city. However, like all those we had passed by during the night, it looked as beautiful as Tyrama. We had barely lost sight of the city when we were treated to a magnificent spectacle. The sun rose before our eyes, in the middle of the river, between two charming hills covered with greenery, flowering trees, copses, and pretty houses that looked like castles. The scene reminded me of the banks of the Saône near Lyon.

Valmor pointed out to me the beauty of the boat that was carrying us, as well as all the little mechanisms for embarking and disembarking, which are always done on foot, without the intermediary step of little boats. There is no possibility of an accident, and the most timid women and children are never afraid in the slightest.

"And these boats," I asked him, "do they belong to your sovereign, too?"

"They certainly do."

"And all the boats that carry merchandise?"

"Those as well."

"And the merchandise also belongs to her?"

"Naturally."

"Please, won't you explain to me . . ."

"Yes, I will explain everything. . . . But look at these people who are waiting to come on board with us."

He had scarcely finished speaking when the boat stopped in front of eight or ten persons who soon became our traveling companions. In this group, there were two women who appeared to be mother and daughter. Valmor rushed up to them, greeted them as if they were close friends, and bade them sit next to us. He sat on my right, between the women and myself. I was not able to see their faces, which were hidden beneath large hats and thick veils; but from the gracefulness of their movements, I thought that both of them, and in particular the younger, must be charming. I could not help trembling when I heard her voice. It was one of those indescribable voices that touch your soul and cause you to shiver slightly. I had not heard such a voice since Miss Mars made me weep with tenderness and pleasure.

I was certain that so pretty a voice could come only from a divine face; however, I would have liked to see it with my own eyes. The longer the face was hidden, the more I desired to see it; but no matter how much I peered, even walking around to look more carefully, the jealous veil and the importunate hat seemed designed to punish my curiosity. My disappointment reached its peak, and I almost cursed that which I could not see when, two hours later, Valmor, who had been paying all his attention to the ladies, came to tell me that they were going to get off at a nearby stop and that he was going to go with them and not return until the next day. Although I had known him for only a short while, I was very sad to see him go. He did not leave, however, without repeating his regrets and his offers of hospitality. He added that his family would be delighted to welcome me if I wished to honor them with a visit, and that he would be very pleased if I felt him worthy of my friendship. His manner, although fervent, seemed so natural and sincere that I was very moved; and he himself seemed so well educated, so good, and so kind that we began, then and there, an affectionate friendship that became stronger and more intimate every day. This friendship, pleasing and precious at first, was destined to become the source of many regrets and much pain for me.

Shortly thereafter, the other passengers and I left the river to get back onto the railroad, and toward eleven o'clock we saw the tops of the thousand buildings of the capital city. Soon, between two rows of high poplars, we arrived at the western gate, a gigantic monument, under whose immense arch I stood without being able to read its inscription or to look at its statues. There I beheld the most magnificent entry to a capital that I have ever seen. Traveling down a long, wide avenue with a gentle slope, like that of the Champs-Elysées in Paris, bordered on each side with four columns of trees, my gaze turned downward toward the city, alighting first on two magnificent columned palaces and then passing between them to lose itself on a wide street that crosses the city. This majestic entryway alone would have sufficed to make me believe in all the wonders of Icaria.

The carriage stopped at the Provincial Hotel, next to which was the Foreigners' Hotel. Although the two hotels were immense, it was easy for compatriots to meet there because the hotels were divided into sections, one for each Icarian province and one for each nation of visitors to Icaria.

"Travelers certainly take up a great deal of space in Icaria," I exclaimed when I saw these immense hotels.

"Do you think they would take up less space," said someone, "if there were hundreds or thousands of little hotels for them in every section of the city?"

I was very disappointed to find no other Englishman there. Because of this, I was even more delighted to make the acquaintance of a young French painter named Eugene, exiled from his country after the July Revolution, who had arrived in Icaria two weeks earlier. Everything he had seen had made him so enthusiastic that he was feverish, delirious. At first, I thought him a madman. I soon discovered, however, that he was frank, warm in his feelings, and of noble heart and soul. He seemed so happy to find a compatriot (for a Frenchman and an Englishman who meet so far away feel as if they come from the same country) that I soon felt kindly disposed to return his friendship.

4 Description of Icaria and Icara

The next morning I was lying on my bed, after taking a bath in the hotel, when Valmor came to invite me, on behalf of his father, to spend the evening with the family. I accepted eagerly because I was anxious to see the people he had spoken of during our trip; and we agreed to meet at four o'clock.

"And that beautiful 'invisible one'," I said to him, "have you brought her back with you?"

"No."

"She must be very ugly to hide herself so carefully."

"Ugly! Yes, frightfully! But you will surely find (for you will see her one day) that there is no one with more pleasant a temperament." As he was leaving, Eugene came in.

"That is the traveling companion I told you about," I said.

"What is his name?"

"Valmor."

"Valmor! How lucky you are, for I have heard him spoken of as one of the most distinguished and noble young Icarians."

"He told me that his father is one of the chief magistrates."

"Yes, I know him. He is a locksmith."

"His sister, Corilla, is one of Icaria's great beauties."

"Yes, the very one, and a charming seamstress."

"What do you mean? A locksmith, a seamstress!"

"Well, why are you so surprised? Can a seamstress not be pretty? And can a locksmith not be an excellent magistrate?"

"But are there no members of the nobility here?"

"Yes, there are many citizens who are noble, famous, and illustrious. They are mechanics, doctors, or any workers who distinguish themselves through some great discovery or service."

"What? The queen's entourage is not made up of members of the hereditary nobility?"

"What queen?"

"The queen of Icaria, the sovereign Valmor kept speaking about, praising her inexhaustible kindness, her concern for the general good, her prodigious wealth, and her total power. I was very pleased to hear of a queen who brings such honor to her title."

"I ask you once again, to what queen are you referring? What is her name?"

"Valmor never told me her name. He told me only that it was the sovereign of Icaria who owned the carriages, horses, hotels, and steamboats, and who transported travelers while watching out for their safety."

"Ah, now I understand," he said, bursting out laughing. "The sovereign you took to be a queen is actually the Republic, the good and excellent republic, democracy, equality. I understand how you thought a queen must possess all the property and power, but how could you have thought. . . ? Ah, Milord, you must abandon all your aristocratic prejudices here and become a democrat like me or leave this country quickly because I warn you that the air we breathe here is deadly for the aristocracy."

"We shall see, we shall see, mister democrat! But before we do, would you like to give an aristocrat a tour of Icara?"

"With pleasure, because I am sure I will be able to 'dearistocratize' you from head to foot. Do you want to see the city without tiring yourself too much?"

"Certainly, if that is possible."

"Well, follow me."

Eugene led me to the big common parlor, where there were many maps of the country and immense street maps.

"First of all, let us take a look at this map of Icaria, which shows only its frontiers, its provinces, and its communes. You can see that Icaria is bordered on the south and north by two mountain ranges that separate it from Pagilia and Miron, on the east by a large river, and on the west by the ocean, which separates it from the country of the Marvols, which you traveled through to get here. You can also see that the territory is divided into one hundred provinces of approximately equal size and population.

"Let us look at a map of one of the provinces. It is divided, as you see, into ten approximately equal communes. The provincial city is located just about at the center of the province, and each communal capital is at the center of its commune. Now, look at the map of a commune. You will see that, apart from the communal capital, there are eight villages and many farms, placed at equidistant points throughout the territory. Now let us look at this other map of Icaria, which shows the mountains and valleys, plateaus and plains, lakes and rivers, canals and railroads, highways and provincial routes. Look here! The great railroads are marked in red, the small in yellow, the grooved roads in blue, and all other roads in black. Take a look at the canals, large and small, and all the navigable rivers or those with canals. You can also see the mines and quarries that are being worked. Look at the provincial roads on this provincial map and the communal roads on this communal map. And now, tell me if you have ever seen a greater number of more easily accessible means of travel and communication."

I was, in fact, dazzled. It was even better than England. Next we examined a superb street map of Icara.

"It is perfectly symmetrical!" I exclaimed.

"Yes," said Eugene. "Plans were specially drawn up in 1784. The construction, begun fifty-two years ago, will not be finished for fifteen or twenty more years. Look here! The city, almost circular in shape, is divided into two almost equal halves by the Tair (or Majestic) River, whose course was redirected in order to enclose it within two almost straight walls. Its bed was dug out so that it could accommodate ships arriving from the sea. Here are the ports, the docks, and the warehouses, so many that they form almost an entire city on their own. You can see that in the middle of the city, the river is divided into two branches that move apart, come closer, and join together once more in the original direction, so that a rather large island, circular in shape, is formed. This island serves as the main square and is planted with trees. In the middle is a palace surrounded by a vast, superb terraced garden with, at its center, an immense column topped by a colossal statue that rises higher than all the buildings. On each riverbank, you can see a large quay lined with public buildings. Both near and far from this central square, you may see two circles, one made up of twenty squares and the other of forty. The squares are almost equidistant one from the other and are spread out throughout the city.

"Look at the streets, all straight and wide! There are fifty large ones that cross the city parallel to the river and fifty perpendicular to it. The others are of different lengths. The ones marked in black, which link the squares, are lined with trees like the Paris boulevards. The ten large red lines are railroad streets. The yellow ones are artificial grooved streets, and the blue ones are canal streets."

"And what," I asked him, "are all those wide, long pink bands I see everywhere between the rows of houses on two streets?"

"Those are the gardens in back of the houses. I will show them to you soon. But first, look at these areas shown by light shades of all the colors that make up the city. There are sixty of them. They are the sixty neighborhoods (or communes) of almost equal size; each is the size and population of a regular communal city. Each neighborhood is named after one of the sixty major cities of the ancient and modern worlds and represents in its monuments and houses the architecture of one of the sixty principal nations. Here you will see neighborhoods of Peking, Jerusalem, and Constantinople, as well as those of Rome, Paris, and London, so that Icara is, in fact, a model of the terrestrial universe.

"Here is a street map of one of those neighborhoods! The painted areas represent public buildings. Here are the school, the hospital, and the temple. The red spaces are large workshops, the yellow ones department stores, the blue ones assembly halls, the violet ones monuments. Note that the public buildings are distributed in such a way that there are some on every street. All streets have the same number of houses as well as buildings of approximately the same number and size. Here is a detailed map of one street. Look here! There are sixteen houses on each side, with a public building in the middle and one at each end. These sixteen houses are similar on the outside or are attached, forming a single building, but no street is identical to another. By now you must have an idea of what Icara is like. Would you like to look at the sketch of a house or public building, or would you rather go out for a short while?"

"Yes, let's go!"

"If you wish, we can take the steamboat below the port and come up the river to the central square."

"Yes, let's go! Let's fly! Let us go see some gardens first!"

We soon entered one of those vast gardens through a magnificent portico, similar to those I had seen in Tyrama. The garden formed a large square set between the houses of four streets (two parallel and two perpendicular) and was divided up the middle by a band of grass between two pathways of pretty, reddish sand. The remainder of the garden consisted of grass that went right up to the walls or planted areas filled with flowers, bushes, flowering trees, and fruit trees. The backs of the houses represented various styles of rural architecture and were decorated with painted trellises of leafy and flowering climbing plants. This ensemble made up a magnificent garden that perfumed the air while charming the eye and formed a delightful public promenade while enhancing the delights of the adjoining dwellings.

"And the city," said Eugene, "is filled with gardens such as this one, as you have seen on the map, between every set of streets behind the houses. The lawn in the middle is often replaced by trees or arbors, brooks, or even canals lined with pretty handrails. The public always enters through four superb gates at the center of the four streets, and each house has its own entrance."

"Really!" I exclaimed, entranced. "These gardens are as beautiful as our magnificent 'squares' in London!"

"What, just as beautiful!" said Eugene. "You mean to say a hundred times better than your aristocratic squares, closed off by walls or high grillwork and hedges that keep even the people's eyes from penetrating them. Here the people stroll in these democratic gardens, pass through on these charming pathways dotted with pretty benches, and enjoy a full view over a charming border of flowers. In addition, each household has exclusive use of its own garden, set off from the others by a simple iron wire that you do not even see. You can see how carefully each little garden is cultivated, how the grass is trimmed, how beautiful the flowers are, and how the trees are planted, trimmed, and shaped in a thousand different forms!"

"What! Every house has its own garden? A great many gardeners must be needed to tend them all!"

"Not a single one, or very few, because each family considers one of its principal pleasures to be the cultivation of flowers and shrubs. At this time of day, you can see only children and mothers, but this evening you will see men, women, boys, and girls working together in their gardens. We must move on if we wish to complete our tour."

"There must be small cabs or hackneys, like in Paris and London. Let us take one to go faster!"

"Take one, take one, you say! There is not a single cab or hackney, not even a carriage in this poor democratic country!"

"What are you telling me?"

"The truth! See for yourself! You will not see a carriage the whole length of the street."

"And there is no omnibus?"

"There are only *staragomi* (popular carriages), which you must have noticed earlier. We are going to take one."

We entered a *staragomi* passing by on the next street. It was a type of double-decker omnibus that held forty passengers seated facing the front, on eight benches with five seats. Each bench had its own side entry. Everything was designed for the comfort of the passengers, to keep the carriage warm in winter and cool in summer, and above all to prevent accidents or risks of any kind. The wheels were placed under the carriage in two iron grooves. Three superb horses pulled the carriage rapidly along them. We passed by a great number of these *staragomi* going down the other side of the street, almost all different in physical appearance, but, nevertheless, much more elegant than the English and French omnibuses. Eugene informed me that half of the streets (every other one) had omnibus lines. Fifty large streets had so many that one came by every two minutes. Thousands of omnibuses had special destinations so that all the citizens were transported everywhere more conveniently than if each had a separate rig.

At the far end of the street, we got onto another *staragomi* on rails that took us below the port. There we took a steamboat to go back up the river to the city center. I felt as if I were back in London, and I felt an inexplicable mixture of pleasure and nostalgia when I saw an immense dock area, canals, other smaller docks, superb quays, magnificent warehouses, thousands of little steamboats and sailboats, thousands of machines for loading and unloading—in short, all the activities of commerce and industry.

"At the other end of the city," Eugene told me, "is another port, almost as beautiful as this one, for the boats that carry products from the provinces."

I was more and more amazed; but I was entranced when, heading farther into the city on this majestic river, filled with a multitude of small craft painted and decked out with flags, I saw, on my right, banks lined with trees and with public buildings and palaces. What thrilled me the most was that, although the river was contained between walls, the banks were irregular and winding, closer or farther apart, and filled with lawns, flowers, shrubs, weeping willows, or tall poplars, and the walls of the quays were often hidden by climbing vines.

Before we reached the central square, we came across two charming little islands, covered with plants and flowers, and we passed under fifteen or twenty superb wooden, stone, or iron bridges. Some were for pedestrians and others for carriages; some were flat and others curved; some had one or two arches, whereas others had ten or twenty.

The central square, with its promenade by the river, its grandiose national palace, its inner garden, and its gigantic statue, took my breath away. Next, Eugene took me to see a strange bridge called the Sagal (the Jump), which was made of parallel hanging ropes attached on one side to the top of a tower twenty feet above the quay and on the other side to the river bank opposite us. Suspended from each pair of ropes was a sort of gondola holding four people. This gondola, slowly moving down the rope, takes passengers from the tower to the opposite bank. A second set of tower, ropes, and gondolas brings passengers back in the same manner. I felt an inexplicable joy (for I wanted to try it) when I saw myself clear, as if in one leap, the abyss at my feet. People would flock to it, as they used to flock to the roller-coaster, if the means had not been found to discourage those who were there only for fun.

I was still dazzled and astonished by everything I had seen when Valmor came to collect me at my hotel at the appointed hour.

"What *staragomi* you have!" I said to him. "Is it your republic, yet again, that constructs the public carriages, like your travelers' carriages and boats, with the citizen's comfort its only concern?"

"You have guessed it."

"And those enormous draft horses that I saw (they are magnificent, as handsome as our great English breeds). Do they and their carriages also belong to the republic?"

"Right again!"

"Your republic is quite the monopolist of stagecoaches, coaches, omnibuses, and transport!"

"Just as your monarchy is quite the monopolist of letters, powder, and tobacco, with one difference. Your monarchy sells its services, whereas our republic provides them free of charge."

"But if all the horses and carriages belong to the republic, your republic must have fine stables!"

"It has fifty or sixty, located at the outer limits of the city."

"They must be quite something!"

"Would you like to see one? We do have the time."

"Onward!"

We got into an omnibus and soon found ourselves in a district devoted to stables. I was amazed! Imagine an immense five-storied stable, in fact five immense stables stacked one on top of the other, clean, washed, painted, as beautiful as palaces, and housing, all together, about two or three thousand horses. Imagine, next to them, immense warehouses of grain and fodder. Imagine immense sheds, each several stories high, to house the carriages. Imagine immense workshops of wheelwrights, blacksmiths, and saddlers, all the workers who take care of horses and carriages. Valmor enjoyed pointing out to me the savings, order, and all the advantages resulting from this new, centralized system. There are no private stables and no sheds next to living quarters! There is no horse manure, fodder, or grain brought through the streets! I was so amazed and fascinated that I would have spent the whole night there if Valmor had not reminded me that it was time to join his family.

We found them seated in the parlor. Four generations mingled there: Valmor's grandfather, an old man about seventy-two years of age who had lost his dear wife several years ago and was head of the extended family; Valmor's father and mother, about forty-eight to fifty years old; his older brother with his wife and three small children; his two sisters—Corilla, twenty, and Célinie, eighteen; and finally, two uncles, one of whom was a widower, and ten or twelve male and female cousins or second cousins of all ages. In all, there were twenty-four or twenty-six people. The old man, although not particularly handsome, had, with his white hair and his open, wrinkled face, an air of nobility and goodness that made him pleasant to behold. Valmor's father gave the impression of strength and dignity. His mother was, of all those present, the one whose face was the least blessed by nature, but she seemed adequately compensated because she possessed in goodness all that she lacked in bodily grace, and she appeared to be the main object of affection.

Almost all the children were charming, in particular a little nephew who often came to sit on Valmor's lap. One of his female cousins was, unfortunately, missing an eye, but two others were extremely pretty. His sister Célinie, with her beautiful blond hair falling in curls around her shoulders and her peaches and cream complexion, looked like a beautiful English woman. His sister Corilla, with black, shining eyes, seemed even more beautiful to me, with all the grace and vivacity of a French woman. Everything shone with magnificence, perfect taste, and exquisite elegance in the parlor embellished with flowers and filled by their perfume. But what made it even more beautiful to me was the serenity, joy, and happiness that shone on all the faces. I could not get over finding, in that parlor, the locksmith and the dressmaker of whom Eugene had spoken.

First, Valmor introduced me to his father, who presented me to his grandfather; and he, like a patriarch, presented me to the rest of the family. At first, everyone joined in the conversation, and they asked me many questions about England.

"I am acquainted with your country," said the old man. "I went there in 1784 to fulfill a mission entrusted me by our good Icar, my friend, and I have fond memories of the welcome I received. Your country is very rich and powerful! Your London is very big and contains many beautiful things! But, Milord, I must tell you that there is one aspect that is certainly hideous, revolting, and shameful for your government, and that is the horrible poverty that devours a portion of your population! I will never forget that when I was leaving a magnificent party given by one of your great lords, I came across the corpses of a woman and her child who, almost naked, had just died of hunger and cold on the pavement." (At this point, the children uttered a cry of terror that made a most painful impression on me.)

"Ah, you are only too correct," I answered. "I blush with shame for my country, and it breaks my heart, but what can be done about it? We have many charitable men and women who give immense sums to the poor."

"I know, Milord. I even know a young gentleman, as modest as he is good, who has just built, on one of his properties, a hospital where his charitable goodness houses fifty-five unfortunate souls." (Here I blushed, but I recovered very quickly, not knowing how he could know my personal affairs.) "Those men do honor to their country and should be blessed! Their benevolence is more valuable, in our eyes, than all their riches and titles. They have even more merit than we do because they have had to fight against the restrictions of a bad social organization, whereas we, thanks to our good Icar, have no more poor people."

"What! You have no poor people?"

"Of course not, not a one. Have you seen a single man in rags or a single house that looks like a hovel? Do you not see that the republic makes everyone equally rich, demanding only that we do an equal share of work?"

"What? You all work?"

"Yes, and we all are happy and proud of it! My father was a duke and one of the greatest nobles of this country, and my sons were destined to be counts, marquises, and barons. Now one is a locksmith, one a printer, and the third an architect. Valmor will be a priest, and his brother is a house painter. All these good girls have a trade, and it does not make them uglier or less charming. Isn't our Corilla a pretty dressmaker? You will go and visit her at her workshop!"

"I am astounded!"

"Ah, Milord. As you have come here in order to learn, we will show you many other marvels! But we can show you neither people who do not work nor domestic servants."

"You have no servants?"

"No one has any. The good Icar delivered us from the plague of domestic servants, while freeing them from the curse of domestic service."

"I am lost. Who is this good Icar, about whom I keep hearing? And how have you been able to do this?"

"I do not have enough time to explain it all today, but Valmor, who seems to have bewitched you into liking him, and his friend Dinaros, one of our most brilliant history professors, will be happy to explain everything to you, to show you everything, and to answer all your questions. Let them guide you in your study of our Icaria."

"Do you like flowers, Milord?" asked one of the mothers.

"Very much, Madam. I find nothing as pretty."

"Nothing as pretty as flowers?" one of the girls said, blushing.

"Yes, Miss. I am sorry to disappoint you. Nothing prettier than . . . certain . . . roses."

"You do not like children?" said one of the little girls, who was sitting on my lap and looking at me with a searching gaze I could not fathom.

"I like nothing better than little angels," I said, kissing her.

"Do you like dancing?" Célinie asked.

"I like to watch other people dance, but I am not a good dancer."

"Well then, you will learn, Milord," said Corilla, "for I want to dance with you."

"Do you like music?" her father asked me suddenly.

"Passionately."

"Do you sing?"

"A little."

"What instrument do you play?"

"The violin."

"We will not pressure Milord today," said the old grandfather. "He will pay his dues another time, but as he likes music, let us sing, children. My dear Corilla, let us show Milord what an Icarian dressmaker is really like."

"But," I said softly, "are you not like those painters who pretend to show you all their paintings and exhibit only their masterpieces?"

"You shall see," he answered, smiling.

The children had already rushed to get a guitar, which one of them gave to Corilla with a charming smile, and Valmor took up his flute to accompany his sister. Without further ado, and without seeming to value her talent, Corilla sang. Her ease, naturalness, grace, and striking beauty, the purity of her pronunciation, her brilliant voice, and her eyes sparkling with wit: everything carried me away. A second song, whose refrain was repeated by all the girls and the children, charmed me even more.

"Our national anthem!" cried Valmor's father. Valmor had already taken up the tune. All the children sang together. The fathers, who were playing chess, the mothers, who were playing at another table, interrupted their games to turn toward the singers; and all of them, carried away by the same spirit, lifted their voices to sing the praises of their country. I was surprised to find myself joining in on the third verse, which led to much laughter and applause. I have never seen anything as delightful. While laughing about my enthusiasm for music, people set the table with fresh and dried fruit, jams, puddings, cakes, and a variety of light drinks. Everything was served by the lovely hands of the girls and was presented with the enchanting smiles of the children.

"Well, Milord," said the lively old man. "Do you think we need lackeys to serve us?"

"Certainly not, when," I added quietly, moving close to him, "one is served by the Graces and the goddesses of love."

I complimented the mothers and fathers as best I could on their families, thanked them for the friendly welcome they had given me, and withdrew, filled with delicious memories. When sleep finally came, gently closing my eyelids, it rocked me with smiling dreams.

5 A Look at the Social and Political Organization and History of Icaria

Yesterday's songs still echoed softly in my enchanted ear and gracious smiles still charmed my eyes when I was awakened by Valmor.

"How lucky you are, my dear friend," I said, "to have such a charming family!"

"It pleased you?"

"Ah! More than words can express."

"What a shame," he said, with an expression that surprised me. "I feel very sorry for you, but I must tell you the truth. This is what happened at the house after you left."

"Come now, tell me."

"Well, my grandfather, although head of the family and free to have as a guest anyone he wishes, does not like to invite any person who might displease even one of his children."

"Could I have had the misfortune of hurting someone's feelings? Tell me!"

"After your departure, he sat us down in a circle and asked if anyone was opposed to your admittance, after mentioning that I had already predisposed the family in your favor."

"Get on with it!"

"I said that I felt I knew you as well as if I had lived for several years with you, and that I had for you an irresistible feeling of friendship."

"Out with it, I beg you!"

"Everybody seemed to applaud, but then Corilla began to speak . . . and you were . . ."

"Rejected!" I cried, leaping off the bed.

"Not at all," he continued, bursting out laughing, "but admitted unanimously, with all the enthusiasm your friend desired. Please excuse this mad joke, inspired by the pleasure I felt at your acceptance into my family. You should be even angrier at Corilla because it was she who gave me the idea. However, to ensure that you will not hold it against her, she commands you to make your formal entrance this evening as friend of the household. You will meet the learned history professor my grandfather spoke of last night: my friend Dinaros, brother of the ugly yet pleasant 'invisible one.' Agreed? Do you forgive me?" (I could only answer by embracing him.) "Just a moment. We must agree beforehand on the conditions; for Corilla's vote hinges on one condition."

"And what is that? Tell me quickly!"

"It is that William will come and announce that Milord has departed. Agreed?" (I embraced him a second time.) "Let us be off," he said, laughing like a madman. "I have acquitted myself of a dangerous mission. I will go and bring my message to the formidable master who awaits me. I will see you at six o'clock this evening."

If the sound of my voice could have made the earth turn more quickly, the evening would have arrived earlier than usual. To wait for it more patiently, I accepted Eugene's invitation to join him for a visit to one of the national printing presses. The sight of this print shop gave me as much or even more pleasure than the pyramids of Egypt. First of all, let me tell you that the republic had it built, and the architect was able to use all the space he needed. Now, try to imagine a building of great length, containing five thousand printers on three floors, supported by hundreds of small iron columns. On the two upper floors, against the walls, are shelves loaded with metal characters of all kinds, brought down or lifted up by machines. In the middle, in one line, are cabinets, placed back to back. A typesetter is seated in front of each cabinet and has everything he needs at his fingertips.

On the side, in a single line, are the beds for placing the compositions, dividing into pages and imposing the forms. Next to each of these tables is an opening, through which a machine lowers the form onto a press, which is on the ground floor. There are three or four rows of cabinets and tables on each floor. It is a marvelous sight. The mechanical presses are located on the ground floor.

To the left of the print shop are immense buildings for manufacturing paper, ink, and characters, and for storing raw or manufactured materials, brought and taken away by canal and moved by machine. There is such a variety of machines that they do almost everything themselves, replacing, so we are told, almost fifty thousand workers. The process is undertaken in such a way that rags are turned into paper that goes directly into the press. The press prints it on both sides and deposits it, all printed and dried, in the bindery located to the right with other immense buildings for assembling, hole punching, and stitching the printed sheets, binding books, and storing them. All the workshops and workers involved in printing are located together in the same section, forming a small city of their own. Almost all the workers live in the neighborhood of their workshops.

"Imagine," Eugene kept repeating, overwhelmed, "what savings of space and time result from this admirable arrangement, to say nothing of the saving of manpower produced by the machines! And it is the republic that has learned how to organize its workshops, its machines, and its workers in this way!"

I was as dazzled as Eugene when I saw this ensemble, order, and activity; and I imagined what this country could produce if all its industries were organized according to the same system. But this did not prevent me from feeling that six o'clock was coming too slowly.

I finally arrived at Valmor's home at exactly the appointed hour, and it was not without emotion that I went into the parlor, where the family had gathered. Imagine my consternation when I saw Corilla jump up, crying: "Ah, here he is! I want to greet him!" and then, running toward me, say, "Come, William, give me your hand, for I want to introduce you to my father today."

"Milord," said the old man in solemn tones, giving me his hand. "As I am full of gratitude for the kind welcome I was given earlier in your country, I am delighted that my household pleases you, and all of us will be flattered if you consider us as friends. By admitting you to our family, among my cherished daughters and beloved granddaughters, I give you proof of my high esteem for your character and my full confidence in your honor. Please forgive the innocent playfulness of my children in treating you already like an old friend." All the children crowded around me, seeing which one could give me the most kisses. I was moved, filled with respect, enchanted, delighted; and the words of the old man were engraved on my heart like sacred, holy words.

"Dinaros will not be coming," said Valmor, "because he is awaiting the arrival of his mother and sister. Would you care to go and see him?" I assented, and we got up to leave.

"Well, that is a fine way to behave!" said Corilla, picking up her hat. "We have but one unmarried brother and one friend of the family, and when poor

Célinie and I want to go and see our friends, these gallant gentlemen leave by themselves, without having the decency to ask us if we need escorts. Stop right there, gentlemen. We will escort you. Célinie, give your arm to Valmor. I will take William's."

Almost intoxicated by having such a charming creature so close to me, I was, nevertheless, quite relaxed with Corilla, although I am usually timid and uncomfortable around women. I do not know what perfume of innocence and virtue seemed to free my soul and to inspire in me a delectable boldness unfettered by any anxieties. "My feelings of affection for your brother and your family," I said to her as we were walking, "and my respect for you certainly merit some response on your part; but you overwhelm me with kind acts and, precious as they may be to me, I cannot help but fear that I have not earned them."

"Ah! I can see through your uncomfortable speech. You are surprised by the rapidity of our friendship. You are shocked by my thoughtlessness, by my madness. Well, you are quite mistaken. Our republic has as many spies as all your monarchies. You are surrounded by spies. Your servant, John, whom you think so faithful, is a traitor. Interrogated by Valmor, he told on you and revealed all your crimes. We know who built, for fifty-five poor souls, that hospital Grandfather was telling you about yesterday. We know who funds a school for the poor girls who live on his land. We know whose name the unfortunate ones bless in a certain county. I also interrogated you without your knowing it, and I ascertained that you love children and flowers, which, to us, is the sign of a simple and pure soul. In short, we know that you have a good heart, an excellent heart. Being that goodness is the most important quality to us, and seeing as Grandfather holds you in high esteem and loves you, we honor you and love you as we would an old friend. I hope that everything is now completely clear. Let us speak no more about it. At any rate, here we are. Let us wait for Valmor and Célinie, for we have walked fast without noticing it."

Valmor and Corilla introduced me to Dinaros, whose facial features appealed to me and whose manners and welcome pleased me even more. The women had not yet arrived and probably would not do so until the next day, so, together with Dinaros, we all returned to the home of Valmor's father, passing through a section of the neighborhood called Athens.

"So you have no shops or storehouses in private homes?" I asked Valmor when we had returned.

"No," he replied. "The republic has large workshops and warehouses, but the good Icar freed us from the shop and the shopkeeper, while freeing the shopkeeper from all the cares that made his life a misery."

"Dinaros," said the venerable grandfather, "explain to Milord the marvels that puzzle him. Set out the principles of our social and political organization.

Tell him about our good Icar and our last revolution. Milord will not be the first to listen to you with pleasure." Even the children stopped their games to listen to their friend Dinaros, and the young historian fulfilled our wish without delay.

Principles of Social Organization in Icaria

"You are aware," he said, "that man distinguishes himself from all other animate beings by his reason, his perfectibility, and his sociability. Deeply convinced by experience that there can be no happiness without association and equality, all Icarians form a SOCIETY based on perfect EQUALITY. All are associates and citizens, equal in rights and in duties. All share equally the duties and the benefits of association. Thus, all make up but a single FAMILY, whose members are united by the bonds of FRATERNITY.

"Thus we form a people, or a nation, of brothers, and all our laws have as their goal to establish among us the most absolute equality, in all cases where this equality is not materially impossible."

"However," I said to him, "hasn't nature herself established inequality by giving people physical and intellectual qualities that are almost always unequal?"

"That is true," he said, "but is it not nature as well who has given to all men the same desire to be happy, the same right to life and to happiness, and the same love of equality, the intelligence and REASON to organize happiness, society, and equality? Besides, Milord, do not be deterred by that objection, for we have solved the problem, and you are going to see the most complete social equality imaginable.

"Just as we form a single society, a people, and a single family, so our land, along with its underground mines and its above-ground constructions, forms but a single domain, which is our social domain. All the property of the associates, along with all the products of earth and industry, form a single social capital. This social domain and this social capital belong indivisibly to the people, who cultivate them and work them together, who administer them together or by designated members, and who then share equally all the resulting products."

"But this is COMMUNAL OWNERSHIP OF GOODS!" I exclaimed.

"Precisely," said Valmor's grandfather. "Does such a community frighten you?"

"No, but people have always said that it is an impossibility."

"Impossible! You shall see . . ."

"Being that all Icarians are associates and equals," Dinaros continued, "they all must practice a trade and work for the same number of hours. All their intelligence is enlisted to discover all possible means of making this work short, varied, pleasant, and without danger. All work instruments and materials are provided through shared capital, and all agricultural and industrial products are deposited in public warehouses. All of us are fed, clothed, lodged, and have our homes furnished by shared capital; and we all receive the same goods, according to sex, age, and a few other circumstances provided for by law. Thus, it is the republic or the community that is the sole proprietor, that organizes its workers and builds its workshops and storehouses.

"It is the republic that causes the earth to be cultivated, houses to be built, and all products made that are needed for food, clothing, shelter, and furnishings. It is the republic that feeds, lodges, and provides furnishings to every family and every citizen.

"Being that we consider EDUCATION to be the basis and foundation of society, the republic provides it to all its children equally, just as it gives them equal nourishment. All children receive the same elementary instruction, as well as the specialized training appropriate for individual professions; and the object of this education is to form good workers, good parents, good citizens, and real men. This is the substance of our social organization, and, based on these few words, you may easily imagine the rest."

"Now you can understand," said the old man, "why we have neither poor people nor domestic servants."

"You must also understand," Valmor added, "how it is that the republic owns all the horses, carriages, and hotels that you saw, and how it feeds and transports its travelers for nothing. And it must also be clear to you that, because each of us receives, as a matter of course, everything he needs, money, buying, and selling are completely unnecessary."

"Yes," I replied, "I understand perfectly well, but . . ."

"What, Milord," said the old man, smiling, "you see the community going full steam ahead, and you cannot believe it! Go on, Dinaros, explain our political organization to him."

Principles of Icarian Political Organization

"Because we all are associates and citizens, equal in rights, we all are electors and eligible for election, all members of the nation and of the public guard. All together, we form the NATION, or rather the PEOPLE, because in our country the People consists of the totality of all Icarians without exception.

"I do not need to tell you that the people are SOVEREIGN and that to the people alone belongs, with sovereignty, the power to draft, or cause to be drafted, their social contract, their constitution, and their laws. We cannot imagine that an individual or a family or a class could have the absurd presumption of being our master. Because the people are sovereign, they have the right to regulate, by their constitution and their laws, everything pertaining to their persons, actions, goods, food, clothing, lodging, education, their work, and even their amusements.

"If the Icarian people could meet all together easily and frequently in a hall or on a plain, they would exercise their sovereignty by drawing up their constitution and laws in that manner. Because this is physically impossible, they delegate all the power that they cannot exercise immediately and reserve all other power for themselves. They delegate to a POPULAR ASSEMBLY the power to prepare their constitution and laws, and to an EXECUTIVE BODY the power to execute them; but the people reserve the right to elect their representatives and all the members of the executive branch, to approve or reject their propositions and acts, to administer justice, and to maintain public order and peace.

"Thus, all public officials are the trustees of the people. All are elected, temporary, responsible for their actions, and removable, and, to prevent ambitious encroachment, no one person may exercise both a legislative and executive function. Our Popular Assembly is made up of two thousand deputies, who deliberate together in a single chamber. It is permanent, always or almost always in session, and every year half of the membership is changed. Its most important laws are, like the Constitution, submitted for approval to the people.

"The executive branch, composed of a president and fifteen other members, half of whom are changed every year, is subordinate to the representative branch. As for the people, it is in their assemblies that they exercise all their rights, elections, deliberations, and judgments. And to facilitate the exercise of these rights, the territory is divided into one hundred small provinces, subdivided into one thousand communes of approximately equal population and land area. You know that every provincial capital is at the center of its province, each communal capital at the center of its commune, and that everything is set up in order that the citizens may diligently attend the popular assemblies.

"In order that no area of interest be neglected, each commune, each province, takes care of its specific interests, and all the communes and provinces together—that is, the people as a whole and their Popular Assembly—look after matters of general and national concern. Spread out among their one thousand communal assemblies, the people take part in the discussion of their laws, either before or after the deliberation of their representatives. So that the people may discuss these matters with full knowledge, everything is carried out with full publicity, all facts are presented statistically, and all matters are published in the Popular Newspaper distributed to every citizen. To ensure that every discussion is thorough, the Popular Assembly and each communal assembly—that is, the whole nation—is divided into fifteen large principal COMMITTEES: constitution, education, agriculture, industry, food, clothing, lodging, furnishings, statistics, and so forth. Every large committee is made up of one-fifteenth of the citizens; and the combined intelligence of a people made up of men who have been well brought up and well educated is continually at work discovering and applying all possible improvements and ameliorations.

"Thus, our political organization is that of a democratic REPUBLIC; it is, in fact, an almost pure DEMOCRACY."

"Yes, Milord," added Valmor's father. "All the people make up the laws, for their own good—that is, for the common good. The people always take pleasure in executing these laws because these laws are their own work and the expression of their sovereign will. And the goal of that unanimous will is always, as we have said, to create social and political equality, equality of happiness and rights, universal and absolute equality. Education, food, clothing, lodging, furnishings, work, amusements, rights of election or eligibility and deliberation: all these rights are the same for all of us. Our provinces, our communes, our cities, our villages, our farms, and our houses are, as much as possible, the same. Everywhere here, in short, you will see equality and happiness."

"But when and how," I asked him, "did you establish this equality?"

"It is too late," replied the grandfather, "to explain that to you today, and you can read our national history, but we can tell you a little of the story if Dinaros is not tired, or if Valmor wants to take over."

"And what about me?" exclaimed Corilla. "Why can I not have the floor as well as Dinaros and Valmor?"

"Yes, yes!" everyone cried. "Corilla, Corilla!" And Corilla began to recount the history of Icaria.

A Brief History of Icaria

"I do not have to tell you that poor Icaria, like almost all other countries, was conquered and laid waste by evil conquerors, and was then, for a long period of time, oppressed and tyrannized by wicked kings and aristocrats, who made workers quite unhappy and poverty-stricken women quite miserable. That is the sad fate of humanity all over the world. Thus, for centuries, we witnessed only frightful battles between rich and poor, revolutions, and dreadful massacres.

"About sixty years ago—I don't remember the year" ("1772," said Valmor)—"the old tyrant Corug was overthrown and put to death, his young son banished, and the beautiful Cloramide put on the throne. At first, this young queen made herself very popular by her gentleness and goodness. But the unfortunate woman let herself be dominated by her prime minister, the wicked Lixdox, and his tyranny brought on a final revolution" ("The 13th of June, 1782," added the grandfather) "after two days of gruesome combat and horrifying carnage. Fortunately, the dictator elected by the people, the good and courageous Icar, was the best of men! It is to him and to our noble ancestors, his companions, that we owe the happiness that we now enjoy. It was he and they who organized the republic and the community, after braving death and carrying out great works to ensure the happiness of our women and their children. You be the judge, William, of how much love we should feel for our good Icar and our good grandfather, one of his best friends, one of the benefactors and the liberators of his country."

At these words, the old man, who until then seemed to be listening enraptured to his granddaughter's story, scolded her gently for an indiscretion that wounded his modesty; but Corilla threw her arms around him, and her grandfather embraced her tenderly.

"It was Icar who roused us," he cried, his eyes moist and shining with tears. "It is to him alone that honor and glory are due! Let us sing, my children! Let us sing to Icar and to our country!" And we all sang their hymn of thanksgiving to Icar and their national hymn.

Back in my room, my head heated up by all I had just learned and seen, I could not cool down my imagination, which raced ahead, imagining or guessing at everything that was still a mystery to me. Nor could I stop thinking about the ease, the eloquence, the grace with which Valmor, Dinaros, and, most of all, Corilla had expressed themselves. I would have liked to banish the night in order to make the walk on which that charming girl had invited me come more quickly.

6   Description of Icara *(continued)*

I had so much trouble falling asleep that I was still asleep when Eugene came into my room like a madman and told me that the night before, by a strange coincidence, he had also learned about Icar and Icaria.

"What a man, or rather, what a god that Icar was!" he exclaimed. "What a people! What a country! Lucky Icarians! Ah! Why did fate not provide us with an Icar after our July Revolution! What wonderful days! They were as wonderful as the two days of the Icarian revolution! Oh, people of Paris! How beautiful, heroic, noble, and magnanimous you were! What a new road of glory and happiness was opening up for my country! Why must it be that . . . Wretched France, France that I flee, that I scorn, that I hate. Oh, no! That I love more than ever!"

He paced the floor as if he were alone. His eyes were filled with tears; and his agitation, which at first had made me laugh, ended up strengthening my feelings for him. When his excitement had abated, he read me one of the letters he had written to his brother. The letter was so interesting and instructive that I asked him to let me copy it; and Valmor's family members, to whom I read it, took such pleasure in hearing it that they wanted to meet the author and gave me permission to introduce Eugene to them. Here is the letter:

A Model City

Throw away your city plans, my poor Camille, but rejoice, for I am sending you, to replace them, the architectural design of the very model city that you have wanted for so long. I regret greatly that you are not here to share my admiration and my wonder.

First, imagine, either in Paris or London, the most magnificent reward offered for the design of a model city, a great competition, and a large committee of painters, sculptors, scholars, and travelers who collect architectural drawings and descriptions of all known cities, who gather the opinions and ideas of the entire population and even of foreigners, and who discuss all the good and bad points of existing cities and the projects that have been entered in the competition. They choose, from among thousands of designs, the most perfect model plan. Imagine a city more beautiful than any before it; then you will have an idea of Icara, particularly if you remember that all the citizens are equal, that the republic does everything, and that the rule always followed is: first the necessary, then the useful, and finally the pleasant.

But where shall I begin? That is my problem. I will follow the rule I just mentioned and will start with the necessary and the utilitarian. I will not dwell on the safety measures taken for public health, for the free circulation of air, for keeping the air pure or purifying it. Inside the city, there are no graveyards, no unhealthy factories, no hospitals. All these establishments are at the city limits in well-ventilated locations, near running water, or in the country. I will never be able to give you an idea of all the precautions taken to ensure the cleanliness of the streets. Not only are the sidewalks swept and washed every morning and kept perfectly clean, but the streets are paved or constructed in such a way that water never collects on them, for there are frequent openings through which the water goes into underground canals. Not only does mud, collected and raked up by ingenious, useful instruments, disappear into the same canals, pushed along by water from the fountains, but all imaginable means are used so that the least possible mud and dust collect in the first place.

Let us look first at how the streets are constructed. Each has eight grooves made of iron or stone for four vehicles abreast, two going one way and two the other. The wheels never leave these grooves, and the horses never stray from the inner track. The four tracks are paved with rocks or pebbles, and all the others with bricks. The wheels do not bring up mud or dust, the horses hardly any, and the machines none at all on the railroad streets.

Furthermore, all the large workshops and warehouses are on canal streets and railroad streets. The merchandise wagons, never filled to capacity, go down those streets only. The grooved streets take only omnibuses. Half the streets in the city take neither omnibuses nor wagons but only small carts drawn by large dogs, for the daily distribution of goods to families. In addition, no refuse is thrown from houses or workshops into the streets. Straw, hay, and manure are never transported, as all the stables and their storehouses are at the outskirts of the city. All wagons and carriages are so carefully sealed that nothing contained in them can fall out, and all the unloading is done by machine, so that nothing dirties the sidewalk and street. Fountains on every street provide the water needed for cleaning, beating down the dust, and refreshing the air. Thus, everything is set up to ensure that the streets are naturally free of dirt, in good condition, and easy to clean.

The law (you may laugh at first, but you will end up admiring this) decrees that the pedestrian must be totally safe, and that there must never be accidents caused by carriages, horses, other animals, or anything else. Now give it some thought, and you will realize that nothing is impossible for a government that genuinely wants what is good.

First of all, spirited saddle horses are not permitted in the inner city; horseback riding is possible only outside the city limits, and the stables are on the outskirts. As for horses used for stagecoaches, omnibuses, and transport: in addition to all the precautions taken to prevent them from getting out of hand, they can never leave their groove or go up onto the sidewalks, and the drivers must slow them down to a walk when approaching any path used by pedestrians to cross the street. These crossings are surrounded by all necessary safety features. They are usually marked by columns that cut across the street to form gates for the carriages and safety zones where the pedestrian can stop until he or she is sure of continuing in safety. I am sure I do not have to tell you that these crossings are almost as clean as the sidewalks. On some streets, the passages are underground, like the London 'tunnel'; on others, there are pedestrian bridges under which the vehicles go.

Another simple precaution, which prevents accidents and which is poorly enforced in our own cities because we do nothing to inform everyone of it and get them into the habit of doing it, is that vehicles and pedestrians alike always keep to the right as they go forward. In addition, you will have realized that, because all the carriage drivers work for the republic and receive nothing from private parties, it is of no advantage to them to risk accidents; on the contrary, it is in their best interests to avoid them. You will also be aware that, as the entire population is in workshops or at home until three o'clock, and as the carriages for manufactured goods move about only when there are few pedestrians, and as their wheels never leave the grooves, accidents caused by carriages or involving two carriages are almost impossible. As for animals other than horses, you will never see herds of cattle and sheep like those that crowd and defile the streets of London, causing thousands of accidents, and causing nervousness and often terror and death, while at the same time habituating people to the idea of slaughter. The slaughterhouses and butcher shops here are outside the city limits. The beasts never enter the city; you never see blood or animal carcasses; and there aren't large numbers of butchers who get used to reacting without fear to human butchery because they are in the habit of dipping their knives and hands in the blood of other victims.

I could not leave the subject of animals without mentioning the dogs, of remarkable size and strength, that the republic feeds, lodges, and uses in great numbers for much hauling, which is done with even less danger than by horses. As all these dogs are well nourished and are always bridled and muzzled or on a leash, they can never can get rabid, or bite, or frighten anyone, or cause a scandal, which, in our cities, can destroy in a minute all the precautions of several years of training.

Everything is so carefully planned that chimneys, flowerpots, and other objects can never be tossed about in a storm or thrown out of a window. Pedestrians are protected even from inclement weather because all the streets have sidewalks, and all these sidewalks are covered in glass, to protect pedestrians from the rain without depriving them of light, and by moveable canvas, to shield them from heat. Some streets, in particular those that run between the big depot storehouses, are completely covered, as are all the street crossings. Concern for safety is so strong that it has led to the construction of covered shelters a certain distance apart on both sides of the street, under which the omnibuses stop, so that people can get on or off without having to fear either rain or mud. And so you see, my friend, that you can travel throughout the city of Icara by carriage if you are in a hurry, through gardens if it is good weather, and under arcades when the weather is inclement, without ever needing a parasol or an umbrella, and with no fears; on the other hand, the thousands of accidents and misfortunes that overwhelm the people of Paris and London every year point an accusing finger at the shameful impotence or barbaric indifference of those governments.

As you can imagine, the city is perfectly illuminated at night, as well lit as Paris and London—quite a bit better, in fact. This is because the supply of fuel for lighting is not exhausted by shops, as there are none, or by workshops, as no one works at night. That means that the light is concentrated on the streets and public monuments. Not only does the gas give off no odor, because a way to purify it has been discovered, but the lighting joins the pleasant to the useful to the greatest extent possible, either by the elegant, varied shapes of the streetlights or by the thousand forms and colors created by the light. I have seen some beautiful illuminations in London, on certain streets, on certain holidays; but in Icara, the lighting is always magnificent, and sometimes it is truly a fairyland.

Here you will find no cabarets, no beer gardens, no cafés, no public houses, no stock market, no gaming houses or lotteries, no haunts for shameful or guilty pleasures, no barracks and guardrooms, no policemen and their informers, no prostitutes and pickpockets, no drunkards and beggars. You will find, however, INDISPENSIBLES that are as elegant as they are clean and convenient, some for women and some for men, where modesty can enter for a moment, fearing an affront neither to itself nor to public decency.

Your glance will never be offended by all that graffiti, all those drawings and writings that dirty the walls of our cities, making us lower our eyes in shame; for children are trained not to ruin or dirty anything and to blush at anything indecent and dishonest. You will not even have the pleasure or annoyance of seeing so many plaques or signs above the doors of houses, or so many advertisements and commercial posters that almost always disfigure buildings. But you will see beautiful inscriptions on public buildings, workshops, and public warehouses, as well as useful notices, magnificently printed on paper of many colors, and posted, by official republican sign posters, on boards designated for this purpose, so that the notices add to the general beautification.

You will not find those rich, pretty shops of all sorts that you would see in Paris and London in all the houses on commercial streets. But what are the most beautiful of those shops, the richest of those stores and bazaars, the vastest markets or fairs, compared with the workshops, the shops, the storehouses of Icara?

Imagine, for example, all the metalwork or jewelry workshops and shops of Paris or London combined to form one or two workshops and one or two stores.

Imagine that it is the same for every branch of industry and commerce, and tell me if each of those stores for jewelry, clocks, flowers, feathers, fabric, fashion, instruments, fruits, and so forth would not eclipse all the shops in the world. Tell me if you would not have as much or perhaps more pleasure seeing them than visiting our museums and buildings that house the fine arts. Well, such are the workshops and stores of Icara! And they are purposely spread out for the greatest convenience of the inhabitants and for the embellishment of the city. To make it even more beautiful, all of them, on the outside, are designed like public buildings, emphasizing simplicity in form and highlighting the qualities of that particular industry.

I have just spoken of public buildings. I do not need to tell you that it is even more likely that all public buildings or utilitarian establishments found elsewhere can also be found here: schools, hospitals, temples, buildings for public courts, all the meeting places of the popular assemblies. We also have arenas, circuses, theaters, and museums of all sorts—all those establishments that have almost become necessary because they are so pleasant. On the other hand, there are no hotels for aristocrats or fine retinues, no prisons or poor houses, and no royal or ministerial palaces. The schools, hospitals, and popular assemblies are palaces in themselves. In other words, all our palaces are dedicated to public utility!

I would never conclude, my dear brother, if I tried to spell out for you everything useful that Icara contains; but I have said enough, perhaps too much, although I am sure that you, in your friendship, will take some pleasure in the details. Now I will get on to the pleasant, where, yet again, you will find variety, the constant companion of uniformity.

Let us look at the exterior form of the houses, streets, and monuments. I have already told you that all the houses on one street are the same, but that each street is different. You will find represented here all the attractive houses of foreign countries. Your sensibilities will never be wounded by the sight of those hovels, cesspools, and crossroads that are found elsewhere next to the most magnificent palaces, nor by the sight of rags by the side of aristocratic luxuries. Your glance will not be saddened by those grillworks that surround the foundations of houses in London and join with the dark color of the brick to give these houses the appearance of immense prisons. Chimneys, so hideous in many other countries, are ornamental here or are not visible, and the tops of the houses are graced by a charming iron balustrade.

The sidewalks or porticos on slender columns that line all the streets, already magnificent now, will be truly enchanting when, as planned, all the columns are garnished with leafy plants and flowers. Shall I try to describe for you the exterior form of the fountains, squares, promenades, columns, public buildings, and the colossal gates of the city with its magnificent avenues? No, my friend. I could not find enough words to paint my admiration, and, in any case, it would take volumes. I will bring you copies of all the architectural designs, and I will limit myself here to giving you a general idea of the city.

Ah! How I regret not being able to visit these places again with my brother. You would see that no fountain, no square, no public building resembles another, and that all styles of architecture are represented. Here you would imagine yourself in Rome, in Greece, in Egypt, in India, everywhere; and never would you become enraged, as we did in London in front of Saint Paul's, at the shops that prevented us from enjoying a full view of that magnificent monument. Nowhere else in the world will you see more paintings, sculptures, and statues than here, in these public buildings, in the squares, on the promenades, and in the public gardens; for whereas elsewhere works of art are hidden in the palaces of kings and the wealthy—and in London, for example, the museums, closed on Sundays, are never open to the people, who cannot leave their work to visit them during the week—here those curiosities of art exist only for the people and are placed only in spots frequented by the people.

As it is the republic that causes everything to be created by its painters and sculptors; as artists, nourished, clothed, lodged, and given all furnishings by the community, have no other motive than love of art and glory, and no guide other than the inspirations of genius, you can imagine the consequences. There is nothing useless and, above all, nothing harmful. Every work of art is created with a utilitarian goal! There is nothing in support of fanaticism and superstition. Everything is created for the people and their benefactors, for liberty and its martyrs, or against its former tyrants and their followers. Here you will never see any of those nudes or voluptuous paintings that hang in our capital cities to please the powerful libertines. By the most monstrous of contradictions, whereas we keep preaching decency and chastity, these paintings present, in public, images that a husband would want to hide from his wife and a mother from her children. And never will you see those artworks created by ignorance or incompetence that the poor sell at a meager price to buy bread, and that corrupt the general taste while bringing dishonor to the arts. Here the republic permits nothing to exist without prior examination. Just as in Sparta they did away with ill or deformed children at birth, here we throw into the darkness of the abyss, without a second thought, all productions unworthy of being illuminated by the rays of the god of the arts.

I will stop there, my dear Camille, although I could have told you a great deal about the garden streets, river and canals, quays and bridges, and the public buildings that have only been started or planned. But what will you say when I add that all the cities of Icaria, although much smaller, are built on the same model, with the exception of the great national buildings that can be found only in Icara? I believe I can hear you exclaiming, along with me: Fortunate Icarians! Unfortunate Frenchmen!

The more I toured the city, the more accurate Eugene's description seemed to me. After I had copied the letter, we went together to visit one of the republican bakeries. We toured five or six immense parallel buildings, one for flour, one for dough, a third for the ovens, a fourth for fuel, and a fifth to store the bread. From there, merchandise carriages distribute it to consumers everywhere. A canal brings the flour and fuel, which machines lift into the storehouses. The flour pours through large pipes into the kneading rooms, while other pipes bring in a constant supply of water. Ingenious machines knead the dough, cut it, and carry it to the ovens. Different machines carry the fuel there, while others move the bread into the last building. Eugene could not stop admiring how much the workers were relieved of toil by this system and the great savings resulting from it.

Although I shared his admiration, my thoughts were occupied with our upcoming walk, and I raced to Valmor's house at five o'clock. Everyone was ready to go, and almost the whole family started off as soon as I arrived. Valmor took the arm of one of his cousins, and the charming Corilla took mine, with such a seductive familiarity that I would have lost my head had I been less steeled against such feelings.

We passed through the garden streets, many of which were filled with girls, children, or men who were watering or working the soil. The more I saw of these gardens, the more delightful they seemed to me: the lawns, the roses and flowers of a thousand varieties, the flowering shrubs, the walls covered with jasmine, vines, lilies of the valley, honeysuckle—in short, greenery mixed with a thousand colors. The perfumed air, the scene of gardeners and children: everything formed a delightful whole.

But the walk delighted me even more: straight or winding gravel paths, vast lawns, shrubs of all kinds, magnificent trees, little groves and flowering bowers everywhere, little elegant benches painted green at every step, grottoes or man-made hills, filled with birds, water flowing in rivulets, brooks, cascades, fountains, sprays; charming bridges, statues, and little monuments: everything that the fertile imagination of the most skilled designer could imagine was there, even birds and animals of all species on the waters and the lawns. And what embellished the walk more than all the marvels of art or nature were the great number of large families walking together: fathers, mothers, and children. Thousands of boys and girls of all ages, all dressed in clean, elegant clothing, were running, jumping, dancing, and playing a thousand games, always in groups and under the watchful eyes of their assembled relatives. You could see nothing but joy and pleasure; you could hear only laughter, joyous cries, chants, and music.

"It seems," I said to Corilla, "that your compatriots have a passion for music."

"Yes," she answered, "and it was the good Icar who gave us the taste for it, as well as for greenery, flowers, and fruits. Since that time, our education has made these passions universal. Everyone acquires a general knowledge of all that pertains to plants and cultivation of the soil. All children, without exception, learn vocal music and know how to sing. Every one of them learns to play an instrument. You will hear music and songs everywhere and at all times, at family and public gatherings, in temples and workshops, at theatrical events, and on walks. We will encounter groups of musicians of all sorts, seated in pretty parlors designed specially for music, as well as many concerts by mechanical devices that replace musicians and imitate them perfectly. All traffic signals are given by trumpet, and thousands of public conveyances depart to the sound of the horn. Do you not find their fanfares charming?"

"Yes, truly charming."

"And you will hear the music at our national festivals with choirs of fifty or a hundred thousand singers."

By then, we had arrived at the bridle path, and hundreds of parties of riders passed by, made up of men and women of all ages, dressed elegantly, although quite differently from our cavaliers and horsewomen of London and Paris. I waxed poetic about the women's grace and horses' beauty. There were superb horses for the men, charming ones for the women, and small, pretty ones for the children.

"This should not surprise you," said Corilla. "Once the republic decided that we would all share the pleasure of horseback riding, it took special charge of training the horses. It even bought the best purebreds from foreign countries. Horseback riding is part of our childhood education, and you will not find a single Icarian today who is not a skilled rider."

"But," I said, "how do you have enough saddle horses for everyone?"

"This is how we do it," she replied. "The republic has only a thousand horses for every communal city, and sixty thousand for Icara. These horses are shared by all the citizens, so that each family can use them once every ten days."

"And all the horses belong to the republic?"

"Of course, and they are lodged in its stables and groomed by its workers."

We talked about everything, about festivals, theater, dance, amusements, customs, and manners of the country. She even told me about the public assemblies and the newspapers, always speaking with such ease and grace that I did not notice it was getting dark while I was taking such pleasure in being educated and in listening to such a charming teacher.

7 Food

It was a day of rest, Icarian Sunday, actually the tenth day of the Icarian week, and Valmor, who had told me about it two days earlier, came early to fetch Eugene and me to accompany his family to the country. I will tell you later about all the ways conceived and put into action by the republic to facilitate these excursions and country picnics Icarians are so fond of from spring to autumn. We all left, some on foot, some on pretty mules, donkeys, or horses, others in omnibuses, and we went to a charming, famous fountain two leagues from Icara on the slope of a delightful hill that overlooks the city.

I cannot tell you what a spectacle the route was, filled with carriages, horses, donkeys, mules, and dogs, walkers and provisions, all going to the same spot. I could never describe the ravishing beauty of the panorama of lawns, bowers, and fountains where nature and art had multiplied their embellishments, nor can I describe the delightful scenes of hundreds of groups dining outside, singing, laughing, jumping, running, dancing, and playing a thousand games.

On the invitation of her grandfather, Corilla described briefly twenty or thirty country walks the Icarian people usually take on holidays or days of rest. She explained to us that all these charming places, which serve today to delight all the people, used to exist for the exclusive pleasure of a few lords, who enclosed them within the walls or moats of their castles and parks. As interesting as Corilla's story was, and as charming as she made it, Valmor caught my interest even more when he told us about the system adopted by the republic for feeding its citizens. I would certainly have summarized it here if I had not found this system perfectly described in another letter from Eugene to his brother. This letter, which I am going to transcribe here, will replace my own narrative. To get right to it, I will add only that the return trip was just as lively and joyous as the departure and the outing, and my heart was filled with the happiness I saw expressed everywhere.

Eugene's Letter to His Brother

Oh, my dear Camille, how my heart breaks when I think of France while seeing the happiness of the Icarian people! Judge for yourself when you learn about their institutions concerned with food and clothing.

FOOD

Everything pertaining to this primary need of man, like all the others, is, in our unfortunate country, left to chance and filled with monstrous abuses. Here, on the contrary, everything is regulated by the most enlightened reason and the most generous solicitude. First, imagine, my dear brother, that there is absolutely nothing to do with food that is not regulated by law. Any particular food item is either authorized or prohibited by law.

A committee of scholars, appointed by the National Assembly and aided by all the citizens, has compiled a list of all known foods, noting those that are good and bad, along with their good or bad properties. Furthermore, the committee has indicated which foods are necessary, useful, and pleasing, and has printed this list in several volumes. Each family has a copy. Moreover, the committee has written down the most appropriate preparation of each food, and every family has a copy of *The Cook's Guide.*

Once the list of good foods has been established, the republic produces them through its farmers and workers and distributes them to families. As no one can have any food other than that which is distributed, it follows that no one can eat food of which the republic does not approve. It first produces the food that is necessary for survival, then the useful, and then the pleasing, with the goal of producing all of them if feasible. The republic divides the food equally among all the people, so that every citizen receives the same quantity of a given food if there is enough for everyone. Each person receives his or her portion in turn, yearly or daily, if there is only enough for part of the population. So everyone has an equal portion of all foods, without exception, from those we call the most crude to those we consider the greatest delicacies; thus, all the people of Icaria are as well fed and even better fed than the richest people in other nations.

You see, my friend, that the government here acts in a very different manner from our monarchy. Whereas the nobility makes such a fuss about a good king who wanted every peasant to have a chicken in the pot on Sundays, the republic here gives to everyone, every day, without saying a word, every food that is seen elsewhere only on the tables of aristocrats and kings!

Not only does the republic raise all necessary animals, fowl, and fish, not only does it cultivate and distribute all fresh vegetables and fruit, but it uses all means of conserving them, drying them, making them into jellies and so forth, before it distributes them as foodstuffs.

And that is not all. The committee I was just telling you about has discussed and prescribed the number of meals, their time and length, their type, and the order in which foods are served, varying them continually, not only according to seasons and months, but even day to day, so that dinners are different each week. At six o'clock, before beginning work, all workers—that is, all citizens—share a very simple breakfast in their workshop (what the workers in Paris call the snack or morning kick), prepared and served by the workshop chef. At nine, they have lunch in the workshop, while their wives and children eat at home. At two o'clock, all the inhabitants of a single street eat, in their republican restaurant, a dinner prepared by one of the republic's trained chefs. In the evening, between nine and ten o'clock, each family eats, in its own home, a supper or light meal prepared by the women of the house. At all these meals, the first toast is to the glory of good Icar, benefactor of the workers, benefactor of families, BENEFAC-TOR OF ALL CITIZENS.

Supper consists primarily of fruits, pastries, and sweets. However, the communal dinner, in elegantly decorated halls that seat one to two thousand persons, surpasses in magnificence anything you can imagine. In my opinion, our most beautiful Parisian restaurants and cafés are nothing compared with the republican restaurants. You will probably not believe me when I tell you that, in addition to the abundance and delicacy of the foods, and the variety of floral and other decorations, there is delectable music to charm the ears while the nose savors delicious smells.

In addition, when young people marry, they do not need to eat up their dowry in a bad nuptial dinner and make their unborn children poverty stricken. The dinners that the husband eats in his wife's restaurant, the wife in her husband's, and the two families at each other's are worthy of the most beautiful nuptial meals in other countries.

You can imagine how much money is saved by serving communal rather than separate meals, savings that can be used to increase the pleasures of the meals. Also, you can see that these communal meals of workers and neighbors have other great advantages, in particular that they lead to fraternization among the masses and lessen women's housework.

Because the republic is most concerned with the happiness of its children, you will not be surprised to learn that it fosters tenderness and kindness by allowing, on Sundays, the families to eat all their meals together at home, to dine with their special friends, and even to spend the day in the country. To this end, the republic has cold meals prepared in the restaurants and delivered to the family homes. The republic also provides additional means of transport when the families want to enjoy the countryside.

In truth, my brother, I do not lie when I assure you that this country is a paradise that brings joy to the soul as well as to the senses; and yet I am furious—I, a Frenchman who adores his country. For my country, I sometimes suffer all the torments of Tantalus!

Well, let us be brave and hopeful! And while we are waiting, let us study! You will certainly want to know how the distribution of food is planned and executed. Nothing is simpler, but this will give you additional cause for admiration.

DISTRIBUTION OF FOOD

The Republic does what is often seen in Paris and London, what our governments sometimes do, and what almost all the merchants are doing now. First of all, you know that the republic grows or produces all the food, receives it, gathers it together, and deposits it in many immense storehouses. It will be easy for you to imagine communal cellars like those of Paris and London, big warehouses of meal, bread, meats, fish, vegetables, fruit, and so forth.

Each republican storehouse has, like our bakers and butchers, a chart listing the restaurants, workshops, stores, hospitals, and families it supplies, as well as the quantity it sends to each. It has, in addition, all the necessary employees, containers, and means of transport, and one instrument is more ingenious than the next. Prepared in advance in the storehouse, everything is delivered to the homes: the yearly, monthly, weekly, and daily provisions.

The distribution itself is quite charming. I will not dwell on the perfect cleanliness that reigns everywhere as first priority, but what I must tell you is that for each family the storehouse has a basket, a vase, in fact, all manner of containers, marked with the number of the family's house, that hold its supply of bread, milk, etc. The storehouse has a double quantity of these containers, so that when a full one is delivered, an empty one can be sent back. At its entryway, every house has a pantry designed for this purpose, where the distributor finds the empty measure and replaces it with the full one, so the distribution can always be done at the same time and, announced by a particular sound, can take place without disturbing the family and without wasting a moment of the distributor's time.

You can imagine, my friend, how much time is saved and all the advantages of this system of mass distribution.

In short, everything is perfect in this happy country, inhabited by men who truly deserve the title of men because, even in little things, they always make use of the sublime powers of reason that Providence has given them for their happiness.

And now, look at their clothing system and admire it, unless you become a bit enraged, like me.

8 Clothing

Continuation of Eugene's Letter to His Brother

Everything I told you about food, my dear Camille, can be applied to clothing. The law controls everything, on the specifications of a committee whose members consulted everyone, examined the clothing of every country, made a list of all items of clothing, including shapes and colors (a magnificent work that all families own), designated which would be adopted and which prohibited, and classified them according to whether they were necessary, useful, or pleasing.

It is the republic that has all the raw materials grown and produced by its farmers; it is the republic that manufactures, in its factories, all the chosen fabrics; it is the republic, once more, that has all the garments made by its male and female workers, and that has them distributed to the families. The republic began by producing only those fabrics that were of greatest necessity. Now it creates all fabrics, without exception, the most pleasing as well as the most useful. Everything that was odd or in bad taste, whether in shape, design, or color, was painstakingly banished. You can imagine nothing purer and more charming than the chosen colors, nothing more gracious and simple than the fabric designs, nothing more elegant and comfortable than the shapes of the clothing. You will find this easy to understand when you remember that there is not a single shoe or hat that has not been discussed and adopted according to a model. And, although you will recall that, because of my passion for painting, I have always been quite fussy about men's and ladies' clothing, I swear to you that in this country I have yet to find a single fault with it.

I have just mentioned the women. Oh, my dear Camille, how you would admire these Icarian men (you who, like myself, are so gallant and passionate with women, the Creator's masterpieces), if you saw how they surround their women with care, respect, and praise, how they concentrate all their thoughts on them, how they work ceaselessly to please them and to make them happy, and how they embellish these women, who are already so naturally beautiful, in order to increase their pleasure in adoring them! Happy women! Happy men! Happy Icaria! Unfortunate France!

It is the women's clothing that you would admire the most. Not only would your avid eye be charmed to see the finest, most delicate, most ravishing fabrics, colors, and shapes you know, but on certain occasions you would be as amazed by the abundance of feathers as you would be dazzled by the sparkle of the jewels and precious stones. It is true that the feathers and flowers are almost all man made, that the jewels are rarely of pure gold but usually of alloys or of other gilded or nongilded metals, and that all the precious stones are manufactured, but what difference does that make? Are these ornaments any less beautiful? Do they adorn any less beautifully the heads that wear them? Are they less precious, particularly when all women wear them equally, and not one of the women can show off any different ones? And these Icarian women, who scorn and despise all conventional beauties and all feelings of childish vanity, valuing only genuine charms and reasonable feelings, are they any less sensitive, attractive, or happy?

Similarly, you would swoon if you smelled the smooth, delightful perfumes given off continuously from the women's and even the men's clothing, for Icarians consider the habit of wearing perfumes not only a personal enhancement but a duty toward others; and you would be astonished at the variety of their oils and essences, their pomades and powders—in short, their toilet waters for men as well as for women—if you did not know that their whole country is covered with flowers, and that nothing is easier or less expensive than making perfume for the whole population. You would think you had been transported into a fairy palace if you saw a republican perfume factory.

Everyone wears the same clothing, so that there is no room for jealousy and coquetry. But do not think that uniformity means no variety. On the contrary, it is in the area of clothing that variety blends its richness most successfully with the advantages of uniformity. First of all, the two sexes dress differently. Clothing for individuals of each sex changes frequently, according to alterations in age and station. Distinctive features of the clothing reflect all the circumstances and roles of the person wearing it. Childhood and youth, puberty and adulthood, celibacy or marriage, widowhood or remarriage, the diverse professions and functions: all are indicated by dress. All individuals of the same social condition wear the same uniform, but thousands of diverse uniforms correspond to thousands of different social conditions. The uniforms differ sometimes in fabric or color, sometimes in shape or particular markings. In addition, although the fabric and form are the same for girls of the same age, for example, the color differs according to their taste or to what suits them. Certain colors are better suited to blondes, as you know, and certain others to brunettes. In addition, each person has many different garments: the simple, comfortable work garment, the one worn around the house, the elegant gown worn in the parlor or at a public meeting, and the magnificent holiday or ceremonial garment. You can see that the variety of garments is almost infinite. In addition, flowers, hats, feathers, jewelry, precious stones, and magnificent fabrics may be worn only at certain specified ages; so you can see that the republic can easily manufacture enough of them for the small number of persons in each age category.

Now, imagine the population gathered together, in their holiday garments, at the circus, on walks, or at the theater; you may be sure that the boxes of the Paris and London operas, as well as the salons and even the courts of those two capitals, offer no more splendid and magnificent a spectacle, and that those tiny groups of privileged society are like tribes of Pygmies compared to the entire population of Icaria.

Shall I tell you about the manufacture and distribution of clothing? You can imagine how easy it is for the republic to know the quantity of raw materials, fabrics, and clothing it needs; to have its farmers produce these raw materials in its domains or buy them in foreign markets; to mass-produce the fabrics in its immense factories, with its powerful machines; and then to have the clothing sewed up in its immense workshops by its male and female workers.

You can probably guess that the shape of each garment is calculated to make its manufacture as easy, rapid, and economical as possible. Almost all clothing, hats, and shoes are made of elasticized material so that they can fit a variety of people of different heights and weights. Almost everything is done by machine, totally or in sections, so that the workers have little to do to finish the garments. Almost all of them are made in four or five lengths and widths, so that the workers never have to take measurements beforehand. All the clothing is made in bulk, like the fabrics themselves, and often at the same time. After that, everything is placed in immense storehouses where each person will always be able to find, without delay, all the garments he or she needs and that are prescribed by law.

I do not have to describe for you the perfect work done by machines or workers who always perform the same operation, or the prodigious savings that result from this system of mass production, or the enormous losses the republic prevents by avoiding capricious and ridiculous changes in fashion. As for clothing distribution, each storehouse has a chart indicating the families it supplies and the quantities it must deliver. It opens an account for each family and delivers what is due after family members have chosen what suits them. Maintaining and repairing the garments is the work of the women of the family, but this work is almost nil, and laundering, which would be more time-consuming, is done by national laundries.

Judge the rest by what you already know! And to end with a wish for your happiness: I wish, my dear Camille, that you may soon have a country like Icaria.

I went back to join Valmor, who was meeting me in the clock-making workshop where one of his cousins worked, and I decided to take Eugene there with me. I need not mention that Valmor welcomed my companion with perfect grace, and that he showed us everything in great detail.

How amazing it was! Everything is together there, from the raw materials lined up in the first storehouse to the clocks, pendulums, watches, and devices of all sorts set out in a final warehouse that resembles a brilliant museum. The special clock-making workshop is a three-storied building of a thousand square feet, held up by iron columns instead of thick walls, which make each floor into one big room, perfectly illuminated by a very simple system of light diffusion. On the bottom floor are enormous, heavy machines for cutting the metals and roughing out the pieces. On the top floor are the workers, divided into as many groups as there are different pieces to make; each one always makes the same piece. You would think you were seeing an army regiment; such is the high degree of order and discipline there. It is also a pleasure to see the shelves, the compartments, and the attached or hanging tools. Valmor's cousin explained to us the movements of this little army.

"We arrive at quarter of six," he said. "We hang our clothing in the locker room I will show you soon, and we put on our work clothes. At exactly six o'clock, we begin work when the bell sounds. At nine o'clock, we all go down to the dining hall where we eat lunch in silence, while one of us reads aloud the morning paper. At one o'clock, work ends for the day. Once everything has been put in order and cleaned, we go down to the locker room, where we find everything we need for washing up, and where we put on our leisure clothes to go and dine, at two o'clock, with our families. Then we have the rest of the day at our disposal. I forgot to tell you that for two hours of work we observe a strict silence; for two other hours, we can talk to our neighbors; and during the remaining time, everyone sings to himself or for others, and we often sing together in chorus."

We left, dazzled by so much reason and so much happiness, and we went to visit a superb public building I will tell you about later.

Soon after I arrived at Corilla's home, a lady came in with six or seven children of different ages, one of whom was a young woman with an angelic face.

Corilla lost no time getting up, running over to her, taking off her hat, and kissing her.

"It is my great pleasure," said Corilla's father, taking my hand, "to present to dear Madame Dinamé the honorable Lord Carisdall, whom my son must have mentioned. He is our friend."

"Then he is our friend as well," said the woman in the most gracious tone.

"As for me," Corilla said in turn, taking me by the hand and affecting a solemn tone, "I have the honor of presenting Mr. William to . . . (I was going to say the charming, as if you needed me to tell you that), to the naughty Dinaïse, whose angelic face conceals a devil, and who would stare me to death if there weren't someone here to defend me."

"You are as mad as ever!" said Miss Dinaïse, blushing.

As for me, I cannot begin to tell you what I felt when I heard that voice: it was the voice of "the invisible one"! I felt myself blush or turn pale. Luckily, the noisy kisses of the children that were running from one young woman to the other kept my discomfort a secret. Imagine my embarrassment when Valmor said aloud to Miss Dinaïse: "You will surely recognize the stroller from the boat, but you do not know what he was saying about you."

"What was he saying?" cried Corilla.

"What was he saying?" cried all the assembled people.

"Can I repeat it, William?"

"Yes, yes!" the voices cried out from everywhere.

"Well, he said . . . he said that, because she chose to be always hidden beneath her veil and her hat, the invisible one must be, without a doubt, horribly ugly." That occasioned a long burst of universal laughter and a continuous volley of jokes about my talent for prediction.

"At that time, I could not believe," I said, almost stammering, "that a human face could appear pretty when accompanied by so divine a voice." My compliment seemed so awkward that, although it made Miss Dinaïse blush even more, it did not stop Corilla and the others from repeating pitilessly: "Ugly, horrible, horrifying." Soon, however, we made music; and Corilla, who went first to set an example, sang even more beautifully than before. Miss Dinaïse did not want to sing, but Corilla encouraged her with such insistence and charming kisses that she finally consented. She sang timidly and badly, but with a voice that made me tremble gently from head to toe.

"Do not judge Dinaïse by her shyness," said Valmor's mother, who was seated near me. "She is witty and well educated. She is a fine young woman, sister, and friend. No one is more affectionate, loving, warm, and intimate. She often ignores her own needs in order to help others. She adores her brother Dinaros, and if she were less untamed, melancholy, or timid with people, she would be as likeable as my Corilla. Her family," she added, "is closely linked with ours. Her brother is Valmor's childhood friend; she herself is my daughter's best friend. She loves me as a mother, and I love her as if she were my own child. I will soon have the pleasure of calling her that, as Valmor is mad about her. Her parents want the union as much as we do, and in a few days we will name the date."

"Enough, enough," said Corilla, approaching us. "It is your turn to sing, William. You may choose to sing alone, with Dinaïse, or with me, but you will sing!"

I could not have done it, and I apologized as best I could.

"You refuse me," she said, "and no one joins me in subduing this man who revolts against my will! Well, I will avenge myself on all of you, and I will fix you! Tomorrow we will go together to see the balloons take off, and we will send Sir Lord off with them. The day after tomorrow, we will spend the evening at Mrs. Dinamé's home, and we will make music. Sir Lord will study this piece during his trip through the air, and if he finds his voice again in the pure air, if he is lucky enough to return, he will sing alone, and then with Dinaïse, and then with me. Thus I command, if the good Mrs. Dinamé assents, subject to ratification by our terrible and fearsome sovereign and master."

Grandfather and Mrs. Dinamé smiled. Her mother said she was mad. Miss Dinaïse seemed to be scolding her, but the children applauded, jumping for joy, and the match was ended.

9 Lodging and Furnishings

I had just written a letter to England when Eugene came in to invite me to see the inside of the home of a family he knew. The mistress of the house was going to give us a complete tour. I accepted, and we went out.

Lodging

Knowing that Icar had a model plan of a home drawn up, after consulting the lodging committee and the entire people and ordering a study of the houses of every nation, I anticipated seeing a house that was perfect in every respect, particularly in the areas of convenience and sanitation. Nevertheless, my expectations were surpassed. I will not tell you here about the exterior and everything to do with the beautification of the street and the city, but will concentrate on features that directly affect the inhabitants of the house.

Everything you can imagine that is necessary and useful—and even pleasing, I should say—is united there. Every house is four stories in height, not including the ground floor, and three, four, or five windows in width. Under the ground floor are the cellars and storage bins for wood and coal. Their base is five or six feet below the sidewalk, and the vaulted ceiling is three or four feet above it. The lady showed us how wood, coal, and all other materials are hoisted by machines from the supply wagons into these underground rooms without even touching or dirtying the sidewalk. She showed us next how all these objects are lifted in baskets or vases into the kitchen and the upper floors by means of openings in the ceiling and small machines that make the use of human power unnecessary.

On the ground floor, there are no shops, no porters' lodges, no stables, no coach houses, no carriage entrances, no vestibules, and no courtyards. Instead, you will find a dining room, a kitchen with all its annexes, a small parlor used as a library, a bathroom with a small home pharmacy, a small workshop for the men and another for the women containing all the implements one usually needs in a household, a small yard for the fowl, a shed for the gardening tools, and the back garden.

The first floor is composed of a large parlor, where the musical instruments are kept. The other rooms and all those on the other floors are bedrooms or rooms designated for many other uses. All the windows open inward and are embellished with balconies. Everything is designed to make the stairs convenient and elegant, without taking up much space.

"What a beautiful view!" I exclaimed, going out onto a terrace bordered with a railing and covered with flowers that crowned the house and formed yet another delightful garden of a different kind, with a magnificent view.

"On beautiful summer evenings," said the mistress of the house, "almost all families gather on their terraces to take a breath of cool air while singing, making music, and having supper. You will see! It is truly enchanting!"

Another small terrace, garnished with flowers, on the arcade above the sidewalk, as well as flowers on almost all the balconies, add even more to the charm of the dwelling and perfume the surrounding air. Not only does rainwater not inconvenience people by falling from the terraces, but, caught in a reservoir or cistern, it is put to practical use as a supplement to water from springs and wells, drawn out easily with the aid of pumps. Eugene and I admired as well the fireplaces and the heating system that spread throughout, economically, an equal, gentle heat without people having to fear the plague of smoke and the scourge of fire.

"These two little statues you see on the mantle," said the lady, "are the ones the republic awarded to those who invented methods of eliminating smoke and fires. You can also see that everything in the building construction and the choice of materials joins together to make these homes safe from fire. As a result, we hardly ever have fires either in our homes or in our workshops, and those that break out are immediately extinguished. Word has it that someone has just discovered a means of making wood and fabrics fireproof when you want them to be."

"Look how the doors and gates roll noiselessly on their hinges," said Eugene, "how they close by themselves, and how perfectly they prevent outside air from entering."

In truth, it was the sanitation system that I admired with the most pleasure, as well as the system designed to spare women all trouble and disgust in housework. There is no precaution that has not been taken concerning sanitation. The lower areas, which are more exposed to dirt, are covered with varnished stone tiles or paint that cannot be dirtied and are easy to wash. Water for drinking and nonpotable water, conducted from high reservoirs right up to the top terrace, are brought through pipes and faucets to all the floors, into almost all the rooms, or are forcibly pumped by washing machines, while all the dirty water and sewage are drawn, without stagnating anywhere and without letting off any bad odor, into large pipes that go under the streets. Those places by their very nature the most disgusting are those where skill has made the greatest effort to diminish all unpleasantness. One of the prettiest statues awarded by the republic is the one you see, in all houses, above the door of a charming little closet; it immortalizes the name of a woman who invented a procedure for expelling fetid odors.

Even the mud that might be tracked in from outside received special attention. Aside from the fact that the sidewalks are extremely clean, many small precautions keep an unclean foot from soiling the rooms and even the threshold of the door to the stairway, while education instills in children, as one of their first duties, the habit of cleanliness in everything. Even the garbage and debris of all sorts are disposed of in such a way that, when they are not being used to fertilize the gardens, they can be removed without the process being disgusting or difficult.

As for housework, which is done not by domestic servants but by the women and children in each family, I could not stop admiring the republic's deep concern for making housework free from any sort of fatigue or repulsion.

"Sweeping up is hardly any trouble," said the mother, "and all other tasks are even less painful. Not only do education and public opinion accustom women to fulfilling our duties with no shame or annoyance, but they make these tasks pleasant and dear to us by reminding us constantly that this is the only way to enjoy the priceless advantage of not having foreign hired help to serve us and our families. Furthermore, thanks to our good Icar and our beloved republic, the collective imagination of our men works ceaselessly to make us happy and to simplify our domestic chores. The two main meals, lunch and dinner, are eaten outside the home and are prepared by national chefs. All the women's and men's clothing and all our other laundry are cleaned in republican workshops, so that we merely have to look after it and mend it and prepare two simple meals that require only the most pleasant preparation.

"Let us go back to see our kitchen! Look at the stoves, the oven, the faucets for hot and cold running water, all these little instruments and utensils, and tell me if you can imagine anything cleaner or more convenient, and if the architect who designed everything to make us love our work is not the most gallant and ingenious of men! Because of this, all our girls like to sing a charming song in honor of the young, gallant kitchen designer."

"The main credit does not belong to the designer," said Eugene, "but to the republic, that most paternal government, that most tender mother, for ordaining everything for the pleasure of its children. Unfortunate France!"

"You are right, my dear friend," I added quickly, to interrupt him and prevent the repetition of his patriotic delirium.

"Yes," said the lady. "In fact, if the republic were ever attacked by our husbands, we would divorce them on the spot, and we women, young or old, would defend it! You may even have the pleasure of hearing our girls make this pledge every morning in another song, for whether they are working at home or in the workshop, they are always singing; and you may be sure that the clothing they wear as housekeepers and workers pleases them more than their leisure or party outfits."

So that is an Icarian house! And all the houses in the cities are exactly the same inside, each housing a single family. The houses come in three sizes of three, four, or five front windows, for families of less than twelve, twenty-five, or forty persons, respectively. When the family is larger (which happens frequently), it occupies two contiguous houses, joined by an inner door. Because all houses are the same, the family next door usually gives up its house willingly and moves to another one, or is forced to do this by the magistrate unless the large family can find two other contiguous vacant houses. In these cases, the furniture being exactly the same, like the houses, each family takes along only its personal effects, moving from one fully furnished house into another. These changes in domicile are so rare that the republic avoids in this way the enormous loss of work and furniture resulting in other countries from the uprooting and transport of all furnishings in constant moves. But the shell and the distribution of space in the house is only one part of the story; and it is the furnishings that we must examine to have a complete picture of a dwelling in Icaria.

Furnishings

The same rules apply to furnishings. We have all that is necessary, everything that is known to be useful (that which we call the comfortable), and that which is pleasing to as great an extent as possible, with choice guided by forethought and reason.

That is why there are parquet floors and carpets throughout. Points and sharp angles are replaced everywhere by rounded shapes to prevent accidents among children and even adults. Throughout the house, the furniture closes up so tightly that dust cannot penetrate it, and it is arranged in such a way, as the lady pointed out to us, that dust can hardly settle on it or can be easily wiped off each day. This good woman also mentioned with pride that the corners and angles of walls or woodwork are carefully filled with plaster or putty to round all edges, so that cleaning tools can be inserted more easily. She also showed us with visible satisfaction all the safety measures taken to protect dwelling places from all the insects that used to live in them and ruin them. I must admit that all these small measures pleased me as much as the most beautiful features of the rooms.

All these rooms are furnished with cupboards, wardrobes, sideboards, shelves, and so forth, and all the walls are designed so that these furnishings are stationary, built in, supported, or firm. They may contain doors only in front that open onto inner shelves or drawers, and occasionally shelves above, which makes for a great savings of work and materials.

All the walls are covered with paper or fabric, or with paint and varnish. They are decorated with framed posters that, rather than being painted scenes, are magnificent instructive prints containing everyday, useful information. The posters in the kitchen, for example, show the most common culinary procedures, so that the cook can find the one she needs in an instant without wasting time consulting a large book. In the bathroom, the posters show the necessary temperature and length of a bath. In the children's nurse's room, they remind the nurse at a glance of the most important safety measures for her and the infant. In the children's rooms, the posters remind them of their daily schedule. Frames contain few painted or engraved pictures because everyone can go to see collections of paintings, engravings, and sculptures in national museums and public buildings. Beds are made of iron and bedrooms are furnished simply, although they do contain everything that might be needed, with dressing rooms for men as

well as for women. The dining room and small parlor are decorated more elabo-
rately, and the bathroom is charming, but the parlor is magnificent.

We already knew that each of the furnishings found in a house—be it a bed,
a table, and anything else—was authorized by law and manufactured and provided by government order. Each family had a catalog or large portfolio containing an inventory of legal furnishings, with prints and engravings showing the
form and nature of each object. We asked to see this unusual book, and we
looked through it with as much pleasure as curiosity. Each of the furnishings, the
lady told us, was chosen from among thousands of its type and adopted during a
competition of model designs. The most perfect one was chosen based on the
criteria of convenience, comfort, simplicity, saving of time and materials, and finally elegance and charm. We were enchanted, in fact, by everything that surrounded us. We admired in everything—the carpets, fabrics, wallpapers, and
furniture of all kinds—simplicity, elegance, and good taste in the choice of color,
design, and shape. What astonished me even more was that all these furnishings
contained the most precious materials: all metals, even gold and silver, all varieties of marble and stone, porcelains and clays, crystal and glass, wood of all
types, fabrics of all sorts and colors—in short, all animal, vegetable, and mineral
products known to man.

As I kept expressing my surprise, Eugene said, "At first, I was as amazed as
you are, but the Icarians have made me realize that the republic considers all that
is produced from the earth of Icaria to be equal in value; the difference comes
merely in the supply. The republic would give families gold or silver shovels as
readily as iron ones if the three materials were equally available. It divides all the
gold and silver equally among the citizens, just as it divides the iron and the lead.
When a material is too rare to be given to everyone, it is given to no one; and if
that material is useful or pleasing, it is set aside for public buildings. Now," he
went on, "don't you see that precious metals, which used to be hoarded in the
palaces of kings and aristocrats, are actually in great enough supply so that every
household can have its share?"

"Besides," added the lady of the house, "alloys of gold and silver, artificial
crystals, and manufactured gems are, in our opinion, as good and as beautiful as
pure gold and silver, diamonds and precious stones; and the republic has enough
alloys and composites to give many to each family. So glass, crystal, stemware,
chandeliers, bronze, alabaster and plaster, artificial flowers, and perfumes—in
short, everything that the republic harvests or manufactures—is divided among
all the citizens. And note how everything to do with lighting has been perfected!
Not only do our lamps, candles, and gas give off no bad odor, but our oils, wax,
and all other materials are scented. Everything joins together to charm the

senses of smell and sight without tiring them. And now, please examine our parlor carefully."

Although I had already seen similar ones, I was filled with wonder when I studied its every detail more carefully. I will not list the charms and beauties here. I will simply say that never in any palace have I seen anything more elegant, gracious, and magnificent than that parlor.

"And all the houses in Icaria are the same!" cried Eugene, who was carried away. "Oh happy country!"

"And this uniformity is not boring," I added.

"First of all," said the lady, "uniformity is a priceless good, even a necessity, and is the basis of all our institutions. In the second place, it is combined with infinite variety in each of its parts. Look! In this house, as in all others, you will not see two rooms, two doors, two chimneys, two wallpapers, or two carpets that are exactly alike. Our legislators were able to reconcile all the pleasures of variety with the advantages of uniformity."

We took our leave, enchanted, after thanking the lady for her kindness and congratulating her on belonging to such a rational and happy people.

I was eagerly awaiting the traveling balloon outing, and Eugene, whom I had invited to join me, was just as anxious to see Miss Dinaïse. Imagine my disappointment when, arriving at Valmor's, I learned that Miss Dinaïse could not come, that she could not even see us the next day, but only the day after that, and that Corilla was at her friend's house and would not be coming with us either. Eugene, Valmor, and I were left on our own, and I do not know which of us felt the worst, although we pretended philosophically to be resigned to our fate.

"How can you steer a balloon while it is in the air?" I asked Valmor while we were walking along.

"Well," Valmor replied, "didn't they say the same thing before the discovery of steamships, the compass, America, and the vaccine, of lightning rods, the steam engine, balloons themselves, and a thousand other things?"

"But you have to find your bearings, and it seems impossible to do that in the air."

"People used to say that other necessary items were impossible to find, and they found them anyway. Furthermore, who says that you must have a fixed point to get your bearings, and who says you cannot find one in the air? You can say, like a blind person, 'I do not see the sun.' But, just as the blind man would be wrong to say, 'There is no sun,' so no one can say it is impossible to steer a balloon."

"And," added Eugene, "that is not a problem today because we are going to see some balloons that people steer at will."

"There were many accidents at first," said Valmor, "just as with steam engines and even the first carriages. Several balloons caught fire, or were hit by lightning, or came down too fast, or fell on pointed objects or into the sea, and many aeronauts perished; but our scientists were so sure that they would succeed that the republic provided them with all necessary means to repeat the experiments. At the end of all these attempts, chance finally led to the discovery of what had seemed impossible. All problems were solved. For the past two years, travel by air has become not only the fastest and most pleasant means of travel, but the one that involves the fewest accidents and least danger."

We arrived just as he was finishing his speech. What a spectacle! In an immense courtyard, filled with spectators, fifty enormous balloons, each holding forty or fifty people in its gondola, decked out in a thousand colors, were waiting for the signal, like fifty mail carriers or fifty stagecoaches. At the signal given by a trumpet, the fifty balloons rise majestically, in the midst of mutual farewells and to the sound of trumpets that sometimes can be heard high in the air. Then, when the balloons reach a certain altitude, different for each, they each set off in a different direction and vanish into thin air, followed for a long time, however, by hundreds of telescopes trained on them.

"You can steer them at will," Valmor told me, "to the right, the left, up or down, and you can slow down or speed up their flight. They often slow down and descend into cities on their route to let off passengers or to take on others. It is even rumored that balloons will soon deliver letters and may even provide telegraphic services as well."

At that moment, we heard the cry: "Here it is!" It was the balloon from Mora whose arrival had been expected, appearing as a point on the horizon. It was soon over our heads, turning and descending slowly into the courtyard, and then letting off its passengers and packages. I will never forget how impressed I was by the sight of the balloons coming and going. The thoughts they engendered threw me into a kind of ecstasy. I felt as if I were dreaming, and I must have looked like a madman.

"At first, this novelty had the same effect on all of us," said Valmor. "Now this sight does not surprise us any more than that of steamboats or horseless carriages, which we see every day. But what will you say a few days from now when you see an aerial festival?"

"I have even heard," said Eugene, "that you have submarines that travel in water like the balloons in air."

"That is true. We have discovered how to imitate the mechanisms of fish as well as birds, and we can move about in the sea, descending to any depth at will, just as we move about at any aerial height. When you read the descriptions of our underwater and aerial travels, you will see that the sea offers to man almost as many marvels as the sky and the earth. You will be equally astonished, I am sure, when you learn about all the other discoveries we have made in the past fifty years, and all the wonders wrought by our own industry.

"Because," he added, "you wish our guidance in your study of our country, I suggest that you examine carefully our system of education. Dinaros, who has promised to explain it to you, has instructed me to tell you that he will be at your disposal tomorrow; and if by chance Mr. Eugene wishes to accompany you, I am sure that our friend would be as pleased to see him as I was to make his acquaintance."

10 Education

Eugene had a prior commitment that prevented him from coming with me, so I went to Dinaros's home alone.

"Milord, you wish to know, in all its complexity, the organization and state of our happy country, and you wish to start by learning about education. You are very right to begin here because we consider education to be the basis and the foundation of our social and political system, and the people and its representatives have given it their utmost attention.

"First, let me remind you that during the era of our regeneration, a large committee planned the organization of public education by looking into all ancient and modern systems and by soliciting all opinions. Then we set up, by law, the different types of education (physical, intellectual, moral, industrial, and civic) and, for each of these, length of time, order of study, and methods of teaching.

"All Icarians, without differentiation by sex or profession, undergo the same general or elementary education, which encompasses the basic elements of all human knowledge. In addition, all those who exercise the same industrial or scientific profession undergo the same specialized or professional education, which consists of all the theory and practice of that profession.

"Education is domestic in that portion delegated to parents within the bosom of the family, and public or communal in that portion delegated to national instructors in national schools. It must have occurred to you that the republic can easily find all the male and female educators it needs, no matter how many, because teaching is perhaps the most honored profession, as it is the profession that is the most useful to the community and has the greatest influence on the common happiness. It must also be apparent that these teachers can acquire easily, in normal schools, all the desirable knowledge and practical skills, in particular the habits of patience, gentleness, and paternal goodness. What you cannot figure out on your own, and what I must make clear to you right away, is that, for fifty years now, because education is exactly the same for each person, and each person is encouraged to teach others what he or she knows, there has been not one father who cannot bring up his sons, not one mother incapable of bringing up her daughters, not a brother or sister who is not educated enough to instruct his or her younger brothers or sisters, not even one man or woman who could not bring up his or her younger compatriots if necessary.

"I will begin with physical education, which we consider the basis of all the others."

Physical Education

"The committee foresaw and discussed everything pertaining to physical education; the people or the law implemented it.

"You should know, first of all, that the republic protects its children not only from birth, but even during their mothers' pregnancies. Right after their marriage, young spouses are taught everything they need to know concerning the welfare of mothers and children. To this end, the republic commissioned works about anatomy, hygiene, and so forth, and developed the necessary courses, which include new instructions for pregnancy indicating all the precautions the mother must take for herself and for her unborn child. The birth takes place in the presence of family members and, almost always, of several midwives. Additional innovative instructions, always prepared by doctors, indicate in the most minute detail everything required for the health of the mother and the physical well-being of the child. And do not imagine that even one mother exists who is unaware of what she needs to know. Because creating children as perfect and happy as possible for the republic is considered the most important of all public functions, the Constitution has gone to great lengths to develop education that will render mothers capable of fulfilling this function perfectly. The republic does not stop at providing mothers with useful pamphlets. Special maternity courses, which they are required to attend, enlighten them more fully on all questions concerning the child. Nothing is more appealing than these maternity courses, given by older mothers trained to teach young mothers who carry happily in their wombs the first fruit of the most pure love, for it is during pregnancy that they attend this course. The only men allowed to attend are their husbands.

During the course, thousands of questions are discussed, concerning not only the breast feeding of the child, its weaning, teething, walking, nourishment, clothing, and bathing, but also the development and perfect functioning of each of his or her organs; for we are convinced that, in a way, the child can be cultivated like certain vegetables and animals, and that the limits of perfecting the human race are not yet known.

"I will add right away, in anticipation of further questions, that, as the mother alone is responsible for educating her children during the first five years of their lives, she is also taught about all matters concerning intellectual and moral education. And we place so much importance on this first maternal education—which is, of course, supervised by the father—that the republic prints the *Mothers' Magazine*, where many useful observations are published. Imagine how great a number of observations of this type are collected when all women and all men are educated well enough to make them.

"You can already see that whereas, in the past, our men and women were just overgrown children incapable of rearing others, our mothers and fathers today are women and men worthy of those titles and perfectly capable of beginning with their children the education that will make true men and true women out of them. The consequences of this first major innovation are incalculable; and you will find a multitude of innovations of the same nature.

"If children are born ill or deformed, all possible care is lavished on them by national doctors in the mother's home or in a special hospital when necessary; and there are few of these illnesses or deformities that the art of medicine has not succeeded in curing or correcting with the help of recently discovered ingenious instruments that the republic always provides without ever considering the expense.

"I do not have to tell you that it is always the mother herself who nurses her child. In the rare case where she cannot fulfill this duty and enjoy this happy act, there are always relatives, friends, neighbors, or fellow citizens who consent with pleasure to become a second mother to the child. To this end, the magistrate and midwives always have a chart of all the women who, in this circumstance, are capable of replacing the mother. The mother never leaves her children either during or after the period of nursing. She always watches over them, nestles them in her tenderness, and, like a benevolent divinity, protects them from all the dangers to which mercenary hands used to expose them. If you only knew how mothers are pampered and cared for by everyone around them, during pregnancy and nursing! how they are respected and honored! how peaceful they are, without cares, without anxiety—in short, happy! and what good milk their happiness and health assure their children!

"You cannot imagine all the discoveries made in the past forty years about the education of children, all the improvements that have been implemented, and all the care mothers take today to develop in their children strength and physical beauty, as well as perfect sight, hearing, hands, and feet! And take a look at our children! Have you ever seen, anywhere, more handsome, stronger, more perfect children? And if you compare the successive generations since our happy revolution, does it not seem that our population has been gradually improving and perfecting itself?

"The mother dedicates herself to teaching her child, from the moment of its birth, all the physical habits he or she will need one day. From ages three to five, all the children from the same street, boys and girls, get together to play and take walks, under the guidance of some or all of their mothers. As soon as the child is strong enough, first at home and then at school, he or she begins all the gymnastic exercises set by law to develop and perfect the limbs and organs. All games are aimed at developing grace, skill, strength, and health. Walking well, running, jumping in all directions, climbing up and down, swimming, horseback riding, dancing, skating, fencing, and military exercises are studied, as well as actual games that strengthen and perfect the body. Some industrial experience and farm-work of the simplest kind produces the same results with the same enjoyment.

"I began by saying 'walking well'—that is, walking with ease, with grace and at length—because, in our opinion, this is a skill, and one of prime necessity, that we learn from earliest childhood, to which we add dance steps and turns of all sorts. All school hikes are like military exercises. Most of these exercises are de-signed for girls as well as boys, even swimming and horseback riding, with suit-able modifications.

"Look at our youth and our entire population! Look at the children, the men, the women, walking alone, or in pairs, or in groups! Isn't it true that our people combine suppleness with strength? Doesn't it follow naturally that gener-ations of children will emerge who are even more robust and handsome than their fathers and mothers?

"But you will see that our intellectual education is in no way inferior to our physical education."

Intellectual Education

"I do not have to repeat that, in this area as well, everything was discussed and decided on by committee and prescribed by the people or by law. You will also remember that books and maternity courses teach young spouses to raise their children well. However, you cannot imagine the care with which, in each family of the republic, the development of the intelligence is observed, studied, and cultivated! If only you could see with what solicitude and what pleasure, particularly during the first years of childhood, the mother at all times and the father after returning from work are concerned with their children's education and vie for their attention with warm caresses. As a result, even before they can speak, the children already exhibit a prodigious intelligence, which allows them to acquire a surprising mass of substantive knowledge.

"Until the age of five, education takes place at home. During this time, mothers and fathers teach the child language, reading, writing, and an extraordinary amount of practical and material knowledge. It is always the mother who claims the happiness and glory of giving to her son as well as to her daughter the first instruments of human knowledge, so that each woman of Icaria is always ready to say, as did the mother of the Gracchi when showing off her children: 'These are my jewels!'

"At the age of five, communal education begins and goes on until age seventeen or eighteen, combined with domestic education; for children do not go to school until nine o'clock, after lunch, and return home at six o'clock, after attending their classes and eating two meals at school. Like the rest of the family, children of all ages are up at five o'clock in the morning. Until eight-thirty, under the direction of the older children, they are busy with housework, personal hygiene, and studies. In the evening, when they return home, they spend time with their family and devote themselves to walks, games, conversation, and study; but all is calculated and combined so that everything has an educational purpose.

"Children get into the habit very early of skillful reading aloud and excellent pronunciation. Later on, they take a course in public speaking so that they are able to charm others by reading aloud a selection of history, poetry, theater, or eloquent speech. As a result, whereas previously there was not one person in a thousand who knew how to read and speak aloud with skill, now you will not find one in a thousand who is incapable of doing so. Listen to our children, our conversations, our professors, our priests, our doctors, our orators, and our actors!

"Children also learn writing from their mother, and from the moment they know how to write, they are not allowed to write illegibly, with the result that you will find many Icarians' writing very well, and many (those who take on the profession of copyist) writing perfectly. You will not find a single example of illegible writing because nothing seems easier to us than writing legibly, and, consequently, nothing is less excusable than not knowing how to do it. We find nothing more ridiculous and impertinent than writing one's name and address or a letter illegibly so that the person trying to decipher the handwriting becomes exhausted.

"Our language is so regular and easy that we learn it without even noticing.

Only the briefest of explanations is necessary to learn the rules and theory perfectly, under the guidance of teachers who make their students practice the grammar, rather than contenting themselves with explaining it. The art of literary writing is a study put off until later, like the art of oratory. However, as soon as the children can write, their mother accustoms them to composing short letters and stories for their absent relatives and for their friends. She also accustoms the children to telling stories orally, answering, forming questions, and even debating. You have been amazed at the ease with which our children recite aloud. You would be even more amazed if you saw the ease and grace of their epistolary writings!

"As for the study of Latin, Greek, other ancient languages, and living foreign languages, we do not want our students to waste precious time in these boring studies, time that can be filled much more usefully. Our scholars can find all ancient and modern books in our public libraries, as well as translations of all these works, at least the most useful ones. Consequently, we can profit from the experience of all eras and all peoples without knowing their languages. As for the study of those languages with an emphasis on either language alone or on literature, it is quite unprofitable when there are so many more useful things to learn, and particularly when you have such a perfect language as ours. In fact, we consider the old custom of devoting all our youths' time to the study of Greek and Latin to be a most monstrous absurdity. We are even convinced that our former tyrants imposed these sterile studies on their subjects only to prevent them from educating themselves.

"We have a certain number of young people who study ancient and modern languages, but only in preparation for the professions of translator, interpreter, professor, scholar, and traveler sent by the republic to foreign countries. Thus, the study of these languages is a profession, and this profession, like all others, is part of specialized education, which starts only at eighteen years of age.

"Linear drawing is one of the first subjects the child studies. Consequently, there is no young man or woman who cannot draw any object; not one male or female worker who, with notebook and pencil always by his or her side, is not always ready to sketch out his or her idea. You cannot imagine how great an impact this skill in drawing has on progress in good taste, the arts, and industry. As for painting, engraving, sculpture, and all related arts, they are professions that entail, later on, their own specialized studies.

"It is the basic elements of the natural sciences in particular that we teach children early: the rudiments of geology, geography, mineralogy, the history of animals and plants, physics, chemistry, and astronomy. Imagine what a nation must be like where, instead of being instructed in the futile old fields of knowledge, all the people have basic elementary knowledge of these magnificent sciences. It is only after all these studies that the children learn about religion and divinity. Elementary calculus and geometry are also taught, so there is not one Icarian who does not know how to count, to measure, and even to make up a scale drawing.

"You know that vocal and instrumental music is also included in general education, and that everyone begins to study music from early childhood. All people here, men and women, children and old people, are musicians, whereas in former times we had almost all foreign musicians. You will never be able to calculate the happy effects of this musical revolution!

"The basics of agriculture, mechanics, and industry are also part of our general education. And all this elementary education is the same, more or less, for girls and boys, although often in separate schools and with different teachers. Our girls have made a mockery of the contempt with which people used to insist that their intelligence was inferior to that of their brothers. Now girls compete with boys in almost everything; and if there are some sciences in which men generally excel, there are several others where the highest honors seem to go to the women.

"Imagine, if you can, the salutary consequences of this revolution in the education of women! You have been going into raptures every day about the exquisite taste of our Icarian women in their dress and in everything they make with their hands, but what is their grace and wit compared with the transcendent genius that places many of our women in the first ranks of medicine, teaching, public speaking, literature, the fine arts, and even astronomy! If Dinaïse were not my sister, I would tell you that her intelligence and her education are far greater than her facial charm. Yes, my dear friend, we cannot compete with them for the crown of beauty, and those charming rulers vie with us for the crown of intelligence!

"At seventeen years of age for girls, and eighteen for boys, specialized or professional education begins, which has as a goal to give each person all the theoretical and practical knowledge necessary to excel in his or her scientific or industrial profession. But general education does not end there because that is when students begin elementary courses in literature, universal history, anatomy, and hygiene, as well as the comprehensive maternity courses I mentioned already and those courses that make up a civic education. All of these courses, obligatory for all young people, last until they are twenty or twenty-one and are taken after morning work.

"Even at age twenty-one, a person has not completed his or her education, for the republic sets up many courses for people of all ages—for example, a course on the history of mankind. Newspapers and books (for we know how to educate ourselves with well-written books) are another means of education that lasts throughout one's life. This complementary instruction is not obligatory; however, there are very few Icarians who do not hunger for it, each one wishing to say, as did the ancient philosopher, 'I learn as I get older.'

"But how can we learn so many things? This is how we do it."

Teaching Methods

"We want to teach the children as much as possible, and, consequently, we use all imaginable means to make the study of each subject easy, rapid, and pleasant. Our great principle is that every learning experience should be a game, and every game a learning experience. So the members of the committee searched their imaginations tirelessly to find and multiply the means to this end; and as soon as experience causes a new method to be discovered, we hurry to adopt it. The beauty and comfort of the schools, the instructors' patience and tenderness as well as their skill, the simple methods, the clear demonstrations, the mixture of study and games: everything works together to achieve our goal.

"As we are lucky enough to have a perfectly regular language, and as everyone speaks it equally well, the child learns it naturally and without effort. However, we follow a certain system, the effectiveness of which has been proven by experience, which regulates the choice and order of words and ideas we communicate to the students, taking care always to show them the object when it is named. From this moment on, and even earlier, in fact, the mother and father are particularly careful to give their dear child no false ideas, no errors, none of those prejudices that used to be planted in the mind by domestic servants or even by ignorant, badly brought up parents.

"You would not believe all the measures the Education Committee has taken to teach reading to the children as quickly and pleasantly as possible. The members deliberated for a long time before choosing the best method. The one they chose, put into practice by the mother, makes this apprenticeship a pleasure the children are so anxious to have that it is the children themselves who demand the lessons. The mothers are so skilled in heating up the children's passion for learning that they must soon be held back. In addition, because our language is written exactly as it is pronounced, with no ambiguous or useless letters, it is much easier to learn to read it. So this first great step in education, which used to cost the student so many tears and so much time and the teacher so much annoyance, is now merely a few months' amusement for the child and his or her mother.

"Need I tell you that the choice of the first books used for learning to read seems so important to us that the republic charges its most famous writers with writing them? We have only one book for children of the same age, and I am going to show it to you" (he went to get it in the next room). "Look, here is *The Children's Friend!* What lovely binding, what pretty, colorful engravings, what beautiful paper and magnificent print! Take it with you and read it. You will see that this book has great simplicity, clarity, interest, charm, and educational value, without a single word, thing, or idea above the child's intelligence because there is not a single idea, expression, or feeling that has not been weighed and chosen by the author. The little book that we used to have, which had won a competition involving a large number of other books, was almost perfect; but this one, adopted only twenty years ago (because we are always making improvements), is a real masterpiece; and as for me, I have never seen a more perfect or useful work, or any statue better earned than the one awarded by the republic to the writer of this book.

"The mother explains everything to the children, questions them to make sure that they understand and know perfectly what has been read. Then, in school, when all the children of the same age are together, the mistress (for it is a woman) has them read and questions them in such a way as to capture the attention of all children equally. If one of them hesitates, another answers, and the mistress provides an explanation only when none of the students come up with the answer. And when, after six months, the children have read—or rather, devoured—this little book, you would be amazed at the prodigious education they already have!

"I do not need to tell you that the mistress is almost a second mother because of the tenderness and caresses she gives each of her little pupils, for one of our great principles requires that teachers always behave with their pupils like the most tender of parents with their children. To scold children, to hate them, and particularly to get angry with them because of a vice or any sort of fault seem to us to be contrary to reason, foolish behaviors that debase the person, making him or her inferior to the child.

"Thus, *The Children's Friend* is the first book that all our five-year-olds read. We have similar books for every age group, and the children's library is made up of very few volumes because we think that a few excellent books the child knows well are infinitely more valuable than a mixture of good ones, and much better than a hodgepodge of mediocre and bad ones. We have even introduced a great innovation in the composition of study books. All our books for the early years, those for geography and figures, for example, which used to be so dry, are written in the form of charming stories.

"Children learn writing according to the same principles, while playing and enjoying themselves, under their mother's direction. She explains to them the reason for everything she is doing and everything she makes them do; for there is always a reason one acts in a certain way rather than in another, and one of our great principles is to exercise the intelligence and the judgment of the children right away, accustoming them to be always reasoning, and then giving them an explanation. Thus, the mother shows her children how they should hold the pen, how they should place the paper, and then explains why; and when the children are gathered at school, their teacher always asks all the hows and whys, what position results in a certain form of writing, and what position is taken to produce a different script. This is the theory of writing; and in all areas of education, even in gymnastics and games, we always unite theory and practice. So now you understand how everyone who knows how to write is capable of teaching it to others.

"This method of exercising the faculty of reason is applied to everything and is used constantly by those who come in contact with the child. Because the goal of this method is to instruct, we never suppress the children's curiosity, but applaud it by answering all their questions and arouse it constantly by asking the children the motive or cause of everything they see. We also train the children never to be embarrassed when they do not know something they have not been taught and to answer without hesitation 'I do not know' when they do not know an answer. You can imagine the results of this habit of examining everything and constantly reasoning.

"Elementary calculus and geometry are taught in school with instruments and methods that make the study charming for the children, particularly because practice is joined to theory and most of the study is done in workshops and national storehouses to get the child used to counting, weighing, and measuring all sorts of materials and products—or, in the country, to teach him or her to measure surfaces and to resolve trigonometric problems on site.

"You certainly do not need me to explain all the methods we have created to teach drawing, geography, music, and other subjects. At any rate, I will show you those when we visit a school. But you must realize that when a whole nation is absolutely determined that the teaching of each science and art be pleasant and within reach of the most limited intelligence, that nation is certainly going to find the necessary means to achieve its goal.

"You will be dazzled when you see our instructional instruments and our museums. I will not dwell on our museums of natural history, minerals and plants, living and dead animals, geology and anatomy (for we have them for all the sciences and all the arts, and, in fact, our great workshops and large national storehouses are actually industrial museums). I merely will mention our geography museums, where thousands of maps and machines of all sorts show the earth in all its diverse aspects, some focusing on countries or peoples, others on rivers or mountain chains; our religion museums, where statues and paintings show the gods and ceremonies of all the different religions; and our astronomy museums, in one of which the most marvelous machine shows the universe in motion and allows you to touch with your fingers and see all the astronomical phenomena that are so difficult to understand otherwise.

"You must realize that with all these methods, with daily walks in the country when it is fine weather, or visits to museums when it is not, there is neither tiredness nor disgust nor difficulty in learning the elements of the arts and the sciences. However, we are not satisfied with instruments and material means to facilitate the growth of the intelligence. One of our most successful methods of education consists in constantly exercising the faculties of thought and judgment, and in making each student responsible for teaching the younger ones what he or she already knows. The teachers explain only what they have to in order to speed up the learning and supervise students in their work, teaching them to think for themselves instead of thinking for them. It is particularly in the art of questioning that the teacher's talent shines—or, more specifically, in the art of using all of his or her students to teach each other. Thus, one student explains or repeats the explanation, another one asks the questions, everyone answers, and the teacher intervenes only when absolutely necessary.

"I must go now. See you tomorrow! If you would care to come back before eight-thirty, we will visit the school in our neighborhood, and I will tell you about moral education."

11 Education (*continued*)

Moral Education

I arrived at Dinaros's house before the appointed time, and we went out together while chatting. "You must have guessed," he said, "that the Education Committee and our legislators provided for moral education in the same way they did for physical and intellectual education. They worked even harder on it, if that is possible, because the soul and heart of a person seem even more important to us than his or her body and mind. You would be amazed if you read the discussions our philosophers and moralists have had on this subject, as well as the immense number of questions they examined and precepts they adopted.

"Once more it is the family, and in particular the mother, under the supervision of the father, to whom the state entrusts the earliest moral education; and, consequently, the maternity courses I already mentioned yesterday teach mothers and fathers everything they must do to make their children, as far as possible, as perfect morally as they are physically. You would be amazed if you saw with what care mothers and all those around them watch out for, examine, and direct the first feelings and the first passions of the young animal, to nip in the bud bad inclinations, and to develop good qualities. Nowhere, I am sure, will you find mothers who are more tender or children who are less likely to cry, scream, get angry, be tyrannical—in short, who are less spoiled.

"The first feeling a mother seeks to develop in her children is filial love, a limitless confidence, and, consequently, a blind obedience whose possible excesses the mother is careful to prevent. It is the mother who teaches the children to cherish their father, and it is the father who helps the children temper their love for their mother with reason. Thus, our children are accustomed to adore and to listen to their mother and father as if they were sublimely well-meaning and enlightened divinities.

"As soon as the children have strength of their own, they are trained to serve themselves and to do everything they can without the aid of another person. Thus, it is with pleasure, for example, that children clean their clothes and their room, without knowing that, in earlier days, they would not have done so without a feeling of repugnance and shame. They are even accustomed to serving their mother and father, then their older relatives, then their older brothers and sisters, and then the friends and strangers that come to the house; and nothing is less annoying and more pleasing than our children crowding around everyone to be of some use. In this way, the child becomes accustomed to all the housework, under the direction of the older children, who have the younger ones do everything they can; and all of these tasks, where everyone teaches and learns, are done amidst laughter and singing.

"Every day, the children are awakened at five o'clock, in the winter as well as in the summer; and for an hour or two, they do domestic tasks in work clothes. Then, always supervised by an older child, the children wash and dress themselves. They are accustomed to valuing cleanliness above all, joining it with good taste, grace, and elegance, not because of vanity but from a feeling of obligation and regard for others. After that, they begin their studies, always supervised by their mother or the elder children, until it is time for lunch and for school. You can imagine how many lessons in care, attention, and skill the child receives during the operations of housekeeping and grooming, and how many other useful lessons he or she is given during study and meals, always mixed with caresses! You can also imagine how firmly the habits of love between relatives, protectiveness and tenderness from older siblings to younger, respect and gratitude from younger to older become rooted.

"I have already told you that, after the age of three, when the child knows how to speak, all the children on a single street, both girls and boys, get together for a few hours to walk or play, supervised by one or several of their mothers, in order to improve their good health: but the principal goal of this gathering is to begin to accustom the children to sociability, equality, and fraternity, habits developed even more strongly as soon as the children start to attend school.

"Here we are at the communal school. What an impressive building it is! What inscriptions, what statues, what a magnificent exterior! Look how much space is around it! Look at the beautiful trees! You will soon see the magnificent interior! Does everything here not proclaim that the republic considers education as the primary good and the nation's youth as the treasure and hope of the country? Does everything here not inspire in the children an almost religious respect for education and for the republic that provides it? Do you see those men going in over there? Those are the teachers entering their common room.

"The nine o'clock bell is going to ring. Let us wait a moment and see the children arriving. Here they are! Look! Here is a street full of children! Don't they look like a small army made up of twelve companies, with different heights, ages, and uniforms? All the children from each family have gone into a building on their street, directed there by an older child; and all the children of that street, meeting in that building, are lined up by age and by school under the supervision of the oldest student of each school, and they leave together to come here, supervised yet again by an older student. This evening, when they leave school, they will line up here, by families, in the order of the houses on their streets, and, as the little troop marches down the street, each family will leave the group to go home, after bidding a friendly farewell to friends.

"See how clean they look in their uniforms according to age, and how happy, yet disciplined, they seem as they arrive at school! Now that you have seen the children of all the streets in the neighborhood pass by, let us go quickly into a classroom."

We entered an immense room, decorated with statues of the men who had rendered the most important service to education; and I was quite surprised to see girls as well as boys.

"Look!" said Dinaros. "Here are all the teachers and the students lined up by schools. Now listen!"

I was delighted to hear those thousands of children singing in chorus two couplets of a hymn, the first in honor of Icar, the second in honor of one of the other benefactors of youth.

"The hymn has more than a hundred couplets," Dinaros told me, "and every morning the students sing Icar's couplet and one of the others; this is how we accustom children to feeling gratitude.

"You are amazed," he said, "to find girls here. Let me tell you that they arrived separately, like the boys; they entered by a different door; and the building is divided into two large, separate parts, one for girls, the other for boys, with a few communal rooms."

"What!" I cried. "Girls from ages five to sixteen in the same room as boys of the same age!"

"Yes, without any problem and actually with many advantages because, in the family and at school, we accustom boys to respect girls, from childhood, as if they were their own sisters, and girls to make themselves worthy of respect by their decency. We consider modesty to be the guardian of innocence and the enhancer of beauty, so we teach children the most modest of behaviors, not only between the sexes but between a girl and her female companions, and even between a boy and his comrades. Now the children are in class. Let us enter this one. See how attentive the children are and how respectful, and with what goodness the teacher speaks to them! See how clean everything is! Not a spot of ink on tables or on clothing! Not a single knife slash anywhere except on the quill pens! That is how strong the habits of order and propriety are!"

After visiting other classes, some made up of boys, others of girls, and others of the two sexes separated by a light partition, we followed the children to the gymnasium, where we saw a multitude of instruments and gymnastic equipment. We also saw a ten-year-old child climb to the top of a thirty-foot pole, detach some ropes fastened to a horizontal pulley, and go sliding down them. We were told that the day before, another child the same age had gotten up to the pulley and had jumped from the thirty-foot height without hurting himself. However, as that was forbidden (because he might have broken a leg), he was going to be tried for disobedience, and we could attend the hearing.

When the children returned to class, we went to see the two swimming schools located in the courtyard, one for boys and one for girls. Dinaros showed me the swimming costumes for each of the sexes and explained that, once the children knew how to swim, they got used to swimming fully dressed, so that they could save themselves if they fell into the water with all their clothes on, and that they were even trained to save another person who might be drowning. No opportunity to teach children to be useful to others was missed.

While waiting for the trial of the disobedient little jumper, we went to take a walk in the courtyard.

"What prizes," I asked Dinaros, "are given to encourage competition?"

"None, neither prize nor crown nor distinction because, as we want to nurture in the children the feelings of equality and fraternal goodwill, we would certainly avoid creating distinctions that would encourage egotism and ambition, on one hand, and envy and hatred, on the other. Moreover, we have so many other methods of nurturing a love of one's studies that we have to repress rather than stimulate the students' passion. The only distinction desired by the students is to be elected the most capable and most worthy to guide and instruct others with the supervision of the teacher. And this distinction is all the more honorable in their eyes because the elections, like the examinations, are supervised by the students themselves, under the teachers' watchful eyes. It follows that we have no idle students; and if by chance there is one, instead of increasing his disgust with studies by heaping extra work on him as a punishment, we increase our gentleness, caresses, and care to inspire him to develop a taste for studies. We have very few students who cannot or will not learn; and when there is one, instead of getting angry at him, we increase our patience, interest, and efforts to help him overcome the unjust inequality of nature. To hate and mistreat the student of little capacity, or even the lazy one, would be an injustice, an irrationality, almost a barbarity that would make the teacher much guiltier than the student.

"We have very few misdemeanors to punish, and all the punishments are light. They consist in the temporary curtailment of certain pleasures or school subjects, and particularly in public blame and publicity. All the children's punishments, moreover, are determined by law, like their homework and their misdemeanors. They are listed in the *Student Code Book*, and to make it easier for the students to enforce this code, it is discussed, deliberated on, and voted on from time to time by the students, who adopt it as their own work, and who learn it by heart in order to follow it more strictly. Five years ago this code was discussed at the same time in all the schools and was adopted almost unanimously by the students.

"When a breach of conduct is committed, the students themselves constitute a jury to hear the case and render judgment. But let us return to the great hall, and we probably will see one of these student trials."

The room was already filled. Like earlier, all the teachers and students were present. One of the oldest students acted as prosecutor; five others would propose the punishment; and the others formed a jury. After stating the facts in the case, a teacher, who supervised the debate, exhorted the prosecutor to be moderate in his accusation, the accused to defend himself without fear, the witnesses to bring testimony without lying, the jurors to bring judgment following the dictates of their conscience, and the judges to apply the law without partiality.

The prosecutor expressed his regret that he was accusing a brother and his desire to find him innocent. But he made it clear that the code was the work of the student population and of the accused; that all its precepts, prohibitions, and punishments had been established in the interests of each and every student; that the accused student could have killed or wounded himself by jumping from the top of the pole; and that the common good demanded that he be punished if guilty or, even more important, that he be absolved if innocent.

The accused young lad defended himself with confidence. He admitted frankly that he had jumped; he recognized that he had disobeyed the law and that he deserved punishment, and he regretted his disobedience. He had been motivated by a wish to show his daring and courage to his companions and by the certainty that he would not come to any harm. Another student came forth to declare that he himself had committed the error of encouraging the other to jump, forgetting that the law forbade it. Yet another student, called as a witness, said that he had seen the accused party jump, adding that he regretted having to make this declaration, which his duty to tell the truth compelled him to do.

The defense counsel admitted the error, but he presented as attenuating facts, and as an excuse, the accused student's admission of guilt, his repentance, and his companions' encouragement. He asked the jury to consider that his friend was the most intrepid jumper of his age group, and that it was his very daring and skill that had made him vulnerable to the encouragement of others. The prosecutor admitted that the accused deserved a prize if one were being awarded for the daring of the jumper; but he asked if it were not precisely to moderate this daring that the prohibition had been set up, and if it were not to those very daring ones that the law must be applied to save them from the dangers of their excessive ardor.

The jury declared unanimously that the accused one was guilty of disobeying the code; but it declared, based on a simple majority, that the fault was excusable. The committee of five proposed the verdict: the only punishment would be publicizing the event within the school boundaries. The assembly adopted this proposition, and the supreme Council of Teachers approved the decision. One of the teachers ended the session by reminding the children that they should not love the little jumper any less, and the jumper that he should not love his judges any less. He reminded everyone that they should give even more love to the republic that was doing so much for their happiness, and that they should love each other even more to please the republic.

I went out, dazzled and heated up by what I had just seen, and I returned home with Dinaros. "What a course in morality in action!" I told him. "Now I truly understand your children, your women, your nation!"

"And, in addition, we have a special course on morality, which everyone takes for twelve years, to learn all his or her duties, all the qualities and virtues to acquire, and all the faults and vices to avoid. This course, which used to be so disregarded and tedious before, is all the more appealing today because we include in it the history of all the great virtues and crimes, in addition to the stories of heroes and famous scoundrels. The most interesting books, written by our most skilled writers, our novels, our poetry, our plays: everything joins together with education to make the people love morality, and the republic, absolute mistress that she is, does not authorize a single immoral work. You might even say that family life is a perpetual course in morality in action, as you called it before, because as soon as they open their ears and mouth, children learn, repeat, and practice only moral actions. Never, for example, will you find a child lying. And why, I ask you, would Icarian children lie when the community makes them so happy? How could they not love this community and equality, when they bring such happiness?

"Farewell. I must take leave of you. I will tell you only one more thing: that a special education magazine, distributed to all teachers, keeps them up to date on all the discoveries and improvements concerning education. But you must come and spend the evening at my mother's house with Valmor and his family, and we can chat a bit about our civic education."

I had not seen Corilla for two days, and, despite my troubled spirit, it seemed that it had been two centuries. I cannot explain what a need I had to see her and to hear her speak. So I went early to her family home to spend a little time there before accompanying the family to Mrs. Dinamé's house.

Corilla was more beautiful and friendly than ever before!

"Ah! Here you are, Sir," she said, coming up to me. "It seems that you are very pleased to see us! How can that be? For two long days, you have not even come to pay your respects to my grandfather! That is bad, very bad, and Grandpa is not happy with you, isn't that right, Grandpa? Well, here you are at last, and we will forgive you. Ah, yes! We are supposed to sing together at Dinaïse's house. Let us see whether or not I will be ashamed to sing with you."

We sang. "Well, that is not too bad," she said, "and it will be better, I hope, the second time." The whole way there, she was charmingly witty.

Mrs. Dinamé's whole small family was there, and we were about forty persons in all. There were so many kisses, particularly from the children, such gaiety, joy, happiness!

"You really are a happy people," I said to Dinaros, whom I had pulled into a corner.

"Probably the happiest on earth," he answered, "and it is a result of our community."

"And of your education."

"Yes, of our education as well, for without it the community in all its perfection would be impossible, and it is our education that prepares us for all the enjoyments as well as for all the obligations of social and political life. You could say that from the earliest years the child is learning to be a citizen. He learns this above all at school, where the discussion of the students' code, examinations, elections, and student jury prepare the child for civic life.

"But actual CIVIC EDUCATION begins at eighteen, when the young person learns the elements of literature, oratory art and universal history. Civic education consists specifically in the in-depth study of national history, social and political organization, the Constitution and laws, and the rights and duties of magistrates and citizens. Every child learns the entire Constitution by heart. There is not one Icarian who does not know perfectly everything pertaining to elections and electors, the National Assembly and its representatives, popular assemblies, and the National Guard. There is not one Icarian who does not know all that a magistrate may and may not do, and all that the law permits or forbids. A person who neglected his civic education would be deprived of his rights as a citizen, but this is a shame and a misfortune to which no one exposes himself. Even the women learn the elements of civic education, so that nothing of interest to them remains a mystery, and so that they understand these matters that occupy their husbands to so large an extent.

"Finally, although we hope we will always have domestic and foreign peace, all citizens are members of the National Guard and are trained in the use of arms and military tactics from the ages of eighteen to twenty-one. This practice greatly embellishes national celebrations; it is similar to gymnastics in its usefulness to the body and to health, and is a complement to civic education.

"At twenty-one, the young man becomes a citizen; and you can see that young Icarians are raised to be good patriots as well as good sons, good husbands, good fathers, good neighbors—in short, real men. I might add that they are men of peace and order; the principal axiom of civic education, an axiom that they are taught from childhood and that they continually put into practice, is that, after a free and complete discussion in which everyone can put forth his opinion, the minority must submit without any regrets to the majority, for otherwise there would be no means of making a decision other than brute force and war, victory and conquest, which lead to tyranny and oppression."

"With your community and your education," I said, "you must not have many crimes."

"What crimes do you imagine we could have today?" replied Valmor, who was listening to us. "Can we have stealing of any kind when we have no money, and when everyone has everything he or she could desire? Wouldn't you have to be mad to steal? And how could there be assassinations, fires, or poisonings when stealing is impossible? How could there even be suicides when everyone is happy?"

"But," I said, "couldn't there be murders, duels, and suicides for other reasons: for example, because of love or jealousy?"

"Our education," Valmor replied once more, "makes men and women of us, and we learn to respect the rights and will of others and to follow the counsel of reason and justice in all matters. Nearly all Icarians are philosophers who, from childhood, know how to control their passions."

"So you see," Dinaros went on, "that with a single stroke the community wipes out and prevents thefts and thieves, crimes and criminals; thus, we no longer need trials, prisons, or punishments."

"Excuse me, Sir," cried Corilla in a severe tone as she came closer to us. "There are thefts and crimes, thieves and criminals; we need courts to judge them and punishments to punish them; and although I am not a history teacher, I am going to prove this to you by an argument that cannot be disproved. Listen everyone!" (All the children gathered round her.) "I have been making myself hoarse with singing for half an hour in order to merit the applause of these gentlemen; and not only have these gentlemen stolen the applause I deserved, but their cackling is preventing others from applauding me. Therefore, you are thieves! (bravos!) What's more, and this is a far more abominable crime, Dinaïse is going to sing. These gentlemen were going to keep on croaking to prevent us from hearing her! They want to force us to listen to them as if they were on a podium, holding forth about the republic and the community! Therefore, you are disturbers of the peace, usurpers (bravos!). I accuse you in front of the august court that is seated here (bravos, bravos!), and I invoke against you all the severity of justice and the law (loud applause); or rather, because I fear the corruption of lying judges (murmurs), I am going to condemn you myself, to be certain that the sentence is equitable (burst of laughter). I hereby declare you accused and convicted of the frightful crime of 'outrage against music.' For reparation, I excommunicate you from the community (murmurs), or instead—for the positive remarks I hear warn me that I was going to punish the innocent along with the guilty—I condemn both of you, jointly and severally, to listen first to the nightingale who is going to sing, and then to sing a nightingale's song yourselves (repeated bravos)."

"Grim bailiffs," she said to the children, "carry out the sentence! First make them be quiet. Afterward, you will hear the condemned men sing!"

Miss Dinaïse sang with discomfort and without confidence, but with a divine voice, which seemed to force people to applaud and which almost made me burst into tears.

"Now," said Corilla, "it is the turn of Mister Nightingale the elder!" (All the children rushed to take him by the hand, pulling or pushing him.) "And he had better sing well, or watch out for the musical police!"

"You are mad, mad!" said Dinaros.

"Yes, mad, that is true; but you, crafty philosopher, have the wisdom to obey folly from time to time."

I was also forced to sing, first with Corilla, and then with Miss Dinaïse.

"Now," said Corilla, "I am going to award the prize, and I will do it with all the impartiality for which I am famous. Attention! The wise and eloquent teacher sang like a nightingale with a cold (bursts of laughter); the big communalist schoolboy sang with Dinaïse like a fox who had fallen into a trap (new bursts of even louder laughter); and Dinaïse sang like a frightened nightingale (long bursts of laughter). As for me, Corilla, who is the bold one who dares to deny that I am the goddess or queen of song? Thus, I await the applause of such an enlightened audience (thunderous applause); and I order that the good little cakes that Dinaïse made be served immediately ("Yes, yes, yes!"), along with all the good things that I saw prepared, so that these lovely singers, who excel in the art of making delicious morsels disappear, have the pleasure of seeing us eat them (laughter and bravos)."

The evening was spent deliciously in games and laughter. Corilla begged my forgiveness for her madness, in a tone that charmed my ear long after I could no longer hear her voice; and I spent the night in enchanting dreams, a little bird flying from flower to flower pursued by a swarm of young girls, fleeing Miss Dinaïse fearfully and allowing Corilla to approach me, only to escape from her happily at the moment her hands thought they had caught me.

12   Work and Industry

Could I be in love with her?" I said to myself in fright as I awakened. "Do I love her, when I can still hear the consul at Camiris advising me to treat the girls of Icaria with an inviolable respect; when, above all, I can hear the voice of the venerable grandfather entrusting his children to my honor? Might I love her, when

I am almost engaged to the beautiful Miss Henriet and want to be true to my promise? Do I love her? Let us see, let us analyze ourselves." And I went out to get Valmor, who was supposed to take me to a masonry workshop.

"Don't you think she is beautiful, witty, lovable, charming?" I said to myself as I was walking.

"Yes."

"Don't you take pleasure in admiring her hair, her eyes, her mouth, her teeth, her hands, her feet?"

"Yes, everything about her pleases me."

"You feel joyful when you meet her, sad when you leave her?"

"Yes."

"During the day, you think about her; at night, you pursue her in your dreams?"

"Yes."

"Unfortunate one! I believe you love her!"

However, the joy that I feel is sweet and calm; the regret when I leave her is without bitterness and without violence. I think of her without feverishness and dream of her without delirium. I greet her without uneasiness; I feel her arm or her hand without shivering. No, I only love her like a sister or a friend! And she? Have I perhaps troubled her rest and her happiness? How guilty and tormented I would be! And yet, when I remember . . . But no . . . In any event, we are going on a walk this evening; and I want skillfully, if I may, to question her heart.

At that point, I went into Valmor's house. He was expecting me, and we left immediately to see the masonry workshop, walking and talking along the way.

"Because we are going to visit workers," he said, "I am going to explain to you our organization of work and industry, for work is one of the most important bases of our social organization."

Work and Industry

"First, let me remind you of several principal facts that are the key to all the others. I have already told you, and I am going to repeat it in a few words: we live in a community of goods and work, of rights and privileges, of benefits and responsibilities. We have neither property nor money nor selling nor buying. We are equal in everything, although that may be impossible in absolute terms. We all work equally for the republic or the community. It is the republic that gathers up all the products of the earth and of industry and shares them equally among us. It is the republic that feeds us, clothes us, lodges us, teaches us, and furnishes us equally with everything that is necessary to us.

"Please remember, in addition, that the goal of all our laws is to make the people as happy as possible, starting with the necessary, then the useful, and ending with the pleasing, without putting any limit on them. For example, if we could give everyone a carriage, everyone would have one; but as that is impossible, no one has one, and everyone can enjoy the communal carriages, which we make as comfortable and pleasant as possible. You will see the application of these principles in the organization of work.

"It is the republic, or the community, that determines, every year, all the objects it is necessary to produce or manufacture for feeding, clothing, lodging, and furnishing the people. The republic, and the republic alone, has these objects manufactured by its workers in its business establishments, all industries and factories being national and all workers being national. It is the republic that has the workshops built, always choosing the most convenient locations and the most perfect plans, organizing immense factories, joining together everything that it is advantageous to join, and sparing no expense to obtain a useful result. It is the republic that chooses the procedures, always choosing the best, and making sure to publicize all discoveries, inventions, and improvements; it is the republic that instructs its numerous workers, provides them with primary materials and tools, and distributes work among them, dividing it in the most productive manner and paying them in produce instead of in money. Finally, it is the republic that receives all the manufactured goods and stores them in vast warehouses, to share them among all its workers or, rather, its children.

"And this republic, which wills and disposes in this manner, is none other than the Committee of Industry, the National Assembly, the people themselves.

"You can certainly imagine the incalculable savings of all sorts and incalculable advantages of all kinds that result from this primary, overall arrangement! Every person is a national worker and works for the republic. All persons, men and women, without exception, practice one of the trades, arts, or professions determined by law. Children do not begin to work until age eighteen for boys and seventeen for girls, as their earlier years are devoted to developing their strengths and to their education. Men can retire from work at sixty-five, and women at fifty: but work is so untiring, and even so pleasant, that few take advantage of this exemption. Most continue their usual occupation or serve in other ways.

"I do not have to tell you that ill people are exempted from work. But, to avoid all abuse of this privilege, the ill person has to travel, or be transported, to a hospital, which, at any rate, is like a palace. I do not have to add that every worker may take a leave in circumstances determined by law and with the consent of his or her fellow workers.

"I have just told you that work is pleasant and not tiring. Our laws spare no effort, in fact, to achieve this end. You have never seen a manufacturer who is so good to his workers as the republic is to its own. There are limitless numbers of machines, to such an extent that they replace two hundred million horses or three billion workers; and it is the machines that perform all the dangerous, tiring, unhealthy, dirty, or disgusting work; everything that causes disgust elsewhere is hidden here with the utmost care or surrounded with the greatest of cleanliness. Not only will you never see bloody carcasses in the streets, or even manure, but in the workshops you will never see a worker touch any revolting object.

"Everything functions together to make work pleasant. From early childhood, education teaches us to love and value our work, the cleanliness and comfort of the workshops, the singing that enlivens them and brings joy to the mass of workers, the equality of work for all, its moderate duration, and the honor with which all forms of work are treated by public opinion, all equally."

"What!" I cried. "All professions are honored equally, the shoemaker as much as the doctor?"

"Yes, of course, and you needn't be surprised, for here it is the law that determines those professions or trades that may be chosen, and all the products that may be manufactured. No additional industry is taught or tolerated, just as no other manufacture is permitted. For example, we do not have the profession of gun manufacturer or the manufacture of daggers in our knife factories. All our professions and manufactures are equally legal and judged, in a certain respect, to be equally necessary. Because the law orders that there be shoemakers and doctors, it must necessarily follow that we have both one and the other. Not everyone can be a doctor, so in order that some people may wish to be shoemakers, the shoemakers must be as happy and contented as doctors. Consequently, we must establish between them, as far as possible, the most perfect equality. Furthermore, as they give the same amount of time to the republic, both must be considered of equal value."

"And you make no special distinction for wit, intelligence, genius?"

"No. Are they not, in fact, gifts of nature? Would it be just to punish, in a way, the person to whom fate gave the smaller portion? Should reason and society not repair the inequality produced by blind chance? Is the satisfaction experienced by the person whose talent makes him more useful not enough in itself? If we chose to make a distinction, it would be in favor of those professions or jobs that are the most exacting, in order to compensate them in some way and to encourage them. In a word, our laws make the doctor as honored and as happy as possible. Why then should he or she complain if the shoemaker is accorded the same status? However, although education already inspires in each person the desire to make himself even more useful to the community, in order to arouse an emulation beneficial to society, any worker who does more than his duty out of patriotic fervor, or who makes a useful discovery in his profession, is the recipient of special esteem, public recognition, or even national honors."

"And what about those persons who are lazy?"

"Lazy persons! They are unknown here. How could there be any when the work is so pleasant, and when laziness and idleness are as stigmatized among us as theft is elsewhere?"

"So it would be wrong to say, as I have heard in France and England, that there will always be drunkards, thieves, and wastrels?" "Given the social organization of those countries, that statement is right, but it is wrong in the context of Icaria's social organization.

"The workday, which was set, at first, from ten to eighteen hours and which has been successively reduced, is today fixed at six or seven hours in summer and six hours in winter, from six or seven o'clock in the morning until one o'clock in the afternoon. It will be further reduced as soon as possible if new machinery comes to replace workers, or if a lowering in the demands of industry (that of construction, for example) results in making a great number of workers superfluous. But the length of the workday has probably reached its minimum because, if some industries decline, other new ones will take their place, given that we will work continually to increase our amusements. Last year, for example, a new piece of furniture was added to our allocated furniture, and a hundred thousand workers were needed to provide it for every family. These hundred thousand workers were taken from the general workforce, and the workday was lengthened by five minutes.

"In each family, the women and the girls do all the domestic chores together, from five or six in the morning to half past eight, and from nine o'clock to one o'clock they devote themselves to their professional work in the workshops."

"Pregnant women and nursing mothers, of course, are exempted from work?"

"You are right. And those women who are chief homemakers are exempted from the workshops because looking after home and hearth is yet another occupation useful to the republic. All the workers in each occupation work together in huge communal workshops, where all the intelligence and reason of our government and people shine forth."

"I have visited several that filled me with admiration."

"Aren't they superb? It is the women's factories above all that you must visit. Have you seen any?"

"No."

"Well, then, I will ask for permission, and we will go to see the workshop of my young sister, Célinie, or Corilla's. The perfection of our workshops will not surprise you when you recall that the design was determined in a competition, after having consulted all the workers in the profession, the scholars, and the entire people. The mobile, portable workshops for all work done outside also contain all possible amenities, as you will see, for we are approaching the masons' workshop that I wanted to show you."

An entire street was under construction there by five or six hundred workers of all trades. On the side was a vast movable shed covered with rain-proof canvas, which contained a cloakroom and a canteen like you would find in the normal large workshops. All the scaffolds on which the masons were working were also covered to shield them from sun and rain. All the materials, stones and bricks, pieces of wood and iron, cement, and even mortar were brought prepared and ready to use.

"All the stones," Valmor told me, "are fashioned in immense workshops located near quarries, with the help of machines that saw them or chisel them. Bricks of all sizes are also produced with the help of machines in immense workshops built on the site from which the clay is excavated. Cement and mortar are also mass-produced in other workshops and sometimes on site, but always with machines. All these materials, brought by canal and stored in large warehouses, are then transported on carts of all kinds to a site near the buildings being constructed. Notice how all these carts are designed for loading and unloading so that nothing is spoiled and nothing is allowed to fall! Notice these portable roads on which the heaviest loads roll and slide effortlessly, and these numerous machines, large and small, that carry everything to the top, to the bottom, and to all sides! Furthermore, you will not see one worker in this crowd of workers in action with a burden on his head or shoulders. Each person has no other task than to control the machines or place the materials. Note also the precautions taken to avoid dust and mud! You will note as well that even the workers' clothes are clean. This morning all these workers—that is, all these citizens—arrived at six o'clock. Almost all of them were brought here by public transport. They exchanged their town clothes for work clothes that were ready for them in the cloakroom. At one o'clock, when they finish their workday, they all will put on their town clothes and take public transport. If you, who have seen only the masons of other countries, were to meet our masons on the street, you would certainly not take them for masons returning from work."

"I imagine," I said to him, "that people wish to be masons here just as much as they would wish to follow any other line of work."

"And all those other than masons who work out of doors are treated with just as much consideration by the republic. They all find their workshop, their tools, their work clothes, and everything they need on the work site. Even the carter himself, as you can see, always has a seat on his carriage. Have you also noted the order that reigns in the midst of this universal movement? Here, as in all our workshops, each person has his place, his job, and one might even say his grade, with some leading others, some furnishing materials to others, and all accomplishing their tasks with precision and pleasure. Could not one say that this ensemble forms but a single vast machine in which each cog fulfills its function without irregularity?"

"Yes. This discipline astonishes me."

"But why should it be astonishing? In every workshop, the regulations are discussed and officers elected by the workers themselves, and laws common to all workshops are enacted by the elected officials of the entire people—that is, by the elected officials of the workers in all the workshops. Each citizen must carry out only those regulations or laws that he has created, and consequently he always follows them with neither hesitation nor reluctance."

"But how are the professions allocated?" I asked him as we were returning home. "Is every person free to choose the one he wishes, or is he forced to accept the one imposed upon him?"

Allocation of Professions

"To answer your question I must first describe for you our system of professional education. You will recall that, until the age of eighteen, all children receive an elementary education in all the sciences, and all acquire the skills of drawing and mathematics. We give them a general idea of all the arts and occupations, of the basic elements (animal, vegetable, and mineral), tools, and machines. And we do not limit ourselves to theoretical demonstrations. We add the practical, habituating the children, in special workshops, to manipulating planes, pliers, saws, files, and other basic tools. This practice, which makes the young person skilled with his hands and which prepares him to learn any occupation, is a genuine pleasure for him, as well as a first job that is useful to the community. Thus, the young man is capable of choosing a profession when he reaches eighteen years of age. Here he makes his choice.

"Each year during the ten days preceding the anniversary of our revolution, the republic, which knows the number of workers needed in each profession through statistical studies, publishes the list for every commune and invites the eighteen-year-old young men to make their choices. If there are too many candidates for one occupation, the occupations are allocated by means of a competition, examinations, and the judgment of the competitors themselves who make up a jury. All the eighteen-year-old young men who spring from the soil of the republic are chosen in this manner for each profession, and therefore for each workshop, on the same day every year. This is the day of the worker's birth, one of our important holidays and great ceremonies. And that is not all. You could say that until that day the young man received in school an elementary, general industrial education. Now that he is eighteen years of age, once he has chosen his profession, his specialized or professional education begins. The length of this education is variable because it requires specialized studies of variable duration for the scientific professions. It is theoretical in that it is presented in courses where the theory and history of each profession are taught. It is practical in that it takes place in a workshop where the apprentice passes through all levels of apprenticeship and begins to pay off his debt of work and usefulness to the community to a greater extent.

"The same is done for young women, to teach them household tasks, to give them the theory and general practices of industries that are particular to women, to prepare them to choose a profession at age seventeen, and to complete their professional education. Imagine what male and female workers emerge from this dual education, both elementary and specialized! Can you imagine the consequences of this system of work in industry?"

"I think I can imagine some of them. All the men must be capable of using their intelligence to extend the frontiers of human industry. All the women must know how to perform perfectly all domestic tasks. All houses are exclusively used as dwelling places and contain no shops. Workshops are located in all neighborhoods, and their exteriors contribute to the beautification of the city. It is to no one's advantage to hide or steal a useful invention. No one need worry about bills to pay or need fear bankruptcy."

"Our system has many other useful consequences. In earlier times, our workers, forced to concentrate exclusively on making money, worked quickly and badly. They often even connived to ruin each other's work in order to procure for each other an additional wage. Thus, when locksmiths, carpenters, or painters were working on a house, the locksmith, for example, ruined the wood or paintwork on the door so that the carpenter or painter would have additional work. Now, on the contrary, it is in the worker's interest to do his work as well as possible. All his movements are marked by caution and reason, and all work is nearly perfect. You can see the feeling of dignity that shines forth from the faces of our workers—or, rather, the faces of our citizens. Each considers his work a public office, just as every officeholder sees his office as work.

"Have you also noticed the regular timetable of our population? At five o'clock, everyone is awake; toward six o'clock, all our streets and public vehicles are full of men who are going to their workshops; at nine o'clock, it is the women and children's turn. From nine to one, the population is either in the workshops or at school; at half past one, the entire population of workers leave the workshops to join family and neighbors in the communal restaurants; from two to three, everyone is dining; from three to nine, all the population fills the gardens, terraces, streets, promenades, popular assemblies, courses, theaters, and all other public places; at ten o'clock, everyone goes to bed; and during the night, from ten o'clock to five in the morning, the streets are deserted."

"So you also have a curfew, that law that seemed so tyrannical?"

"Had the curfew been imposed by a tyrant, that would indeed have been an intolerable humiliation; but adopted by the entire people in the interest of health and good order at work, it is the most reasonable, useful, and well-executed of laws."

"Yes, I understand, and I can see how happy your workers must be."

"So much so that the descendants of our former aristocracy are proud of their titles of locksmith, printer, and so forth, which have replaced those of duke or marquis."

All these details, told with a grace that doubled their worth, were of great interest to me. They did not, however, prevent me from being impatient to ask Corilla those questions that would put my mind to rest. Imagine my annoyance when, on encountering Mrs. Dinamé and her daughter and son who had come to fetch Corilla's family to go on the walk, I heard Corilla say, "I want to ask the professor some questions about history, so I will take his arm. Mr. William, offer your arm to Dinaïse."

Valmor had taken Mrs. Dinamé's arm. I would have liked to find an excuse to withdraw, but because this was impossible, I offered my arm as politely as I could. I would have willingly begun an argument in order to escape. That is how embarrassed I was to be near this charming young woman who was said to be even more endearing than pretty, and whom I had so desired to see when I had heard her voice. She seemed as disconcerted as I was, and her discomfort made mine even greater. After walking for a time, sometimes saying nothing, and sometimes speaking about the beautiful weather and the beautiful trees, I thought I would please her by speaking of Valmor. I praised him with all the warmth inspired by the most sincere and passionate friendship because she seemed to be listening to me with feeling and pleasure. She in turn spoke to me of her friend Corilla, praising at great length her wit and gaiety, expressing the most tender attachment to her, and affirming that no one deserved more to be loved and to be happy. Imagine my surprise when she added that Corilla was impatiently awaiting the arrival of one of her brother's friends, a young man whom she loved and who was going to marry her!

"Miss Corilla is going to get married!" I cried.

"I thought you knew," she said with an embarrassed air.

Thus, I learned by accident the secret that I had wanted to know. I do not know (for the human heart is unfathomable) if this discovery caused me pain or pleasure. It did plunge me into an irresistible reverie and a vague unease that I could not understand. I accompanied Miss Dinaïse back home, but her sweet voice was unable to restore the calm in my soul; and I felt such a strong urge to be alone that I took my leave as soon as the possibility arose.

13 Health, Doctors, and Hospitals

How charming you are, William! You are leaving us to accompany Dinaïse home, and you have not come back to say good-bye to me! I am so angry! I certainly wish to forgive you, but you must come to seek your pardon in person. Come this evening, at eight o'clock, to take me to Dinaïse's home. Do not forget to come! I will tell you something that will bring you pleasure. Come!"

This note threw me into a new state of bafflement. "What do this anger and this pardon mean?" I asked myself. "What does she want to reveal to me? Might it be her marriage? Might she be a flirt? No, no, she is totally ingenuous. We shall see!"

After lunch, I went to visit the neighborhood hospital with Eugene and a doctor of his acquaintance who was taking us there. I thought we would be obliged to leave my poor friend there, to cure him of the fever caused by his continuously increasing enthusiasm for everything he was discovering in Icaria. I must admit that I myself was more and more delighted, and that I shared completely the feelings he expressed when recounting our visit to his brother; I will add his letter to this document in a moment, after recounting my discussion with Corilla.

Corilla was ready when I arrived, and we left immediately.

"Come" she said, taking my arm. "Come and let me share my joy with you! You know that my brother loves Dinaïse. He is crazy about her, the poor boy! But you also know that she is kind, good, amiable, charming! I do not need to tell you this, for when you heard her and saw her for the first time, you found her voice divine and her face angelic. Yes, she is an angel with her parents and her friends, and if she were less modest, less distrustful of herself, less wild or timid with people she does not know, she would be perfection itself."

"Does she love Valmor?" I asked.

"How could she not love him, a boy who is so good, so well educated, held in such high esteem, the brother of her best friend, the best friend of her brother, a boy with whom she has virtually been raised? Oh, we would all be so miserable if she did not love him! What pain she caused me from time to time by letting slip that she would never be able to leave her mother and that perhaps she might never want to take a husband! She seemed to be fleeing from Valmor, while showing him much affection when they happened to be together. Poor Valmor did not dare speak to her of his love. All of us, my relatives and his, want this union almost as much as my brother does; we did not dare to press her to declare her consent. But happily those unfortunate days are now in the past. She has begun to spend more time with us recently. Her brother and mother give us the most flattering hopes. They doubt her consent no longer, and we have just decided that the day after tomorrow both our mothers will ask of her the 'yes' that will overwhelm us all with happiness. You will have a chance to see one of our marriages! And to be sure that I will have an escort who pleases me, I choose you in advance. You will be my cavalier, William."

Although I shared most sincerely her wishes, hopes, and joy concerning Valmor, I felt dissatisfied and even a trifle annoyed with her silence about her own feelings. "And you have no further confidences to share with me?" I said to her.

"No", she replied.

"None?"

"No, not a single one."

"You are concealing your own marriage plans from me!"

"What? My mother told you about that the other day."

"Never."

"Oh, yes she did!"

"No, she did not, I tell you."

"I was sure she did."

"And this marriage pleases you?"

"It will ensure my happiness. He is the finest of men! You will certainly grow to like him when he arrives in two months. In the letter my father received from him this very morning, he says that, from the description we have given him of you, he already shares our warm feelings for you. He will be one of the best husbands, and I will be one of the most perfectly happy wives!"

"And I, who would I be if I loved you?"

"If you loved me? You? Ho, ho, ho!" (She burst out laughing.) "And the beautiful Miss Henriet, who loves you, whom you love, whom you have promised to marry, and whom you will marry in eight or ten months?"

"You are laughing! But if, I repeat, if I loved you!"

"What do you mean by that?" she said fearfully. "What reproaches, what regrets, what remorse! How miserable I would be! William, my lord, I beg you, give me your assurance quickly!"

"Yes, it is true. I love you. I cherish you. I love you as the most tender of brothers, as the most respectful and devoted of friends."

"Oh, now I can breathe again," she said. "What a weight you have lifted from my shoulders. You are so good to me. I was sure of it! But what a lesson for my daughters! Farewell, my friend. Do not come in. Go home now. Take your leave! I must run to tell my mother how happy your friendship, my new brother, makes me, your sister!"

"Holy friendship," I said to myself as I walked away. "As of yet, I know but you; but when you give us such a friend, you alone deserve our worship and our homage!"

And now, here is Eugene's letter to his brother.

Health, Doctors, and Hospices

Would that you were here by my side, my dear brother Camille, you whose heart is so full of love for humanity! Would that you were near your friend to share his admiration and his regrets, his transports of delight and his pain! I have just visited an Icarian hospital with one of their foremost doctors, who was kind enough to give me a complete tour and to explain everything to me. Listen!

I will not describe for you the immense building, rather the magnificent palace, situated on a small airy hillock, in the center of a vast and charming garden traversed by a lovely stream. The republic seeks to join utility, convenience, and charm in all its public buildings, which are always constructed according to a model plan, so it will be easy for you to imagine what an Icarian hospital is like: an institution designed to receive not poor, destitute persons, but all citizens without exception (when they have a serious illness), all of whom have more than adequate lodgings of their own. I do not lie when I tell you that the interior is as magnificent as that of a superb palace. It is even more beautiful than that of the houses, for the republic is of the opinion that her ill citizens should be treated even better than those who enjoy good health.

In the midst of greenery and flowers, you see statues of the men who have given the most service to the art of healing. But what I admired with great emotion were the precautions taken to avoid noise, bad odors, and, in general, anything that could affect adversely the ill patients. Above all, there was much thought given to supplying what would bring pleasure to the patients: for example, harmonious, soft music produced by an invisible machine; pleasant smells; and colors and objects always restful to the eye.

I admired as well the mobile beds, flexible in all directions, the innumerable instruments and machines invented to carry the patient and put him in any position that might relieve him, either to avoid accidents and pain or to facilitate operations and dressings. It seemed throughout as if the most ingenious and tender mother had set up everything possible to banish suffering from the bed of her beloved child. If only you could have seen the care taken to make remedies less bitter, dressings less painful, even operations less frightening and cruel. You could say that the patient here is treated like the favorite of a benevolent deity.

I was deeply moved, and yet nothing amazed me when I remembered that the republic had charged the Health Committee to arrange everything to the advantage of the patients, sparing no expense. Nothing surprised me when I reflected upon the fact that there were no mercenaries and no poor people in this hospital, but only citizens who cared for the patients as if they were their own children, and patients who saw only brothers around them. Moreover, every patient, his family, and his friends have the consolation and pleasure of seeing one another as often and for as long a period of time deemed acceptable by prudence and by the doctor. When the nature of the illness requires it, the patient is isolated in a separate room, but ordinarily the beds are placed in vast halls. When the family comes to visit, the patient's area is quickly transformed into a closed room into which one may enter without being seen.

See how everything is well placed for serving the patients! The doctors, surgeons, pharmacists, and nurses live at the circumference of the hospital, virtually in the hospital itself. Because staffing is so adequate, the employees do not become too fatigued, each of them having to work only six or seven hours a day. Every day, doctors visit each patient three or four times on a regular basis; and in the intervening hours, to handle unusual cases that may arise, there are always enough employees at the hospital, in addition to young doctors who are always available in the halls to dress the patients' wounds, to monitor them, and to call the doctors whenever they are needed. All visits are carried out by at least three doctors, and a surgeon performs all operations in the presence of two others. In serious cases, all the doctors and surgeons of the hospital are brought in for consultation.

You can imagine how much to his or her advantage it is for an ill or wounded person to be treated in the hospital, for, despite the amenities he would find in his home in the bosom of his family, he has at his disposal at the hospital an endless number of advantages that could not possibly be found elsewhere. In fact, citizens take themselves to or are taken to the hospital only for fairly serious illnesses. All families are familiar with these maladies, for they are clearly indicated by doctors or in books on hygiene. Mild illnesses and pains that do not require a doctor's intervention are treated within each family. Heads of families, who have taken a hygiene course and are able to consult books written for them, can recognize perfectly well the cases where a doctor's intervention is necessary, those cases where none is needed, the treatment to follow, and the formulation of remedies, most of which are prepared in the small home pharmacy.

This universal knowledge of hygiene, when combined with the small pharmacies in each home, is an invaluable innovation. Whereas in earlier times families did not know how to prepare the simplest remedies, prescribed by doctors who did not go to the trouble of explaining how to prepare them, not a person today does not know perfectly well how to prepare the most common remedies. Whereas most of these remedies were often prescribed cavalierly or inappropriately, there is not one remedy today that is not applied discreetly and appropriately.

I will give you one example, the footbath that patients or their families often use without the doctor's order, or that doctors prescribe without finding out whether or not anyone knows how to prepare it. You know as well as I do that a footbath may be taken in a thousand ways. It may be too hot or not hot enough, too long or not long enough, in too much or not enough water, and so forth. Only one of these thousand ways is helpful, and all the others are harmful and sometimes fatal, yet ignorance always chooses one of the latter. How many accidents result from this! In Icaria today, there is neither man nor woman who does not know how to prepare a footbath perfectly.

Hygiene for the teeth has been developed to such an extent, for example, that the care one takes of them every day, from childhood on, protects them almost completely from the painful and dangerous maladies that used to be so common. Another great and valuable innovation is that every workshop where the work in question may lead to accidents has a surgeon on call with a small pharmacy so that the required first treatment may be applied in the moment following the accident. Doctors rarely make home visits, and then only in extraordinary cases, particularly in the city (they do make more visits in the country). For these urgent or long-distance trips, saddle horses are always available to them in a small national stable attached to each hospital.

It is, therefore, at the hospital where doctors treat all the patients who need their care. All surgical operations, in particular, are performed at the hospital. The result is an immense advantage for the art of medicine, which you can no doubt guess: all former doctors or surgeons, as well as young doctors and students, can and do attend and assist at important operations and treatments of all serious illnesses. They all profit from each other's experience, and this experience is as wide as possible because every doctor or surgeon sees all the patients of any particular neighborhood or commune.

And here is another great innovation worthy of your admiration! Convinced that there were innumerable serious drawbacks because only males were visiting, assisting in delivery, operating on, and treating women, the Icarians determined that there would be as many female as male doctors and surgeons. Only women would visit, assist in delivery, operate on, and treat women, and male doctors would be reserved exclusively for male patients. You cannot imagine how many advantages result from this medical revolution!

You are aware that a woman can possess as much intelligence and education as a man; that she is usually more patient, gentler, and, above all, more affectionate; that she is likely to inspire more confidence because she will be less likely to offend modesty; and that she may even have a more thorough knowledge of those maladies peculiar to her gender. But, you may say, what about the courage and physical strength required—in particular, in surgical operations? As for courage, women are not lacking in that. More accustomed than men to suffering and to seeing suffering, they know how to use tenderness in helping the sufferer bear her pain and sensitivity in sympathizing with pain and giving consolation for it. As for strength, women have enough of it, just as they have sufficient skill, particularly after training in surgery, for all normal cases; and if, in a few rare cases, the intervention of a man becomes necessary, it is the female surgeon herself who solicits this aid.

The republic, therefore, has no male obstetricians but only females; no male surgeons and doctors for women, but only females. When women become seriously ill, they are, like men, taken to the hospital. Thus, each hospital is made up of two similar, separate buildings, one for women, where only women are present, and the other for men, where only men are present.

Here is another innovation. Almost all women are delivered of their babies in the hospital, where they are brought several days before the birth and where they stay afterward for as long as necessary. Fearing that this innovation would be distasteful to many women, the republic postponed its implementation until education and public reason had convinced them that this measure would have no real drawbacks, and that their children, they themselves, and the nation would benefit greatly from it.

You can imagine that this system makes the recording of births very simple. The birth is registered in accordance with the declaration of the midwives, at the hospital, with no need for going elsewhere and at the very moment of birth. It is also obvious that, in this community, there could be no motive for hiding or suppressing the birth and the civil status of a child. A small number of women, however, still give birth at home, but always in the presence of at least three midwives, and the exceptional cases where women are treated outside the hospital are more numerous than for men. Young children up to five years of age are usually still treated at home, exclusively by women, little boys as well as little girls. Older children are treated in the small infirmary at school or in the regular hospital.

As for the chronically ill or the elderly who can be cared for as effectively within their families as in the hospital, their relatives surround them with tenderness. You are never confronted with the revolting spectacle of a blind man reduced to being guided by his dog or his walking stick and to begging for alms, an indictment of society and nature. On the contrary, there is nothing more touching than the sight, on the promenades, of elderly fathers pulled in pretty little carriages by their sons and daughters, or children pulled by their brothers and sisters, followed by their fathers and mothers.

You may be sure that all the hospital services—its kitchen, laundry, and baths—are immense and magnificent, but what would charm you the most are the means used to bring food, medications, baths, and water right to the beds of the patients, with the aid of machines, without noise and almost without manpower. You would be even more amazed at the pharmacy, its laboratory and its army of pharmacists. Envision, if you can, its immense size when I tell you that there is but one pharmacy in each neighborhood or commune, and that this pharmacy provides not only all the medications required by the hospital, but all those that make up the small home pharmacies as well.

But you have heard nothing yet, my dear Camille. You must learn about the training of doctors. At seventeen and eighteen years of age, girls and boys who wish to practice any field of medicine or surgery take an examination based on their elementary education. All those who are admitted to the program take a general course at a special medical school, the goal of which is to impart to all students of medicine comprehensive knowledge of the current state of medicine and surgery. After a second examination, each student chooses medicine or surgery and takes two years of specialized courses. Following a third examination, each surgeon or doctor chooses, yet again, from among a great number of specializations and takes a further year of courses particular to his or her discipline. Thus, there are general doctors and specialists, some for children, others for the mentally ill, and yet others for each of the principal illnesses, just as there are general surgeons and then dentists, ophthalmologists, gynecologists, and other surgeons who specialize in each principal operation. Only following a fourth examination does the student earn the title of doctor or national surgeon, and only then can he or she practice his profession. And no one can complain about the length of his studies because every student is supported in full by the republic.

Can you imagine what manner of persons these doctor-surgeons are, and these surgeon-doctors, and these dentists, who are as well educated as the most brilliant doctor and surgeon put together? Also (perhaps you will laugh, but it is true), the dentist's skill and practice are so advanced, children are so used to taking care of their teeth every day, and dentists visit every family so frequently that Icarians hardly ever have atrocious pain or tooth loss anymore.

Add to all these methods everything you can possibly imagine to facilitate and perfect the study of medicine: anatomy museums containing in bone, skeleton, wax, and sketches all the parts of the human body and the effects of all diseases; craniology museums containing thousands of unusual skulls, with the observations to which they have given rise, museums of comparative anatomy containing the skeletal structures of all animals, surgery museums containing all instruments and all operations, and so forth. Add to this the joining of practice to theory. As soon as they have received sufficient instruction, students attend, in the hospitals, all treatments and all operations, and they are responsible for dressing wounds and keeping an eye on the patients.

Finally, take note of this great innovation: all cadavers, without exception, are dissected in an immense amphitheater, in the presence of all the students, under the supervision of one or several doctors or surgeons who have treated the dead party. A case study written up for each dissection states all useful observations without mentioning the person's name. It took the republic a long time to overcome prejudice against these dissections, just as it took time to overcome prejudice against giving birth in hospitals in the presence of many other women. But the republic finally succeeded, by the irresistible power of education and public opinion, in convincing all persons that their birth and their death, like their life, should be dedicated to the good of their fellow citizens. The first converts ordered their own dissections, but others forbad it. Today, reason has won out permanently against prejudice. These two great and major events, birth and autopsy, are imbued, moreover, with a sort of religious respect, by order of the republic. For many years, the names of women giving birth and persons being dissected were unknown to the spectators. Today, even the bodies of deceased women are reserved for the sight of other women, for the body of a woman is a sacred relic that should never be profaned by the eye of a man. Naturally, the autopsy reports of female surgeons are published, just like those of their male colleagues.

I will speak to you on another occasion about funeral practices. I will tell you here only that instead of being abandoned to putrefaction and worms, a person's remains are sent up to heaven, transformed into flames, which need no cemetery and fear no desecration.

I would never finish this letter, my dear brother, if I told you all the advantages that result from this system of funeral arrangements, births, and observations of cadavers by doctors and surgeons from all fields, some examining the heart in particular, and others the liver or other parts of the body. Let me just mention, regarding births, that not only are they now performed without any vestige of danger for the mother or for the child, but doctors know how to prepare for them and make them so much easier that the pain is greatly reduced. Nowadays, they are even capable of performing operations on the bodies of children, which greatly influence their health, strength, and physical and intellectual perfection. As for the autopsies, the discoveries they have engendered prove that they are of great benefit to humankind.

I do not need to tell you about the magazines of medicine and surgery, which publish all observations, improvements, and discoveries, nor need I remind you of the national pharmacies and of the art of pharmacy. You can certainly imagine the revolution in this important profession: the education of pharmacists, their theoretical and practical instruction, and above all their perfect honesty, stemming from their highly respected position and their dedication to earning the public's esteem unhampered by any possibility of personal profit. You may even have guessed that their art has progressed to the point that they have neutralized everything that used to be repellent in their remedies and have even rendered most of them pleasant to take.

You may also have guessed that home nurses receive all necessary instruction. I must tell you that this profession is generally practiced by individuals who, because of bad health, are prohibited from marrying and who, unable to provide the nation with citizens, dedicate themselves to the preservation of the citizens already there. The republic, on the other hand, goes to great lengths to provide these people with all other means for happiness, and the patients worship them as if they were ministers of the Divinity.

Judge, my friend, all the consequences of all these revolutionary changes in medicine, surgery, hygiene, and pharmacology! The results are such that many illnesses thought to be incurable are easily cured today, others have completely disappeared, and death from illness has been greatly reduced. Not only have the Icarians procured vaccines from foreign countries to prevent the plague that caused the masses to be disfigured when it did not send them to the grave; they also have imported or discovered many means to prevent other plagues almost as devastating. Just as the genius of education teaches the stutterer to speak with ease, the deaf to hear everything with their eyes, and the blind to see everything through touch, so the surgeon gives back speech to the mute, hearing to the deaf, eyes to the blind, and limbs to many unfortunates who had lost them; so that in Icaria today there are scarcely any persons who are blind, or deaf, or mute, or toothless.

It is the republic that furnishes to every person all the tools and remedies necessary for his or her health! And all these tools are perfect because no one would profit from making or distributing inferior ones. Nothing is more unusual than the store where they are kept, where a skillful surgeon-doctor distributes them in accordance with the patient's needs. If only you could see, for example, with what care the oculist chooses the lenses appropriate to a person with imperfect sight, almost always giving a different lens for each of the two eyes! Rest assured that these lenses are given only to people who really need them. You would never see in this country the ridiculous fashion of wearing useless, harmful lenses! Nor would you have occasion to become angry, as you often did, about a habit as useless and disturbing to its practitioner as it is annoying and disgusting for the bystanders, as expensive for the poor as it is ridiculous for young men and women—the dirty tobacco habit—for it is truly a filthy habit! Here, the only people you will see smoking or taking snuff are that very small number to whom doctors have distributed tobacco as a necessary remedy.

To all these improvements that medicine has made to public health, you may add, my dear Camille, all those resulting from the new social organization. For example, there are no more unhealthy workplaces, nor is there excessive work for children, women, or men, and there are hardly any accidents anywhere. Poverty and bad food no longer exist, nor do drunkenness and intemperance. Gout, consequently, has been almost eradicated. Violent passions hardly exist anymore, nor, consequently, do madmen. There is no longer any licentiousness, and, consequently, we have eradicated those shameful maladies that ravaged so many in secret!

And finally, I will add that we no longer see those deadly habits that, from childhood, enervate the body, deaden the intellect, wither the heart and the soul, and perhaps do more harm to humanity than the plague. The republic, the Education and Health Committees, fathers and mothers have done so much and are still working so hard at it that this enemy of youth has almost entirely disappeared!

What an incalculable revolution in public and individual health! For one hundred ill persons in the republic before the revolution, there is now only one. And what a difference in longevity! A happy childhood without work, an adulthood without fatigue and without cares, and a prosperous old age without pain have almost doubled the human life span. And what a difference in the rate of population growth, which has increased steadily because of the fecundity of our women, all of whom are married, robust, and happy, and because the young people of today are not decimated by infanticide or war, massacres or death by torture, assassinations or duels or suicides. The population has grown from 25 million inhabitants of Icaria in 1782 to nearly 50 million, not counting several colonies!

And that is not all! Most admirable of all, perhaps, is the improvement in the purity of the blood, the shine of the complexion, the beauty of the figure. You know how abundance or need, calm or anxiety, happiness or indigence influence physical beauty and intelligence. You know that the children of the rich are generally more beautiful than poor children, and that certain populations are beautiful, whereas others degenerate because of poverty. Calculate, then, how all these innovations and the degree of happiness experienced by the Icarians have influenced their physical and moral improvement. In the first few days following my arrival here, I could scarcely believe my eyes when I saw such robust, majestic men, such beautiful women, such handsome young men, such ravishing girls, and children one would take for angels. But today nothing surprises me!

You should know, in addition, that for fifty years a large commission called into being by Icar and composed of doctors and of the most skilled of men has been working around the clock to perfect the human race, with the conviction that the human being is, in every way, infinitely more perfectible than other animal and vegetable life. First of all, the republic invested this commission with the authority to determine the cases where a young man or woman would give birth only to unhealthy children; and the law forbids them to marry. It orders the individual's parents not only to warn the other individual and his or her family but to oppose the marriage. It charges the magistrates with reminding all parties of their obligations before the ceremony takes place. Although this law is sanctioned by public opinion only, no infraction of it has ever occurred; such is the strength of education and public pressure.

But that is not all. Of everything I have seen or learned here, nothing has amazed me more than the work, experiments, observations and discoveries, successes and hopes of this Commission on Perfectibility, whose journal is read with avid interest by all scholars. When I think about it, nothing arouses my anger more at the members of the aristocracy and monarchy who, for centuries, neglected totally the perfecting of the human race, while they worked so hard to perfect breeds of dogs and horses and strains of tulips and peach trees!

And look at the inconsistency! Marriage between brother and sister is almost universally prohibited. For what reason? Because we know that if brothers and sisters married for several generations, their children would become more and more degenerate. Thus, we recognized the necessity of mixing bloodlines, mixing families, and crossing races. And yet we limited ourselves to prohibiting marriages between close relatives. Here, on the contrary, the republic, the good republic, the National Assembly, the Commission on Perfectibility, and the entire nation think and work continuously for the improvement of the human race. A brunette chooses a blond, the blond a brunette, the mountain dweller a girl of the plains, and, often, the northern man a southern girl. The republic negotiates with several of the most beautiful foreign nations to obtain a great number of children of both sexes, which it adopts, raises, and marries off to its own children. And the superb results of these experiments notwithstanding, I dare not reveal to you the far-reaching hopes of the Icarian scientists concerning the physical and intellectual perfectibility of humanity.

And all these marvels that send me into transports of admiration also overwhelm me with sorrow when I think that the sun of July could have brought out fruits as beautiful as these from the fertile earth of our beautiful country, and that it produced only riots and civil war, fusillades and volleys of gunfire, banishments and deaths, while creating corrupt spirits, enslaved souls, and cowardly hearts! Oh my brother! Oh my country!

14 Writers, Scholars, Lawyers, and Judges

I was about to go out when Valmor came in, beaming with joy.

"I am so happy," he said to me, throwing his arms around me, "that I had to come and share my joy with you, for now we are almost brothers because my sister is almost your sister! And I am going to treat you in a brotherly fashion, just as I expect from you all the proofs of a fraternal friendship. My happiness must be your happiness, just as your pain will be my suffering. Corilla revealed all yesterday. She told us everything after you left, and I don't know which gives me the most joy: my sister's feelings of friendship for you or Dinaïse's affection for your friend. How impatiently I await her consent! How long these two days will seem to me, although her brother and mother have as much as promised me her consent. Oh, my friend, how happy I shall be! If you only knew what a treasure she is, what an angel! You have seen and heard her, but you do not know her spirit, her soul, her heart. If you knew her as I do, you would understand my enthusiasm, my transports of love. Perhaps you would love her yourself. But then, I would slay you!"

"Good, very good," I said, laughing. "How well the Icarian, the wise man, the philosopher, controls his passions! How quickly you jump to conclusions, my poor Valmor. Here we have, in Icaria, a Cain, a homicidal priest!"

"Yes, if . . . but Miss Henriet is there. And you would be immortal," he added, embracing me once more, "if you could die only by Valmor's hand! But let us speak seriously. We will all spend the evening together, and Corilla begs you to come early. Don't forget!"

Just as he finished speaking, Eugene entered, laughing.

"Haven't you heard?" he said. "I almost got into a fight yesterday!"

"A fight, in this country? You're joking!"

"Yes, it still makes me laugh. He was red with anger, that gross animal who arrived a few days ago from who knows where, that so-and-so whom you must have noticed with his long beard and pointed tuft of hair."

"And what was the serious subject of the quarrel?"

"You shall see. We were talking about a charming song about women. At that moment, someone said that all Icarian songs were lovely because no one could have any work published, not even a song, without the permission of the republic.

" 'You are surely mistaken,' exclaimed the man with the pointed tuft of hair, rudely interrupting him. 'It is impossible that the republic would censor as the monarchy does, quite impossible!'

" 'I know nothing about it,' I said in turn, 'but I believe it is also true that you can write only with the permission of the republic.'

" 'Well, you are wrong to think that!'

" 'However, isn't it possible that this censorship might be a consequence of the principle of community?'

" 'That would be an absurd consequence!'

" 'But it seems to me that the republic might permit only certain people to publish works, just as it permits only pharmacists to prepare drugs.'

" 'Then your republic, which you praise to the sky, is more tyrannical than a tyrant!'

" 'But, Sir, freedom does not mean the right to do anything regardless of the consequences. Freedom consists in doing that which does not harm other citizens, and certain songs may be moral poisons as deadly to society as physical poisons.'

" 'You are an enemy of freedom of the press!'

" 'No, Sir. I am for it in oppressive monarchies, but in the Icarian republic . . . '

" 'You are an aristocrat in disguise!'

"I was about to take the lout down a peg or two when a burst of laughter from the listeners, upon hearing me called an aristocrat, made me laugh as well and put an end to the discussion. Well, William, what is your opinion on the matter, you who hobnob with scholars," asked Eugene, addressing me, "or, rather, what do you think, oh learned Icarian?" he said, turning to my friend.

"William will answer your question," said Valmor.

"My word, I do not really know," I answered, "but I think, as you do, from what I have seen of the Icarian organization, that the composing of works, no matter what they be, must be a profession like medicine. I think there must be national scholars, writers, poets, just as there are national doctors, priests, and professors. I am even convinced, now that I think about it, that only the republic publishes books because only the republic has print shops, printers, paper, and so forth; and surely the republic publishes only good works. No one can sell books because no one has money to buy them. No one can have books distributed free of charge, and, surely, once more, the republic cannot distribute bad books. Yes, your arguments to the lout seem irrefutable. I am convinced that nothing may be printed without the consent of the republic. I see no disadvantage in this innovation, which, at first glance, might amaze you; for who would complain about being unable to have a bad book published, a book that would be scorned and left unread, when everyone is fed, clothed, and lodged by the republic? And if a good citizen, devoting his leisure time to the public good, were to compose a useful work, who would believe that the republic would not be quick to accept it and to have it published?"

"As for me," Eugene continued, "not only do I see no negative points, but I see great advantages to this system. I imagine that the job of writer is considered one of the professions, and that at seventeen or eighteen years of age the young man or woman who wishes to follow this profession is authorized to choose it only after an examination that tests his or her aptitude for it. The future writer, I expect, then undergoes, for five or six years, the necessary specialized education; his or her works are published only when they are in accordance with the law, upon approval by the appropriate committee. Would this not ensure that writers would not come out with bad books, when they have all possible opportunities to compose all the good works they might desire? Thus, the republic would have national historians, novelists, poets, and songwriters, just as kings used to have pensioned writers. The republic would ask them to write all the works it judged useful, independently of those they might have conceived spontaneously. There would be neither licentious novels nor obscene songs. It would be profitable to no one to rush to write a mediocre work; and this system, applied to all the branches of writing, science, and the arts, would lead to perfection. When all is said and done, such is the Icarian system."

"Both of you have guessed well," said Valmor, "and I note with pleasure that you understand our organization; but let us see. Go on."

"Because all boys and girls," I continued, "learn the basic elements of all the sciences and all take a literature course, it is obvious that all Icarians without exception have ideas about everything and know how to express their ideas in oral or written form. The perfection of the Icarian language and the habit of terseness that every Icarian acquires from the earliest age must surely increase their writing skills. There is certainly no worker who is not capable of sending to the commissions and to the newspapers well-written notes containing useful observations. It is probable that a great number of workers, after finishing their required tasks at the workshop, compose well-written works in all genres, the best of which may be accepted and printed by the republic."

"That is correct," said Valmor.

"As for the many professional scholars (chemists, geologists, mechanics, physicians, astronomers, and so forth), that is certainly another matter. For a long period of time, starting when they are seventeen or eighteen years of age, their specialized studies must be in such depth and of such a sublime nature that, in all branches of science, twenty-five-year-old scholars are already in full possession of their field of knowledge both in general and in all its parts, and therefore may dedicate the remainder of their long and happy lives to experiments and discoveries that challenge the limits of that art or that science. Among this mass of scholars will be found those who experiment, those who apply the knowledge, those who teach it, and those who write treatises and articles for scientific and industrial journals."

"Very good," said Valmor.

"And, like the locksmiths, printers, and other workers, writers (historians, poets, and so forth), scientists (such as chemists and astronomers), and artists (painters and sculptors, for example) will have immense workshops. These workshops, with huge rooms for tests, competitive examinations, and discussions, will be built according to specific models."

"Very good."

"And the republic," added Eugene, "will spare no expense for experiments, tests, laboratories, museums of chemistry and other fields, practical or pleasurable applications, teaching, writing of treatises and journal articles, printing and distributing adopted works."

"Very good."

"And all the works," I added, "will be assigned, adopted through competitions or chosen by scholars, so that, among a great number of good and excellent works, the best will always be chosen."

"Very good, very good."

"And the republic," continued Eugene, "has the chosen works printed in order to distribute them free of charge, like all other works, some to scholars only and others to all families, so that the citizen's library is made up of masterpieces only."

"Very good."

"And the republic," I added, "was able to rewrite all the books that were imperfect—a national history, for example—and to burn all the old books judged to be dangerous or useless."

"Burn them!" said Eugene. "If my lout could hear you, he would accuse you of imitating the ferocious Omar, who burned the library of Alexandria, or that Chinese tyrant who burned the annals of his country to put his dynasty in a more favorable light."

"But I would reply to him," said Valmor, "that we do in the name of humankind what his oppressors were doing to its detriment. We have ignited a fire to burn bad books, whereas the brigands or fanatics lit the bonfires to burn innocent heretics. Nevertheless, we have saved, in our large national libraries, a few copies of all the old books in order to be reminded of the ignorance or madness of the past and the progress of the present."

"And happy Icaria!" cried out Eugene, who was heating up by degree. "Happy Icaria has advanced with giant steps on the route of progress for humankind. Happy Icaria no longer contains anything bad, not even anything mediocre, and has almost arrived at perfection in everything, whereas my unfortunate country, which could also have taken to flight like the eagle, is tormented and stirs restlessly like Prometheus on his rock, bound by a despotism as deadly to other nations as it is to my compatriots."

"What a good young man," said Valmor when Eugene had gone out. "How he loves his country, and yet how magnanimous he is."

After dinner, Eugene accompanied me to Valmor's home. Mrs. Dinamé and her family were there, and although Eugene had already visited several families in Icaria, he seemed to me to be quite uncomfortable when he found himself, by chance, between Corilla and Miss Dinaïse. They seemed to be trying to outdo each other in friendliness toward him, and they complimented him on his letters to his brother, from which I had read to them. The grandfather, in turn, complimented him on his gallantry and on his favorable judgment of Icarian men. "And of Icarian women," added Corilla. Valmor told them about our little morning scene, and everyone had a good laugh when he spoke about the lout with the pointed tuft of hair who had called Eugene an aristocrat.

"Because you have guessed everything about our writers and scholars so accurately," said the grandfather, "let us see if you can make as good a guess concerning the education of our jurisconsults and magistrates."

"Of course! That is easy!" I replied.

"Well," said the old man," "we shall see."

"Your men of law must follow the same path as your scholars," I said. "At eighteen or seventeen years of age, young people—for perhaps you have female lawyers as well as male" ("And they are not the least skilled," said Corilla) "— who wish to pursue this career are admitted to higher learning only after being tested on their elementary education."

"Good," said the grandfather, smiling.

"Once they are admitted, they dedicate themselves for five or six years, in law schools and under the tutelage of skilled professors, to specialized studies pertaining to legislation."

"Good," said the old man.

"Good," repeated all the other people.

"They learn not only all the national codes of law, but even the history of ancient and foreign legal systems."

"Good, good," cried out the whole group, applauding.

"They are taught procedure as well as law, and practice as well as theory. They are taught the habit of clear reasoning and are trained to express their opinions prudently. It is not to their advantage to mislead their clients, as they are given their sustenance by the republic; therefore, they give counsel and defend only those cases they judge as just. They are never obliged, as they had been previously, to debase themselves by pandering to prosecutors they scorn in order to obtain from them a few bad cases to plead."

"Very good. Very good," everyone cried, laughing even louder.

"And the solicitors are almost as well educated as the barristers and no less honest. Even the bailiffs are noted for their education, their politeness, and the beauty of their penmanship."

"Very good, very good," exclaimed Valmor, laughing even more.

"And the judges, chosen from among the most experienced and honored lawyers, join virtue to skill and are worthy ministers of justice and the law, the criminal judges above all."

"In what country do you think you are, my dear William?" cried Eugene, bursting out laughing. "Are you dreaming? Are you mad? Have you forgotten that we are in Icaria, in a country of community, where there may be neither crime nor trial because there is neither money nor property?"

"Good," said Dinaros, rubbing his hands.

"What purpose would be served by codes and laws about property, sales, mortgages, bills of exchange, or bankruptcies? What purpose would be served by a code of criminal procedures or a code of civil procedures? Are all these enormous codes not bad books and insipid works of fiction?"

"Good, good!" cried Corilla.

"And when a moment ago these women were applauding you," he added, laughing even louder, "you did not see, my poor William, that they were laughing at your affability." Everyone was giving me a cunning look.

"And I," I answered, "I maintain that this is how men of law must be trained in Icaria . . . if there are any, but I know as well as you do, my dear laughing friend, that there can be none here; and while you were being amused by my affability, you did not notice, any of you, that I was laughing at your credulity!" At that point, everyone laughed even louder.

"Thus," Eugene continued, "those caricatures, those masks in black robes, their pretty, fresh, pink cheeks peeking out from under the powder of their large wigs (we have seen many of them, William, haven't we?); those bands of harpies with grasping fingers, those bands of famished crows: they are seen no longer in the paradise of Icaria."

"And that army of judges or executioners," I added, "wearing red robes to hide the blood in which they are covered, those miserable men who used to find the truth guilty (we knew many of them, didn't we, my poor Eugene?): to what hell have they been banished since they disappeared from Icaria?"

"How happy you are!" Eugene continued, addressing the grandfather. "No more lawyers, no more solicitors, no more notaries or stockbrokers or brokers in Icaria! No more bailiffs, or bailiffs' assistants, or gendarmes, or policemen, or informers, or jailers, or executioners! No more large or small judges, robed in red and black, fanatical followers of tyranny and hellhounds of Lucifer!!! Oh, community, what God was ever as benevolent as you!" Poor Eugene did not notice that the girls were laughing a great deal at his enthusiasm.

"We do have, however," Valmor said, "crimes, penal laws, and trials."

"But what crimes," said Eugene, "can a person commit here with your community and the happiness in which it bathes you? Theft? Impossible. Bankruptcy, forgery? Impossible. There can be no gain from murder, no motive for arson, violence, or even verbal abuse. There is no cause for conspiracy. In truth, I see room only for an excess of virtues or for peccadilloes."

"But we have serious crimes," added Dinaros.

"What crimes, pray tell?"

"Well, tardiness or inexactitude in the completion of some duty, a distributor who did not send a sufficient amount, someone who asked for more than his due, a wrong caused by imprudence!" (At this point, Eugene burst out laughing.) "One of the crimes we consider to be among the most odious is slander."

"Ah! You are certainly right! When it is premeditated, calumny is a theft, a cowardly assassination!"

"But in our country slander hurts only he who slanders. We defend the slandered party like we would defend a victim attacked by assassins, and an unproven accusation makes no more impression than if it had never been made."

"Therefore, in Icaria, you cannot say: 'Slander and some of it will always remain'?"

"Something would, in fact, remain: a prejudice against the slanderer, but absolutely nothing against the slandered, no more than if, when someone said that Dinaïse was horribly ugly . . ."

"What? Who is the scoundrel who dared . . ."

And all the children pointed their fingers at me or yelled out: "It's William! It's William!"

"Our education," Valmor continued, "instills in us such a horror of slanderers; the feeling of fraternity developed by our upbringing is so lasting that, in the past twenty years, you would not be able to find even one example of calumny; on the contrary, sometimes citizens are occasionally taken to task because they have not reported a misdemeanor they witnessed."

"And what are the punishments for the infamies that besmirch your unfortunate country?" asked Eugene.

"They are terrifying," replied Valmor. "The declaration of a misdemeanor by the court, censure, publication of the verdict to a greater or lesser extent (in the commune, the province, or the republic), forfeiture of certain rights and privileges in school or workshop or commune, exclusion for a long or short period of time from certain public places, even from the Citizens Home. . . . You appear to be laughing. Well, I want you to know that our upbringing trains us to fear these punishments as much as people in other lands fear the shackles or the scaffold. (I once saw a little girl yelling in despair because her mother had sentenced her to eat her slice of toast with jam upside down.)"

"Do you not even have prisons?"

"We have no need whatsoever for them."

"But," I said in turn, "what if there were a brute whose violence was threatening the public safety?"

"We have no brutes of that sort, and if we did, we would treat the individual at a hospital."

"But finally, no matter how selfless and wise you generally are, could there not be a murder or two caused by a lover's jealousy?"

"No."

"But you know as well as I do, someone . . ."

"Who, who?" called out the girls. "Be quiet! We would treat the would-be murderer like a madman." (In England, all suicides are attributed to temporary insanity. Otherwise, the cadaver would be dragged on a rack and deprived of a grave.)

"So," said Eugene, "you have no need of that infernal apparatus that we call the Police."

"Speak for yourself," I said, "and label your police as you will; but have some respect for our English policemen, whose only task is to watch out for thieves and drunkards, and who, each evening, make sure that the doors of shops and houses are locked so that everyone may sleep safe and sound."

"Admire instead," he replied, "the republic of Icaria, where no one need lock a door, and where there are no drunkards, no thieves, and no policemen."

"You are mistaken," said Valmor. "Nowhere on earth are there more police-men, for all our public servants, and even all our citizens, are required to oversee law enforcement and to pursue or denounce the persons whose misdemeanors they witness."

"And you do not fear the hatred or vengeance of the accused against the accuser?"

"Never, for, on the one hand, a person accuses another without passion or malice, and, on the other hand, the accused knows full well that it is the law that requires the accuser to do his duty in the public interest. If, by chance, the con-demned party allowed himself to feel resentment, it would be a new misde-meanor, a revolt against the law, and a hostile act against the people, which would kindle universal indignation. You will see an example of this. Today's paper con-tains a verdict that has just been handed down on a case of this sort by the Popu-lar Assembly in one of the communes in our province."

"Corilla," said the grandfather, "read us this verdict, or, better yet, give the paper to my little Maria, who will show these gentlemen how well Icarian chil-dren know how to read."

The sweet little girl, hardly seven years old, read this for us with a pure pro-nunciation, an intelligence, and a grace that charmed us as much as those quali-ties brought pleasure to the old man. Here is the judgment:

A Judgment in Icaria

"The reporter of the Censure Committee states that T——, previously censured by the Assembly for a misdemeanor he himself admitted, based on information given by D——, has accused the latter, in absentia, of acting with malice. The reporter adds that this imputation would bring dishonor on D—— if it were justified, but that the Assembly remembers D——'s conduct when he came before it. No one may accuse him of malice and, therefore, T——'s accusation appears to be false and slanderous. This slander against a citizen who was only doing his duty is even more serious because it could disturb the public peace and turn citizens away from obeying the law and doing their duty to the people. In conclusion, T—— deserves to be punished if he is found guilty.

"The reporter then points out the informer and the witnesses. The president invites them to come before the bar and questions them. They confirm the facts of the case. The accused, brought before the bar, confesses to the principal facts, bringing to light only a small error on the part of the witnesses. He declares, in a strong, deep voice, that the law is eminently practical and fair, that D——was only doing the duty of a good citizen, that he deeply regrets having given in to a first impulse of annoyance, but that he wishes to correct his erroneous behavior by exhorting his fellow citizens to apply the law in his case. A few members take up his defense, without, however, excusing his behavior entirely. Then the reporter attacks him, while recognizing, on the other hand, the nobility and patriotism of the repentance his public ally expressed.

"The president then consults the Assembly. 'Is T——guilty of slander?' The Assembly replies in the affirmative. Everyone rises. 'Are there extenuating circumstances?' An almost unanimous 'Yes' is heard.

"Finally, the reporter and two other members of the Censure Committee quickly deliberate among themselves and propose, as full punishment, the publication of the proceedings in the communal newspaper, with the names of the parties, and the publication of the verdict in the provincial and national newspapers with full anonymity. This proposition is unanimously adopted by the Popular Assembly."

"What?" said Eugene while I was hugging the little reader. "It is the Popular Assembly that serves as the court?"

"And why not? Do you not keep repeating that a citizen should be judged by his peers—that is, by his fellow citizens?"

"By all of them?"

"Why not? Is a court of two or three thousand not worth more than a court of two or three?"

"And the Popular Assembly judges all misdemeanors?"

"Oh, no! We have other courts. Every school is a court for judging the misdemeanors committed in the school. Every workshop judges the offenses that occur there. The National Assembly judges those offenses that are committed within its body. Each family constitutes itself as a court of justice to judge family misdemeanors. You can see that there is no area where courts and justice are not in existence, and that there is no other land where delinquents can boast that they are judged by their peers to this extent."

"Are women judged by courts made up of women?"

"And why shouldn't they be? Women's infractions committed in the workshop are judged by the members of the workshop, who are far from being unskilled judges. For other infractions, elder women in their families judge women. And if they committed a serious misdemeanor, the women would appear before the Popular Assembly."

"But the women of Icaria are . . ."

"Angels, aren't they?"

"And your popular assemblies do not often have the pleasure of seeing them appear before the bar."

"Never. You may even have figured out," added Valmor, "that little errors committed during communal dinners, in the national restaurants, are judged by the assembled diners; and because these diners are all the citizens from each street, who meet every day as a matter of course, they judge on a daily basis all small public infractions committed the day before by the inhabitants of their street."

"That is very convenient and certainly expeditious," I said, "but what if many of the judges happened to be inebriated?"

"Inebriated? You are forgetting that you are speaking about Icaria! Add to all these courts the fact that every citizen has the right and the duty to intervene personally with two persons whose discussion is degenerating into a dispute, and that those two persons must separate as soon as the third exhorts them to do so in the name of the law, which works like magic. In addition, whenever we have a difference of opinion, we are in the habit of choosing a priest or any other fellow citizen to be a friendly-arbitrating-arranger".

"Well," exclaimed Eugene, "I see that Discord and the Furies may stay in their hell or breathe their poisons in other places, not here."

"We even have," added Dinaros, "a court for the deceased."

"That suits me just fine," Eugene exclaimed, "for nothing revolts me as much as the triumph of crime. I have often wished that the cadavers of tyrants could be exhumed so that these tyrants might be judged and condemned to eternal infamy."

"This court," continued Dinaros, "was instituted based on a proposal by Icar. In the first year of our Regeneration, the National Assembly decreed that all the historians of Icaria meet each year for a month to pass judgment on controversial points in history, following discussion, and to judge past men and events. This historical tribunal passed judgment first on the record of the most important historical figures of Icaria from 1772 onward, and then on earlier persons, and then on the most renowned foreigners, while always searching religiously for the truth."

"So you have an official biography of all the illustrious men of antiquity?" I asked him.

"We have for all our compatriots; but, although the work was started fifty years ago, it is not yet complete for other countries. In addition, we have a museum of history, a veritable temple to justice, a sort of pantheon or pandemonium where, following the decisions of the Censure Committee, the National Assembly awards glory to the former friends of the people and infamy to the enemies of humanity. There you will see Icar at the head of the glorious and Lixdox at the head of the infamous."

"I will visit it," exclaimed Eugene, "for I would go to hell itself to see the wicked and the tyrants unmasked and humiliated there!"

"Happy Icaria," I added, "which gives the nations, finally, an example of justice! Unfortunate France, where the only example given is that of infamy!"

Eugene's latest sally made the young people laugh a great deal. The old man, who feared, perhaps, that their gaiety would appear as mockery, assured my friend the democrat that the entire family valued and loved his frankness, warmth, and patriotic enthusiasm.

15 Women's Workshop, Novels, and Marriage

Valmor could not sit still, for the poor boy was so impatient to learn his fate from the lips of Dinaïse. He spoke to Eugene and me for more than hour about her perfect divinity, his love, and his happiness. "But," he finally exclaimed, "here we are, chatting, when we should be on our way! Let us leave immediately, or we might arrive too late!"

"Are you coming with us?" he asked Eugene. "No, I have things to write."

"Come now, you can write tomorrow. Come see our pretty female workers in their workshop!"

"Your female workers!" exclaimed Eugene. "Oh, I'm coming! Give me two minutes. I will be right back." We took the omnibus, and ten minutes later we were going into the milliners' workshop.

What a sight! Two thousand five hundred young women working in a single workshop, some seated, others standing, almost all charming, with beautiful hair piled on their heads or falling in curls on their shoulders, all wearing elegant aprons over their elegant dresses! In their hands brilliantly colored silks and velvets, laces and ribbons, flowers and feathers, superb hats and gracious bonnets! Here were workers who were as well educated as the most well brought up women of other countries. They were artists, and their habit of executing designs gave them exquisite taste. They were the daughters and wives of all the citizens, working in the republican workshop to beautify their fellow citizens or, to be more precise, their sisters.

Valmor pointed out to us one of the daughters of the first magistrate of the capital and, further on, the wife of the president of the republic. His sister and Miss Dinaïse's sister were right near us. It never would have occurred to one of the young women that she might be superior to any of her companions. Everything was set up for the convenience and enjoyment of this youthful female band, the flower of the nation! What lovely decorations were displayed everywhere in the workshop! What sweet perfumes could be smelled there! What a delicious harmony could be heard from time to time. Everything pointed to a nation where women were adored and to a republic more attentive to the pleasure of its daughters than to the happiness of its other children.

One of the female directors explained the laws of the workshop to us, its special rules decided on by the workers, the participatory election of all its leaders, the division of labor, and the distribution of workers. You might have said that this was the most disciplined of armies! Another directress told us that fashion never varied. There were only a certain number of different forms for hats, caps, turbans, and bonnets. The model for each of these forms had been chosen and decreed by a commission of milliners, painters, and so forth. Each model had been so designed that it could be made larger or smaller to accommodate nearly any head without the necessity of taking specific measurements of each.

Because the republic wants every task to be done as quickly as possible, each hat, for example, has been designed so that it is split into a great number of pieces. All of these pieces are manufactured in great quantities, so that workers have only to sew and attach them together and can finish a hat in a few minutes. Each worker is used to doing the same operation all the time, and this repetition doubles yet again the speed of the work, while making it perfect. The most elegant headdresses are conceived by the millions at the hands of our pretty creators, like flowers in the rays of the sun and the breath of the wind.

Although the rules prescribe silence for the first hour so that the leaders can give instructions to all and lessons to the apprentices, the silence that reigned was so deep that it amazed me even though I was already aware that the tongues of women gathered together wag no faster than those of men, and that women know how to keep quiet and even how to keep a secret just as well as their unfair accusers. But I trembled when, as the bell sounded the last chime of ten, those 2,500 pretty mouths opened to sing a magnificent hymn, far too short, in honor of good Icar, who had recommended the cult of womanhood to his compatriots, saying that this was the cult of the divinities on whom their happiness depended. In the midst of all these voices, I thought I could pick out that of Miss Dinaïse, and I would have been convinced that it was hers if I had not known that she were elsewhere. After that, several voices sang a song full of grace and wit about the pleasures of the workshop. I wish I could remember the joyous refrain that the entire workshop repeated with the most charming gaiety. The hour of song was over in a flash, followed by another hour of silence, during which we were amazed by the order that reigned in the midst of the leaders' movements as they made their way through all the rows.

I would have liked to spend the conversation hour among the 2,500 neighboring workers. I would have liked to see the lovely workers putting down their pretty aprons, hiding their lovely heads once more under their pretty veiled hats, and getting back into the omnibuses that would take them to the many neighborhoods of the city. I also would have liked to see the adjoining buildings, the immense warehouse for fabrics and other materials necessary for the workshop, and the immense storehouses for hats, bonnets, and other completed goods. But Valmor had to leave, and we went out with him, although the directress invited us to stay.

"All the women's workshops," Valmor said as he was leaving us, "those of the seamstresses, the florists, the makers of undergarments, the laundresses, and so forth, are virtually identical to this one. It is as if you had seen them all."

"No, no!" cried Eugene, "I would like to see all of them, over and over again!" And during our trip home, although I may have shared his admiration for Icarian gallantry, his enthusiasm often made me burst out laughing.

When I arrived back at the hotel, I found the following note: "We will have, at four o'clock this afternoon, the 'yes' we have so desired. Come, come! I want to tell you the news myself. Corilla."

Imagine my surprise when, two hours later, I received this second note, unsigned, but whose writing I recognized as Valmor's: "Do not come. Tomorrow morning, at five o'clock, be at the entrance to North Garden." Why this change in plans, this new date, meeting place, and hour? I do not understand. Let us go anyway! I rushed to Corilla's home. "They are not available." I rushed to Mrs. Dinamé's. "They have just left for the country."

Uneasy, worried, not knowing what to do with my anxieties or where to go, I walked straight ahead without thinking until I found myself, quite by chance, on the banks of a stream, on one of the great walkways of Icaria. Coming upon a bench in an isolated spot and wishing to rest for a few minutes, I decided to begin reading a novel that Corilla had lent me. This reading was of such interest to me that I devoured the little book, not stopping until the final word. Illustrations, story, anecdotes, style: everything about it was charming.

It is true that the subject was extremely interesting in and of itself: marriage, its success or failure, the qualities and duties essential to the spouses' happiness, the unpleasant consequences and disasters that result from each of their faults. You can imagine what gracious portraits, piquant little stories, and useful lessons might emerge from such a subject. It was a most charming treatise of moral education concerning marriage for young people, spouses, fathers, and mothers. It was for this reason that the novel had been chosen by the National Assembly. All national writers, indeed all citizens, had been invited to present their projects, and this one had been chosen from a large number of entries. I am sorry I am unable to summarize the plot, but the intrigue is so concise that I could not possibly analyze it. I would prefer to limit myself to a few reflections, rather than to mutilate such a charming composition.

I will begin by two primary observations. The first is that, because in accordance with the communitarian system dowries are as unknown in Icaria as patrimony, young people and their families never consider personal fortune as a factor in marriage and look only at personal qualities. The second is that, because all boys and girls are equally well brought up, all would make good spouses, even if couples were formed by drawing lots. However, young Icarians, who consider marriage the paradise or inferno of this life, accept a spouse only when they know this person perfectly well. In order to know him or her, they keep company for at least six months and more often from childhood or for a long time because a young woman cannot marry until she is eighteen and a young man until he is twenty. In order that girls may study the character of their future spouses, they are given total freedom to converse and to go for walks with boys of their own age, but always under the watchful eye of their mothers, on the promenades as well as in the parlor. Education inspires in men such respect for women and

makes the women so used to it, and public opinion would condemn an infringe-
ment so severely, that two young people in love could be left alone without danger. However, in addition to the extreme vigilance of the mother, the family, and
the general public, and the virtual impossibility of avoiding being seen by the
human eye, education leads Icarians to consider it a crime for a girl to avoid the
eye of her mother or to keep anything secret from her. The young man confides
as fully in his father.

Because the mother and father always know their child's earliest feelings and
the feelings that another child might have for theirs, any inappropriate friendship would be nipped in the bud. Moreover, fathers and mothers are never motivated by personal gain to oppose a marriage their child desires, and children are
used to heeding their parents' advice as if they were tutelary gods.

As soon as marriage is imminent for a young woman and man, they are
taught all the duties and obligations it entails. Mothers and fathers take charge of
this task, supported by books, priests, and priestesses. The spouses know perfectly well that they are joining together for life, that they give themselves to
each other without reservation, that both pain and pleasure must be shared, and
that the happiness of each depends on the other. They commit themselves voluntarily, and with full consciousness, to fulfill all these duties. But why speak of
duties to spouses who admire and love each other? All the precautions that have
been taken so that they will always love each other—their upbringing, the
woman's education, which makes her capable of discussing everything with her
husband and of accompanying him anywhere, their family life, the new parents'
affection, their mutual love, the activeness of a life full of work and without idleness, above all the happiness they enjoy at the hands of the republic and the community—are these not of greater value than all sermons and legal measures in
guaranteeing the fulfillment of their duties? And the masterpiece of the social organization Icar gave to his country, is it not to have made all spouses virtuous
without effort? Virtue is so easy for them that you cannot even call them virtuous, for this title must be the reward of the unfortunate woman who, for the sake
of duty alone and to remain faithful to a detested tyrant, resists the man whose
admiration has captivated her heart. It would be as painful for an Icarian woman
to betray her beloved husband as it is for this unfortunate woman to cause her
cherished lover to despair. The Icarian woman is modest enough to be satisfied
with being happy without competing with that unfortunate woman for the rewards of virtue.

If, however, by chance, happiness seems to escape the couple, the parents,
who could not help but notice, would be the ones to bring to bear duty—or
rather, reason and wisdom—to convince the unhappy spouse or both of them

that it is in their true interest to be resigned to their fate and to be mutually accepting of shortcomings, just as a mother puts up with faults in her children without rejecting them. It is at this point that the priest or priestess comes over occasionally to reinforce, through the authority of his or her words, the family's tender exhortations, which encourage the spouses to seek happiness or, at least, peace in virtue. The novel, which gave me such pleasure, contains two charming portraits on this subject. One is of an unhappy woman who conquers the affection of her husband and finds happiness once more through patience, sweetness, and skill; the other is of an equally unhappy woman who increases her misery tenfold by abandoning herself to vengeance.

Those few spouses who are not happy in their union continue to follow the dictates of reason; they never fail in their commitments and duties to the republic, which offers them the opportunity to divorce when their families feel there is no other recourse. This frees them to look for another conjugal tie, which may provide the happiness they did not find in the first.

Because the republic considers marriage and conjugal fidelity to be the basis of order in families and in the nation, it provides its people with an excellent education and a guaranteed livelihood for their families and themselves, and it facilitates both marriage and the remedy of divorce. That same republic stigmatizes celibacy by choice as an act of ingratitude and a suspect state, and it declares that cohabitation and adultery are crimes for which there is no justification. This declaration suffices, without the necessity of supporting laws, because our education makes all citizens view these crimes with horror, and public opinion would accord the criminal no mercy.

Furthermore, the republic has gone to great lengths to assure that cohabitation and adultery are physically impossible. Consider for a moment our family life and the layout of each city. Where could adultery find a safe haven? The novel I was just speaking about presents a horrifying picture of the difficulties, the anguish, the remorse, and the general condemnation to which an unfortunate woman who allows herself to be seduced is exposed. This portrait, however, appears today to be purely imaginary, for if a few rare cases of divorce have been seen in recent years, it has been twenty years since even one woman has been guilty of breaking these laws.

Public opinion here does not imitate the unjust and cruel inequities of former times and other countries that, while treating the seducer leniently, acted and continue to act without mercy toward his victim. On the contrary, public opinion and the law are doubly inflexible toward the seducer, who is the principal guilty party. To seduce a girl by promising to marry her and then to violate one's promise, to cheat her, and then to abandon her would be—against the girl, her family, and the republic—a treason, a theft, an assassination, a crime more odious than all other crimes that used to exist here and still exist elsewhere. Instead of finding that people admired him for his skill, the seducer would encounter only scorn and imprecations. Instead of feeling triumphant and laughing with impunity at the tears and despair of his victim, he would be faced with a certain amount of pity for her and universal excommunication for himself.

Nothing is more frightening than the portrait in this novel of the seducer of a married woman. He is sullied by public execration and is treated like an assassin by all women, like a thief by all husbands, and like an enemy by all families. In the book, there is also a flirtatious widow who takes pleasure in inflaming the passions of a few young men and finds supreme happiness in having at her feet the corpse of a man who has killed himself for love. She is rejected everywhere as a firebrand and a poisoner.

Despite the charm that the author's talent poured into his portraits of inestimable moral value, their didactic purpose has been realized to such an extent that you cannot find any models today, for, in all Icaria, you cannot cite one example of adultery or cohabitation, even through weakness. Abduction is unknown, for how could the abductor carry off his prey? Seduction itself is virtually impracticable, for what could the seducer offer as bait? There are no more of those scandalous trials for denial of paternity, for annulment of marriage on account of impotence, or for divorce on account of harmful bodily treatment. A husband who beat his wife would be a monster that the women would stone or tear to pieces! Our new language does not even have words for abortion, infanticide, and exposure of a newborn child; that is how impossible these horrors seem.

In Icaria today, there are only chaste girls, respectful boys, and faithful, respected spouses, enjoying a happiness of which my novel gives the most delightful picture, painted from life, while showing that of all the nations of the earth, ancient and modern, the Icarian nation is certainly the one that enjoys the most fully all the delights with which nature has imbued love. I am obliged to admit that all these marvels are results of the republic and community. Like Eugene, I feel disposed to cry out: Happy Icaria! Happy Icaria!

16 Dinaïse Does Not Wish to Marry
Valmor's Despair

When I arrived, worried, at the entrance of North Garden, I saw Valmor at some distance from me. He was walking with large strides and appeared greatly agitated. As soon as he heard me, he ran to me. "Are you my friend?" he cried, beside himself. "Come, follow me! I am fleeing from Icaria! Do not abandon an unfortunate, a very unfortunate man," he repeated, throwing himself upon me before I was able to answer him. "She does not love me, William! Yesterday morning I was the happiest of men, and now I am the most unfortunate! She does not love me! For more than ten years, I have concentrated all my hopes on her, all my affections, all my future happiness, and she does not love me! Her brother and mother were fostering in me an illusion that was keeping me happy; and a word has destroyed my happiness forever. Oh, my friend, my sorrow and that of my family and sister make me so miserable! We all surrounded her with our love, and her refusal overwhelms us all with desolation. If your friendship causes you not to abandon an unfortunate man, you will see joy among us no longer, but only consternation and sadness."

When I showered him with affection and protestations, trying to give him some hope, he said, "No!" and pressed my hands. "Your friend has no more hope! If she hated me, I might have some hope, but she holds me in her affection. And how could such a good heart hate a childhood friend who treats her with such tenderness and respect! She is made desolate by my despair and by my family's pain. The affliction she causes her mother and brother almost drives her to despair. But she declares, crying, that she can accept no husband at all. What makes us despair is that this angel of innocence and beauty, this angel usually so modest, so timid, sometimes joins to her affectionate complacency and angelic timidity the most firm and inflexible character. Knowing all the misery she would cause all of us, she fought for a long time, hesitated for a long time; and her refusal, which costs her so dearly, makes us despair even more, for it seems invincible and irrevocable."

After allowing him to breathe out his pain for a long time and showing him how much it afflicted me as well, I attempted to offer him some consolation by appealing to his reason, his courage, and his love for his mother and sister, whose distress he should soothe by the example of his strength in the face of misfortune and his acceptance of irremediable misfortunes. I obtained his word that he would not leave, and I spent the whole day with him. My friendship seemed to soothe him a trifle; and the members of his family—above all poor Corilla, whose depth of sorrow broke my heart—entreated me to accompany him to the country, where Dinaros was supposed to take him the next day for a few days.

17 Agriculture

All three of us left via the gate through which I had entered Icaria, and soon, after speeding along on the railroad, we reached the river by which I had arrived. Valmor seemed deeply moved when we passed the place where Miss Dinaïse had disembarked. I felt troubled as well when the boat stopped to put us down at the spot where she embarked and where I saw her—or rather, heard her—for the first time with her mother. I felt even more moved when Valmor said to me, "Do you remember? It was here that she came in right near us on the boat. How the future was smiling on me then. And today!"

We passed by several farms that appeared charming to me. "What beautiful weather!" exclaimed Dinaros. "What beautiful countryside!"

"Yes," replied Valmor, "and yet the sun bothers me, and the greenery pleases me even less; nature has no more charms for me."

"Come now, my friend," Dinaros continued, "take courage! Are you not a man? Will you be the wise Valmor no longer?"

After walking for more than an hour, we arrived at another farm located at the foot of a hillock. "She was coming here when we met her with her mother," Valmor told me. "I used to draw near her with such happiness when I would travel here with her and her brother. And now I know not what thick, heavy air . . ." He could not go on.

Mrs. Dinamé's father, Mr. Mirol, a close friend of Valmor's father who lived at this farm, had been told of our arrival by a letter from Dinaros. The air of affectionate attentiveness, and yet of sadness, with which his family welcomed us almost brought forth Valmor's tears. "I came here several times with her," he repeated to me, taking me aside, "and the sight of these spots will do me much good and . . . much ill."

Mr. Mirol's family was very large. There were more than forty persons: he and his wife, five sons and their wives, fourteen grandsons and ten granddaughters, three of whom were married and five or six very young great-grandchildren, in addition to three or four who were of school age. One of the grandsons, almost nineteen years of age, would soon complete his education.

During dinner, which was sad and silent at first, the grandfather asked his grandchild questions pertaining to his studies and education. He asked him which animals were harmful to farming. The young man named, without a moment's hesitation, all the quadrupeds, birds, insects, and worms that cut roots and eat seeds, leaves, fruit pips, flowers, and mature fruits, or that attach themselves to useful animals. Then he recited the facts about the most important of these animals: their birth, their habits, and the procedures used to destroy them. One of his older brothers told us, in a similar vein, the facts about useful animals, with all the peculiarities of their training, feeding, diseases, and principal qualities. One of the girls spoke about silk worms and their charming production. A glass hive filled with honey, whose beauty and excellence were much praised, gave rise to a talk by the girl's mother on honey and bees. And during the recitations by these four principal orators, each of the listeners added a few interesting details. Although I knew Icaria well enough to be shocked by nothing, I was, nevertheless, surprised by their ease in storytelling and their elegant pronunciation, as well as by the scope of their knowledge.

"You are surprised," Dinaros told me, "to find such farmers, both male and female; but Valmor will tell you this evening about the education of our farm laborers" (for we had decided to make Valmor speak as much as possible to distract him), "and then you will understand all the marvels you will have the pleasure of seeing here."

After dinner, Mr. Mirol wanted to give me a tour of his home. I found it to be, in its layout and furnishings, exactly the same as the townhouses, but larger and with one advantage: all sides of the house have windows that bring light into the rooms. Several of these rooms accommodate guests such as relatives or friends. The kitchen, where dinner as well as the other meals are prepared, is larger and better equipped than its counterpart in the city because country folk are brought up to be better cooks than city folk. The living room is as magnificent and larger than its counterpart in the city of Icara and spacious enough to accommodate the families of two neighboring farmers when they wish to pay each other a visit. I noticed that the walls throughout the home were covered with maps and beautiful printed posters showing all the most useful and common agricultural precepts.

"You see," Mr. Mirol said to me, "that we country folk have no reason to envy our city brothers, and that we are no more dazzled and uncomfortable when we visit them than they are disgusted or deprived when they arrive at our homes, for we all have the same interior furnishings. It is true that we do not have a constant view of their superb public buildings, but they do not always enjoy the magnificence of nature. Moreover, we may go to the city as easily as they may come to the country. Like the city folk, we have all the large and small stagecoaches, which travel continuously up and down the highway. In addition, we have our saddle horses and open carriages, which take us to the stagecoaches or even right to the gates of the city, where we leave them in national stables and sheds and take the omnibus. As you have seen, our roads are so beautiful, our horses so rapid, and our farms so close to the communal cities, that two hours always suffice for the round trip so that we may easily attend all popular assemblies, schools, courses, and even cultural events. In addition, special carriages from the city bring us on a regular basis everything we need in food, clothing, and furnishings."

We were leaving the house as he was speaking, and he showed me that all its sides were different, so that each house appeared to be four different houses, bringing together all possible architectural features. "No farm in the commune," he added, "resembles another in its external features, but all are equally attractive. And look at the walls of the farm buildings, all adorned elegantly, although simply, with painted trellises, garnished with greenery and flowers. Aren't they charming? And soon you will see the dairy, the chicken coop, and the rest. But first, come and see the garden and the orchard.

"Here is the important part: the vegetable garden, which is the department of my dear Elisa and my nephew Elois. My Elisa is a skilled cook, as you have already seen, and she will prove it to you even more! My friend Elois is a skilled gardener. Look at the beautiful vegetables of all varieties! In forty years, almost all of them, because of astounding progress in cultivation, have doubled and tripled in size and quality. Look at these cloches, these hotbeds, and all these inventions of people brave enough to dare to help nature!

"Now you are in the kingdom of my kind Alae and her good little brother Alvarez. Admire these roses of a thousand varieties, these carnations, these flowers of all sorts that charm our eyes while providing honey for our bees before going to fill our national perfumeries. This is the palace and the royal court where the majestic Alae assembles her richest subjects, for you will see and smell other flowers everywhere, beautifying and perfuming the whole domain of the republic. Go no further! Here is the hive. The workers that labor in these workshops of straw and glass, as wild and ferocious as they are marvelously skilled, might make you feel the sharpness of their stingers. How much they prefer the care of my dear Camille to the indiscreet curiosity of an English lord.

"Here you will see our espaliers, and further on you may see our strawberry patch and all the fruit shrubs. These are the estates of Frasie and her cousin

Comar, for each is minister here, or prince and princess, and reigns as an absolute monarch over his or her subjects (but don't think that we miss despotism or monarchy). Now then, Valmor" (who had almost fallen in a little brook), "don't you remember our waterways and our garden anymore? In earlier times, Milord, we had a great deal of trouble irrigating, but thirty years ago we discovered the secret of penetrating the very depths of the earth and digging wells there to make springs, rivers, and underground lakes bubble forth. We were so successful that we have all the waters we need, everywhere, for our houses, gardens, meadows, and fields. Our irrigation tools are so convenient that, without making yourself tired or wet, you may give yourself the pleasure of spreading the freshness of life on our flowers and vegetables. And if you like fishing, you will have the additional pleasure of finding all our streams, rivers, canals, and reservoirs filled with fish of all sorts that we take great pains to maintain.

"Here is the orchard! This is my empire and that of my old and faithful empress, but we are so lacking in tyranny that we are hardly obeyed, and it is our very children who come to steal from us."

"What beautiful trees!" I cried. "What beautiful cherries!"

"And what would you say about the other fruits in the autumn?" Dinaros replied.

"Ah! Ah!" continued the old man. "We take care. We think carefully about our task at hand. We do the same for our trees as we do for our vegetables and flowers. We have our nurseries, where we choose the most beautiful plants. We graft the best species. We remove everything that is or becomes defective. We turn over the soil, and we water. With the pruning knife always in hand, we trim and cut off all useless, parasitic branches; we take off all overabundant leaves; we defend our pupils against all their enemies; and from their birth until their old age, we pamper them like children. Consequently, you should not be amazed that they are handsome and well brought up and that their gratitude is proportionate to our solicitude. Moreover, you will not see a useless tree or hedge. In our fields, wherever a fruit tree would be more useful than anything else, you will see a fruit tree, and you will see fruit trees without number in the country. But night is falling. The evening will be beautiful. Let us go join the children on the terrace, where we will enjoy, while resting, the magnificence of the setting sun."

We went up to the highest level of the house, where we found the family gathered among the flowers and a large table in the middle under a canopy that opened and folded at will. The view of the surrounding countryside and neighboring farms, lightly illuminated by the dying beams; the rays of the sun still gilding the tops of the trees and the hills, whose lower extremities were disappearing in the shadows; the clouds and the sky painted a thousand colors; the cries of the animals returning to the stable or greeting the end of day; the songs of birds celebrating the hour of repose and sleep; the sweet smell and freshness of the air; the beauty of the sun, which seemed to promise us a lovely tomorrow as it majestically disappeared beyond the horizon: everything came together to put me in a state of delightful ecstasy.

"Well now, Milord," said Mr. Morel, "do we not have our theatrical spectacles here in the country, too, and do you think they are less magnificent than the city opera? If only you could see a beautiful summer storm here: thousands of flashes inflaming the distant vast horizon, suddenly illuminating the deepest darkness and presenting to our dazzled eyes the image of creation emerging from chaos at the command of the creator's single voice! If only you could hear, in the midst of the most total silence, the bolts of lightning and the crash of the thunder repeated by our mountain echoes! But soon you will see millions of lights that will illuminate the endless vaulted ceiling of our immense living room, and then the moon, even more resplendent, who will try to eclipse them to rival her brother!"

"I saw her here," Valmor whispered in my ear, "admiring all these beauties; and I admired them, too, for my heart was filled with hope and happiness, but now . . ."

"Come now, Valmor," said Mr. Morel. "Milord is amazed that farm laborers here are so skilled, so show him that it is the natural result of our education, and that, in order to know nothing, we would have to be as stupid and stubborn as our donkeys. We are going to sit around the table, and we all will listen to you with the greatest of pleasure. Begin!"

Valmor tried to make excuses at first. "I am your father here," added the old man in a paternal tone, "and consequently I command you. We are waiting impatiently. Go on, go on, begin, Valmor!"

"You know, my dear friend," he said finally, addressing me, "that until eighteen years of age for boys and seventeen for girls, all Icarian children receive, as a group, the same elementary and general education. Because agriculture is considered in our country the most indispensable of the arts, the republic wishes that all citizens could, if needed, be farmers, and that all be taught and brought up in such a way that they could fulfill this task. The knowledge essential to the farmer is deemed, moreover, essential for citizens of all professions. Consequently, all children learn the basic elements of agriculture. And because we wish, as much as possible, to join practice to theory, we take the children to the countryside daily to teach them about the products of the earth and to have them observe agricultural labor. These trips are as charming as they are instructive. The strongest children, those more than fourteen years of age, are even taken to the countryside as workers to do certain easy tasks such as ridding the fields of stones or helping bring in the harvest; and these tasks are charming pleasure parties as well.

"At eighteen or seventeen, the child of a farmer is free to choose another profession, if a family in the city agrees to adopt him or her, just as a city child may become an agricultural worker if a farmer will accept him or her into his family; but the children of farmers prefer to become farmers like their fathers. At that point, the children who choose agriculture have one year of special theoretical and practical education, which they then complete upon the paternal farm, and which is designed to make them as perfect farmers as possible. Thus, the farmer studies and knows all forms of metals, rocks, and particularly soil, their elements and their diverse characteristics; all varieties of plant products and their qualities; all instruments and their advantages; and everything pertaining to seasons, winds, all forms of bad weather and how to avoid them and secure the crops against them. Not one farmer may be ignorant of any information pertaining to animals, harmful and useful, domesticated or wild, as well as the diversity of animal products.

"The farmer's daughter learns the same material and knows everything that may be of interest to her in agriculture, in particular everything pertaining to milk production, fowl, vegetables, flowers, and fruits. Note as well that because each province or each commune has land of varying qualities, and consequently different products—one having vineyards and another fields of grain, for example—the provincial and communal schools direct the education of their young farmers to these types of soil and their products. In addition, because each farm has its own set of land statistics and, consequently, a production specific to its own small domain, each farmer's instruction is concentrated, finally, on that particular speciality.

"You should be amazed no longer, now that you know about the education, knowledge, and skill of our farmers, both male and female. And do not tell me you are still surprised that they are able to learn so much, for, if you think carefully about it, you will realize that children can certainly learn many things until they are nineteen or eighteen, particularly when their education is carefully undertaken from the moment of their birth. Moreover, the education of our cultivators, like that of all our workers and all our citizens, does not stop with school but continues and increases for the whole lifetime. After leaving school and returning to the farm, the young man and woman find the most experienced and affectionate instructors there: their fathers and mothers, uncles and aunts, brothers and sisters.

"They also find there, magnificently printed by the republic, all the books and treatises they have studied, a vast *Agricultural Encyclopedia*, a large number of gardeners' guides, florists' guides, and so forth, and finally the *Journal of Agricul-*

ture, which informs them of all the discoveries and all the improvements occurring every day throughout the republic. You can imagine what observations, what inventions, what improvements must come forth from such a large population of farmers who are so enlightened and so habituated to using their powers of reason. For, if you compare our farmers today to those of yesteryear, who were as brutish as their livestock, you will understand that we have as farmers millions of skilled men and women instead of stupid beasts, and that our agriculture, therefore, has progressed more each year for fifty years, and particularly in the last thirty years, than during all previous centuries put together.

"Progress in all branches and in every respect is so great that we ourselves need to keep in mind the cause so as not to be amazed by such strides. You would be even more astounded if I told you about the astronomical observations made by our country folk, from their terraces, or, rather, their observatories. Here, for example . . ."

"Good, very good, my dear Valmor," Mr. Mirol said, interrupting him. "We should forget both supper and our beds listening to you, but you must be tired, and tomorrow we will have the pleasure of seeing each other again, provided you give us once more the pleasure of listening to you."

I myself was very pleased, for aside from the subject's interesting nature and Valmor's charming speaking manner, his melancholy rendered even more touching that voice which, by its very nature, already reminded me a little of the penetrating timbre of Dinaïse's voice.

We had not yet had the time to examine the sky and its constellations when one of the girls came to tell us that supper was served. After this delicious collation, Valmor led me to bed in the same room as himself, where I spent a long time without sleeping, for that unfortunate man could not prevent himself from speaking to me of his misfortune and of the qualities and perfections of the one whom his love had fashioned into an angel.

18 Agriculture *(continued)*

Awakened early, I took Valmor through the farm buldings, where Dinaros soon joined us. We visited in turn the varied stables of many domestic animals, the manure storehouses, the carriage houses, the sheds for machines and irrigation implements, the workshop for repairs, the vast storehouses for the rough harvest, the barns for preparing it, and the depots for the products ready to be transported to the city. We ended with the farmyard, the chicken coop, and the dairy.

Had I not known that the farms had been built according to a model plan, like all the other workshops of the republic, I would have admired this one even more than the house, for in those places where one usually sees only disgusting filth, disorder, and poverty, I found all the cleanliness, order, convenience, and elegance I had noted everywhere else. Valmor, who was explaining everything to me, had me admire the large and small plows and the numerous machines recently invented to facilitate, shorten, and improve farm labors and to spare the laborer almost all exhaustion by replacing his arms and shoulders by animals or inanimate instruments, so the farmer's role is reduced almost to that of intelligent director and enlightened organizer. On the other hand, a single man does as much today as ten or twenty previously and does a much better job.

"The mule," he told me, "the donkey, and even the dog are living machines that carry burdens, replacing men, on the narrowest of paths. Also, the cultivator's work clothes, as warm in winter as they are cool in summer and always waterproof, are, like those of any worker, so clean and even elegant that you take pleasure in seeing him. I need not add that the work clothes of the female farmer are as charming as those lovely farmers themselves in the midst of the plants, flowers, and fruits of their countryside."

We met two of Dinaros's female cousins in the dairy, where the whiteness of their skin rivaled that of the milk, and their rosy cheeks seemed like roses placed next to lilies. How clean it was, that dairy garnished with vases filled with milk, cream, butter, and ten varieties of cheese. And how pretty and lively the farmyard was, freshened by a reservoir filled with aquatic birds, its circumference fitted with airframes for flocks of birds of many species. What handsome roosters, proud and jealous like sultans in their harems! How all these diverse nations rushed forward at the sight of their pretty mistress showering them with kindnesses!

"Look, here is her cherished hen," Valmor told me, pointing out a magnificent hen, white as snow. "Ah! If only you could have seen her in the midst of these birds! How happy she seemed to give them the grain that the most daring came to peck from her hand. With what rapture did I watch her one day, through these bushes, she laughing and happy to spread happiness around her! I will never see her that way again!"

After lunch, Mr. Mirol himself wanted to take me around the fields of the farm. First he showed me, on a magnificent map of the farm that covered the wall of one of the rooms, the garden to the right, the buildings behind, and, in front, a meadow crossed by a river and bordered by a grove of tall trees.

"Yesterday," he said, "we saw the garden, and this morning you visited the buildings. Now we are going to go over the meadow, which will take us to the tree nursery and to the woods, and we will come back by way of the fields. We do not have any useless luxury lawns, but have you ever seen a more beautiful carpet than this meadow studded with flowers and whose green expanse, dotted with red, white, and blue, renders even more striking the handsome yellow of the rape that borders it? Look at those animals over there that revel in their feed in mobile pens that free us from the task of watching them. Furthermore, this meadow, as big as it is, would be far from adequate for us if we did not have, almost everywhere, other artificial meadows, other grasses, and other vegetables sown before or after our other harvests, for the art of varying cultivation and sowing has been developed to such a degree that we have succeeded in producing, each year, an even greater variety of produce in every field, without ever letting the field lie fallow.

"Look at this lovely pool and this lovely river, where soon we may take a boat ride. Note as well with what care my sons have leveled the banks, so as to minimize all danger. Higher up, where the bank is bordered by a steep ledge, they put up a small barrier to prevent falls, for although all our boys and girls learn to swim, the republic orders us to work on the banks of all our rivers, canals, and any body of water in order to prevent accidents."

After crossing the river on a lovely bridge and passing through the rest of the meadow, we arrived at the tree nursery and then at the woods, or, rather, at a grove whose trees seemed magnificent to me. I was amazed to see that they were cultivated and tended to like those in the orchard.

"How old do you think this grove of trees is?" Dinaros asked me.

"Sixty or eighty years old," I replied.

"Thirty-five," he said.

"But," said Mr. Mirol, "I must tell you that the republic has adopted a totally new system concerning woodlands. It has had taken out all those that were located inconveniently, that were too difficult to tend, or that could be replaced by more advantageous products. It partially cleared the others, leaving only those groves that were intermingled with crops, farms, or industries, taking out all the bushes from these groves and cultivating the remaining large trees. Then, in all the farms without groves, it caused groves such as this one to be planted. I chose the spot and prepared it. After that, I took from the tree nursery the species and the plants that I felt would be the most appropriate and useful, and I transplanted them. Since that time, I have never stopped cultivating them, pruning them, tending them, as formerly we treated only the grape, the hops, the poplar, and some aristocratic trees; and you can see how beautiful they are! Thus, we have neither vast woods, nor thickets, nor undergrowth as formerly; but all farms have groves, quite apart from the fruit trees in the orchards or scattered among the fields, and in addition to the other trees that often border the rivers, canals, and roads. Thus, we have at least as much wood for burning, and at any rate at least as much as we need, with the advantage of having many more fields, many more fruit trees, and many more beautiful woods of all types for all our industrial needs. And we have added to all these advances the equally important advantage of having rid the country of almost all the animals that were dangerous to man or harmful to agriculture. In addition, we have found the way to sow or plant small shrubs and trees on bare mountains that formerly displayed only stones, to bring or to create there a form of soil and vegetation, thus overcoming their sterility.

"Here we are on our fields. You will notice my children and our neighbors scattered everywhere, for, from the first to the last day of the year, there is always something to do outside or inside, so that we have to work only six or seven hours a day, like city folk; but our work, which we do at will or according to the weather, is so pleasurable to us that we are always busy. I am tired of speaking. Valmor, tell your friend about our lands."

"First of all," said Valmor, "see how everything is cultivated so as not to waste an inch of land. Look. Not only are there no bramble bushes, no thistles, not a useless plant or herb, but there are no fences, no walls, no sterile hedges. There are only ditches, irrigation channels, and essential lanes and paths. This pretty border of currant and blackcurrant bushes used to be a large, ugly, crumbling wall that ate up ten feet of earth on either side. Calculate, if you will, the cost of walls, railings, fences, and stone ditches, and you will see the savings of all sorts that result from the elimination of enclosures.

"This lovely embankment that you see over there at the edge of the road, adorned with the leaves and flowers of an excellent vegetable plant, used to be a thicket, thorns, and a caterpillar nest. And see how the roads, paths, ditches, even the furrows are in a straight line. All our fields, as much as possible, are elongated squares, which makes cultivating easier while saving ground. This was not difficult to do because, as you know, the terrain of each farm was traced out at will by the engineers of the republic. And see how smooth the surface is, even when it follows an incline. You will see no protuberances or cavities. You will not see even a stone. You will never see a more perfect crop, more beautiful ears of corn, more beautiful hemp plants, more beautiful rape.

"And look at these beautiful byways, these irrigation channels so carefully dug with the spade and cleaned out, these lovely paths lined with stones and lightly sanded. Is it not satisfying to see everywhere the work of men who think everything out, who seek perfection in everything, and who bring to everything as much good taste as reason? Does not this entire farm seem to be a single, superb garden whose pretty paths provide a delicious promenade?"

"What did you say?" said Dinaros. "All of these farms together form a single garden; all these fields are but an endless walking path."

"You are right," Valmor took up again. "We have as few enclosures as we have legal trials because we no longer have private property. And each farmer may walk on neighboring farms, just as the city folk may walk throughout the countryside. And you need not fear that a single person will allow himself to touch or to trample anything beneath his feet. Our system of education accustoms us from childhood to respect everything. Moreover, when city folk, who, in any case, have everything they need in the city, come to a farm, there is not one farmer who would refuse to give them flowers and fruit."

"But," I said to him, "all farms cannot possibly be as pretty. What about those in the mountains, for example?"

"In the mountainous regions," he replied, "there are even more charming farms, embellished by the thousand charms of the site, by picturesque views and clear waters bubbling or falling in cascades. It is true, however, that there are some less-fertile and naturally less-pleasant mountains; there, above all, the republic concentrates all its efforts and solicitude in order to correct the apparent injustices of nature through the charity of the arts. I do not need to remind you that in those regions there are communal villages exactly the same as all the others, whose territory contains the same number of farms of the same size. Nor do I need repeat that the houses of these mountain farms are the same as the others and that the buildings are similar, according to their destined use. It is not necessary to add that these farms also have their particular gardens, vegetables, flowers, and fruit. The cultivation and products are not, in fact, the same in nature, quality, or quantity, but everything is cultivated equally and well. Each farm produces as much as it can and, in fact, produces a great deal, for the art of cultivation has become so advanced! All of these farms have their own charms; each one is pleasant for those who live there or visit; each is useful to the republic. And if you want my opinion, the places that were the most deserted and infertile at the beginning are the very ones that please me the most today because of the miraculous transformations that genius has wrought."

"But it may happen," I said, "that some farms may have too many workers and others not enough. What do you do then?"

"First of all, you have to understand that intelligent men, brought up to be industrious and useful, always find something to do to make that which is already good even better. And then, if a farmer really finds himself without work, he can do a different kind of work, even on his father's farm, or help a neighboring farmer. As for those who need steady or momentary help, they can always get this help from neighboring farmers or from young city folk who come voluntarily to join the family, or from their friends, or from school children, or from other city folk who never shy away from the pleasures of country work."

"Go to the left, Valmor!" cried Mr. Mirol. "Let us go back past the espaliered trees. I want to show them to Milord." In fact, he showed me some very unusual espaliers. They were not walls, but moveable partitions that reflected the heat in the most efficient way for ripening the fruit and that could be removed so that the trees would not be burnt by too strong a sun. We rested for a few minutes under the trellises and the charming bowers, where we breathed sweetly scented air under a vault of leaves and flowers.

"How beautiful she was beneath her wide straw hat," poor Valmor whispered to me, gripping my arm, "the last time I saw her picking strawberries here! Oh, my friend! May you never be as unhappy as me!"

During dinner, Mr. Mirol turned the conversation to the harvest, hunting, and fishing, addressing as usual his daughters or granddaughters, whose words seemed to give him great pleasure. One of the girls told us how they went about the haymaking, harvesting, grape picking, and the gathering of vegetables, flowers, and fruits. First, she explained that each farmer chose the appropriate time for each harvest, and that he always arranged it so that it could be completed in a single day to be sure of good weather. When he needed help, he got it from neighboring farmers, whom he helped in turn, from school children, and from his city friends, who never refused because harvest day was always a day for pleasure and celebration. For this reason, every farm had footgear and headgear for forty or fifty guests, with the necessary implements. She told with charming grace how all these temporary male and female farmers would arrive from the city in omnibuses or stagecoaches, with their foodstuffs carried by little mules.

Then, in a spirited way that often evinced from us a group smile, she described the joy of the boys and girls as they arrived, their laughter as they got dressed up, their shouts or songs as they worked, the gaiety of the country meals, the joyous and zany ceremonies that began the work, the dances and games that lasted long into the night, always beneath the watchful eye of parents who were as joyous as their children. This gracious recitation brought back, without a doubt, happy or painful memories to poor Valmor, for several times I thought I saw a tear shining in his eye.

Another girl told us about the hunt, not for large wild animals, because they have no more hideouts and have been destroyed, but for harmful birds, for whom all manner of traps are set, and in particular for insects. Like her sister, she made us laugh a great deal by telling us the story of one day when, in the whole territory of the republic, they hunted a type of bird that was eating up a quarter of the wheat harvest. The species of bird was totally destroyed within a single day. She made us laugh even more by telling of the hunt of an insect that comes in great numbers at a certain period. This hunt takes place on a single day in all the farms of the republic, and almost all the city folk rush to the country as if they were participating in the most precious harvest. One of the boys also told us about the repair of a road common to several farms, explaining how all the farmers and their children, joined together in a single group and directed by a single general, usually completed the operation in two or three days.

After dinner, we took Dinaros, who could not stay with us any longer, back to the boat. I was very sad about this because, in the short time we had spoken together, I had discovered in him goodness and friendliness in equal measure to the knowledge I had already seen; and the affection he had for Valmor made both of them even dearer to me. He seemed as appreciative of the friendship I offered his friend as if Valmor were his brother and made me promise to come and see him often upon our return. Poor Valmor almost fainted when he embraced him to say farewell. "How cowardly I must seem to you," he said to me afterward. "But I will become a man once more, you will see!"

As we returned by way of five or six farms, one more rich and beautiful than the next, I waxed poetic about such an abundance of richness and beauty.

"And what would you say," he told me, "if you were to compare the prosperity of our agriculture today with its former poverty! Our progress does not amaze me, but it is immense, incalculable. Wherever we look, everything has been perfected, admirably perfected! Land suitable for cultivation has been almost doubled in size by the clearing and cultivation of areas that were formerly neglected and lost. This very land has been almost doubled once again by the most perfected art of cultivation, mixing, and fertilizing, and by the multiplicity of successive plantings on the same land during one year. All of our products are not only more abundant in number and volume, but are incomparably superior in quality. We even have many extremely useful new species. For example, you have seen in the garden a type of gigantic melon, more exquisite than any of our earlier fruits. Well, thirty years ago we did not have even one of these. The first ones brought here from a neighboring country were mediocre in both taste and size, but today they are as big as they are delicious, and they are so abundant that all Icarians may enjoy them.

"Everything I am telling you about fruits may be applied to animals and their products, as well as to all vegetables and their products. The republic has spared nothing to obtain from foreign countries all the best of agricultural methods, types of vegetable, and races of animal. Thus, our horses, our beef cattle, our sheep and their wool bear no more resemblance to their former selves than do our grains, vegetables, fruits, and flowers. In a word, when you take into consideration all the improvements, can you imagine how much the total agricultural production has risen in fifty years, according to national statistics?"

"How should I know? Five times?"

"Twelve! And you can verify it for yourself. Knowing that, you may not be surprised to discover that the population has almost doubled, and that all fifty million Icarians are housed, nourished, and clothed, as you have seen."

"Nothing surprises me anymore."

He was going to go on when we noticed Mr. Mirol, who had promised to come to us with some of his children. He wanted to take us to a charming fountain, he said, but we were tired and went to bed early. I was still thinking about everything I had seen and heard when Valmor fell into an agitated sleep, murmuring fragments of sentences, or rather, inarticulate sounds, among which I could barely distinguish "Good, beautiful, angelic . . . eternal regret."

19   Agriculture *(continued)* and Commerce

Before breakfast, while Valmor was writing to his sister, Mr. Mirol showed me the pictures and maps covering the walls of his library. One was a large printed map of the commune, with the communal city approximately in the center, surrounded by villages, with marks for all farms, routes and byways, rivers and mountains. He pointed out farms where only grapes were harvested, and others with only wheat, as well as several mines and several large manufacturing plants. He spoke at length of a very odd factory one league from his farm, which he offered to show me after breakfast. Another picture was the inventory or map of the farm, which showed where everything was located.

A third poster, whose writing I most admired, done by one of the national scribes, contained the statistics of this particular farm, showing everything it had produced the previous year, what had been saved for the farmer's consumption, and what had been put into the national stores. I marveled at the large quantity of production, and I understood perfectly well how agriculture could give to the re-public everything needed for nourishing, clothing, lodging, and furnishing splendidly all its citizens. Yet another poster contained the list of products needed by the republic for the present year; and, on this list, Mr. Mirol showed me that they asked for less of one product, more of another, and a trial run of a new product.

Then he explained to me how the products were transported to the republi-can warehouses, some by his wagons, others by national wagons. As for vegeta-bles, poultry, dairy products, and fruits that have to be transported to the city every day, each farmer has the necessary baskets and containers, and he places them at set times by the side of the road, where a variety of national wagons suit-ably equipped come to collect them to transport them to the city.

The factory we went to visit was an earthenware factory, located on a vein of earth that is unique to the republic, half a league from the communal city. All the pottery for the republic is made there and almost the entire population of the communal city is employed there, brought back and forth each day in five min-utes on a railroad. What a variety of workshops and machines! What movement! What bustle! Look at all the storehouses to store temporarily the completed vases! What activity in packing them! Look at all the wagons to transport them to all the communes of the republic! If we had spent the whole day there, we would not have had the time to see and to admire everything.

"I see," I said upon returning, "that you have no need of trade."

"Certainly not," replied Valmor. "The republic asks of each commune the agricultural and industrial production for which the nature of its land and its lo-cation best suit it. It is the republic that takes from each commune its surplus to distribute it to others, and that brings to the commune what it lacks by taking that commodity from all those that produce it. This is exchange or, rather, shar-ing and distribution of products, and no one could do it as well as the republic.

"Imagine, as a case in point, a rich and skilled merchant with a powerful company who effectuates a trade exchange between two communes, two provinces, or two countries, buying from each one its surplus products and sell-ing to it that which it lacks. You may well imagine that the republic is capable of doing the same and even better because all merchants joined together could never have the republic's power, unity, and, above all, the cooperation and volun-tary support of the entire people.

"All necessary means of transport, carts and horses, steam wagons and rail-roads, boats and canals: the republic has them! Carters, ferrymen, and agents of all kinds: the republic has them, and they all are faithful workers because it feeds them and houses them magnificently. Its wagons often travel, without stopping, from one end of the country to the other, but their drivers and horses do not leave their commune or province and are replaced by others. What speed! And the wagon that leaves full never returns empty! And look at the storage! Every commune has its communal storehouses, which house, first, that portion of its produce that it will consume. Then there are provincial depots and national depots, which receive the excess so that it may be transported to other communes and provinces or to foreign countries.

"As for advance planning and designing methods of preventing shortages, how could any group be as effective as the republic? Who else could know of all the accidents that threaten the harvests, the needs of each province, and what must be asked of each province in the best interests of the others? Who could compete with the republic's power in foreign trade? The republic does not deal with private parties but with the foreign governments themselves, at least with all those who are its allies. The republic first decides which products it should export and which it should import; the people themselves or their representatives make this decision, and then the government negotiates the exchange. The republic does not cultivate or manufacture products that it may easily obtain from another country if its agriculture and industry may be utilized more effectively for other products. You can imagine the savings and the advantages that result from this system for the happiness of the people!"

That evening the conversation came around to the pleasures of country compared to city living. "I do not know," I said, "whether city folk are more or less happy than country folk; what I do admire is that, as difficult as it is to be as happy as the first group, it is impossible to be happier than the second. If the Roman poet were alive today, instead of saying 'O fortunatos nimium sua si bona norint, agricolas' (O happy country folk, if only they knew their happiness—you know your Latin better than I do), he would say: 'Happy are the farmworkers because they know how to appreciate all their happiness!' "

"You are right," Mr. Mirol replied. "And so I do not miss the palace I used to have in the city, or the castle of my earldom, or my hunting, not even my box at the Opéra. If you wish to get up before four o'clock tomorrow morning, I will lead you to the great oak on the summit of the hill to contemplate the sunrise, and you will see that our morning spectacle is every bit as good as the evening amusements in the cities!"

20 Religion

A quarter of an hour before daybreak, Mr. Mirol, Valmor, and I were on the mountain. "What magnificence," I exclaimed, "precedes the appearance of the Sun! Look how Venus herself, who has shone to guide the shepherd, disappears before him! How charming Dawn is! How right is the cheerful imagination of the Greeks in portraying Dawn as a young goddess with vermilion cheeks and rosy fingers, scattering dew, flowers, and sweet perfumes around her, tinting the wispy clouds with her brush steeped in a thousand shades of the most delicate red, announcing the arrival of her master, and finally opening the immense portals of heaven to let him pass through. He comes near, without yet appearing, and already his powerful rays enlighten, warm, and rejuvenate the plants that turn green once more and stand tall, aided by the sweet breath of the zephyr. The flowers open once more their perfumed calyxes, the birds bear witness to their gratitude and joy by their concert, and the workers spread out gaily in the awakened countryside. Finally, here he is, surrounded by fire and light, eclipsing all around him, illuminating the sky and the earth, dazzling the eye that is daring enough to stare fixedly at his splendor and his brilliance. See how he soars upward to travel majestically through the immense circular vault of the azure skies on his sparkling chariot, drawn by four swift and superb steeds, escorted by the Hours, and spreading everywhere torrents of heat, light, and life! He is the father, the benefactor, the god of nature receiving almost everywhere the tributes of his creatures and the adoration of all mortals."

"And all this is but illusion and lies," exclaimed Valmor, sighing deeply, "as is happiness upon this earth! This sun, which your imagination renders so swift and generous, is only a little lamp or a little stationary heater, attached to its post to light and heat our little earth and a few other atoms turning around it, next to the billions of other suns and other earths, each with its place and its function in the universal workshop. It is this universe that we must admire, this workshop, eternal in duration, immense in space, without beginning and without end, without limit in width and in height, where innumerable armies of workers of all sizes and all species swarm around innumerable machines, suspended and piled one on the other without disorder. Some—infinite in volume, in weight, in speed, and in power—are millions of times larger than the Earth and yet fly millions of times faster than a cannonball, whereas other creations, infinitely delicate and finely crafted, are millions of times smaller than the most imperceptible mite."

Valmor seemed beside himself with enthusiasm. We were careful not to interrupt him, and I deeply regret being able to recall his words only imperfectly.

"And yet once we believed," he went on, "that this sun, this little lamp, this little stove, was a god! All those innumerable suns, would they also be gods? But who would have created those gods? Who would rule over them? Who would have created their empires and their subjects? For I cannot conceive of an Earth that was not created, or a god that would not be a creator or a father! Thus, I must believe in a unique God, creator, father, architect of all the rest of the universe.

"And, on the other hand, who is this architect who drew up the plans of this universe and constructed it? From where did he take the building materials and the workers? How did he have the power to create these prodigious machines and to manufacture this marvelous handiwork? Why, for what purpose, for whom did he create so many machines and marvels? And this creator, this architect, this father of gods and of men: Who created him? Who is his father? When, where, how, from what was he born? How may we comprehend omnipotence, eternity, infinity? And, on the other hand, how may we also comprehend the limits to space and duration, the beginning and the end of the universe, the limits to the possible and to the impossible?

"Must not there be a God? Could matter exist by itself and from all eternity? This infinite power, this admirable order that presupposes the infinite intelligence and foresight of an infinitely skilled worker, all the marvels of the organization of animal, vegetable, and mineral—might these be merely a quality of matter? The varied plumage of the birds, the marvelous structure of the eye, the gracious form of the mouth, all the admirable parts of the admirable human machine, might they have formed themselves, like salts and crystals? But how can we conceive of the marvels of crystallization itself more easily than of the existence of a God? Moreover, is this not merely a question of vocabulary? For this quality of matter, would it not have all the attributes that we ascribe to the divinity, the all-powerful, the infinite, the eternal? This quality, this matter, would it not be that which we wish to express by such overly vague and indefinite expressions as *God, divinity, nature, supreme being?* For me, the divine is this *first cause* of which I see the effects, to whom I lend a human face in order to understand it better and to be able to speak about it more easily. I cannot, however, with my limited senses and my imperfect powers of organization, perceive and know either its form or its essence.

"I bow down before the divine, deeply aware of my imperfection and my inferiority. I understand that I am lacking a sense, like a deaf or a blind person, through which I might hear or perceive it. And when my weak intelligence pushes too hard to pierce these mysteries, I feel that my reason becomes clouded and falls into madness, just as my weak eyesight becomes dazzled and makes me faint when I insist on staring too fixedly at the glare of the sun. I admire its marvels! Sometimes I find subjects for admiration everywhere, even in the mire and the mud from which thousands of animal or vegetable organisms emerge; and sometimes I no longer admire anything, or, rather, nothing surprises me, and I am ready to discover even greater marvels.

"I am inclined to bless its goodness (if I may use, when speaking of it, an expression that is usually applied to man), without, however, being able to explain why this all-powerful divinity condemns the innocent child to pay with atrocious pain for the teeth that it needs, nor why this selfsame divinity makes me so miserable today, I who hate no one, I who have never done harm to anyone, I who cherish all my fellow men, I who do not discriminate among people in my love, giving but a stronger part of that same tenderness to my parents and my friends. Why does this divinity cause me to suffer so much today?"

(I thought he would not be able to continue, for his heart appeared so oppressed at that moment.)

"I would like to believe in its justice in another life, in its eternal rewards for the good and punishments for the wicked; in order not to blame the divine, I sometimes need to believe that the misfortunes of the oppressed will be rewarded by happiness of another sort, and that the insolent triumph of the oppressors will be transformed into humiliation and suffering. I need to believe that tyrants will be punished, without, however, desiring eternal torment for them. And if I speak of tyrants, that is concerning only other peoples, for we have done more than curse them and condemn them. We have banished them forever from our land, without waiting for an afterlife to create happiness for mankind.

"I often take pleasure in believing that the soul is a divine emanation, when I contemplate the power of the reason, intelligence, and genius placed in such a little head and so weak a body. I take pleasure in believing that the soul is immortal, for I see in nature only transformations without annihilation, and I cannot bear the idea that so beautiful, so perfect, so angelic a creature . . ."

His emotion prevented him from completing the sentence, and he hid his face in his hands. The old man, to distract his young friend from his sorrow, took both of us by the arm and led us to a delightful grotto, which was a few steps farther on the other side, on the incline of the hill.

"Do you have any philosophical materialists in Icaria?" I asked him to get him going.

"Yes, a few."

"And you put up with them?"

"What do you mean, do we put up with them? What harm can their belief cause when everything is regulated by laws, and they obey the laws? Of what importance can any religious belief of a few individuals be when the entire nation is happy? Moreover, are not our beliefs independent of our will? Are you free to believe or not to believe? Should not beliefs be respected as much as tastes? For too long, our ancestors were superstitious, fanatical, intolerant, given to persecution, and bloodthirsty. For too long, religion, invoked as the salvation of humankind, was itself the plague. Are not executions and wars caused by differences in religious beliefs as absurd as conflicts between those who prefer red currants to strawberries and those who prefer strawberries to red currants? Would not the persecution of philosophical materialists be as great an act of injustice, of oppression, of barbarity, of madness, and of rage as the persecution of those who hold minority opinions in thousands of questions concerning astronomy, medicine, and other sciences?"

"So you have several religious sects?"

"Yes, and because we are on a subject that interests you a great deal, judging from the questions that you ask me every day, I am going to describe our religious system to you, if you wish and if my venerable friend gives me leave to do so."

"Speak, speak!" we replied in unison.

"Pay attention, for this is one of the masterpieces of our good and divine Icar, who treated people prudently and patiently until he had brought them all to share his beliefs. What I am going to tell you about is therefore, like all our institutions, the handiwork of the entire people. Now listen carefully, for here, as in almost everything else, we have created a radical revolution, and we have built everything anew as a consequence of the principle of community.

"First, we replaced the expressions *god, divinity, religion, church,* and *priest* by new expressions that were so perfectly defined that they could not give rise to any ambiguity. Second, here again, as in everything else, education forms the basis of the entire system. Until the ages of sixteen and seventeen, children never hear discussions about religion and are not mustered under any religious banner. The law permits neither parents nor foreigners to influence children before the age of reason. It is only at that age, at sixteen and seventeen, when their general education is almost complete, that the philosophy teacher, and not the priest, exposes them, during a year, to all religious systems and beliefs, without exception."

"But what curb is there on the actions of children and young people?"

"To what curb do you refer? Why is a curb necessary? This curb used to be necessary years ago, but what crime, what misdeed could a child do today? Is not his good conduct guaranteed by his education, by the affectionate caring of his teachers, by the enlightened tenderness of his parents, and by the happiness he is led to enjoy every day? Ask our venerable friend if we ever have occasion to rebuke severely the children of Icaria. At seventeen or eighteen years of age, each person adopts, based on complete knowledge of the possibilities, the belief that seems best and chooses freely the religion that suits him or her. No matter what that belief may be, it is respected. No matter what the cult may be, it is permitted; and as soon as a sect is large enough to have a temple and a priest, the republic provides both. Do not imagine, however, that the sects are great in number. In religion as in politics, as in morality, as in everything, truth, if not absolutely, at least relatively, is one. Our republic marches toward unity in religion as in all other matters because the influences of education, reason, and debate naturally lead each person to espouse the beliefs of the most enlightened, which become the universal belief. Possibly, even probably, we will continue to modify our religious views as we have already done and as we certainly will modify our scientific and industrial knowledge. But now, and in the past fifty years, sects are rare among us, sectarians are few in number, and it could be said that nearly all Icarians hold the same religious belief."

"And what is this belief?"

"Let us suppose that today, in our present state of enlightenment, the most educated, judicious, and wise men and women meet in council, as did the Christians of yesteryear, to discuss, free of all personal considerations, all the different religious beliefs in order to choose the most reasonable. You may well imagine that such a council may declare, if not unanimously, at least with a large majority, that it adopts one particular belief."

"Yes, I can conceive of it, but what is this belief that you have universally adopted?"

"It would take too long to expound it now because we cannot broach such a subject without going into all the details, and I would not like to wound your religious sensibilities."

"Have no fear and tell me what this belief is."

"Please do not pressure me on this matter today. I promise to explain it to you later. What I can tell you now is that religion is no longer the province of either the government or the state, and that it is totally separate from them. It has no civil authority, and it is not exempted from the law under any circumstances, but, on the other hand, the law intervenes in religious affairs only to protect freedom of belief and to maintain the peace. Thus, we acquire all the benefits that religion can bring while avoiding the harm that, all too often, religion has directly caused or for which it has provided the occasion. In fact, our religion, whether in its popular or its universal form, is no more than a moral and philosophical system and has no other use than to lead men to love one another as brothers, while setting forth for them as a rule of conduct these three precepts that contain everything else: 'Love your neighbor as yourself. Do not do any wrong to others that you would not want done to you. Do unto others all the good that you wish for yourself.'

"Our worship itself is very simple. Everyone admires, thanks, prays to, and worships the divinity as he or she pleases, within the confines of his or her own home. We also have temples where we go for instruction or to worship together, but we think that justice and fraternity, and by extension submission to the general will and love for country and humanity, are the form of worship most pleasing to the divinity. We believe that the person who worships and pleases the divinity the most is he who knows how to be the best father, the best son, the best citizen, and, above all, who knows best how to love and venerate woman, the masterpiece of the creator. We believe that the deprivation and suffering that fanaticism imposes are insults to divine goodness. We believe as well that nature in its entirety is the most beautiful temple where we may offer our homage to the Supreme Being.

"Our worship is, therefore, without any ceremony or practice that smacks of superstition or that has as its purpose to give power to priests. There are no fasts or self-mortification, and there is no penitence, either voluntary or imposed. If a person commits an error that causes any sort of harm, he is punished by the very action of righting that wrong and by doubling his effort to be of use to his fellow citizens and to the nation. We would find it absurd to pronounce prayers in an unknown language or even in a language other than our own, just as we would find it almost idiotic to recite official prayers that each one of us had not composed for himself. Our temples—without graven images, handsome, and, above all, comfortable and healthy, as are all our public establishments—are designed principally for preaching and for religious instruction. And to finish in a word, I will add that our priests have no power, even spiritual. They can neither punish nor absolve. They are only preachers of morality, religious instructors, counselors, guides, and consoling friends, happy when they themselves do not need consolation and counsel."

After these words, he seemed to want to stop, absorbed in a deep melancholy.

"What!" I said to him. "You wish to be a priest, and therefore you know that information concerning your priests is what interests me the most, and you say no more about them! Teach me about their education, their reception into the priesthood, their ministry!"

"Well," he said in a voice tinged with sadness and friendship, "you may listen once more. Let me tell you first that we have priestesses for women, just as we have priests for men. What I am going to tell you about priests applies as well to priestesses. The priesthood, like medicine, is a profession and, if you will, a public function. At eighteen years of age, when general education has been completed and when each person chooses his or her calling, the young man who wishes to be a priest takes an examination to see whether or not he possesses the necessary education, disposition, and personal qualities. If he is admitted as an aspirant, he undertakes special studies in eloquence and morality, philosophy, and religion until the age of twenty-five. During this period of study and testing, he dedicates himself as well to educating the young. He must marry before reaching the age of twenty-five in order to be as free as possible from passion, and so that we may judge whether he can serve as a model to others in all social positions.

"At age twenty-five, he is examined once more to make sure that he is worthy and capable of counseling and consoling those who may have need of consolation or counsel, for, although Icarians are brought up to become men worthy of that name, although fathers, mothers, and friends are very capable of being counselors and comforters to their children and their friends, the priest's voice is sometimes useful in extraordinary circumstances and produces an even greater effect because it is so rarely heard. Because the priest should be a counselor and a leader for the unfortunate, a second father for the young, a brother for those of his own age, and a friend for others, we insist that he be a man most distinguished for his prudence, wisdom, patience, and persuasive talents.

"If the examination at age twenty-five is successful, the aspirant is designated a candidate, and it is from among these candidates that the citizens of each neighborhood then elect their priest. They elect him for only five years in order to be able to remove that person whose virtue does not render him constantly worthy to serve as a model to others. It is virtue above all that we require of a priest, and the more we honor him, the more we demand that he be virtuous. It follows that the more virtuous he is, the more he is honored."

"And so we are anxious," said the old man, interrupting him, "that you turn twenty-five, for no one, my dear Valmor, passed the aspirants' exam more splendidly. No one has had greater success as a teacher. No one has been more universally loved and esteemed. No one is more confident of being named a candidate and of being unanimously elected a priest. You can see how happy this makes me, I who am your grandfather's oldest friend, I who love you as I would one of my own children!"

"Ah!" exclaimed Valmor, who had seemed to me to be quite agitated for a long time. "Why do you speak to me of public matters? I no longer merit the esteem that was my ambition and that I once deserved (for, as heaven is my witness, what heart is purer than mine?). How could I counsel others to rule their passions, I who allow myself to be in thrall to my own? With what effrontery would I dare to encourage another to bear a misfortune with resignation, I who am so weak and so cowardly? But what misfortune has ever equaled my own, tell me, you who are her grandfather, you who know her soul?"

And his pain, so long under control, finally erupted, like a torrent that breaches its dike, and the unfortunate one burst into tears. Oh, how the tears of a man are painful to his friends! We both cried with him. But he was ashamed and annoyed by his tears. "Look," he said, showing us his chest, which was red and almost lacerated by his hands. "Look what I did to fight my tears and to punish myself for my weakness!"

"Cry, my child, cry freely with your friends! I also suffered in my youth, and I feel compassion for your suffering. I, too, have cried, and I know that if we are tempted to blame the heavens for making us suffer, we must recognize at least that tears are a gift of nature."

"Yes, now I feel relieved of the weight that was oppressing me."

"Now let reason and courage prevail. Was my daughter Naira not an angel as well? And we who cherished her, did we not have to bear our loss?"

"Ah! If Dinaïse had died, perhaps I would be less miserable!" (And his tears began once more.)

"Now, Valmor," the old man said to him in an almost severe tone, "be brave! It is time to be a man. It is time to show virtue, and one is virtuous only when one knows how to triumph over adversity. Instead of saying, 'I am weak and I no longer want to be a priest,' Valmor, you must say, 'I will be a priest, and I want to be worthy of being one.' "

"Yes," he exclaimed rapturously, "yes, I will be worthy of the priesthood, and I make a commitment to it before you, her grandfather, who should have been my own. Please pardon for a moment longer my pain, which is only too justified!" (And he fell into the old man's arms, bursting into tears once more; and the old man cried with him.)

"I feel better," he said finally. "I feel stronger. I will triumph. I will overcome it, but give me the time to fight! Tomorrow, perhaps even this evening, we will leave. I will not flee from her. Soon you will be pleased with me."

Poor Valmor. He will still have much suffering and many rude assaults to sustain, but he will have consolation, and I, who helped to console him today, I will soon be overwhelmed by the weight of inconsolable pain. He will be cured, and I will be prey to a misfortune without remedy. His heart will be able to beat once more with pleasure and happiness, and I, miserable one, I will drink to the lees the chalice of human misfortune!

21   Valmor's Cure, Milord's Anxiety

I had brought Valmor back to his family, who did not know how to express their gratitude for the friendship I had shown him by accompanying him to the country. Corilla, above all, made even more sensitive by her sadness, intensified her caresses and her affection toward her brother and me. One hour after we arrived, Valmor wanted to go and see Dinaros. That evening we returned together to the home of Mrs. Dinamé. Everyone tried to act as they had before the fatal discussion. Valmor and Dinaïse did not try to avoid each other. However, Valmor no longer surrounded her with attention as he had before, and everyone seemed to work together to keep both of them occupied, some people gathering around Valmor, and the others around Dinaïse.

I myself approached Dinaïse several times when Corilla was with her, and I could not keep myself from secretly pitying Valmor because she had never seemed so ravishing to me. I was surprised to find her less shy with me. Her tone seemed almost affectionate. It even seemed to me that, like Corilla, she wanted to show her gratitude for the care I had taken with Valmor. But as she became bolder, I was no less flustered when I dared to look upon her, and above all when I heard that voice that made me tremble each time I heard it. I often thought of all that Valmor had told me about her, and I understood more clearly his enthusiasm and his despair. I was even amazed at Valmor's tranquility. However, at one point I thought I saw him turn pale and heard his voice change as he looked at her, but that was merely a momentary flash.

"Well," he said to Corilla and me as we were leaving, "are you satisfied with Valmor? If only you knew how much I suffered and what battles I fought! I thought I was stronger! How weak is man! But it has been done, I have triumphed, and I am sure that I will continue to triumph. I will give you back your peace of mind, my dear sister, and you, my dear and faithful friend." (And he squeezed my hand affectionately.)

I should have been pleased with Valmor's state, with his caresses, and with Dinaïse's welcome, but how strange is the human heart! I went away sad and troubled, without understanding the cause of my sadness, and without suspecting that the vague anxiety that oppressed me presaged misfortunes that would overwhelm me, just as a stifling atmosphere is often the precursor of a storm.

22 The National Assembly

Corilla, Dinaros, and I had agreed that, in order to distract him, I would take Valmor out as often as I could, and I had made him promise to explain to me in more detail their political organization and to let me see it in action. His grandfather having told us that the next session of the National Assembly would be of interest, I asked him to take me there with Eugene, whose company I knew he enjoyed. We called for him early and left while chatting, after promising to return later to the house, where we probably would find Mrs. Dinamé and her family.

"The National Assembly," Valmor told us as we were walking along, "is the greatest source of power after the people. You will see that it is composed of two thousand deputies elected for two years, half of whom are replaced every year. Because each of the thousand communes that make up the republic has two deputies, each elects one deputy every year. All elections take place on the same day, the first of April, throughout the republic. They all are decided in a single session, after the lists of candidates have been drawn up and discussed in two preceding sessions ten days apart. Because all citizens acquire the habit of taking active part in public affairs in the popular assemblies, and almost all fill communal or provincial offices, with the most skilled filling almost all these offices in turn; and because the deputies are chosen from the most notable among these skilled persons, you can imagine that the representatives are almost all men ripened by age and experience, who are the cream of the country in talent, virtue, and patriotism. If a few young men appear among them without having passed through the ranks of lower offices, as some have done, it is because they are men of genius.

"The National Assembly is permanent, like the people and like the popular sovereignty that it represents. It is in session for nine months and takes three vacations of a month each, during which times it is represented by a Watch Committee, which would recall it if necessary. The representatives are convened and dissolved at times ordered by the Constitution with no other order than the mandate of the sovereign people. All are housed and fed together in the National Palace. On another day we will visit their lodgings and refectory, and you will see that they are treated no differently from all other citizens. Their conference room and everything designated exclusively for their personal use are in no way exceptional.

"But look carefully at the public building, the National Palace" (we were approaching it then), "and tell me, you who have traveled so much, whether you have ever seen a more beautiful imperial or royal palace. We sent out everywhere for architectural designs, which we prepared and discussed for four years. It has been completed for only twenty-two years, after twenty-eight years of work. Icar and the republic had said together: let the National Palace be the most handsome public building on earth! And here it is! But let us enter quickly because the hour for the session draws near."

I will not attempt to describe the interior. I do not believe that any throne room in any monarchical palace could be as majestic, as superb, as magnificent as this room for the deliberations of the representatives of a People that is at once emperor, pope, and king! Several vast galleries hold more than six thousand spectators. There is not a soldier, not a guard, not a weapon, but only music, at once imposing and delectable. At five minutes of four, the president, the vice presidents, and the secretaries, preceded by numerous sergeants at arms and followed by the two thousand representatives, entered the hall superbly attired and took their respective places in majestic silence. These two thousand deputies seated on semicircular benches forming an amphitheater, the six thousand spectators seated above them, the brilliant costumes, the elegant and brilliant attire of the women, all those handsome, graceful faces, the rostrum in front, the officers behind and farther up, the president in raised position among them, the inscriptions and the statues, the sparkling chandeliers and the banners, the music and the silence (in the midst of which a voice seemed to cry out: 'It is here that the happiness or misfortune of a great people is decided'): all formed a spectacle that neither the sterile magnificence of a court nor the vain extravaganza of an opera could offer.

Four o'clock was striking when a superb old man, in citizen's dress, appeared above the president and pronounced these words in a solemn voice: "Representatives of Icaria, remember that the people have sent you here for the sole purpose of working for their happiness, and that your brothers have chosen you to be an example of all the virtues."

Then the president declared that the Assembly was in session. "Chief Sergeant at Arms," he said, "Are all the representatives in their places?"

"No."

"How many are missing?"

"Three."

"Who are they?" (The sergeant at arms named them.)

"I declare to the Assembly," added the president, "that the first two have sent me the reasons for their absence, and I will transmit their letters to the Censure Committee. Does anyone ask for a temporary release?" Four deputies rose and gave their reasons. The Assembly excused three and sent the fourth to the Censure Committee. A reporter then read to the platform, in the name of the Furnishings Committee, his report on a projected law, which would add a new piece of furniture to the set of furnishings of every family. He declared that the committee was unanimously in favor of adoption and briefly summarized its arguments. No one asked to speak against this project. The Assembly voted without discussion by sitting or standing and adopted the law unanimously.

A new reporter was at the rostrum when the door of the hall opened with a ringing of bells that attracted all eyes and ears. "Watch carefully," Valmor told us. "It is the third deputy whose absence the head sergeant at arms has just declared."

"But why," I said, "this noisy door instead of a door that opens without interrupting the speaker?"

"It is so that the Assembly will notice the entry of the tardy one. You will see in a moment!"

The reporter, who had stopped speaking until the deputy was in his seat, finished his report. After the Assembly's vote, the president said to the deputy, "Representative B———, you have not given your fellow citizens a good example of punctiliousness in the execution of a duty. What is your explanation?" The deputy put forth the reason for his lateness. "Assembly," the president said, "do you want to send this man to the Censure Committee?" Everyone remained seated. "Does the Assembly accept the explanation?" They rose to a man.

"But this ceremony is already a severe punishment," I exclaimed without troubling to keep my voice low.

"Sir," an old man next to me said politely, "I have come to hear our representatives and not your reflections. Kindly do not deprive me of my rights!"

"Pardon me," I replied, for he was right.

Fifteen to twenty-five proposed laws were adopted in the same manner, and some were rejected without discussion, by unanimous vote of the committees and of the Assembly. Next a reporter came to declare that his committee had adopted a particular project only by a two-thirds majority. After him, a counter-reporter, who had been chosen by the minority of this committee to explain the motives of their opposition, presented his report. Several speakers then spoke for and against the project, expressing themselves with extreme terseness. Because the Assembly was not unanimous, the minority that stood to support the opposition was counted and found to be 105. These names were rapidly recorded, so that the 1,895 who made up the majority in favor of the law would be known. At that point, the session was recessed for a quarter of an hour.

"My neighbor's rebuke was deserved," I said at that point to Valmor, "but my comment was justified nonetheless. Your door with bells and the interruption of the speaker are a real punishment for the latecomer."

"Ah," he answered. "We do not take our duties lightly! The functions of a representative are not a game for us! You have heard the man of the people remind the National Assembly that its members must exemplify all virtues. The deputy who fails voluntarily to fulfill his duty seems far guiltier to us than another citizen, and public opinion is so unyielding on this point that, ten years ago, a deputy was unanimously excluded from the National Assembly because he failed just once to attend the Assembly without a legitimate reason. Therefore, no one misses the Assembly, and out of two thousand deputies you saw but one latecomer."

"Ho! Far be it from me to censure this severity," I replied. "On the contrary, I approve of it with all my heart and I admire it."

"It appears," said Eugene, "that your committees play an important role in legislative work. How do they function?"

"You know that the National Assembly has fifteen principal committees, each made up of one hundred and thirty-three members. These are subdivided into sixty subcommittees of thirty-three members each. All these committees and subcommittees have their designated fields of interest and conference rooms. All proposed laws are distributed to them according to their specialty to be examined and discussed separately and without delay. The sessions of these committees are public and take place every day in the morning, from ten to one o'clock, and the sessions of the Assembly take place in the evening from four to eight o'clock and sometimes as late as nine o'clock. Although these committees are supplied with all the statistics they might desire, and although they are in constant contact with analogous committees of all the popular assemblies, they often conduct inquiries under the aegis of the Chamber, and publicly question both officials and citizens. In addition to those, they even organize special commissions, to which they appoint nondeputized citizens who gather information and give their advice. These free commissions, along with the committees, have rendered invaluable services in the organization of the community. When a committee has finished its deliberations, its reporter writes up his report immediately, and it is handed in, printed, and distributed ten days before being read and discussed, with the exception of emergency cases, which are exceedingly rare."

When the session started again, I had the pleasure of hearing an animated debate on a serious issue that had been sent back to the popular assemblies for their opinion, and on which these assemblies, like the committee, were divided. It was a question of deciding whether it would be appropriate to work seven and one-half hours a day instead of seven, and to have a day of rest every five days instead of every ten days, so that the citizens could enjoy the countryside more often. The two most skillful speakers had been chosen by the minority and the majority to debate the opposing opinions. They subjected each other to questions, objections, reasons, and arguments for more than half an hour, replied twenty times one to the other, came to agreement eventually on many points that had originally divided them, and finally agreed on a trial period during the three summer months, putting this new compromise to a vote in the popular assemblies. The National Assembly, having listened silently to them, as a tribunal listens to two lawyers, adopted almost unanimously their opinion.

I then had the treat of a somewhat rare spectacle, that of the president of the executive body being called in by the National Assembly and appearing before its tribunal to give it the information it required about the state of a negotiation ordered by the Chamber with five foreign governments concerning a colonization project that they would undertake together. The president read some letters, answered all questions, and let it be known that three of these governments had accepted the proposals of the republic, and that the other two would soon accept them. He then retired with the same rites that had accompanied his entry.

"The president never refuses," I asked Valmor during a second intermission, "to appear at the invitation of the representatives?"

"To refuse," he replied, "would be a revolt, and the National Assembly would revoke his powers and put him on trial. The National Assembly is the sovereign, or the representative of the sovereign. The president is its subordinate, the executor of its laws, elected by it and responsible to it. In addition, every year the National Assembly calls on the president, on a day of its choosing, for a report about the execution of all the laws. It frequently calls to account the ministers as well."

"And all your foreign affairs are conducted in public as well?"

"Certainly! Could there be a secret kept from the National Assembly? Would this not be absurd, being that the Assembly is sovereign?"

"What if the president maintained that the public welfare required that a given affair not be known to any?"

"Absurd, audacious lie of despots and tyrants! If the president were to declare that the affair required secrecy, the Chamber would see to it itself; and if there were a doubt, the Chamber would name a special commission that would be brought into its confidence and would report directly to the Chamber. When the Chamber judges that more or less total publicity is appropriate, no one can hold to the contrary. In addition, such a problem has not come up since our revolution, and all our foreign affairs have had the same measure of publicity as all other matters."

When the session resumed, the Chamber expedited a great many items. It distributed among its committees some petitions that had been proposed by popular assemblies, and other proposals made and publicly read by its own members. Finally, it fixed the order of the day for the morrow and retired as it had entered, leaving all the spectators deeply respectful and our Eugene in transports of enthusiasm.

"If every session is as full as this one," I said to Valmor as we were going out, "what a great number of laws your National Assembly must enact every year during its nine-month session."

"Yes," replied Eugene, "but all of its laws are, like these, certain to be in the interests of the people, and consequently I think that you will not complain of their number."

"Eugene is right," said Valmor, "and to convince you of it, when we are back home, I will show you the list of the laws enacted last year."

"But," I replied, "I have always heard that the legislative branch should neither administer nor consolidate power, and here I see that the National Assembly does both!"

"No," replied Valmor, "our National Assembly does not administer. It only discusses, decides, and orders many administrative acts, just like all legislators do, and we only regret that it cannot deliberate on everything because what harm can there be in these laws being enacted by two thousand legislators instead of by a few general executors or by a single one? Is it not even more to our advantage that the laws be examined by the most enlightened body, the one that, in addition, can consult all other bodies and the entire people? You say that the National Assembly consolidates power? So much the better! May it establish unity and equality throughout, while always being sure to avoid the disadvantages and to bring together all the advantages of consolidation. A scourge under despotism and tyranny, the consolidation of power is a benefit within the republic and the community!"

When we arrived at the house, Dinaros told us that we would not see his mother and sister, whom Corilla was with, and Valmor gave Eugene the list of laws enacted during the past year. Eugene read it aloud.

" 'A law ordering the inclusion of a new vegetable on the list of foodstuffs, cultivation, and distribution. Ten other laws concerning food, clothing, lodging, and furnishings. A law ordering improvements on all routes. Five other laws in the same category for canals and rivers. A law ordering the creation, printing, and distribution of a chronological, alphabetical table of all human inventions. A dozen laws of the same sort. A law ordering construction and experimentation involving an antihail project. Fifteen laws for increasing useful and pleasant conditions for women in their workshops and elsewhere. Forty laws ordering the construction and use of new machines in national workshops.' That is enough, I think."

"No, no, go on," said Valmor.

" 'Fifteen laws for improving education. Two laws ordering the manufacture and distribution of certain objects to a savage people to attempt to civilize it. A law proposing to the Congress of Allied Nations the conducting of geological digs together.' "

"Enough, enough!" The two or three hundred other laws also had as their goal the general welfare.

"Well," said the grandfather to me as we went home, "are you satisfied?"

"Enchanted," I answered, "and amazed! I did not hear a single piece of eloquence, and I saw nothing dramatic; but I admire the reason, wisdom, decency, dignity, and terseness of your representatives. They seemed like judges in court, always attentive, silent, and remaining in their seats. Not an interruption or shout, not the slightest noise to disturb the speaker or the listeners. On the contrary, there was total considerateness and a display of esteem and fraternity. Your popular assemblies, your public officials, and your citizens must certainly find models there! That is what I have always desired. That is what overwhelms me and delights me!"

"I cannot understand your amazement," replied the old man. "What you see here is no different from what you see in our schools, in our workshops, in our theaters, in all our public meetings. Could the elected representatives of the people possibly be less reasonable than school children? Remember that from childhood onward, our education provides all of us with the physical and moral habits necessary for persons in society, and, above all, for the citizen in assembly. The habits of listening silently, replying briefly, and never annoying your neighbor are quite easily formed. What seemed harder at first was to train the body to be able to stay seated, silent, and attentive for several hours; but by working on these habits from childhood, we succeeded completely in cultivating them. As for politeness, fraternity, exactitude, and the fulfillment of all duties, it would be a crime for our elite to give to others a scornful example."

"Oh, how fortunate you are!" exclaimed Eugene. "How fortunate you are!"

"We are even more fortunate in this respect," replied the old man, "because the exact opposite prevailed before our revolution of 1792. During that time, shameful and painful to the memory, the great majority of deputies made a mockery of their duties. Those who were lavish with promises in order to get themselves elected spent weeks and entire months without coming to the Chamber, putting their pleasures or self-interest before their duties. Every day many of them arrived after the session had begun and left before it ended, and often (and this scandalized the public) the theater was full of deputies, the legislative hall was empty of legislators, and the president was reduced to ending the session because he was almost alone in the hall. During the discussion, you could see them walking about in the room, coming and going at any given moment. At their benches, they would read the newspaper, write letters, or chat with their neighbors. All you could hear was the opening of doors, footsteps, and talk and noise of all sorts, so that those who were not listening to the speaker prevented the others from hearing him and prevented him from speaking freely. Our young people today cannot get over their amazement when we tell them the story of those times of discord and oppression. They can barely believe that there was so much lack of consideration, impoliteness, and grossness even among the elite and the flower of the country. But this monstrous piece of nonsense, this reversal of all reasonable ideas, was, unfortunately, only too real and too normal then. Those people who would have choked to death rather than make a sound in the presence of a singer or a dancer made as much commotion as a crowd of drunkards when their duty brought them into the so-called sanctuary of the law. There was no school, no guardroom, no barracks, no cabaret, not even a fair where you would not have found more decency and order than you often found in the solemn assembly of legislators!"

"But Grandfather!" exclaimed Valmor.

"Let me go on, my son," said the venerable old man, taking up the subject once more and becoming even more animated. "I know how much these truths make you blush for our country, but the shame and folly of the past raise even further the wisdom and glory of the present; and it is good to remember the vices and misfortunes of our former regime to appreciate better the virtues and happiness that we owe our Icar. It is good to show our young friends what we were before, so that they may judge the miracles our community has produced. I will go on.

"The legislature was divided into two factions: the majority, which defended the interests of the aristocracy, and the minority or opposition, which defended the interests of the people. These two parties formed two separate camps, two enemy armies who threatened each other by glance, gesture, and voice; who threw curses and insults back and forth; who applauded their speakers like fanatics or who yelled to prevent their adversaries from speaking; who grunted or screamed, burst into laughter, or tapped their feet like madmen or lunatics; who bared their fists and made war whoops like heathens attacking the enemy trenches; who enacted a law like soldiers overwhelm a citadel in the midst of confusion and a terrible tumult; who killed themselves two by two in duels; and, finally, whose only intention was to injure the other party when they were not actually physically engaged in doing so.

"You shudder, my children, at the tale of such horrors. But everything was turned upside down in that time of tyranny, civil war, and abominations. The ministers, who should have been the elite of the elite, often set, at the tribunal, an example of telling the most obvious lies, proclaiming the most immoral maxims, pouring out insults and slander, praising treason, and rewarding murder! And those ministers had the nerve to heap praise upon themselves, to give themselves the highest tributes, to claim for themselves all wisdom and virtues, to accuse the people of ignorance and stupidity, to treat as imbeciles, ninnies, muddleheads, and anarchists those who defended the popular interest. And their majority always drowned out their voices with applause and bravos. And those same ministers, seated at the head of their majority like generals before their soldiers, gave them the order or signal to applaud or mumble, to stand up or sit down. And that majority passed for the ministers all the laws of tyranny, terror, and blood that they demanded and accorded all the millions they desired for the queen and her three children.

"But, you may be wondering, what was this majority? Of what sort of animal was it composed? Of groveling, domesticated, and voracious ones; of foxes, gluttonous beasts, kowtowing dogs, chameleons, and lynx. You would surely have found all the species in that menagerie. It was a handful of rich men (barely two hundred of them), chosen by another handful of the rich (thirty or forty thousand of them), who were, in fact, chosen and appointed by the ministers, who controlled the electorate through their influence and through the appointments or favors they gave out and promised. They chose for deputies the aristocrats who had the same self-interest they did. They chose their agents or those public officials who were the most faithful to them (that is, who were most faithful to their own positions): chamberlains, horsemen, captains of the guard, eunuchs, high officers or senior servants of the Crown, even the queen's handsome pages. It even appeared for a moment that they would choose as legislators, to represent the sovereign, her pretty chambermaids and her beautiful ladies-in-waiting. But they were content to appoint themselves, and in several decisive circumstances their voices made up the majority and therefore the law.

"It seems like a dream when I think of it, and sometimes I can barely trust my own memory. We used to call that machine a representative government, but, as you see, it was nothing more than a vulgar farce, if you'll pardon the expression, a real comedy, and a comedy that cost the unfortunate people dearly, for it was really the queen, or rather her ministers, who made the laws. The ministers were more absolute than an autocrat, more despotic than a sultan, and far bolder in striking and stealing millions than they could have been without their shadow deputies serving as fronts for them and giving them everything in the name of the people.

"In addition, whereas today our National Assembly enacts laws only for the good of the people and for humanity, you would tremble if I cited the laws passed in our unfortunate Icaria during the ten years from 1772 to 1782. Budgets, a civil list for the queen, privileges for her two sons, a dowry for her daughter, and laws of terror, all favoring the royal family and its servants, the ministers, and the aristocracy, all against the people. And if, because of fear and villainy, to make themselves popular they consented at first to a few laws that seemed in the popular interest, the deputies revoked them one by one or altered them or failed to execute them. And see how all modesty is trampled upon when despotism succeeds in robbing everything of its morality! This majority, these deputies who supposedly were sent to supervise and take the ministers to task, never left the ministerial lodgings or even the queen's palace, where they rushed like starving hordes to the dinners and galas of the Court and courtiers. These people vied with each other to see who would be superior in flattery, adulation, servility, and baseness. You will find it hard to believe that these deputies, sent there to deliberate on the happiness of the people, discussed in all seriousness one day for two hours whether feathers did not suit the queen better than flowers. And to make the seducing and the buying of favors complete, the ministers procured for themselves, their wives, and their children stations, privileges of all sorts, the most puerile gradations, little ribbons of all colors, and little crosses of all kinds, while they disenfranchised and ruined those deputies who, putting their own conscience before personal gain, voted against them. After dividing the Chamber in order to control it, they threw the majority against the minority like street urchins who urge on one dog against another. They did not even permit the minority to speak or, above all, to put forward a single proposition!"

"But," I said to the old man, "what was the reaction of the spectators to these debates and of the people who read the reports of these sessions?"

"They said that it was a school for scandal and immorality, a lair, a cavern, a den of thieves, a plague-ridden home, a lunatic asylum, an opium den, a wicked place in need of purification."

"Did the people not petition, as they do in England?"

"Petition, but whom? How could they petition the ministers against their acquiescent and servile deputies? Or the queen, against her acquiescent and servile ministers?"

"And the people never met together, as in England, to deliberate in public meetings?"

"But the law (that is, the rich, the deputies, and the ministers) crushed assemblies and meetings."

"And the press did not cry out on behalf of the people, as in England?"

"But the law (that is, the aristocracy) gagged the press."

"And did not the people vilify those who sold them down the river, while pretending to represent them, as in England?"

"But the enemies of the people surrounded themselves with bands of thugs and ruffians!"

"And the people did not cry out against the minister, as in England, where the great Duke of Wellington was obliged to put gratings, doors, and iron shutters around his townhouse?"

"What about the hail of bullets and the provost marshals?"

"Was there then no remedy, as in England, where the people undertook so successfully their parliamentary reform?"

"What are you talking about? Did heaven not send us Icar and the community forty years before sending you what you call your reform? And although I admit that you may feel justified in taking pride in it, what is that little reform worth compared to our radical regeneration? We can barely stop ourselves from laughing when we hear you talk here in Icaria of your English radicalism. I have seen with pleasure, I will admit, your proud candidates appearing humbly on your hustings out of doors, before the assembly of all the people, exposing their feelings and their principles, as if to pay homage to the people's sovereignty. But why are these same people disdainfully excluded on the morrow when it is a question of voting and electing? Why, moreover, do the parties slander each other so ignobly? Why do the contestants insult each other so grossly? Why these cries, these howlings, these outrages? Why such base and savage violence by the people against those who are going to be their legislators? Why this daring and impudent corruption of the vote by guineas, which contains in and of itself all corruption and immorality, which transforms your elections into a grand lie, which dishonors both your rich corrupters and your poor corrupted, and which suffices to demonstrate without a doubt the fatal influence of riches in the face of poverty? Speak no more, my poor, unfortunate Milord, of your reform, of your elections, of your supposed assembly of the English people, particularly when you have just come out of a session of our Icarian National Assembly. Do you not agree, democrat Eugene?"

"Oh, yes," replied Eugene, whom I had seen blush, turn pale, and hide his head in his hands several times. "Yes, I envy, I admire this Assembly, these legislators, this people, or, rather, I admire this Constitution, education, and community, which have so transformed your electors, deputies, and ministers. And when I think about it, my blood boils. But it is not against men that I feel hatred and anger; it is against the horrifying social and political organization that perverts rich and poor, elector and deputy, even minister and monarch, creating misfortune for the aristocrats and despair for the people."

"Good, Eugene! Bravo, bravo!" said the old man, holding out his hand to Eugene.

Although the conversation was of great interest, everyone seemed sad. Even the children were mirthless, as if everything were languishing in the absence of Corilla and Dinaïse.

23   Icarian Peerage, Provincial Assembly, and Pantheon

Can you imagine," I said to Valmor, "that Eugene spent the night in the Chamber of Deputies in Paris, and that he woke up red with anger?"

"Well," said Valmor, "to cool his blood, I will take him to see our House of Lords, if he wishes."

"What!" cried Eugene, heating up once more. "Lords in Icaria! You are making fun of me!"

"Not really. We have lords who sanction or reject the most important laws passed by the National Assembly. And our House of Lords is not made up of a few hundred lords but of several thousand. We have not one House of Lords, but a thousand."

"You do not understand," I told Eugene, "that their lords are their citizens, who are all equal, and that their thousand houses of lords are their thousand communal or popular assemblies."

"So much the better," replied Eugene, "and I would like to see them right away, although I have already observed a few."

"Calm down! The Communal Assembly does not meet until tomorrow. Moreover, I would like to show you beforehand a session of our Provincial Assembly."

"What! I said to him. "You have a Provincial Assembly as well?"

"We certainly do," he replied. "Each province has its assembly in its own palace, its palace in the center of its own provincial capital, and its capital in the center of its ten communes. These provincial assemblies are composed of one hundred and twenty special deputies elected by the communes. They are organized along the lines of the National Assembly: each one changes half of its deputies annually, each one is divided into fifteen committees, and each one holds its sessions in public."

"But that makes each one a little Chamber of Deputies," I said. "What if one were to decide to set itself up as a rival of the National Assembly?"

"Never," replied Valmor. "Each has too few members; it meets for only four months, divided into four sessions of ten days each, with long recesses; it deals only with matters expressly laid down by the Constitution. In essence, it is subordinated to the National Assembly, as a province is to the nation. Its first duty is to supervise the execution of the laws in every commune of the province. It can discuss and make decrees only to expedite and ensure the carrying out of the laws or to regulate certain matters of interest only to the province."

As a session of the Provincial Assembly would only be a replica in miniature of what we had already seen in the National Assembly, I chose instead to visit the History Museum or the Pantheon.

All the life-size figures were made of tinted wax, with genuine hair, eyes, and dress, which produced such a complete illusion that you felt you were in the midst of a meeting of live people. Each one held a different posture, and many, by means of concealed devices, made movements that rendered the illusion even more believable. Eugene went into raptures over the perfect human resemblance.

"Yes," I said to him, "but these costumed wax statues are not nearly as worthy of our admiration as statues of marble or bronze."

"Ah!" he replied. "The triumph over a difficult medium in art does not interest me. What I value above all is its reproduction of real life, for that should be the goal of all painting and sculpture. Now, where is the portrait, bust, painting, or statue that can represent a person or a head as well as this wax?"

"Besides," added Valmor, "do not imagine that such perfection in these wax statues is an easy matter! Examine these forms, these hands, these heads, this flesh, these postures. Let me tell you that our most skillful sculptors and our most adept painters have masterpieces here that have won major competitions. Even the costumes require more skill and talent than you appear to recognize, both in terms of exactness and application. Nowadays, our actors and painters come here to learn how to costume the classical characters they wish to represent on stage or in their paintings."

In the Pantheon first and then in the Pandemonium, we strolled through I do not know how many rooms containing the most famous personages of all nations, thus passing in review eras and countries, benefactors and scourges of the human race. A month would have been necessary to do justice to this pageant, and our rapid overview merely tired my head while dazzling my eyes. Valmor pointed out in particular contemporary Icarian figures, telling us that it was like seeing them in the flesh, for the resemblance was that striking. I had expected that Icar, the idol of Icaria, would have an inspired expression and that Lixdox, whose name is never pronounced without horror, would look like a demon or thief; but Icar's only exceptional feature was his face's serenity, and Lixdox was merely an ugly, one-eyed hunchback who seemed more cunning than wicked, although he was, in fact, as wicked as he was ambitious and hypocritical. As for the young queen Cloramide, I will never forget her image, nor will I forget Eugene's stupefaction when, upon seeing her, he cried out, "How closely she resembles Dinaros's sister!"

Valmor blushed, and his very obvious discomfort threw me into an inexplicable torment. I have never seen anything as charming. Never, I believe, did a more beautiful forehead wear the diadem; never did more beautiful hair wind around a crown; never did more majesty and grace sit upon a throne; never did a sweeter glance pierce the hearts of the people; never did more lovely a mouth smile more enchantingly. Only Dinaïse's voice was missing, and I listened, fully expecting it to slip out of the half-opened lips.

"The poor woman!" I cried. "What a misfortune, what a shame that she had Lixdox for her minister!"

"What a misfortune," said Eugene, "that she held the title of queen, a title that can pervert the best of hearts!"

I could not get my fill of contemplating that beautiful image, and it was with regret that I found myself pulled away by Eugene and Valmor. I will return often to visit this museum!

24 Popular Assemblies

I refused to go with Eugene, who wanted to take me to see a public building, and I returned alone to the Pantheon, where I spent the morning visiting the various rooms once more. I returned again and again to the beautiful Cloramide, and each time I felt even more strongly that Eugene had been right in saying that she had the same features as Dinaïse. After dinner, Eugene, who was sulking because I had not gone with him, finally consented to accompany me to pick up Valmor so that we could attend his communal meeting together.

"If the whole Icarian people could meet in Icara," Valmor told us, "we would have no National Assembly, just as we would have no Provincial Assembly if the population of a province could meet in its principal city. It is for this reason that we have no separate Communal Assembly, for all the citizens of each commune can easily meet in the communal palace. Thus, the people of each commune constitute their own assembly or council when dealing with purely communal matters. In a word, they exercise their sovereignty and conduct their own affairs. First, they take all measures necessary to ensure, within the commune, that all laws of the National Assembly and decrees of the Provincial Assembly are enforced. In addition, in constitutionally determined cases, they enact ordinances that regulate the special workings of the commune. The people meet regularly three times a month, every ten days, and in special session each time they are petitioned to do so by a certain number of citizens or magistrates. The regular meetings take place on designated days and at fixed times throughout the republic so that the entire nation is assembled at the same moment. They always begin at four o'clock in the evening, after work and dinner. On assembly days, all other public places (theaters, concerts, scientific courses, museums, and so forth) are closed because all citizens, without exception, must attend the assembly, which usually lasts until eight or nine o'clock. If you were to go out in an hour, you would find only women and children in the streets and walkways, as you will already have noticed. Any men that you might see would be foreigners. You would find only a few omnibuses in operation, driven by young people who are not yet citizens."

"Does no one miss the assembly?" I asked.

"No one. You must understand that, because all citizens are fed by the republic, and all workshops close at one o'clock, no one has any motive or excuse for failing to fulfill his duty. It would be a cause for shame, a kind of theft committed against the republic, one of the most serious of misdemeanors. But this is an offense that is never committed because we are used to considering our assemblies a right of which we are proud and which we jealously protect."

"Look," he said, showing us a printed page. "Here is the agenda for today. You can see that we have many matters to take up today: eleven communal, five provincial, and eight national. But we will expedite them, for all these matters were announced in the meeting before last and were sent to special committees that examined them right away and passed in their reports in the last session. The reports were then placed on the agenda for today, and on the following day they were distributed to each one of us."

"Your assembly is divided into committees like your National Assembly?"

"Exactly. It is split up into more than sixty committees or subcommittees. Matters pertaining to the specialty of each are sent directly to it, so that the committee may examine them separately before the upcoming session. Thus, we are prepared to vote, particularly because we have had the opportunity to discuss all these matters, either in our workshops or in our parlors."

"Ah! I see here," I said, "the proposal you told me about to enlarge the hotel for foreigners."

"Yes, I made the proposal at the session before last so that it would be known in advance and discussed today."

"But what is all this flurry about?" (For we had come in some time before, and now the crowd was rushing into the room.)

"It is the citizens taking their places, for four o'clock is about to sound and the session is about to begin. You can see the president and the members of the board seated in their armchairs. It would be a grave mistake to come in late, and you will see not a soul who is remiss in promptness."

Valmor left us to rush to his place, after promising to join us for a moment at the first recess of the session. The room was immense and magnificent, filled with more than ten thousand seated citizens. You would have thought it was a small, or, rather, a large House of Representatives, for there were five or six times more citizens than deputies; but the spectators' gallery was much smaller, and it was filled almost entirely with women.

Once the session had been opened, marked only by the clock in the midst of deep silence, the citizens took care of communal matters and then went on to provincial and national affairs in the order indicated on the agenda. For each matter at hand, they began by reading a very brief report from a specific committee. Most of the items were voted on without discussion, by standing or sitting, and were passed by a large majority. A few were debated by a small number of speakers, who spoke standing in their own places. In this way, the assembly proceeded to elect five or six communal officers from a list of candidates decided upon and published at the last session. Other elections were announced, and each citizen was invited to submit his candidates before the next session. After the communal and provincial affairs had been expedited, the session was recessed for half an hour, and we went to take a walk on the surrounding square with Valmor, who had joined us once more.

"What silence!" Eugene said to him. "What calm, what order, what speed! I am dazzled by it!"

"But you are always dazzled, my dear Eugene," Valmor replied, "and I do not comprehend your surprise. Are not silence, attention, order, and terseness accepted by everyone as obligatory so that we may expedite our affairs and use correctly our right of assembly? Why should we not be calm? We have no exclusive interests, no parties, no political passions. Do not forget the influence our general and, above all, our civic education has on us. Our elections are the same.

Would you be amazed to know that we have no intrigue concerning posts that are responsibilities, and that we have no corruption surrounding electors who have nothing to gain from candidates who have no bribes to give?"

The session continued with matters concerning the entire nation, several of which had been sent by the National Assembly to the people for their advice or approval. Among these matters was a question presented by a provincial citizen at his Communal Assembly, where the matter was discussed, after which it was taken up by all the assemblies of that province. It was then sent to the National Assembly, which returned it to the assemblies of all the other provinces. The discussion was longer than before, more speakers spoke for and against the issue, and the vote was given by yeas or nays, so that the National Assembly would know the exact number of yea and nay votes in the thousands of communal assemblies throughout the republic—that is, so that the will of the people would be known. Now that all items on the agenda had been dealt with, the president proposed to the assembly the agenda for the next session. Ten or twelve proposals were presented by various members. Some pertained to communal affairs, others to provincial, and the rest to national matters. All were sent to their respective committees. Among these, I noted one by a cobbler who was proposing a method of lessening the workload in the national printing houses. He suggested that the printers should compress into a single letter all those words that were repeated with high frequency in the same work, such as the words *National Assembly, people's representatives, republic, government*, and so forth, which are repeated thousands of times in printed matter concerning legislation.

"You may well laugh at me again," said Eugene as we went out, "but I am nonetheless dazzled by everything I have witnessed."

"Good! You will be able to enjoy the same pleasure tomorrow, for our stenographers have copied down all the proceedings, and you may read them all in our communal newspaper."

"I love," added Eugene, "the frankness and daring of voting publicly by standing or sitting or by saying 'yea' or 'nay.' "

"What daring? Do we need courage to express our opinion? Do we have anything to gain or lose? And if we needed courage, would our education not provide it? I will not permit you to be amazed by the initiative accorded each citizen and by the right he exercises to set forth in his assembly all his ideas on communal, provincial, or national matters, for nothing is more reasonable and more natural."

"Do you wish me to admire only that which is neither rational nor reasonable?"

"Oh, well. Admire as much as you will because our education and social organization do not lead you to figure out how many thousands of useful ideas must come out of our popular assemblies!"

"It follows that you have no use for the right of petition!"

"Naturally. Each citizen presents his petition only to his own assembly. If the assembly adopts it, it becomes the petition of that assembly to the National Assembly. If it is rejected, it may be presented another year or right away to the assembly of another commune. In this way, all good ideas are assured exposure, and bad ideas may not obstruct the work of the National Assembly."

Valmor wanted to speak to us about newspapers, for he felt that their perfection was a result of the citizen's right of proposal. However, because he had to take his leave, he put off until the morrow speaking to us in greater detail about that matter.

25 Newspapers

As soon as we were together once more, we took up our conversation about newspapers, and I was very surprised to hear Eugene attack them vehemently.

"Certainly," he said, "freedom of the press, with all its excesses, is necessary in the face of aristocrats and royalty. It is a remedy against intolerable abuses. But the freedom of newspapers in certain countries that William and I know well is such a fallacious freedom and such a frightening remedy! Here is what we find in most newspapers: monopolies, monetary speculation, self-interest, partiality, slander and insults one cannot counter, lies, false rumors and errors one cannot erase, journalistic contradictions, and doctrinal uncertainty and confusion. What muddle, what chaos, results from the multiplicity of newspapers! One's political and social organization must be truly detestable to choose so abominable a defender of one's own interests to fight it."

"We have," said Valmor, "almost nipped this evil in the bud. First, we have established a social and political organization that has made hostility on the part of the press unnecessary. Second, we permit each commune and each province to have only one newspaper respectively. There is only one national newspaper. Third, we have entrusted the editing of newspapers to officials elected by the people or their representatives. These editors have no self-interest, and their posts are temporary and may be taken from them. We have extirpated the entire root of this evil by ordering that newspapers consist only of reports of proceedings. They may contain only accounts and facts, without any discussion by the journalist. Like any other citizen, the journalist may submit his opinion to his Communal Assembly, which discusses it and supports it or refutes it. When each person is able to publicize his own opinion by submitting it to his assembly, why should he be permitted to publish that opinion in any other manner, which might leave dangerous errors uncontrolled? Our freedom of the press is, in fact, our right to bring forth proposals in our popular assemblies. The opinions raised in these assemblies constitute our public opinion! And our press, which makes known all our proposals, all our discussions, and all our deliberations with exact figures and minority opinions is, in the fullest sense of the word, the expression of our public opinion."

"Yes, I admire it, I admire it, I admire it!" said Eugene once more.

"Add to what I have said that our elected journalists are some of our most skilled writers. They stake their reputation on recounting the facts and analyzing discussions with clarity and order, as dramatically as possible and, above all, with the most perfect terseness, so that they omit nothing important and use not one unnecessary word. You have already noted the beautiful paper, the convenient format, the magnificent printing, the distribution of various items. Compare these with your English or French newspapers! Yes, admire them, admire them!"

"And why, when you reprimand me so often for being dazzled, do you want me to admire them now? I do not want to admire them! Great marvel indeed: that a newspaper be made more competently by a republic and a community than by a shopkeeper-journalist!"

"Ah! You are right," said Valmor, smiling.

26 Executive Branch

Our first fundamental rule," Valmor told us, "is that the executive branch is essentially subordinate to the legislative branch. The executive branch, or Executive, is charged only with executing the decisions, orders, and will of the legislative branch, and it always acts in the name of the people and of the National Assembly. It follows from this tenet that it is accountable, responsible, and subject to dissolution. You will see, as well, that it is, by its very essence, elected and temporary. Another radical principle is that this power is never entrusted to one man but to a body that we call the Executive, which has a president. Thus, we do not have a president of the republic, but only a president of the executive body, the executive of the republic. Every legislative body has its executive. We have, therefore, a national executive, one hundred provincial executives, and a thousand communal executives.

"The National Executive is composed of sixteen members who are called executor generals (one greater than the number of principal committees of the National Assembly). Each of these executor generals is a sort of minister, with his own department, and their president is truly a president of a council of ministers. In the capital, in the provincial capitals, and in every communal capital, the national executive branch has all the minor officials it needs. The sixteen executor generals are elected for terms of two years. Half of the National Executive is replaced each year, like the National Assembly. The people do the electing from a triple list of candidates elected by the National Assembly. All the other minor officials are elected, some by the Executive itself, and others by the National Assembly, with the vast majority elected by the people. Therefore, the Executive's responsibility, in regard to the actions of its minor officials, is limited to that which may actually arise from its own error.

"The executor generals and their president are housed in the National Palace, next to the National Assembly. All their departments and offices are there also, or in the same neighborhood, so that communication between the National Assembly and its Executive is extremely easy. I do not have to tell you that the members of the Executive have no guards, no civil list, and no special treatment, no more than that accorded any other official. The executors are fed and lodged no better than any other citizen, for, in our country (I believe I have already told you this), all public service is a profession; or, rather, all professions are part of the public service. Public service is nothing more or less than a duty from which no one is exempted without just cause, and officials are often not exempted from their regular work. The Executive has no means of seduction or corruption, intimidation or usurpation."

"And the president of the Executive," I said to Valmor, "who replaces the kings of yesteryear, does he not feel humiliated by his subordinate position?"

"Humiliated? If our presidents were former princes from the former royal family, they might feel deposed, but all our presidents and their colleagues have been, and still are, workers. Like all our representatives, our officials, and our citizens, our current president, a most venerated man and former president of the National Assembly, is a mason who took up his profession again in the interim period and all of whose children work in the workshops. It has not occurred to a single one of our presidents that it might be humiliating to be subordinate to the National Assembly or to the people.

"Fearing a confrontation between the two powers, or of one trying to usurp the other's position, we first considered setting up a conservative body, which would assure the balance between them and would watch over the defense of the Constitution; this precaution seemed unwarranted, however, and experience has proven that we were right to reject it.

"I will mention only briefly the Provincial Executive, charged with the execution of laws and decrees concerning provincial interests. This Executive is organized like the National Executive and is made up of members elected by the people of each province, from a list of candidates presented to them by each Provincial Assembly.

"As for the Communal Executive, it is composed of sixteen members, one of whom is president, all elected by the people of the commune, each responsible for a specific area and for overseeing minor officials. These minor positions are very numerous, so that every person can fulfill his function as well as possible, so that his official duties can be added to his work without being too heavy a burden, and so that the greatest possible number of citizens can get used to managing public affairs. Schools, hospitals, fixed or mobile workshops, stores, public buildings, theaters, streets, promenades, and the countryside: all of these are filled with special officials.

"However," said Eugene, "you have no army, no generals, no active national guard, no policemen, no sergeants at arms, and no informers because you have no civil disturbances, no political parties, no uprisings, and no conspiracies?"

"Certainly not."

"Nor do you have jailers or executioners because you no longer have crimes or prisons?"

"Certainly not."

"Because you no longer have taxes, or currency, or customs, or charges, or city tolls, you no longer need an army of receivers and payers, or an army of customs officials, or an army of fiscal agents?"

"No, but that does not prevent us from having collectors, receivers, and distributors of all agricultural and industrial products, workshop directors, and officials of all kinds to protect the citizens and to safeguard their interests and even their pleasures. All of these officials are elected annually by the people. They attend all the assemblies and are always prepared to account for their actions."

"They do not consider themselves government servants, obliged to work for its interests against the good of the people? Do they not have an arrogant attitude toward the people?"

"What absurd nonsense!" replied Valmor. "They are representatives of their fellow citizens, and they treat each citizen with the politeness, consideration, and respect owing a sovereign people and its members; and each citizen treats them with the respect he himself owes to the people and its representatives. In principle, we wanted a citizen to be able to stand up to an official who was overstepping his authority, but we chose instead to oblige the citizen to obey without resistance any official who might speak in the name of the people and the law. The citizen is then permitted to bring that official before the citizens' bar, where abuse of power is punished."

"Public officials do not, then, enjoy the revolting privilege of immunity?"

"On the contrary! Having been elected because they were the men most worthy of their office, it follows that officials must be an example of all social and civic virtues, and, above all, they must abide by the law and act according to the dictates of brotherhood. Their errors are more serious than those same errors committed by other citizens. The higher the office held, the more serious the error. To break the law is a crime, particularly for those who make it or for those who are charged with enforcing it. And the widespread publicity that twisting the truth or the abuse of power would engender, and the censure and removal from office that might result: these are considered such serious punishments that you never see a citizen making himself liable to pursuit by another citizen, just as no one fails to treat an official with deference and respect. Such is the strength of our education and of public opinion."

"You mean," said Eugene, "that the benefits of community are without number!"

27 A Wedding, a Ball, a Dance

Corilla and Dinaïse had been invited several days earlier to the marriage and wedding ball of a mutual friend, and their two families were also invited because in places of public amusement you never see a girl without her mother, a mother without her daughter, a husband without his wife, or a wife without her husband. At first, we thought we would give our excuses, fearing that it would be too painful for Valmor to attend this ceremony. However, Valmor, who had guessed the reason for our refusal, insisted that we accept the invitation, declaring that he felt his spirit was strong enough to withstand all trials from that day forward. Each family could bring two foreigners, so I accepted gratefully Valmor's offer to accompany them, and I had the honor of being Corilla's escort. She made me promise to dance with her and with Dinaïse.

We arrived at five o'clock at the matrimonial palace, where all the families living on the married couple's street soon gathered, for they were entitled to attend, in addition to several families of friends who had received special invitations. Mrs. Dinamé, who arrived at almost the same time, sat near us. All the family members were wearing their holiday clothing. This mixture of men and women, old people and children, and girls and boys made up a charming company. All the girls looked beautiful and pretty to me, but Corilla looked the most beautiful, and Dinaïse the prettiest. It even seemed to me that the many looks directed toward them confirmed my opinion, and, though I know not why, this gave me a secret pleasure.

The ceremony was short, for Icarians do not wait until this moment to instruct the future spouses about the seriousness of the commitment they are making and the duties they will have to each other and to the republic. The magistrate, dressed in his solemn uniform, addressed them with a touching speech, which served as an indirect lesson to all the listeners. After that, he conferred on them the title of husband and wife and placed their union under the protection of the community. We then passed into the ballroom, which was in the same building.

This public ballroom is the most gracious, elegant, and magnificent room you can imagine. The gilding, mirrors, wall coverings, candelabras, lights, flowers, and perfumes: everything made it an enchanted place. All around it, many spectators were seated in armchairs in tiers. All the public rooms are set up so that everyone can see and be seen easily. The room may be made longer or shorter at will by means of a light, mobile floor-to-ceiling partition.

The young married couple inaugurated the ball by dancing and waltzing alone. They were not intimidated by everyone staring at them and admiring their gracefulness and skill because everyone knows how to dance and to waltz. The children danced together next, and then the young men, the young women, the men, the women, and even the old people, for all of them loved to dance, and a ball is always organized like a drama or ballet where everyone has a role to play.

Icarian dance consists primarily of figures and turns. The citizens' dance differs in essence from that performed in the theater, just as the men's dance is not the same as the women's. After the children, a young man danced alone for several minutes, then two of them together, then three, and then all the young men, divided into groups. The young women followed suit. Some of them accompanied themselves with castanets and others with a variety of instruments. Several old persons, male and female, performed dances that were humorous in character. After that, waltzes of different sorts were danced, but the men danced with men, and the women with women. Only a husband had the privilege of dancing with his wife. At first, I thought there would be few waltzers, but all the boys danced together and all the girls, and many husbands with their wives. This variety produced a charming effect. Finally everyone danced together, all ages and sexes, forming the most lively of spectacles. The ballroom was next to the restaurant, which had sent over, for refreshments, fruits and liqueurs that all Icarians like and that were presented to the mothers by their little boys and to the fathers by their little girls, always beginning with the oldest persons.

"It appears," I said to Corilla and Dinaïse, "that you all love to dance. You probably never have balls like in Paris and London, private balls whose principal attribute is to provide a meeting place for so many people, even strangers, that the last to arrive must stay at the door or on the staircase, while the earlier arrivals, pressed together in narrow halls, stomp on each other's feet or suffocate without being able to dance."

"We are not that mad," replied Corilla. "We dance rarely in our parlors and only when two or three families made up of close friends have gotten together. We dance only when we can dance comfortably."

"But we dance often in Icaria," added Dinaïse, "because every marriage has a ball like this one for all the families living on the streets of both spouses and for all their friends. Every street has eight or ten marriages every year, so you can see that every family attends this number of marriage balls annually. Every winter we also have four or five balls where each street gets together just to dance."

"And we also have summer balls," Corilla continued, "on all the promenades. Each family can join in for an hour, dancing and watching the other dancers out of doors under archways of plants and flowers, in the midst of which lights of all colors and forms produce a magical effect."

"In addition," said Dinaïse, "we have country dances, which are rounds and 'courantes' made up of runs, jumps, and turns rather than dance steps, but we love them passionately because we can do them anywhere, in the country and on the promenades, any time that several families are gathered."

"What do you do for music?" I asked.

"We almost always use a mechanical orchestra, like this one that you find charming, although it is out of sight and there is not a single musician. In the country, we dance to the flute or the flageolet, which all the dancers play in turn, or to the lively singing of the male and female dancers."

I knew that Corilla danced brilliantly, but Dinaïse's dancing seemed even more ravishing. Although I could dance quite well with Corilla, I was so upset when I had to dance facing or next to Dinaïse, and particularly when I felt her hand, which seemed to be burning up, that I missed the figure and lost the beat. I stepped on someone's feet, I bumped into others, and I mixed up the entire *contredanse*. This made Corilla and everyone in our vicinity laugh a great deal, while Dinaïse seemed as embarrassed as I was ashamed and annoyed. However, I soon took my revenge, and I danced so well that I heard only flattering murmurs. The ball ended with a dance done by a single dancer so that the other dancers could rest before leaving. All the families left the ballroom by a quarter past nine.

"The best dancer brought me here," Corilla said jokingly to Dinaïse, "and he will take you home." I was thus obliged to offer her my arm; and, perhaps for the first time, I accepted that obligation with pleasure, for I needed to make excuses for my clumsiness, which had seemed to displease her but which, I told her, only brought out even more the brilliance of one of the female dancers. Her response, made in a voice that affects me emotionally whenever I hear it, and that seemed even sweeter and more penetrating than ever, was so generous, while, at the same time, witty and modest, that I took my leave of her less displeased with myself.

28   A Horseback Ride

I was so agitated all night that I was unable to sleep. I was so tired and so . . . oh, I do not know what it was that led me to refuse several invitations from Eugene, who wanted me to go out with him. I was sorry to disappoint him, but I felt a certain need to be alone, and I went to see the statue of Cloramide at the museum, while waiting to join Dinaïse and Corilla on the horseback ride that they had proposed. The long-awaited hour having finally arrived, I raced to Corilla's home, where Dinaïse and her brother soon appeared, and ten or twelve of us mounted our steeds. The weather was brilliant. I felt an indescribable joy upon being, for the first time in many months, on a steed that seemed impatient at being reined in, and I felt sure that I would freely admire everything surrounding me. The graded, watered-down route through a green prairie, filled with pretty cavalcades, was charming. Some groups were walking their horses, some trotting or galloping, while some young men were amusing their companions by executing all sorts of extraordinary equestrian turns. It was delightful for me to be reminded of one of my rides at Hyde Park, where I rode between a young duchess and a charming marchioness. I admired a young female Icarian who had just been at the workshop and who now, on horseback, could compete in elegance and skill with the most brilliant female member of our beautiful English aristocracy.

I could not keep from admiring the aplomb, the ease, and the gracefulness of these Amazons, who were almost all quite pretty. Above all, I could not take my eyes off my two companions, each in turn, and I felt almost as much pride as I did pleasure in finding myself placed between those young women who seemed more beautiful than all the other beauties. I was a trifle anxious when Corilla proposed that we break into a full gallop and talked us into it despite Dinaïse's misgivings, she being less daring and on a more spirited horse. I even felt a few moments of fear, which made me move my hand toward her horse's bridle, but I soon saw that she was not afraid, and I let myself feel the pleasure of flying, so to speak, between two charming Amazons, or, rather, between two angels. I was drunk with it! But the ride ended, and when I was alone again, I felt ill at ease, empty, agitated in a way I had never experienced before.

29   Milord Loves Dinaïse; The Story of Lixdox, Cloramide, and Icar

I was still in bed when Eugene came in, looking serious.

"Ah, well, I've had enough of this. Tell us frankly, what is wrong with you?"

"Nothing," I replied, amazed.

"Nothing? That is impossible. I do not know how you are acting outside, but for quite a while you have seemed like a stranger to me. You have changed: you avoid me and refuse my invitations. It appears that my presence and my friendship bother you. Speak. What have I done to you?"

"But I do not understand, my dear Eugene, for I love you more every day."

"Perhaps. But you are sad, even dour. You seem to have your cursed spleen. Does it upset you to be away from your England? Are you homesick?"

"But you are wrong, I assure you."

"For the last few days, you have been impatient, agitated. You cannot stay in one place. As soon as you go out, you return. As soon as you have returned, you go out again. You seem to be unaware of it, but your mood and your personality have changed. You no longer seem so sweet, so good, so accepting of others; and your poor valet, John, who loves you so much, has suffered more than once from your agitation."

"What are you saying? You are upsetting me!"

"You no longer sleep, you hardly eat, you are getting thinner. There is something at the root of this, I am sure. And you will not even confide your troubles to your friend!"

"But you are mistaken, Eugene. There is nothing wrong with me."

"There is something wrong, something seriously wrong, I am sure. Have you received some bad news from England? Have you learned of some major monetary loss? Has Miss Henriet been unfaithful to you?"

"I have received no upsetting news."

"No one has offended you?"

"Certainly not."

"Well, my dear man, you must be lovesick. Now I may rest easy. You will be leaving soon, and the sight of Miss Henriet will soon cure you without the need of medicine."

"You are really a skillful doctor if you think it is Miss Henriet who is making me ill!"

"Then it is not Miss Henriet!" he cried. "Oh, unfortunate man, it is an Icarian woman whom you love. It is Miss Corilla . . . or Miss Dinaïse!"

"Hold your tongue!" I told him. "You are mad!"

"Yes, one of us is mad, but it is not me; or, if I am mad, then I am only mad about Icaria and its community, which nothing prevents me from worshipping with all the strength of my soul. But you, poor William! Oh, I suspected something of the sort when I saw you expose yourself so often to two fires! I did not dare look at either one or the other, for fear of being burned by both. But an Englishman is much more courageous. Ah! I am no longer surprised that yesterday, during the horseback ride, you did not notice me when I waved to you. You were unable to see anyone, dazzled as you were between two shining suns! Poor William, poor William, how I pity you!"

It was no use denying it. Eugene persisted in his opinion, without being able to pin it down to Corilla or Dinaïse. I had tried in vain to fool myself. I could no longer pretend, either to myself or others, that the passion that had been ignited in my breast was not real. It is true that images of Miss Henriet and Corilla were almost always joined in my dreams to those of Dinaïse, but certain differences left me in no doubt as to the true state of my heart. Nothing in my life was comparable either to the trembling that Dinaïse's voice always made me feel or to the discomfort I felt in her presence, the pleasure I had felt when I was near her these last few days, or the sadness I had not been able to dispel after leaving her. It became clear to me at this point that I had loved her for a long time without being aware of it, and that Corilla's beauty and warmth had been but a momentary diversion that had confused me. I felt that my passion, weak and undisclosed at first, had become too devouring to remain hidden, and I saw with terror the abyss into which I was blindly throwing myself. I soon resolved to find my salvation in flight and to leave Icaria immediately.

"But," I said to myself, "what if she loves me? The other day, when I was in her brother's office, she came in and fled immediately, pale and trembling, as if she had not been aware that I was there . . . yet she knew that I was! Why this pretext, this curiosity, this uneasiness? But what madness! Her coldness toward me, her embarrassment, her resolution not to marry, her refusal to marry Valmor. But . . . it has been only since my arrival that she has rejected Valmor's wishes . . . and if, perchance. . . !"

I spent the whole day in a state of the most violent agitation, trying to make sense of my recollections, unable to determine her feelings for me, and yet pausing from time to time at the delightful thought that I might find favor in her eyes. But the thought of the torment Valmor would feel if he knew I was the loved one, the suspicions he would have about my loyalty, and the charges Corilla and her family could bring against me caused my indecision to cease; and, tormented by a burning fever, my brow covered with sweat, I swore to flee Dinaïse forever. However, because I had promised to spend the evening at Corilla's, whose grandfather wanted to tell me about the history of Icar, I thought it would be acceptable for me to go there one more time with Eugene.

Imagine my surprise and my torment when I saw Mrs. Dinamé, whom Corilla had gone to fetch, and Dinaïse, more attractive than ever! What torture when I saw her draw near me and say to me in an indefinable voice, "You are pale, Mr. William. You seem to be suffering. What is wrong?" What torture it was to feel Eugene's eyes almost always on me, although he looked away as soon as I turned toward him. And what further torture it was to see her go up to Valmor and speak to him in an unusually affectionate manner. Being jealous was all I needed!

"Well," said the grandfather a little later. "Because Milord has been so interested in the portraits of Icar, Cloramide, and Lixdox, we must tell him their story. Will you begin, my dear Corilla?" Corilla began to tell the story of Cloramide and Lixdox. Afterward, she forced Dinaïse to tell that of Icar. What grace, what charm, what a voice! And I was obliged to control myself, to let nothing show of the thousand feelings that shook and overwhelmed my soul! And I was going to flee from her forever! No, no one will ever understand my pleasure and my torment! I was too upset at the time to remember the stories told by Corilla and Dinaïse. Here is Eugene's summary, although he himself was quite distracted.

The Story of Lixdox and Cloramide

"After the expulsion of the old tyrant Corug, in 1772, the Icarians chose, or rather received, as queen the young and beautiful Cloramide, who was presented to them or imposed upon them by Lixdox, the head of one of the aristocratic parties. Brother of the dethroned king, immensely rich and powerful, little, ugly, one-eyed and hunchbacked, devoured by ambition, full of wit, education, eloquence, skill, and even genius, Lixdox had been working for a long time to supplant his brother and master. Secretly supported by a part of the aristocracy, as treacherous and deceitful as he was ambitious and tyrannical, he made full use of every ruse and base deed to trick the Court and the people and to make himself popular.

"While shedding hypocritical tears about the faults and misfortunes of his brother the king, he quietly incited his partisans, or, rather, his accomplices, to have the king condemned and beheaded. He had his sister-in-law the queen secretly assassinated and all their children poisoned, with the exception of the youngest son, whom faithful servants succeeded in taking to the court of a neighboring king. Lixdox could have ascended to the throne easily. His many partisans among the nobility and the people were calling on him to do so with great cries, but he felt it would be safer and easier to reign under another's name; so, still pretending to be completely disinterested, he proposed the election of a queen, his choice being the countess Cloramide, who came from one of the most noble of families.

"Cloramide, barely twenty years of age, was, perhaps, the most beautiful woman in the country, as you have seen from her portrait that hangs in our History Museum. Never had a queen been more deserving of being called divine. She was praised unceasingly for her goodness of character, her fine qualities and virtues, as well as for her perfect appearance. Widow of one of the most celebrated generals, with whom she had three charming young children, a daughter and two sons, she was reputed to be the best of all possible wives and mothers. Unassuming yet magnificent, magnanimous yet noble, she had all the qualities necessary to seduce and captivate the nobility and the bourgeoisie, rich and poor alike. She was the one most capable of seducing the public, and for this very reason the skillful Lixdox had chosen her.

"As for Lixdox himself, because he had only one child, whom he was educating on his own, he pretended to aspire to no more than the sweetness of private life. Not only did his partisans never stop praising his virtues as husband and father, his talents and great abilities, but innumerable deputations and documents arrived every day pressuring and entreating him to be the counselor, guide, and prime minister to the queen. These praises and supplications were secretly purchased and directed by none other than Lixdox himself; but to hide more completely his ambition and to trick the credulous, he resisted for a long time, feigning poor health. He even pretended to be ill for a fortnight, and when he finally accepted, he declared that he was sacrificing himself for the good of his country in order to give in to the general will. As he had absolute power over Cloramide, he was the one who governed. The queen, whom he probably planned to get rid of later, was but an instrument of Lixdox's rule.

"For a time, the queen and her prime minister, using all means at hand to gain popularity, managed, in fact, to retain the public's approbation. But when Lixdox—supported by the rich and by a powerful neighboring king, who garrisoned three hundred thousand soldiers on the frontier—thought he was powerful enough to end the charade, he stopped hiding his aristocratic and despotic plans and spoke only of intimidation and terror. For a short while after that, the queen, whose beauty and apparent goodness he was still exploiting skillfully, served as his mantle, his shield, and his lightning conductor. In the end, his tyranny became so violent and bloody, and the queen herself, corrupted by him, became so despicable and odious that popular execration broke out in conspiracies, assassination attempts, and insurrections until, in 1782, the people finally had the good fortune to crush their tyrants. After the battle, two of the ministers were massacred by the people in fury; the other four ministers, who were fleeing disguised as valets and women, were triumphantly brought back. Cloramide was arrested by her own guards in her palace, and Lixdox, searched for everywhere, was found disguised in the rags of a scullion. Those who had condemned so many innocent people were judged in turn. What a transformation! The adored queen, the insolent and cruel Lixdox, the pitiless ministers—all were brought to their knees before the representatives of this same people they had called subject!

"You may want to read those tragic proceedings, which tore a thousand cries of horror from the audience when they heard the declaration: 'On the 13th of June, when he received the false report that he was victorious, Lixdox, reclining nonchalantly on golden cushions and smoking the most delicious Arabian tobacco, took his sultan's pipe out of his mouth to pronounce coldly these abominable words: "Let Icar and the ten other revolutionary chiefs be brought under my balcony so that I may see them torn apart by my horses."

"The Popular Assembly unanimously declared Lixdox and his minions to be perjurers, traitors, usurpers, thieves, and national assassins. However, considering the queen to have been manipulated and Lixdox as the true king who had pulled all the others along with him, the Assembly sentenced Lixdox and the other ministers to death, and the queen to life imprisonment. The Assembly ordered Lixdox to be brought to his execution barefoot, in his shift, his face covered by a black veil. He would witness the execution of his accomplices, after which he would have his hand severed and his head cut off. The president of the republic was given the power to commute the sentence. After that, the Assembly ordered all the villains as a group to pay a billion écus in indemnity to the people, thus providing a salutary example by dooming to mendicancy the children of those who had not feared to reduce millions of widows and orphans to beggary.

"Following Icar's proposal, the people commuted the death penalty. Abandoned by their former flatterers, in total ignorance of all that was happening outside their cells, Lixdox and his accomplices were led to the place of execution in the midst of a huge crowd whose majestic silence froze with astonishment those among the condemned who had not been paralyzed by fear. When they all were placed together on the scaffold, their sentence was read to them and then its commutation. Lixdox had his head shaven at the hands of the executioner and was exposed to public view in an iron cage. I will not tell you the curses heaped upon him by women demanding of him their children or husbands. Those who hurled the most mud and curses were precisely those poverty-stricken people he had drawn into his party by tricking them, and the shopkeepers who, as a result of his calumny, had acted in the most enraged and cruel manner toward their brothers. The other ministers were imprisoned for life, and Cloramide was given her freedom after a month of begging at the door of the National Assembly. This was the end of the wicked Lixdox and the unfortunate Cloramide, a striking example of the calamities that injustice and ambition bring down upon the heads of the people's oppressors! Now you will see how different was the fate of the good Icar."

The Story of Icar

"Love of humanity was Icar's ruling passion. From earliest childhood, he could not see another child without running to caress him, kiss him, and share with him the little that he had. In his youth, he could not see an unfortunate soul without personally suffering the man's misery and without consoling him. He was often seen to give his own bread to the poor person that he met along the way. On one particular day, finding a young man almost naked and dying of the cold on the pavement, he gave him his own clothing that he had had for only two days. He returned to his father's home, overcome with joy, but almost naked. The father, who was poor and a brute, furious that his son had lost the winter clothing he had gone to such pains to acquire, whipped the child until he drew blood. On another occasion, at a fire that daunted the bravest of onlookers, people were terrified to see Icar throw himself into the flames and, clothing afire and right hand badly burned, emerge with a child in his arms.

"Son of a miserable carter, carter himself for many years, he had experienced all the miseries of the worker and the poor. An impassioned reader, he devoted to his reading all the time that children and workers of his own age spent at their games. As soon as he had begun to read a book, he had to read it to the end. He read while walking, on the highways and byways, even during his meals and throughout the night, despite his father's prohibitions and anger. Philosophy books were his favorites. He devoured them like young girls devour romantic novels. Everything fired his imagination and led to useful conclusions, which remained engraved in his mind. The first words of the Christian prayer 'Our Father' began to convince him that all men are brothers and equals, that all should form a single family, and that all should love each other and help each other as brothers. An unexpected inheritance suddenly made the laziest and most wicked of his neighbors pass from the depths of poverty to opulence; at the same time, lightning reduced to poverty the richest, most hardworking, and most charitable of his neighbors. These events gave Icar his first glimpse into the viciousness of a social organization in which fortune or poverty depend on a whim of fate. It was while examining a stonemason at work and while reflecting on the steps taken by an architect to prepare the construction of a house that Icar understood for the first time how an entire country could be administered effectively. It was, finally, while leading his cart through a vast monastery that he first realized that all the inhabitants of a country could work and live in community.

"I will not go into the details of the strange twist of fate that led him to become a priest, having realized that there was no finer aim in life than to dedicate oneself to the salvation of one's fellow men. Nor will I tell you how he was brought from his province to the capital. His education, his tender soul, his warm heart, and his ardent imagination soon made him a famous preacher. Filled with pain and overcome with indignation at the horrifying poverty of the workers whose hovels he visited, he attacked, from the height of the preacher's pulpit, the vices of the social order, the insensitivity of the rich, and the degeneracy of the Christians. He invoked unceasingly the name and words of Jesus Christ in favor of equality, of fraternity, and even of communal ownership of property. His eloquence made such an impression that his superiors forbade him to preach and condemned him to inaction and silence. He left the church and published several pieces against its abuses; his writings drew new persecutions from the government. He was exposed to public view on a scaffold, like a thief, because he had said that Jesus Christ was the most daring propagandist and revolutionary ever to appear on the earth. Far from humiliating him or cooling his zeal, this outrage merely increased his enthusiasm.

"After studying in depth the problem of social organization, examining all ancient and modern, foreign and national philosophical systems; after meditating on the doctrine of Jesus Christ and on the thousands of religious communities based on that doctrine; after drawing up the outline of a new political and social organization based on the principle of perfect equality and communal ownership of goods, he became convinced not only that this new organization was the only one that could lead to human happiness on this earth, but that this same organization was not impracticable.

"A pamphlet he had published that favored community led to his being arrested once more and almost cost him his life. Like the early Christians, he was accused of conspiring and of advocating regicide and civil war. Like them, he was called an anarchist, a drinker of blood, and an enemy of the people and of humanity. However, he was given a choice of death or his freedom if he retracted his statements. He replied that he preferred to die, like Socrates and Jesus Christ (and like Thomas More, the English chancellor), rather than deny a truth that would one day conquer the world. Half of the judges found him guilty, and the others acquitted him, although declaring his doctrines to be senseless.

"Having acquired unexpectedly an immense fortune left to him by an uncle who had just died in the East Indies, he vowed, in a fit of saintly enthusiasm, to dedicate his fortune and his life to the regeneration of his country. His exaltation was even greater because he felt that the rebirth of his country would bring about the regeneration of the whole of humanity. From this moment onward, he became a revolutionary and propagandist like Jesus Christ, ready to devote himself, like Jesus, to the happiness of men, and ready as well to fulfill a secondary role if he could find a man who, by his name or his genius, could play the main part of rallying the masses and causing the reform to triumph.

"In addition, from that moment onward, Icar surrounded himself with educated, charitable persons who aided him in his writing and his works. Icar directed them, in particular, to research and bring together all the ancient and modern, foreign and national judgments for or against community in order to present to the people not only his own views but the whole of human thought on this issue, the single most important issue for the happiness of humanity. His hopes were fulfilled when he discovered, on the list of favorable judgments, the greatest names in the history of legislation and philosophy.

"Finally, from that moment onward, he left no stone unturned in an effort to increase his already great popularity. I will not go into detail about his methods, but within a few years his frugality—unchanged despite his recent and sudden opulence—the simplicity of his clothing and manners, his affability, the renown of his great fortune, the use he made of it, devoting it entirely to the popular cause, his indubitable love for the people, his battles against tyranny, his courage and skill: all of these attributes won him the confidence and affection of the people to such an extent that he became the recognized head of the party of reform and revolution. He had enough influence to prevent individual attacks and premature, imprudent attempts; but when an act of manifest tyranny seemed to him to provide a suitable opportunity, he was the one who gave the signal to begin the insurrection, inflaming by his example as well as by his proclamations the courage and patriotic devotion of a people in revolt. After a relentless, bloody battle that lasted two days, the 13th and 14th of June 1782, the people were victorious, and the brave Icar, slightly wounded, was proclaimed dictator by popular acclamation.

"Now with the power in his hands, and with no other plan than that of bringing about the happiness of his country, he did everything to win universal trust even more completely in order to stop the massacres, to reestablish order, and to organize the people into a single body, in order to assure the triumph of the revolution without and within, and to accomplish, finally, his great project of radical reform and regeneration. It was he, the dictator, who proposed to his fellow citizens social equality and justice, the communal ownership of goods, and the democratic republic, with a temporary organizational plan that would be in force for fifty years. After a terrible war against a coalition of all the neighboring kings, after horrifying reverses followed by a decisive victory, after the general peace enacted in a People's Congress, all his projects were adopted with enthusiasm, and the immense work necessary for the bringing to fruition of community was begun in all parts of the country.

"Many provinces and communes already had a communal regime, and more than three million poor people were enjoying the benefits of the new organization when, on the 7th of January 1798, in the sixteenth year in the era of our regeneration, after having seen that his great work would certainly be accomplished, the best and the most benevolent of men ever to be honored by humanity died at the age of fifty-nine. Never did a man receive more unanimous praise during his life and after his death. A simple magistrate of his village after having been dictator, a plain citizen (for he had wanted to serve as an example of goodness in all social situations), he could not leave his home without being greeted by public acclamation and without receiving with each step the most touching demonstrations of love and respect. He himself often said that he was the happiest of mortals.

"At the news of the fatal event, all citizens, without exception, spontaneously stopped their work or recreation and went into mourning. Never were so many tears shed at the death of a king. The National Assembly decided that his body would be brought to the capital. His funeral rites would be celebrated that very day in all the communes of the republic. The republic would be in mourning for a year. Every year the people would celebrate his birthday. A statue of him would be erected in the main square of every city. Finally, a bust of him would be placed in all national buildings and his portrait in all homes. Thus, he who always opposed the public display of his effigy is the man whose image has been the most multiplied and venerated after his death. Up to that point, the two-day anniversary had been marked by only two celebrations: the festival of martyrs and that of victory. Now the National Assembly decided that a third festival would be added, one that Icar had always opposed: a commemoration of his dictatorship. The Assembly even decreed that the nation would give up its name to take on that of Icar; that the country would henceforth be called ICARIA, the people ICARIAN, the capital ICARA, and its inhabitants Icarians.

"Many people thought that Icar was a second Jesus Christ and wanted him to be worshipped like a god, invoking, to prove his divinity, the same proofs brought forth more than eighteen hundred years earlier by the first worshippers of Christ. But Icar had never put himself forth as a god, and his admirers were content to venerate his memory as a genius, a benefactor of humanity."

30 Theaters

Are you mad, waking me up so early?" said Eugene, rubbing his eyes. "I was sleeping so well. Because love keeps you from sleeping, must you trouble the sleep of those who do not have the good fortune to be in love? Poor William, as I told you already, you are madly in love! And you are foolish in thinking that you have enough skill to fool all of us. You are mad to love an Icarian, whom no foreigner is allowed to marry. There is no point in denying it: you love Dinaïse. Yes, it is Dinaïse whom you were pretending not to look at last night, not Corilla, upon whom you pretended to train your eyes."

"But I am leaving," I told him. "I am fleeing from all Icarian women. I am fleeing from Corilla and Dinaïse."

"You are leaving! Bravo, William. It will make me very sad, but I will rejoice for you, my dear friend, for there are enemies that one can conquer only by fleeing from them and dangers that wisdom counsels us to avoid rather than to confront stubbornly; and if you take with you the arrow that pierced you, at least no new arrows will come to make the wound incurable and mortal."

I accepted his offer to accompany me to the frontier, and we agreed to leave Icara in two or three days. Although I wanted to leave without saying farewell to anyone, and without even seeing either Corilla or Valmor again, I could not bear to be alone, so I yielded to Eugene, who had been pressuring me for a long time to accompany him to the theater, which he had promised to attend with a family he knew. Eugene's friend, Almaes, seemed to me a charming young man, and his sisters were very pretty young women. The hall was full, and the play generated universal interest, but how lonely I was in the crowd! How long the performance seemed to me! How ill at ease I was in the midst of all those faces glowing with happiness! I could not take part even in the conversation between Almaes and Eugene on the theaters of Icaria. No matter how interesting that conversation may have been, I could not possibly tell about it had I not the possibility of borrowing Eugene's journal in order to transcribe it here.

Extract from Eugene's Journal

THEATERS

"Tell me," said Eugene to Almaes, "how you organize your shows, considering that, on the one hand, nothing is sold, and on the other hand, all citizens have the same rights?"

"Have you not guessed?" replied Almaes. "Come now, you can work it out for yourself. What would you do? Let us see!"

"Well," said Eugene, "the whole population of Icara, including the provincials and the foreigners who are there, must be able to see the same show without paying?"

"Yes, without a doubt."

"It follows also that each citizen must be assured of getting a seat as soon as he comes in, without being obliged to wait at the door?"

"Certainly."

"Well then, how many inhabitants and travelers might want to see the show?"

"Approximately nine hundred thousand."

"How many spectators can the hall hold?"

"Approximately fifteen thousand."

"Then a play must have sixty performances so that every one may see it?"

"Yes, more or less."

"I assume you know the number of families in Icara and the number of people in each of them?"

"Yes, exactly."

"And therefore, you know how many families have thirty members, how many twenty-five, twenty, and so forth?"

"Yes, without the slightest error."

"Therefore, the theater administration can fill each performance with a certain number of families of thirty, twenty-five, twenty, and so forth, and a certain number of provincials and foreigners?"

"Yes, very easily."

"Well then, the rest is also easy. Family and individual tickets can be made for each performance and distributed by lot. Every family and every separate individual will have tickets, and each person will know in advance which performance he or she may attend."

"Very good, that's it! However, what if the date of my performance were inconvenient for me?"

"You would then look at the table of ticket distribution and find a person or family that would like to exchange tickets with you."

"Exactly, you have guessed it."

"We do the same," said Almaes, "for all our theaters and plays. We follow the same procedure for all public curiosities, for museums and scientific courses, and even for the sessions of the National Assembly. We have the same system for horseback riding. Each family can enjoy it only every ten days because we have only enough saddle horses for a tenth of the population. As you can see, nothing is easier than the distribution of life's pleasures, which, like food, are given out equally and free of charge."

"But," said Eugene, "as each family sees only one performance in sixty, the people must go a long time without attending the theater, mustn't they?"

"That is true for a show they have already seen," replied Almaes, "but families can enjoy museums, scientific courses, walks, social evenings, and even some other type of show. Let us see. What would you do if you were the republic and you wished to give the people the pleasure of attending shows as often as possible?"

"I would set up," said Eugene, "shows of all sorts: tragedy, drama, comedy, opera, dance, song, music, and equitation."

"Well, that is precisely what we have done. We have forty or fifty theaters of the same size for all imaginable varieties of show. The family that likes attending shows can enjoy this pleasurable activity almost every day because you can find shows even in the open air and on all the promenades. You have certainly seen in no other nation as many marionette theaters, pantomimes, and above all Punch and Judy shows that delight children. You will never see such lovely entertainments elsewhere because here the republic directs them and spares no expense to make them charming in every way. Nor will you see elsewhere so many *wonderful plays*, as we call them, where physics, electricity, light, chemistry, astronomy, and conjurers of all sorts produce more wonders than have ever been seen before."

Fifteen of us left in an omnibus (because the public vehicle service is so perfectly organized that special omnibuses are designated in each neighborhood to take and bring back the families that go to the theater), and we got out further along, under the covered portico. The entrances, the stairs, the corridors: everything seemed wide, convenient, and magnificent, and set up purposely to prevent accidents.

"What an immense hall," said Eugene upon entering it. "I have never seen such a gigantic hall in any other country!"

"All of our theaters are built to hold the greatest possible number of spectators," replied Almaes. "Our architects had at their disposal the scale drawings of all the theaters in the world."

"And are the acoustics good?"

"Judge for yourself. You will not miss a single word because accurate transmission of sounds is the first priority for an auditorium, and that is the first objective of our builders."

"Are all your other theaters without boxes, like this one?"

"Yes, all of them. The box is essentially an aristocratic and privileged item, and we are democrats who cannot bear even the shadow of privilege. The box takes up a great deal of space, and we want all the space available for the citizens. The box is a firetrap, and everything in our theaters is set up to avoid fires. Do you not like these semicircular benches raised one above the other to form an amphitheater?"

"I certainly do! We are seated very comfortably, and we can see the audience as well as the theater itself. This mixed audience, these beautiful outfits, these decorations: everything is magnificent. The opera houses in London and Paris are no more beautiful than this one!"

"Well, all of our theaters are as vast as this one, and if you could visit them all at this hour, you would find that they are all filled with such an audience. Our children's theaters, which are almost as big as this one, might appear even more beautiful to you than this one."

The curtain soon rose. Tomorrow I will try to summarize the play; I will only say a word about it today. The subject is an historical one. It is the famous Gunpowder Plot against Lixdox in 1777, and the famous trial of Kalar, who, although innocent, was found guilty of being the instigator and leader of the plot. The partisans of the young pretender Corug are incited to conspire by Lixdox through his agent, a devoted courtier who betrays them. Lixdox, however, wants to save the true conspirators, who are aristocrats, and arranges to compromise Kalar, a well-known democrat, and to have him found guilty. We see the meeting between Lixdox and the courtier, the planning of the plot, a count pledging to carry it out, the count's attempt, his arrest, his interrogation in prison, the maneuvers used to convince him to accuse Kalar, his assumption of the false identity of a charcoal burner, Kalar's interrogation in his cell, his refusal to answer questions, and his courage.

"How well this actor plays the role of Kalar!" Eugene said to Almaes when the curtain had fallen at the end of the first act. "How well he speaks his 'I wish to say nothing,' which he repeats twenty times and which always sounds fresh! What beautiful stances! What grand gestures! Even his silence is eloquent! Moreover, all the roles are well acted, and the overall effect is perfect."

"But you cannot judge the actors by these roles, for they are too easy," replied Almaes. "We have excellent actors, and that is easy to understand because they undertake this profession only out of a natural inclination, and, for a long time, they receive the training most capable of developing their talent. All of our actors and actresses have distinguished themselves by their literary and dramatic training. As they all are fed and clothed by the republic, they are in no hurry to make their debut and may do so only after an examination has declared them fit."

"Actors are a class of people held in low esteem in my country, and they are usually worthy of little esteem."

"That is probably your fault, for here, where dramatic art is a national profession like medicine, where the actor is brought up, nourished, and treated like any other citizen, he is neither more nor less respected than any other person. No woman in our country would ever think that an actress, a dancer, or a singer might not be as good a wife, a mother, or a daughter as she herself. In addition, you can see how respectfully the public behaves! Talent is applauded, but silence is the only reaction permitted in the face of imperfection."

The second act portrayed the trial and the sentence. We saw the court of lords and the debates; we saw the false charcoal burner, the provost marshal, the high-court judge, the lords, and a gatekeeper, who was a false witness, joining against Kalar, who defended himself energetically. The heroism of a young girl who refused to bear false witness produced tragic scenes. The despair of the wife and daughter of Kalar produced a heartrending scene; and Kalar's devotion had a quality of the sublime that electrified all the spectators.

The curtain had scarcely fallen before the names of the actors appeared in order on magnificent transparencies. Those who had just played Kalar, the false charcoal burner, and the two young girls were greeted with unanimous applause. The other actors received more or less applause or were greeted with silence. Then, on other transparencies, the names of the characters in the historical drama appeared. Those of Kalar and of the gatekeeper's daughter brought forth an acclamation and enthusiasm of which I did not think the happy Icarians capable. The names of Lixdox, the treacherous courtier, the false charcoal burner/count, the provost marshal, the high-court judge, the court, and the gatekeeper brought forth boos, whistles, and curses that created for a few minutes a new and quite unusual spectacle.

"This play," said Eugene to Almaes as they were going out, "has little worth as a dramatic composition. The author seems to have done no more than dramatize a historical event, but I can understand the interest and enthusiasm that this drama inspires within you; and if you have many plays in this genre, I can understand the moral and patriotic usefulness of your theater."

"This drama," Almaes replied, "was written shortly after the revolution. I believe it was put on for the first time in 1784. Since then, it has been performed only every eight or ten years, but we have many other plays in the same genre. One in particular arouses even more excitement. Its subject is the trial of our last tyrant, Lixdox, in 1782. I have not seen it yet, but it is said that nothing is more splendid than our most celebrated actor when he reveals, one by one, all the indictments against tyranny. The last act shows the tyrant exposed in an iron cage in the public square. It is said that nothing is more dramatic than the curses of the people against the guilty one.

"Moreover," Almaes continued, "our theater is infinite in its variety. We have plays in every genre, including jolly, comic, burlesque ones, but all our plays have a moral, patriotic purpose. There is not a single play that would be inappropriate for children and girls. The theater is a school where the teachers are the fine arts themselves, charged with joining all their talents together to instruct while they amuse. You will not be surprised to learn that we have discarded almost all our old plays, and that new plays must be commissioned or approved by the republic. They are written by authors inspired only by patriotism and genius, and supported by the most perfect education."

"Well, amidst all these perfections," said Eugene, "do you know which pleases me the most?"

"No."

"It is the thought that the audience, so decent and dignified, is not an assembly of the elite, but is made up of citizens picked at random: in a word, the people."

"And what is so admirable about that?"

"In England, as in France, in almost all theaters, you hear yells, whistles, an appalling cacophony, even while the actors are in the middle of a scene; and quarrels, even fights, are common."

"Well, I will say once more that the fault is yours. We used to be as rowdy and mad as your people, and your people could be as wise and calm as we are today."

"Ha! I am only too aware of that," Eugene replied, sighing. "Our deadly social organization engenders only vice, disorder, and poverty, whereas your benevolent community engenders only perfection, virtue, and happiness!"

31 Historical Drama
The Gunpowder Plot and the Trial and Sentencing of an Innocent Man

If I set aside a place here for the analysis of a historical drama, it is not in order to hold it up as an exemplary literary work. My single purpose is to give you an idea of the morality of the Icarian theater, which is dedicated above all to reminding the people of the vices of the old system of social and political organization, and to demonstrating their mortal but inevitable consequences, particularly in the matter of justice. Here is the synopsis:

Act I

SCENE I

A small room almost entirely dark. You cannot make out the two characters whose voices you hear, but you know that they are Lixdox and the Duke of Coron, his favorite.

Terrified by the conspiracies and attempts on his life being plotted every day, either by nobles who have remained faithful to the cause of the exiled young pretender (the son of Corug) or by the foremost democrats who are devoted to the public good, Lixdox searched for the means of spreading terror among his enemies. After consulting all the Machiavellian traditions carefully gathered for centuries and compiled in a large book, Lixdox conceived the plot of setting up a horrible conspiracy, to which he would try to attract the most dangerous nobles and through which he would compromise the most formidable leaders of the people. Once his plot had been set up, he needed a trusted friend, a second self, to carry it out. He chose the Duke of Coron. The duke fabricates insults and a break with Lixdox; he feigns anger and a desire for vengeance. Setting himself up as the leader of the hostile nobles, he pets, incites, pushes, and provokes them, while visiting Lixdox almost every day to report his successes. Everything is going according to plan. Twelve of the foremost nobles, each of whom has decided to conspire, are supposed to meet that very night at the duke's table.

"What a role you are making me play!" says the duke to Lixdox. "Provocation, perjury, treason, informing, infamy!"

"You are saving the state, the throne, religion, and your friend. My gratitude will be without limits. You and I alone will know the truth. Fortune and glory await you!"

SCENE 2

The curtain rises on a superb banquet hall in the duke's chateau, where twelve other nobles, seated at the table, are speaking passionately about the prime minister.

"Yes" says the duke. "After all I have done for him, he refuses my request that my daughter become chambermaid to the royal princess! He is an insolent traitor whose ingratitude and affronts I will never forgive!"

"He is a hypocrite, a liar, and a traitor!" says a marquis.

"He is an impious man who aims to proclaim himself God!" says a prelate. "He is the Antichrist, perhaps Satan!" says another priest. "He had my son killed!" says a weeping baron. "The scoundrel stole my mistress from me!" says the Count of Gigas angrily. "He killed his son and his king! He had the queen and his nephews imprisoned!" says another.

The duke: "He is despised, hated, detested!"

The count: "If he were burned to death, no one would mourn him, for no man has fewer friends and more enemies!"

The duke: "No man has been the object of so many conspiracies and assassination attempts!"

The count: "Those who fail are mourned as martyrs!"

The duke: "He who succeeded would be hailed as a liberator, but there are only victims!"

The count: "The conspirators have all been fools. There is one certain means of success!"

All: "What is that?"

The count: "You know that a charcoal burner lives in a cellar under the queen's palace. Well, twenty barrels of powder in that cave, and a brave soul who sets a fire on the day of a royal audience. The queen and her children, the tyrant, his accomplices, and their followers: all of them would be eliminated with a single blow!"

The duke: "Yes, but where is that brave man?"

The count: "He is here!"

The duke: "Who is he?"

The count: "Me!"

All: "Down with tyranny! Glory to the liberator!"

However, several of the men have doubts. They are afraid that the aristocracy will be dishonored, but the count and, above all, the duke, remind them quickly of all the examples of conspiracies, poisonings, and regicides committed not only by nobles and bishops, but by princes of royal families, sons of kings against their fathers, kings and emperors or popes against other sovereigns or other popes; and the assassination attempt is decided upon. The count will disguise himself as a charcoal burner. He will take over the cellar of the charcoal burner who is currently living there. He will bring twenty barrels of powder there and will hide them under a pile of wood. He himself will set fire to a wick that will leave him time to escape before the explosion. The others will prepare everything for the restoration of the Pretender. It is the perfidious duke who proposes that the conspirators make an inviolable pledge to each other. All swear devotion and fidelity, carried away by passionate eagerness.

SCENE 3

It is the duke's room, dimly lit by a lamp. He has just dismissed the conspirators and is about to go to the palace, where Lixdox is waiting to hear what has taken place. But what should he do? What is in his best interest? Should he betray those who have sworn allegiance? Or should he betray Lixdox? He meditates upon these questions for a time, while pacing the floor of his room, and goes out without having made a decision.

SCENE 4

The cellar. You can hear the noise of the courtiers' carriages, and then the ringing of the chapel bells. A charcoal burner arrives. It is the count. The twenty barrels of gunpowder are there, under the pile of wood. The royal audience is about to begin. The sounds of trumpets and fanfares announce the appearance of the queen and Lixdox in the midst of the nobles. The count lifts up a stick concealing one of the ends of the wick. He will have five minutes to get away through a back door. All of a sudden the trumpet sounds. He trembles. He rejoices in the fact that he will be sending to kingdom come a usurped throne, a usurping queen, a tyrant, a court, an entire monarchy. The fire burns in his hand. With his other hand, he seizes the wick. It bursts into flames. But now terrifying yells come from under the pile of wood. A large group of soldiers emerge and fall upon him. Five or six fall dead at his feet. He races with lightning speed to the staircase and is about to disappear, but other guards come down and bar his passage. He strikes out once more, causing some to fall, and falls down in turn, bathed in his own blood. Soldiers take the dying man away; others are horrified to discover the volcano that was designed to make the earth tremble. And then one of the guards notices that the wick was tampered with and cut through the middle!

SCENE 5

A dark, dirty cell, a little straw, an unfortunate man in a shift uttering sharp cries forced out of him by pain. It is the count once more! The judges, guards, and courtiers who surround him hurl curses at him. But he sees nothing, hears nothing, and answers not a word. They want him to remain alive in order to name his accomplices and to perish on the scaffold. Physicians and surgeons rush around him, operate on him, tend his wounds, and make him drink a liqueur. He is revived, he breathes, he looks around him and seems to hear and see.

"Your name?" the Grand Inquisitor asks him. "Miguf," replies the unfortunate one in a scarcely audible voice.

"Your occupation?"

"Charcoal burner."

"Your country?"

"Pirma, in Cassie, three hundred leagues from here."

"Was your plan to kill the queen?"

"No, to kill the tyrant."

"What harm did His Excellency do to you?"

"He is oppressing the people."

"What was your purpose?"

"To save the country and to serve humanity."

"Scoundrel!" someone said. "Monster!" said another.

"Who are your accomplices?"

"Everyone, a hundred, none."

Insults, curses, threats: nothing can shake his resolve. He has no accomplices, and he demands the death sentence as the beginning of his immortality.

SCENE 6

We are in another cell. We can see another wounded prisoner. It is the duke! Lixdox and he agreed that he would be arrested in order to allay all suspicion. He would kill one of the men charged with arresting him, he would inflict upon himself a light wound, and the rumor would be spread that he had been gravely wounded in the fight. A few days later, they would declare that a mistake had been made, that the dead soldier had used illicit violence, and that the duke had merely exercised his legitimate right of defense. They had agreed that the list of the conspirators would be placed at one of their homes so that the police could find it. All measures were taken to ensure that Kalar, one of the leaders of the Democratic Party, would be gravely compromised by some supposed revelations.

A man wrapped in a coat soon enters the cell. It is Lixdox in disguise! He tells the duke what has happened. All the conspirators are in flight or have been caught. The police have found the list at the house of the man whom the duke had designated guardian of the list. They have been careful to keep all the circumstances secret and to confound public opinion by spreading a rumor that the horrible assassination attempt is the infernal work of the Democratic Party. The charcoal burner, Miguf, is but the unfortunate tool of this party. The courtiers, still horrified by the peril that threatened them, cry out for the extermination of the revolutionaries. Lixdox's supporters cry out almost as strongly. The Pretender's partisans also cry out against the anarchists. The democrats are intimidated. Lixdox and the duke are drunk with joy upon seeing the complete success of their maneuvers. But it is of greatest importance to have Kalar condemned and to indict the entire Democratic Party. How may they accomplish this goal? Here is the plan that Lixdox has conceived and that he expounds to the duke.

"You will have," he says, "a meeting with the count. You will tell him of your arrest, the soldier's murder, and your own wound, and then you will reprimand him for his lack of caution. You will tell him, and the papers will report, that his actions and his mysterious behavior around the cellar aroused the suspicion of a policeman. They entered the cellar with a skeleton key during the night, and thus everything was discovered because of his error. You will add that one of my confidants came to tell you, on my behalf, that I will pardon the count, that I will free you, and that I will cease to pursue the other conspirators on the condition that the count implicate and bring to justice as his accomplice Kalar, our common enemy. You will add that, if this comes to pass, the count's true name will never be revealed. He will be known only by his false name and occupation (Miguf, a charcoal burner from Pirma in Cassie). The demagogues alone, in particular Kalar, one of their leaders, and the unfortunate charcoal burner, their agent, will take the blame as the execrable authors of this abominable act. To support the count's accusations against Kalar, we will suborn one or two false witnesses; and in order to deceive the other ministers and judges, you must be responsible for carrying out these acts concerning the count and the false witnesses." Lixdox tells the duke that he will become prince, and the duke accepts this position. At this point, the treacherous Lixdox goes out, while the perfidious duke prepares to confer with the count.

SCENE 7

We are in the duke's cell once more. He is in bed. A man arrives who can barely walk. It is the count! They have told him most mysteriously that the duke was arrested, that he had killed a soldier, was gravely wounded and on the point of death, and that they were in adjoining cells. The count wishes to see him. At first, the duke refuses, and then he gives permission.

The treacherous duke heaps recriminations upon him. He reproaches the count for having lost everything by his own error and for having compromised all his friends. Duped by this treachery, the count makes excuses, almost throws himself at the duke's feet, and asks his pardon. The duke relents and becomes affectionate, and then he tells of Lixdox's message. Lixdox has the list; he knows everything. All is lost, even their party, even the cause of the legitimate sovereign. "However," adds the duke, "Lixdox wishes to be generous and to exercise clemency. As for me, I rejected indignantly his proposition to save myself by condemning an innocent man. I will know how to die with courage! I have resigned myself to it!"

The count, however, would like to save all his friends, his party, and his sovereign's cause. Moreover, is not every democrat a guilty man, a criminal, and a scoundrel? Now it is the count who encourages and begs the duke to accept Lixdox's offer in the name of all their companions. It is the count who praises the clemency and generosity of the tyrant! The duke continues pretending to resist. He consents, finally, but only in order to save the count, their friends, and the honor of the nobility. He hands over to the count Lixdox's plan to accuse Kalar. The count reads the plan. It contains the supposed life story of the charcoal burner, Miguf, his links to Kalar, and their conspiracy. It also details the actions that the false Miguf must follow in order to defend himself and to accuse Kalar.

Lixdox, the duke, and the count will be the only ones party to this secret. The judges will be prevailed upon to grant Miguf a favorable verdict. All anger will be directed against Kalar. The judges will be even more vehemently against him because many of them will be fooled like the public, and they will truly believe him to be the instigator and leader of the infamous plot. The count consents to everything and prepares to study and to play his role of charcoal burner. At first, he will continue to say that he has no accomplices. He will deny that Kalar is guilty; and then, appearing to yield to the voice of his conscience, he will admit the whole truth and will formally accuse Kalar of being the inventor, the instigator, and the leader of the plot. The count will reproach Kalar for having dragged him into the conspiracy. He will accuse him of cowardice. As for the duke, he will be given his freedom and will seek out two false witnesses.

SCENE 8

Another cell. Many guards bring in a handsome man, his clothing torn, his head bare, his expression sad but resigned. One guard hits him with a cane, another with a riding crop. One pulls his mustache, another his sideburns. It is Kalar! They throw him on the straw, and the jailer leaves him a little black bread and water. Left alone, he bemoans his fate, but he will know how to suffer in the cause of freedom.

"The judges are going to come and interrogate me," he says. "What will I answer them? Judges! What am I saying? They are enemies, thieves, assassins! I am in a den of thieves, surrounded by traps. No, I will say nothing here!"

The Grand Inquisitor, the provost marshal, the chief justice, the ministers, lords, and guards soon arrive.

The Grand Inquisitor: "Do you know Miguf?"

Kalar: "First of all, of what am I accused?"

The chief justice: "Of being one of the authors, inventors, and directors of the infernal gunpowder plot. Do you know Miguf? Answer me!"

Kalar: "Here is my answer. I am innocent!"

The provost marshal: "Do you know Miguf? Answer me!"

Kalar: "I have nothing further to say. If you claim that I am guilty, it is up to you to prove my guilt. Set me free or give me a speedy trial, and then I will answer your questions. Here I will deny nothing nor admit anything. I will not answer as long as I do not have my own counsel and as long as I am not in the presence of the public."

The Grand Inquisitor: "But we are only asking you for the truth. You have no need of counsel in order to answer questions about facts that concern only you personally. You are in the presence of the court here, and because you are innocent, it will be easy to acquit yourself."

Kalar: "I do not wish to answer."

The chief justice: "But it is in your best interests to answer in order to prove your innocence!"

Kalar: "I do not wish to answer."

The provost marshal: "It is the duty of an accused party to enlighten the court."

Kalar: "I do not wish to answer."

A minister: "Are you not afraid of disobeying the court?"

Kalar: "I do not wish to answer."

A lord: "You are provoking the court." (Silence.)

The chief justice: "Have you no confidence in me?" (Silence.)

The provost marshal: "It will be thought that you are guilty!"

The chief justice: "You are only hurting your own case. See here, let us be reasonable."

Kalar: "I wish neither to discuss, nor to reason, nor to answer."

The chief justice: "What I am asking you cannot compromise you."

Kalar: "I do not wish to answer."

A minister: "You would be released with all due speed!"

A lord: "Those who have advised you to remain silent are not your friends!"

Kalar: "But you . . . I do not wish to answer."

A lady of the court: "You are acting against your family's best interests."

The provost marshal: "Xirol and Yard, your friends, have been arrested. You are acting against their best interests."

The chief justice: "They will know that it is you who are delaying their release!"

The Grand Inquisitor: "Your silence is useless and can only compromise you, for the witnesses have revealed all."

A minister: "Your codefendants are not acting as you are. While you are sacrificing yourself out of generosity for them, they are confessing all and are accusing you!"

A lord: "We know everything that you have done. Your obstinacy can only lead you to perdition, whereas we would take your frankness into account."

Kalar: "Once again, I do not wish to answer at all."

Anger, threats, cajolements: nothing can shake his resolve.

"It would have been easy for me to answer them," says Kalar when he is alone, "and I was often tempted to crush them or to confound them, but I am more secure because I have avoided their traps."

However, the chief justice soon returns. "We are alone," he says to him. "It is no longer as a magistrate that I speak to you, but as a man who admires your courage and your valor, who wants to help you. I will even confess to you that in the depths of my heart, I share your opinions and your feelings."

Kalar: "I have no friends in prison. I do not engage in idle chatter in prison. I do not wish to answer. Leave me alone!"

"They will condemn me nonetheless; I know it," he says, throwing himself on his pallet. "But I will make them see that they are assassinating me, and my death will not have been in vain for my country!"

Act II

SCENE I

An immense courtroom, old and dark, lit by mournful lamps. One hundred judges, preceded by many lictors, the two defendants chained together and dressed in black robes, many soldiers, witnesses, and numerous spectators appear in turn. The judges' benches are raised. Those of the defendants, facing the judges, are at their feet. In the middle of the room, we see the barrels of powder and the wick. The judges are all lords of the court, all prominent officers of the Crown, all those whom the powder was supposed to blow up. Their magnificent attire, the soldiers' uniforms, the variety of costumes, the great number of spectators on stage form an imposing spectacle. The false Miguf appears insolent. Kalar seems dauntless and calm.

The chief justice interrogates Miguf. Miguf confesses his crime. He admits its seriousness. He sheds tears of repentance. He throws himself on his knees and asks the pardon of the queen, the ministers, and the lords who are going to judge him. He sings their praises. He invokes virtue, honor, fidelity to the sovereign, even religion. He inveighs against the revolutionaries and the anarchists whose deadly doctrines have led them astray. Finally, he accuses Kalar of having drawn him in and of having provided him with the means of committing the crime. He accuses him neither out of vengeance nor to obtain his own pardon. He does so only to follow the dictates of his conscience, to help the court, and to serve the state by intimidating the conspirators by the example of his remorse, his torture, and his revelations against his companion in crime. The judges and spectators encourage him ten times over by murmurs of approbation, bravos, and applause. The chief justice and provost marshal praise him solemnly for declaring the truth so frankly.

It is Kalar's turn to be interrogated. Everyone believes or pretends to believe that he is guilty. All around him he sees only rage directed against him. The chief justice and the provost marshal interrogate him in a threatening manner. What will become of him? Before answering their accusations, he begins by impugning his judges: "You are the generals of the aristocratic camp," he says, "and I am a soldier of the democratic camp. It is you, moreover, whom the barrels of powder were threatening. You are my enemies, and you cannot be my judges!" But the court rises in anger and orders him to reply.

"As God is my witness, I am innocent. I have nothing to say. Prove that I am guilty!"

"Miguf swears it!" the chief justice replies brutally.

"Miguf! He has contradicted himself twenty times. He has admitted that he had been mistaken, and even that he had lied."

"But today he tells the truth!" cries the provost marshal.

"You know that Miguf is a foreigner, a thief, a forger. He is an assassin who killed twenty policemen. He is a regicide who wanted to assassinate the queen and all of you. He is an infamous scoundrel and a monster; and you set his testimony against me!"

Miguf, pale and trembling, looks as if he may retract his statements; but murmurs, stamping feet, and yells from all sides bear witness to the judges' anger against Kalar. The provost marshal, the chief justice, and other lords bombard him with objections, questions, reproaches, and threats; unruffled and steadfast as ever, however, Kalar answers all of them vigorously.

"Answer Miguf's accusations!" the provost marshal says to him, rising angrily.

"Is not a regicide a monster in your eyes?" replies Kalar. "You wish me to lower myself to answer Miguf, a regicide, a monster!"

"It is the court that is interrogating you," says the chief justice, "and it is the court that you are insulting."

"The court! You profane the name of justice! I see here only enemies, and not one judge!"

"The Law orders you to reply!" the provost marshal cries out.

"No!" replies Kalar, "and he who accuses me is trying to trick me so that I will bear witness against myself! That is an abomination!"

Several witnesses to the facts are heard. The gatekeeper of the house inhabited by Kalar declares that he saw Miguf entering Kalar's home several times and saw Kalar give Miguf a letter that was found on him and that might compromise Kalar. The court cheers and appears triumphant.

"What say you to this overwhelming deposition?" says the chief justice, raising his head.

"Miguf did come to visit me" (cheers from the judges), "and I am convinced now that he was plotting some infernal machination against me" (murmurs); "but he never spoke to me of any plot, and he is an infamous impostor! I never gave him any letter! The witness is an infamous liar! He is a false witness!"

The provost marshal: "All scoundrels tell the same tale."

Kalar: "And so do all innocent men!"

The chief justice: "Was the witness your enemy?"

"He always treated me respectfully." (Cheers from the judges.)

A lord: "Then why would he bear false witness?"

"I do not know. Perhaps his testimony has been bought!"

The provost marshal: "You are slandering the magistrates!"

"I gave no letter to Miguf, and this man is a false witness!"

"Well then," says the chief justice, "you will now hear from a child, the image of innocence and candor!"

The daughter of the gatekeeper, a child of twelve, is then brought in. "My child," the chief justice says to her in a caressing tone, "you saw Kalar give a letter to the charcoal burner Miguf, did you not?"

The child hesitates, turns pale and blushes. She is urged on, cajoled, encouraged, and threatened.

"Your father told this to us. Is your father a liar?"

The child hesitates again and starts to cry. Then, urged on to corroborate her father's statement, in a weak voice, she says "Yes." (At this word, the judges tremble with joy.)

"You have heard her," the chief justice cries out triumphantly. You see how difficult it was for an innocent one to proclaim the truth that points to your guilt."

"I see," replies Kalar, "that one innocent person is being tortured in order to condemn another innocent person!" (The lords cry out in anger.)

"Look carefully at the accused," says the chief justice to the child. The child does not dare raise her eyes.

"Look at me, my poor child," Kalar tells her in a tone that is impossible to describe.

"He is the one!" she cries. "Yes, he is the one! But I did not see the letter change hands." (After these words, this cry, she falls down, wracked with frightful convulsions.)

There is widespread astonishment, confusion, and agitation. The child is taken out, and the session is suspended for a few moments.

The child returns once more; she is urged on once more; she denies once more.

"But you swore before the Grand Inquisitor that you saw the letter, and, a short while ago, you repeated the charge here. Were you lying then? Take heed!"

"I was encouraged to do so. I was told that my deposition would do harm to no one."

"But who encouraged you? Speak up!" The child hangs her head and weeps once more without answering.

"We will not countenance such a scandal!" cries the provost marshal. "Either the father or the daughter is a false witness! We ask that the session be suspended for half an hour, and that both be put in solitary confinement with no access to other people. The truth will out!"

SCENE 2

A wretched cell, with frightening instruments of torture. The child arrives, bathed in tears. Soon afterward, the provost marshal, the chief justice, several lords, and even a duchess enter the cell. The child is caressed and flattered. They try to frighten her.

"You saw the letter," they say to her. "That is the truth. Tell the truth. Your father will be dishonored, lost. He will be sentenced to the galleys or perhaps even to death! You are killing your father and your mother to save a miserable soul who will be found guilty in any case!"

The mother arrives as well, crying, shouting, in despair. The father is brought in in chains. Everyone joins together to try and force a confession. The child finally promises to confess and is taken out in order to be brought back to the session.

SCENE 3

The court is in session.

"The two witnesses," says the chief justice, "were locked up separately, in two different cells. Without having conferred with each other or with any other person, they have had the time to reflect, and now we will certainly know the truth." (The father and daughter are brought in. Anxiety is painted on all the faces.)

"Do you persist in affirming that you saw the letter change hands?" the father is asked.

"Yes."

"Did your daughter see the letter changing hands? We ask you to tell nothing but the truth."

"Yes." (The court rejoices.)

"Your father has just told the truth," the chief justice says to the girl. "Follow his example. Tell the truth! You saw the letter change hands?"

The child, still troubled, hanging her head, crying, says in a barely audible voice: "Yes . . ."

"We cannot hear her!" shout several judges. "What did she answer?"

"She replied 'YES,' " says the chief justice. (Cheers break out noisily from all the benches.)

"You are not judges," Kalar cries out, "but bloodthirsty tigers!"

At that point, the provost marshal, the chief justice, and several judges join together to hurl invectives at Kalar. They tell him that the girl's testimony is overwhelming because it confirms the testimonies of both her father and Miguf.

"You have seen the girl's struggle," shouts the provost marshal. "She is the one who finds you guilty!"

"No, no, no!" the girl cries from her seat. "I saw nothing! I saw nothing!" And she falls down in a faint. (There is universal astonishment and irritation on several benches). The girl is lifted up and taken to the middle of the room. She is bombarded with questions. But a piercing cry is heard. She falls down once more. She has bitten her own tongue! The session is suspended, at that very moment, in the midst of the greatest confusion.

When the session resumes and several other witnesses are heard from, the provost marshal sustains the accusation. He praises the repentance and sincerity of the false Miguf, presenting him as a victim of Kalar. Miguf is almost a hero, or an angel. In Kalar's case, he finds a thousand proofs of guilt. Miguf's contradictions, lies, audaciousness, and curses against Kalar are considered proofs of Kalar's guilt. The young girl's hesitations, retractions, and final catastrophe are also proofs. Kalar's silence, denials, protestations of innocence, and courage are even more proofs against him. Kalar is the principal guilty one, the only guilty one, a scoundrel of whom the earth must quickly be purged!

The false Miguf, certain of saving his own life, takes the stand only to ask hypocritically to die to expiate his crime, and to exhort the people to cease from engaging in conspiracies. But Kalar, certain of being sentenced to death, protests that he is the victim of an infernal machination that he cannot unearth. "You are an assassin!" he says to the provost marshal. "You are an assassin!" he says to the chief justice. "You are all assassins!" he says to the judges. They try to silence him in vain, and soldiers cannot force him to sit down.

"My death sentence was decided well in advance!" he cries. "It is democracy and a friend of the people that the aristocracy wishes to give into the hands of tyranny! I will die a martyr!" (They come to put a gag over his mouth.) "But someday the people will avenge my memory!" The soldiers take him away, and the court retires to deliberate his sentence.

SCENE 4

The deliberation chamber. The judges are seated. "There are no proofs," some of them say. "His accuser is obviously lying. Moreover, Miguf is an accursed scoundrel whom we cannot believe. Kalar is innocent. We would bring dishonor on ourselves. He would be a martyr!"

"He is guilty," say the others. "He is a scoundrel, an anarchist, a revolutionary!"

Lixdox enters at that point and entreats them to keep in mind reasons of state and the salvation of the queen and the nobility, attacked daily by demagoguery. A verdict of guilty is essential! Royal clemency will do the rest.

"Is Kalar guilty?" asks the chief justice. Almost all the judges rise. And the two accused men are condemned as parricides.

SCENE 5

The false Miguf is in a clean, elegant, well-furnished room that serves as his prison cell. "Poor Kalar," he says to himself. "But he is a democrat!" The duke rushes in and tells him the sentence. In fact, he has come to set him free. An unfortunate soul who has just hanged himself in his cell will be put in his place, and the court newspaper will announce that Miguf strangled himself.

SCENE 6

Kalar's wretched cell. He is in chains. He is sleeping, exhausted. The jailer comes to wake him up and to strap him down even more tightly. The executioner arrives and reads him his sentence. In half an hour, he will be broken on the wheel, torn apart, and burned at the stake. Kalar hurls curses against the court, society, the aristocracy, and tyranny. He imagines with horror the despair of his wife and daughter. He remembers their virtues, their fine qualities, his love for them, and their love for him. These memories bring forth tender feelings. The image of his death makes him shudder, but love for his country gives him back his courage.

One of the queen's ministers comes in and offers him a pardon if he will bring an accusation against another leader of the Popular Party who has just died. He refuses indignantly. A second lord arrives and asks only that he admit his guilt. He seems to think about it. His chains are removed. But he refuses once more.

"Only ask for clemency!" they cry to him. At that point, his wife and daughter appear and throw themselves, crying, into his arms. He kisses them passionately. The lord shows him the pardon signed by the queen and explains that she has as her only condition that he . . .

"Ask for clemency?" Kalar cries. "That would be to admit that I am guilty, and I am innocent!"

His wife has her arms around his neck; his daughter is at his feet, holding out the pardon that the lord has put in her hands. He hesitates; he fights; it appears that he will consent.

"Oh my country!" he cries. "What a sacrifice I am making for you today!"

"Let him be broken on the wheel and torn apart!" says the lord to Kalar. His wife and daughter are shrieking. He frees himself violently from their embrace and pushes them away. They faint. He races off to go to his death, and then he comes back, as if in a trance. He picks up his daughter and bursts into tears, pressing her passionately against his chest. We can hear only a few fragments of words: "Freedom . . . country . . . people . . . tyranny!"

"Pardon! Ask for clemency!" cry all those surrounding him.

But he rushes off once more and disappears forever, leaving all eyes filled with tears, all brows covered with sweat, and all souls filled with anger against tyranny and with admiration for devotion to freedom.

32 Jealousy and Madness; Reason and Devotion

I have not seen them for two days, and I must leave this evening (May 24), leave her forever without letting her know the pain she has caused me! I will simply write to Valmor, telling him I will be away for a few days and apologizing to his family and friends. Later, I will write once more to beg their pardon for leaving

Icaria without thanking them. How they would pity me if they knew the torments I am enduring!

I had begun my letter, but my blood was coursing through my veins, and my head was burning like a volcano about to crack open; soon a glacial cold wave made my flesh quiver and my teeth chatter. My eyes clouded over; my fingers let the pen drop, and . . . I have no idea what happened next.

Illness, Delirium, and First Awakening

What a dreadful sleep! What unending insomnia! How horrible are the night and the chaos! Black whirlwinds disappear and reappear ceaselessly, and the eye keeps following them without ever being able to reach them! "Is it you, Eugene? Why have you forsaken me for so long? I saw Dinaïse crying! What was wrong with her? Where is Dinaïse? When will my voyage be over? My bones and my limbs are broken! But where am I?"

"At the home of a faithful friend," replied Eugene, squeezing my hand gently. "Rest some more, my dear William! Sleep peacefully!" That voice, that hand, friendship's sweet touch seemed to pour freshness and life into my veins. But soon afterward, I fell back into nothingness.

Convalescence

I am being reborn, and good Eugene has just told me that I have been ill, but that I will soon recover. I thought I was in England, but I am, in fact, in a hospital in Icara. They do not wish me to speak as yet.

He Learns What Has Happened

My forces are returning, and Eugene, who has taken care each day to tell me what is going on, has just told me the whole story. For seven days, a raging fever put my life in danger. I recognized no one, not even Eugene or Valmor. It was not Dinaïse whom I saw, but Corilla, who was weeping. The doctors are no longer anxious, but I must be prudent and careful if I wish to be in a healthy enough state to make my departure.

Indiscretions During His Delirium

Pressured by my questions, Eugene has just confessed to me that in my delirium I kept repeating Dinaïse's name, and that Valmor, who was there at the time, was so painfully affected by this that he left abruptly and never came back to my bedside. But never a day passed when Corilla did not send someone by several times to find out how I was. Good Corilla! Poor Valmor! As long as Dinaïse does not find out about my involuntary indiscretions! But why does Dinaros not come to visit me?

All Is Revealed

My hair has turned white. However, I am well enough for Eugene to permit me to read a letter from Corilla. Let us read it quickly.

Corilla's Letter to Milord

"May 30. Finally, my dear William, you have recovered! If you only knew how many tears your illness has cost me, and how happy I am about your recovery! However, I should probably despise you, poor unfortunate soul. How much anxiety you have caused everyone! What desolation you have sown in two families who welcomed you with affection. What pain you cause my poor brother! What pain you have caused Mrs. Dinamé, Dinaros, and my poor friend Dinaïse!"

"The pain I have caused Dinaïse?" I cried. "What has happened to her? Hide nothing from me, Eugene. Eugene, speak to me! How is Dinaïse?"

"Better."

"She was ill? How? Why? Tell me everything, my dear Eugene."

"Calm yourself! I will tell you everything. Corilla and Dinaïse were together when Dinaros informed them of your sudden illness. Dinaïse did not allow herself to show any emotion, while Corilla appeared deeply affected by the news. But the next day, when Valmor added that in your delirium you had been saying 'Miss Henriet' frequently, Dinaïse, as if hit by lightning, fell on the floor, writhing with convulsions."

"She loves me." And I myself fainted. "Where is she?" I cried as soon as I had regained consciousness.

"She has been at her mother's home for several days, but she was at the hospital for a long time, almost as gravely ill as you were."

"She loves me! But what about Valmor?"

"Valmor has been away for a time and, I hope, will be returning soon. But calm yourself, my dear William! Rest!"

"Poor Valmor! Eugene, we still must leave! But if only you knew what a balm the news that I am loved has been for my soul."

After a few hours of rest, we finished reading the letter.

The End of Corilla's Letter

"What pain you have caused Mrs. Dinamé and Dinaros and my poor friend Dinaïse, who will never regain her composure! We are quite miserable today, William, and it is I, perhaps, who suffers the most, for I suffer cruelly because of the unjust way you are being treated. One of my aunts and her husband are accusing you of being the cause of all our misfortunes. Mrs. Dinamé is often very angry and blames me for having introduced you to her family. Dinaros scarcely dares to utter a few words in your defense, and Valmor is furious with you. Ah! It was only my courage and the intense friendship I feel for you that kept me from cursing you myself when I saw Dinaïse at the point of death, everyone in tears, and my brother, my beloved brother, almost mad with despair!

"But my heart was never deceived about you. I know you better than the others do. I was positive that you were not guilty in the least, and that we had only nature and fate to blame. Eugene (Oh, how you should love him, that good Eugene!) has revealed the whole story to me, and because of that, I, your friend, have found new strength to defend you. I have soothed the good Mrs. Dinamé. Dinaros will come to see you soon. I have written two or three letters to my poor Valmor, and I hope that my tenderness will reawaken his reason. My aunt and uncle are still stubbornly against you, but we will bring them around. Let us wish not, my friend, for happiness, for I fear that is no longer possible for us; but let us hope that we will be able to help each other find consolation in friendship. As for me, I will be strong and courageous as long as you save a little friendship for the young woman who holds you in such esteem. Corilla.

"P. S. I do not know whether or not you persist in your plan to leave as soon as you are completely recovered. Perhaps it would be wise to do so; but I beg of you, dear William, do not leave without saying farewell! Moreover, let there be no farewells!"

"What a friend!" I cried, embracing Eugene. "There would be no happier mortal on earth than I if the friend of Corilla were also the husband of Dinaïse! But Valmor! Poor Valmor! We must leave soon, Eugene, and without saying farewell!"

A Note from Corilla

"June 3. Eugene tells me that you beg me to tell you everything about Valmor and Dinaïse, and that you have promised to be wise and courageous. I am giving in and am sending you a letter from the unhappy woman. Courage, William! You promised!"

Dinaïse's Letter to Corilla

"1st of June. You must be very tired, my dear friend. You have spent so many nights without sleeping, at the foot of my bed, and here I am, tiring you even more with my letters! But when I do not see you, I must write to you or hear from you, my cherished Corilla. How are you? Come here quickly, so that I may embrace you to show you how much I love you! Tell me that you are coming back. I have slept well. What dreams I have had! I will tell them to you. I am better, quite well, very well. You saved me by the single word you whispered in my ear! Do not bring your aunt here anymore. I do not wish to see her again! Is it my fault that I had no control over my heart? Everyone tells me of Valmor's sterling qualities, talents, and virtues. No one knows and appreciates his soul more than I do. No one finds his character and manners more pleasing. I did love your brother, at least I thought I did; and I still love him, as much as I love you, as much as you yourself love him. I would have married him. I felt I could make him happy. I would have been happy to be his wife. I had no way of knowing that another man could bring forth such different feelings in me.

"But William appeared, and from that moment on my whole being has been turned upside down. Why? I do not understand it because I already loved Valmor, my childhood friend, the brother of my dearly beloved friend, whereas William was a foreigner on whom I had never laid eyes before, and toward whom I felt as indifferent as he felt toward me. He never told me he loved me. He never let his feelings show. I did not know he loved me. In fact, I thought I meant nothing to him. Nevertheless, when I saw him, I felt a discomfort I had never experienced before. When I compared him to Valmor, reason turned me toward your brother, but an irresistible power pushed me and pulled me toward your friend. You loved him, too, Corilla, while still loving your brother! Valmor loved him, too. All of you loved him, even my brother and my mother!

"My poor mother! How desolate she is because of Valmor! How her pain causes me to suffer. Take pity on me, Corilla, for my heart has many wounds and bleeds painfully when I see my mother cry. The unfortunate woman does not dare to scold me! This morning, however, after your departure, she almost accused me of having hidden my love from her. But you know full well, Corilla, that I was not conscious of it myself, and you were as ignorant of it as I was. When I saw him for the first time on the boat, with your brother, I hid myself without thinking, as if a secret premonition were warning me that he was an enemy advancing toward me in order to put me in his thrall. After that, as you yourself noticed, I almost always avoided him. You reproached me for my uncivilized behavior and for my frightened look. Without the dagger thrust that caused me to be jealous (and I blush to think of it), I would probably still not know that I loved him.

"He loved me, too, without knowing it and without willing it. He was going to leave without declaring himself, without knowing my feelings. He was sacrificing himself for me; he was sacrificing me to Valmor and to honor. Only fever and being near death revealed our love to you. Your aunt, who has probably never loved, blames us rather than pitying us. Ah! That injustice quiets my natural timidity and gives me daring and courage! Now I feel that my soul is made of fire, and that I have enough energy to confront misfortune. Yes, I love him! Yes, I am happy to know that I am loved! Yes, whether he leaves or stays, I will love him forever! I may die of unhappiness, but neither my aunt nor anyone may take away my love for him or my friendship for you!

"But Valmor, good Valmor, poor Valmor! I have told you before, and I repeat it once more: I still love him as much as ever! You must not think that his misfortune could make me happy. No, my friend, I swear to you and to him that I will never cause him the misery of seeing me as the wife of another man. I, poor, feeble creature that I am, wish to be for him an example of a person who seeks happiness in pure and blessed friendship. In that way, I will be able to love both of them, to love you all, and still to cherish my Corilla with all the power of my soul. Dinaïse."

I cannot begin to tell you the feelings that reading this letter brought forth in me. No, I can find no words to give you an idea of my emotion, discomfort, admiration, happiness, and delicious tears. I cannot express the pleasure and transports of joy I felt when I read the letters that followed. I do not know how it is that so many passionate emotions did not kill me!

Corilla's Second Letter

"June 6. Good news, my dear William! Valmor is coming back! I am sending you all his letters and one of the letters I sent to him. Act wisely!"

Valmor's First Letter to Corilla

"Mola. May 24. Reassure our mother, my dear sister. I beg her forgiveness for the uncertainty I am causing her. I traveled two hundred leagues in twenty hours: on foot, on horseback, by carriage, by railroad, by boat, even by hot-air balloon. I am exhausted, broken, worn out, and my brain is more tired than my body; but I am pleased to have found repose in exhaustion. I was suffocating! I will write to you tomorrow. Answer me right away, care of the post office in Valdira."

Valmor's Second Letter to Corilla

"Mola, May 25. Oh, it was wise for me to flee! I did not recognize myself anymore. I would have committed an unwise act. Yes, my sister, I even entertained the horrible thought of killing him, her, and myself after them. A few hours later, while running in the countryside, I still had (I am ashamed to admit it) the most frightful temptation. But tell me, my dear sister, has there ever been unhappiness equal to mine? I welcome him. I shower him with friendship. I treat him like a brother. I confide my love to him, and he steals my happiness from me! I was almost cured, and he reopens all my wounds! No sooner do I hear that he is ill than I rush to his side, sacrificing my rest and my sleep, in order to hear him repeating over and over again that he is my unashamed rival! And when I try to forget my suffering in order to think only of the well-being of an ingrate, she herself tells me that she prefers the traitor to me! Insensitive to ten years of love, unfaithful to her childhood friendship, breaker of her vows, she pushes away my tribute on the hypocritical pretext that she has made a vow never to marry. A few days later, the perfidious woman throws herself at the feet of the first foreigner who gives her any encouragement! They love each other, Corilla! They would die for each other! They will be happy and victorious! They will be able to laugh at my naïveté, my trust, my tortures! No, no, I will not be the only unfortunate one! I am returning to Icara! They will see me soon!

"P. S. I am reopening my letter. No, my sister, I am not coming back yet. I was mad! Luckily, enough reason has returned to me to allow me to continue on my way."

Corilla's Reply to Valmor

"Icara. May 26. Your letter, my dear brother, caused my mother and myself to shed many tears. How I pity you, my poor Valmor! How unhappy you are! Both William and Dinaïse would be very guilty if they deserved your reproaches, and I would certainly hate them, I who felt such deep friendship for them! But, my friend, one may often be deceived by appearances. What if you were wrong? What if they were innocent? What if William had never betrayed you? What if Dinaïse. . . ? Perhaps you will never see my poor Dinaïse again, or William, who was on death's doorstep this very morning. Eugene has made a clean breast of it to my mother, my grandfather, and me. Listen carefully to me, my brother!

"Three days before the crisis, William himself was not conscious of his feelings for Dinaïse. Eugene suspected something and made his friend aware of those feelings. Thinking only of you and the misery he would cause you, William resolved to leave Icaria and to say nothing to Dinaïse about his feelings. He planned to leave without even saying farewell. He was to leave three days later with Eugene, who planned to accompany him to the frontier. But a few hours before the time of their departure, fever prevented him from leaving; and you know the rest. Well then, my dear Valmor, you whose mind is usually so superior to ours and whose heart is always so true, tell me this. How could we call that poor William a deceitful traitor? Is he not, on the contrary, a faithful, honorable, and devoted friend?

"You may reproach him only with seeing Dinaïse unwisely; but think, my friend! Is he not the first victim of this misfortune? Are we not the cause of it? In the first place, you kept talking to him about the perfect qualities of your loved one. My mother and I kept praising Dinaïse's laudable traits. We made him party to our deep friendship for her. Yes, my dear friend, you must blame your mother and, above all, your sister, for those two women (who would sacrifice their lives for you) introduced Dinaïse to William and exposed him to the danger of becoming miserable forever. As for that unfortunate Dinaïse, whom we all cherish, you know, my brother, that nothing would have made us happier than her love for you. Nothing could hurt me more than the impossibility of calling her my sister. I would have looked upon her with horror if she had been an ingrate, a deceitful, unfaithful woman! But believe your Corilla. I am sure that she did not know her own feelings, and that she is the victim of a kind of fate. I am certain that she has the most sincere and tender affection for you. I have not been able to ask her any questions since she has been ill, but I know her well enough to dare to swear that she will never marry William. Poor girl, she may well reproach us for destroying her peace of mind and her happiness!

"Take pity on her, then, my brother, my good brother! I am merely a woman, but I am your friend. If the voice of friendship is not strong enough, listen to your own reason. Remember your thoughts, your courage, your resolve to control yourself, your vows to Mr. Mirol, your combats, and your victory! Your wisdom had cured you. The discovery of a fact you did not know has reopened all your wounds. It is jealousy that is leading you astray! I cannot believe that this passion worthy only of vulgar souls would get the better of Valmor! No, my brother, no! You must be an example to all of us of courage, justice, goodness, and virtue. You owe it to us, and you will not disappoint us! Do not forget that your sister will not sleep until she has received an answer from her beloved brother. Corilla."

Valmor's Third Letter

"Valdira. May 29. I have just received your letter dated the 28th. He is dying! She is dangerously ill! And he was leaving because of me, without telling her that he loved her! Is it really true? Oh, Corilla, my sister! Run quickly to William. No, rush to Dinaïse's side! Hurry! Write to me, write to me!"

Corilla's Letter to Valmor

"Icara. June 2." (This letter, mentioned in the previous one, contained a copy of Dinaïse's letter that has already been presented.)

Valmor's Fourth Letter

"Valdira. June 3. Rejoice, dear Corilla, for you have done me a world of good by informing me that they are both out of danger. I have just received your letter dated the 2nd and the copy of Dinaïse's letter. What? William still plans to leave, and Dinaïse is sacrificing her love on my behalf? How unworthy I am compared to them! My head is still too heated up for me to answer you right away. I need to walk, to run in the fresh air. I will write to you soon, and you will be pleased with what I have to say!"

Valmor's Fifth Letter

"Valdira. June 4. I will take vengeance on myself! I will punish myself! I have just reread your letters and that of Dinaïse. I have reread them ten times, devouring and kissing them. How weak and fearful I am! How unjust and mad! How cowardly and violent! But I will be avenged upon myself! Yes, it was jealousy, blind, stupid, ferocious jealousy that led me astray and made me inhuman. But I will be avenged upon myself!

"Oh, my dear sister, how grateful I am to you! How proud I am to be your brother! With what pleasure I will press you in my fraternal arms! Embrace William! Press Dinaïse to your heart! I want to repay the sacrifices they have made on my behalf. I have resolved to do it! I will make it my happiness to see that they are happy! Let them love each other while keeping their friendship for me. I will probably have more battles to fight, efforts to make, and pain to bear. It will still take me time, so I will not return to you right away. I will overcome this or die, and I expect that I will be victorious. I only hope that I can make you all happy once more, and that I can repair, as much as possible, the harm that I have involuntarily caused you. One thing of which I am sure, my beautiful and good Corilla, is that your brother will always love you tenderly."

Recovery

Seven days later, on June 11, two days before the national holidays, Valmor returned. Dinaïse was completely recovered. I was so close to full recovery that his arrival gave me back all my strength. He embraced us all so effusively and tenderly that we began to experience, after those most dreadful two weeks, a happiness that we had believed lost forever. However, Dinaïse persisted in her vow never to marry; I still planned to leave; and it was Valmor who encouraged us to renounce our dual decision.

Unable to persuade us at first, he declared that he wished it, he desired it, he begged for it, he insisted upon it, he ordered it, and that he would figure out a way to force us to renounce our decision. While we were laughing at this new madness that had come to replace the first, he added with a triumphant air: "And what if I were to marry within the month? What if I were certain to marry a woman who would make me happy, and whom I were certain to make happy, a wife who would entrust me with her happiness? What if I were to marry Alae, Dinaïse's cousin, who has always held me in high esteem, and whom I have always liked a great deal?" (Imagine our amazement!)

"Well," he said, "everything is settled. Before I returned, I spent four days at the home of Dinaïse's grandfather. I told him everything. Alae, who was well aware of my feelings, did not reject my proposal. Both our families have given their consent, and in two months we will celebrate three marriages on the same day. And now that I have spoken my piece, be silent!"

Corilla gave us the signal by throwing her arms around his neck. We embraced him with a passion that is impossible to describe, and we began then and there a new era of happiness, along with the festivities that were being prepared to celebrate the anniversary of Icaria's era of happiness.

33 Prelude to the Anniversary Celebrations
School, Workers', and Civic Birthdays

Tomorrow is the anniversary of Icarian rebirth. It is heralded by three events of immense popular interest. As the year begins on the 13th of June, the day of the People's Rebellion, it is on that day that three birthdays are celebrated: the school birthday for all children who are five years old; the workers' birthday for all eighteen-year-old boys and seventeen-year-old girls; and the civic birthday for all twenty-one year-old men. This morning, on magnificent posters, in every commune, the list of all new students—that is, of all the five-year-old children—was displayed. The list was also posted of all the new workers—that is, of all eighteen-year-old boys and seventeen-year-old girls—with the different professions that each had chosen during the competitions that had taken place within the last few days. This evening the list will be posted of all the new citizens who will have been admitted to civic life today. This ceremony is so interesting that Valmor wanted to take us there along with Eugene, who has become our inseparable companion.

Civic Reception

All three of us arrived at the Communal Palace just as the session was going to begin. "The person you see in the armchair," said Valmor, "is the president of the communal Popular Assembly. Seated at his right is the president of the Communal Executive. At his left is the priest. The men surrounding them are the popular magistrates. Those handsome boys who are seated in the first row are all the young men of the commune who have had their twenty-first birthday. They will be received as citizens. The men of all ages you see behind them are their godfathers. These are family friends who present them to society (for this is truly our birth into society) and who will serve as their counselors and friends throughout the rest of their lives. The higher benches are occupied by all the young men of the commune who have had their twentieth birthday. They are required to attend this ceremony and to attend faithfully, during the year, the popular assemblies, in order to complete their civic education. Next year they will be proclaimed citizens and will be allowed to exercise all their rights and duties. The other spectators are, like ourselves, people who are interested in this ceremony."

When the music had ceased (for in Icaria, delightful music is heard in all places of public assembly, as well as in church), the president opened the session and gave the floor to one of the magistrates, who gave a short speech about the importance of this civic ceremony. After that, the secretary began to call the roll of the young citizens and their godfathers. The president and the members of the bureau asked fifteen or twenty young men, chosen by lot, questions on the Constitution and the rights and duties of a citizen. I do not need to add that all of them answered with confidence and dignity. The president then read them the Civic Oath (devotion to country, obedience to the law, fulfillment of all duties, and fraternity with all fellow citizens) and emphasized the importance of this oath. He reminded them that the republic requires that a citizen take this oath only once, no matter what offices he may hold thereafter. All citizens take this oath at the same time, while standing and holding out both hands.

The president, in the name of the republic, then proclaimed them citizens, members of the sovereign people, electors eligible to hold office. He ordered that their names be inscribed on the poster of members of the Popular Assembly and the National Guard. He also ordered that the uniform of citizen be distributed to each of them, and he himself gave the symbol of citizenship to their godfathers. Each attached the symbol to the chest of his young friend, while a patriotic song was played. The president ended this majestic ceremony with a short speech on the love that Icarians should have for their republic. Almost a million new citizens were born in this manner, at the same moment, in the sixty communes of Icara and the thousand communes of Icaria!

Everything is in motion for the great anniversary of the revolution. Tomorrow's festivities must be a faithful reenactment of that event. The two armies are getting organized to put on the historical drama. One represents the royal guard, the other the insurgent people. The companies, the small troops, the bands, and the patrols are getting ready and receive the orders of the day. The posts and roles are distributed. Some play Icar and his generals, others Lixdox and Cloramide. Materials for barricades are piled up in the Arena of the Rebellion located near the large watchtower containing the bell that sounded the alarm on the morning of June 13, 1782, and is the only tocsin left in Icara. A wooden replica of the former palace of the queen has been erected at one of the ends of the large Arena of Victory. Everything is ready. And the sun, setting beautifully, promises to be even more magnificent tomorrow, to complete the reenactment of the two brilliant and glorious days.

34 Anniversary of the Revolution

First Day: Rebellion, Combat, Victory

The air is pure. The sun, more sparkling than yesterday, seems like a god who wishes to illuminate the freeing of a great people. Starting at five o'clock in the morning, I hear the bell, followed by cries and drums sounding the alarm. I run with Eugene to fetch Valmor and Dinaros, as we had planned, and the four of us run to the sound of the tocsin. No sooner have we gone out than we meet many bands of young people who are singing hymns of combat and freedom, putting up a proclamation of rebellion by Icar, and running around, waving little black flags, and crying, "To arms! To arms, citizens!" We soon notice an enormous black flag floating on the high tower where the alarm bell's electrifying sound doubles in intensity. We see citizens coming out and placing proclamations on the tower. There are thousands of them, all written by hand and all different. Each person has made his or her own. Patrols of the royal guard are crossing with bayonets, firing into and dispersing the crowds. Bands of citizens are carrying corpses, crying, "Vengeance! To arms!"

But the troops resist. Rifle fire answers rifle fire. Barricades are formed everywhere, with ropes, chains, poles, and carriages. Shooting takes place on both sides of the barricades. We are forced to fall back and to take other streets. At that point, the firing of small firearms and cannons begin; and finally, we hear, from all sides, fusillades and cannonades, mixing with the tocsin, the drummed alarm, and cries of "To Arms! To the battlefield of the rebellion!"

All these new experiences both overwhelm and please me, but Eugene is so electrified by it that he seems to have gone mad. "Let us run, let us run!" he keeps repeating. "I feel like I am back at the 27th of July!"

Continuing on our way, we meet up with bands of runaways, some of them rebels, others soldiers. We also meet bands of prisoners, some made up of citizens being taken away by guards, others made up of disarmed royal guards led off by citizens who have taken their weapons. We are stopped several times ourselves, first by rebels who want to take us with them, and then by soldiers who take us prisoner, but we manage to escape. We arrive with the rest of the crowd at the battlefield of the rebellion, and we get up onto raised bleachers that surround the arena and are filled with interested onlookers. A third of the population are spectators, while another third are actors in this immense drama.

Many of the rebels are already in the arena, where we can see the uniforms of the bourgeois guard. Orators harangue those who gather round them. We see the continuous arrival of citizens, women, and children dressed in costumes of workers or the bourgeoisie; they are carrying all sorts of weapons and instruments. Icar is on horseback, in the middle, organizing them and inciting them to combat. Dinaros points out, next to Icar, one of his aides-de-camp, who is better dressed than Icar and appears wounded. I see that it is Valmor's grandfather. The tocsin, the drums, the trumpets, the cannon, and rifle fire are never-ending. Finally the fusillades and cannonades come closer. The rebels who are in combat with the royal guard flee from them. Barricades are set up to stop the soldiers. The first barricade is spiritedly attacked and defended, and finally taken, as is the second. The third, beneath our eyes, is the scene of a heroic combat. The cannon resounds in our ears. A child plants a flag on the barricade, braves the fusillade for a long time, and finally falls as if pierced by shells. The soldiers cry victory and are going to climb the barricade. The sound of the tocsin intensifies along with the danger. The trumpets and drums give the fighters new strength. Icar dashes forward at the head of the bands he has just organized in the arena. They all rush forward singing the "Hymn of Combat," and the guard is repelled. The shooting is wild in front of the first barricade formed by the soldiers, but the barricade is taken once more. Shouts, trumpets, and cannonfire fading into the distance announce that the victorious rebels are pursuing the royal guard toward the Arena of Victory. The noise ceases. We hear only intermittent rifle fire. The Arena of the Rebellion empties out. Everyone goes home when the heat of the day is upon us.

Just after three o'clock, we all leave together, with Dinaïse, Corilla, and their two families, to go to the Arena of Victory. The whole population is going there as well, some as actors, the others as spectators, everyone in the most perfect order, following the route and the location of each neighborhood indicated in the program. Everyone is guaranteed a good seat with excellent visibility. There are no policemen or informers, but only ceremonial stewards elected in each neighborhood who are both respectful and respected. The great arena is immense, larger than the Champs-de-Mars in Paris. The ground is perfectly level, made up of a sort of wetted mastic that turns neither to mud nor to dust. All around the field, beginning at ten feet from the ground, are clean, comfortable terraced bleachers raised in a circular amphitheater, on which a million spectators can sit. They are protected by a light cover, which looks like a thousand tents held up by thin columns.

The people of each of the sixty neighborhoods of Icara, the provincials, the colonials, the foreigners and their ambassadors, and the different magistrates all have their assigned seats and their flags, of all different colors. The thousands of flags floating under the thousand tents, the great number of spectators, and the variety of clothing already create an impressive scene. But the inside of the arena creates a second superb spectacle. It is filled with royal troops in uniforms of red, green, yellow, black, and so forth, uniforms of the infantry, cavalry, and artillery. The queen's palace, located at one of the exits, is filled and surrounded by cannons and soldiers.

Soon the tocsin begins again, and fusillades and cannonades resound and come closer. Five or six hundred thousand spectators fill the stands when, at about four o'clock, the fighting becomes heavy again beneath our very eyes. We see the royal army maneuver to get into battle formation. Cloramide, Lixdox, and the Court, in magnificent costumes, prancing around on superb horses, review the troops and go to great lengths to elicit cheers. The cannonade and fusillade, closer still, make it clear that the royal guard is retreating. The tocsin, trumpet, and drum sounding and beating the charge, the fusillade from the rebel side growing stronger, and the rebel cries let us know that they are not far away.

The royal vanguard arrives, fleeing in disorderly fashion. Soldiers, horses, and cannons are thrown together. A few pieces of artillery defend the entrance and fire continuously; but children, slipping past the columns of the porticos or slithering on their bellies, manage to capture a battery of artillery, which the citizens soon turn on the royal army. Some of the people's cavaliers capture another nearby battery by rushing it at lightning speed with their horses. Then the soldiers barricade themselves in, but the rebels arrive en masse, some wearing their workers' and bourgeois costumes and carrying arms of all sorts, others barely clothed at all. The barricade is attacked in the midst of a lively fusillade supported by the rebels' cannon. A girl climbs the barricade and is the first to appear at the summit, waving a flag, next to a young man in military dress. Their appearance is greeted by a multitude of cheers, and the barricade is taken.

The main part of the royal army sets off at this point and advances against the attackers. The two armies face each other, one made up of a mass of soldiers, the other of little bands, in the midst of which we see Icar on horseback, surrounded by his aides-de-camp, among whom we see Valmor's grandfather. The fusillade and cannonade from both sides begin again, but several cavalry and infantry regiments turn their rifles and sabers in the opposite direction, bend down their flags and join the citizens, shouting, "Long live the people!" The spectators applaud and cheer. The rebels reply, crying, "Down with tyranny! Long live the citizens' army!"

Frightened by these defections and cries, the royal guard and, in particular, the foreign guard retreat into the palace or flee behind it. Icar, moving forward at the head of his men, falls from his horse as if wounded by a shell; but he soon reappears, and his wound merely inflames the popular passion even more. At this point, we see the attack on the palace, the assault and the climbing of the walls, where the attackers perform all manner of amazing gymnastic and military feats. Finally the palace is taken after a frightening fusillade and cannonade. A hundred trumpets piercing the air from the height of the palatial terrace announce that the rebels may now seat themselves upon the queen's throne. Red uniforms and court regalia are thrown from the windows by the victors, and the royal flag falls to the accompaniment of the spectators' applause. Soon the queen, arrested by her own guards, is brought out by them, amidst cheers and bravos. The villainous Lixdox, whom we saw a few minutes ago in a gilt costume and who has just been found hiding in a charcoal pile, is brought out dressed as a scullery maid amidst boos and curses. The palace now bursts into flames. Floods of smoke and flames pour forth in all directions from the windows. Stockpiles of gunpowder explode. The columns burst apart and come crashing down in the midst of a dazzling light.

Suddenly thousands of trumpets make the air resound, followed first by hundreds of drums, and then by innumerable bands of a thousand instruments each. Toward nine o'clock, royalty is extinguished in the ashes of its palace, as songs of victory are chanted by fifty thousand victorious rebels and echoed by more than eight hundred thousand witnesses of their combat and triumph. And the people, escorted by many bands of drums, trumpets, and musicians who circulate in all the neighborhoods, return home, singing hymns to freedom and to the nation! I will not even attempt to describe the passionate enthusiasm and admiration that this first day brought forth.

Second Day: Funeral Rites—Old Martyrs, Heroes, and Recent Victims Are Honored

From early morning, the great bell, the cannon fired from time to time in each neighborhood of the city, and lugubrious drums resounding in all the streets at the same time announce a grand ceremony of funeral rites. All citizens, women, and children put on their mourning garb and the national flag is draped in black everywhere. People everywhere are reading or declaiming elegies for the old martyrs and the most recent victims; all citizens have been encouraged to compose elegies. After five o'clock, sixty funeral processions, each made up of four or five thousand persons, leave from Icara's sixty neighborhoods, while seven or eight hundred thousand spectators seat themselves in the grandstands of the great arena. Each of these processions includes several bands of musicians;

a band of young women carrying baskets of flowers; a band of young men carrying crowns and garlands; three bands representing wounded citizens, unwounded fighters bearing arms, and those who distinguished themselves by heroic acts; white horses draped with black flags; carts carrying the wounded; other carts carrying coffins; still more carts carrying the wives and children of the dead; communal magistrates; and battalions of National Guard, on foot and on horseback.

In the middle of the arena is an enormous funeral pyre surrounded by a hundred altars on which incense is burning. The names of the principal victims are suspended under funeral wreaths; beneath them are the names of the heroes and those of a hundred of the old martyrs. These three categories are set apart from one another by their relative height and by their different colors. At six o'clock, the bell and the cannon announce the arrival of the first procession. It enters the arena with horses and carts several abreast, and stops near the funeral pyre. While the coffins are carried there, drums roll and funereal notes issue forth from the musicians, girls throw flowers, boys throw wreathes, and the National Guard lower their arms and flags. The procession then starts up again, circles back, passing the next one, and stops near the gate through which it entered, taking up a position perpendicular to the funeral pyre. The girls are in front, followed by the boys, drums, musicians, National Guard, horses, and finally the carts, with their backs to the stands. The wounded men who are on foot, the heroes, and the fighters go to sit in the front stands, and the magistrates are seated in turn. The sixty processions parade in this manner in an uninterrupted flow, one after the other, forming one immense procession. At that point, Icar arrives wounded, on horseback, followed by the entire National Assembly, all in high mourning, and they take their places around the coffins.

Up until now, the gradual arrival of the funeral processions and their different aspects formed an animated, imposing spectacle. Now that all the processions have taken their places, toward eight o'clock, the arena itself is the most magnificent spectacle. We can see the funeral pyre in the center, a hundred altars around it, and hundreds of wreathes and inscriptions suspended above it amid clouds of incense, surrounded in turn by the immense circle of the National Assembly. In one direction are sixty perpendicular rows made up of the sixty separate processions; in the other, a multitude of different circles: a large circle of girls dressed in white, a similar circle of boys dressed in black; a circle of drums and musicians; two circles of uniformed National Guard, on foot and on horseback; circles of white and black horses; a circle of empty carts; another of carts filled with widows and orphans. Above them, the stands are filled with circles of the wounded, heroes, and fighters, followed by twelve mixed circles. Above everything, we can see the top of the thousand tents on which are mounted thousands of flags. And every person sees everything and is seen by everybody. Every person is both spectator and actor in the spectacle!

Now the funeral rites begin. At the signal, we hear the lugubrious sound of the great bell, followed by the long roll from the drummers' circle and the sound of sixty musical bands. Incense is lit once more and burns even more strongly, and Icar and the members of the National Assembly throw funeral wreathes on the coffins of the martyrs, heroes, and victims. After that, they take their places in the stands, while all the other circles move closer to the funeral pyre. What magnificent harmony now makes the air come alive! Throwing flowers toward the funeral pyre, the circle of young girls sings the first couplet of a hymn glorifying the victims, heroes, and martyrs. The boys repeat the refrain with the girls. Throwing wreathes, the boys sing the second couplet, and the girls repeat the refrain with them. Lowering arms and flags, the National Guard sings the third couplet, and the boys and girls repeat it. They all sing the fourth couplet, which is repeated by all six hundred thousand spectators. And then, to the sound of a hundred trumpets, fifty feet above the funeral pyre, a dazzling light appears with these words in letters of fire: "The nation adopts their children and their wives." At the same moment, sixty stars appear and shine over the sixty groups of carts carrying the widows and orphans. And then, to a further trumpet fanfare, the National Assembly, the provincials and colonials, the people and magistrates rise together to ratify the adoption. The inscription then disappears and is replaced by another, which says: "Glory to the heroes!" Sixty stars shine above their heads. All the spectators rise once more to the intonation of hymns and the sound of music. Other stars and ceremonies follow, with these inscriptions: "Honor to the wounded! Honor to the fighters!"

Finally, to the sound of the great bell, cannons, drums, music, and songs, the funeral pyre bursts into flames and becomes the site of an immense, superb fire whose flames, alternating red and violet, illuminate the sky and the arena. Following this dazzling light, we see torrents of black smoke and a deep darkness, in the midst of which suddenly appear once more the names of the victims, heroes, and martyrs, illuminated by wreathes of sparkling stars; and, higher still, this inscription in enormous letters of fire: "Immortal glory to our revolutionary martyrs!" Everything is extinguished, but there is more to come. Even farther up, four or five hundred feet in the sky, we see a hundred large wreathes of light held up by a hundred large balloons, and an immense wreath formed by the luminous cord that joins together these hundred balloons arranged in a circle.

The people go home beneath their porticos, now darkened and without lighting, to the sound of sixty bands, which move through the sixty neighborhoods. I will not attempt to describe the emotions of this population, dazzled, electrified, carried away with passion and gratitude for patriotic devotion.

Third Day: Icar's Dictatorship—Triumph

The cannon and the great bell, now accompanied by a harmonious carillon, announce a festival of triumph. During the whole morning, we see bands of musicians moving through the streets, some on foot, others on horseback or on carts. We hear nothing but battle fanfares, victory tunes, and songs of triumph.

By four o'clock, almost the whole population of Icara and its sixty neighborhoods or communes, 100,000 provincials, 10,000 colonials (among them almost 8,000 black or copper-colored persons), and 25,000 foreigners have gathered in the grand Arena of Victory. They all are seated in large groups set apart by their costumes, colors, and flags. Here are the 2,000 deputies who make up the National Assembly, the 100,000 provincials, the 10,000 colonials, the 720 deputies making up the provincial assemblies of the six provinces of Icara, the communal magistrates of its sixty neighborhoods, and the 25,000 foreigners and their ambassadors, in seats of honor, between the National Assembly and the people. On the grandstands occupied by the people, we see, in front, circles of children, girls and boys, who will go down into the arena to dance and sing.

Soon more than 300,000 members of the National Guard arrive, infantry and cavalry. They make up the National Guard of the sixty neighborhoods or communes of Icara and are seated with their sixty bands on the bleachers, with equal spaces left between them. The sixty brigades of National Guard take their position in the center, facing the spectators. The public officials all have impressive costumes. All the citizens are wearing their holiday outfits. Ornamentation of all sorts—feathers, brilliant fabrics, and dazzling stones—are displayed today to embellish the beauty of the spectacle. Everywhere we see garlands of plants and flowers and waving, unfurled flags. In the center, we see a hundred altars burning with incense at the feet of a very tall woman who represents ICARIA and who is seated on a raised throne. You will see nothing more magnificent than these brilliant costumes, superb plumes, horses, shining weapons, sparkling helmets, and flags! And I am seated between Dinaïse and Corilla, who are as decked out and beautiful as divinities. My soul, drunk with happiness and hope, is open to all the joy admiration can bring.

The bell, the cannon, and the sixty musical ensembles announce the opening of the festival: the dictatorship. Now we see entering the arena a band of fighters made up of men, women, and children, some on foot, others on horseback, all carrying different weapons, some dressed in a variety of outfits, others in shirttails, crying out: "Icar for dictator! Icar for dictator!" They acclaim loudly a man in their group, mounted on horseback, who is playing the role of the wounded Icar. Corilla, her eyes shining with joy, points out her grandfather near Icar. Icar and his procession go around the arena, among the spectators and the circular front of the National Guard. As they proceed to the sound of drums and music, the national guardsmen lower their flags and present arms, chanting: "Icar for dictator!" They parade around the arena a second time, turning toward the stands, and all the spectators rise and intone the same chant. Their voices mix with the sound of the drums and music.

Now the ceremony of triumph begins. The victorious rebels, who were accompanying Icar when he arrived, now go back through the opposite gate and pass under a triumphal arch that had been hidden until then under a piece of fabric and is suddenly uncovered. The rebels carry as trophies or drag along on the ground the emblems of royalty: pieces of the destroyed throne, courtly dress, and noble coats of arms. They move around the arena to the sound of the bell and its carillon, cannons, drums, trumpets, music, and songs of victory, under a rain of wreathes, laurel wreathes, and flowers thrown by the people from the stands. The rebels drag in the queen, led by the members of her guard who arrested her; her ministers, some in embroidered costumes and others disguised as lackeys and beggars; nobles in magnificent, torn costumes; and finally Lixdox, in the scullery maid's outfit, locked in a cage on a cart that puts him in full view. Nothing is said to the queen; but her ministers, her courtiers, and, above all, Lixdox are greeted everywhere with hisses and curses. Finally, the victors come in on horseback or on carts, followed by Icar on a triumphal cart, his head bare, at the feet of Icaria, who is adorned with a magnificent mantle and a brilliant crown.

Now that the triumphal ceremony is over, Icaria and Icar move to the center, she on the throne, he on the first rung, to preside over the games and physical contests that are beginning. Sixty poles come out of the earth. For a quarter of an hour, spectators laugh at the boys who try, one after the other, to climb up the poles and who keep slipping down until finally one of them reaches the top. The poles disappear, and the laughter increases at the sight of boys who are running a sack race. Most of them fall before they reach the finish line. Other games follow rapidly and are the cause of even more joy and laughter. These are followed by a variety of races for boys and girls, horses and carts, all taking place to the sound of the trumpet. Horseback riding displays are next.

Now comes the review of the National Guard, which was organized by Icar a few days after the revolution. Mounted on a superb horse, escorted by Valmor's grandfather and a few generals prancing about on spirited horses, Icar rides rapidly by the front of the line between the guard and the spectators. This is followed by military maneuvers, during which the National Guard executes a thousand different infantry and cavalry formations. Next the members of the National Assembly, organized and convened by Icar after the revolution, leave their seats and parade before Icar and Icaria in a hundred squads of twenty deputies each, carrying the hundred provincial flags and the thousand communal ones. Lined up around the hundred altars, surrounded by the national guardsmen, the representatives pledge to uphold the republican, communitarian CONSTITUTION presented by Icaria and Icar. The pledge is repeated by the National Guard and by the spectators, who, all standing and bareheaded, have both hands outstretched.

Now twenty thousand children, from six to ten years of age, come down from the stands into the arena, pass between the brigades of the National Guard, and form a first central circle. Thirty thousand girls and thirty thousand boys, from ten to twenty years of age, come down in the same manner and form two other circles. Some are wearing flowers and wreathes, others scarves and garlands, branches and flags. Now the ballet begins. It consists of dances and rounds for eighty thousand dancers, who execute a thousand turns while throwing flowers and wreathes toward Icar and Icaria, waving their branches and scarves, their garlands and flags. Now the song begins. First the twenty thousand children, and then the thirty thousand young women and the thirty thousand young men, and finally more than a million voices sing a hymn of gratitude to the community. The concert begins. The bell and its carillon, and then cannons on all the city squares, followed by five or six hundred drums, and then five or six hundred trumpets, and then sixty bands scattered throughout the stands, and finally all the bands and nearly ten thousand instruments placed together in a group around the center make the arena resound, first with various tunes of victory and triumph and then with the most sublime harmonies.

Night has fallen. An immense firework display has been prepared on frameworks placed throughout and hidden by garlands, leaves, and flags. Soon the sky seems to be burning with a thousand fires that burst into the air from all sides and cross each other in all directions, displaying a thousand colors and shapes. The finale is the most gigantic and magnificent bouquet imaginable. The festival is not yet over. When the people leave the arena, accompanied by the sixty musical ensembles, they find their porticos decorated with garlands and flags, the usual lighting replaced by illuminations (always run on gas) that display a thousand colors, inscriptions, and shapes, on the streets as well as on the façades of public buildings or on the leaves of trees in the public promenades.

And that is not all. When we arrive at Valmor's house, we all go up onto the terrace, where supper had been prepared before we left. While eating, we enjoy a spectacle that is even more magnificent in its own way. We see that all the terraces are illuminated and filled with families having supper, laughing, and singing. All the balustrades are outlined by lights, as are the tops of the illuminated public buildings. And then, to signal the time for retiring to bed, the wide vault of the sky, darkened by night, appears suddenly to be inflamed by thousands of fireworks of all colors thrown in all directions by a hundred balloons scattered five or six hundred feet above the city. The balloons pour a great rain of stars and fires on the city.

It is certain that after such a spectacle, there is nothing more that the eye might take pleasure in seeing.

35 Festivals, Games, Amusements, Luxury

When Eugene and I arrived at Mrs. Dinamé's home, where we planned to spend the evening, the two families were seated outside in the garden in the midst of green shrubs, flowers, and their sweet perfumes. Dinaïse, dressed in her gardening clothes, was planting and sowing flowers, while the children watered and Corilla supervised by giving orders. Corilla motioned to me and I drew near.

"You see," she said in a low voice, "what a coquette Dinaïse is! She has put on work clothes so that you will see that she is even prettier in them than she is in her party dress, and than I am in my society frock."

"You are mean!" Dinaïse replied.

"You are cunning!" said Corilla.

"You are a flatterer!" they both told me when I remarked, as I moved away, that they both were charming.

"Well, young men," said Valmor's grandfather, "how do you feel today? I will not ask my friend Eugene if he slept well, for I am sure that he shot rifles the whole night, but you, Milord, are you still feverish? Do you know that yesterday and for two days before that you seemed as mad, as passionate, I mean, as our friend Eugene?" he continued, smiling. "How our festivals fired you up!"

"How can you not catch fire," said Valmor, "when you are under fire, between two fires, and surrounded by fires?"

"Yes, my son," the old man said, laughing. "You are lucky that Dinaïse and Corilla cannot hear you! Do you think, Milord, that our Icarian festivals are less beautiful than your English ones?"

"Oh, yes!" cried Eugene. "English festivals are certainly beautiful! The aristocrats attend court receptions in beautiful costumes and are brought in hand-some carriages. They have the incomparable pleasure of waiting in line for hours on end to have the honor and pleasure of making a humble bow to the king, the queen, and some royal brat in a cradle, if there happens to be one. Festivals, in-deed, where you have the pleasure of catching your death of cold in a church to hear four or five hundred musicians; horse races where many people lose their fortunes through wagers; a few military reviews where they shoot off a few can-nons or rifles; great dinners in gilded parlors or large luncheons in parks. And for the people? Nothing, absolutely nothing, with the exception of those motley processions on the day of the patron saint of some corporation; the sight of a few monotonous illuminations in bad taste on the king's feast day; and, for those few people who can take a day off work, the sight of fancy carriages, lackeys, and the luxuries of the aristocracy!"

"But, Eugene," said the old man, "do you think that our festivals are less beautiful than your French festivals?"

"Oh, yes, they are certainly beautiful!" I replied before Eugene had a chance to do so. "Adulations for the king, for Charles X as well as for Napoleon. Arches of triumph for a prince who is a child or coward, as if he were a hero; balls and dinners for the aristocracy; and, for the masses, reviews that they do not get to see, pitiful fireworks displays of which they can see only half, standing painfully on tiptoe and mixing with the crowd, in danger of being suffocated, crushed, or robbed. Oh! I almost forgot the policemen stationed throughout in order to em-barrass, annoy, and have a go at the spectators. I also forgot to mention the sausages and the wines made available to the people so that others can enjoy see-ing them beat each other up and get drunk! And I almost forgot the anniversary of the famous July Days. Yes, the July Anniversary is a great one!"

"Ah!" cried Eugene in a deeply upset voice. "Do not speak to me of the July Anniversary! We do not have one anymore! In fact, we never had one. It is only in Icaria that I have seen the anniversary of a Popular Revolution! This one alone can be called an anniversary! Here is a nation that has not renounced its works! Here is a government, born on the revolutionary barricades, that is not unfaith-ful to its origins. This government does not erase the traces of bullets shot by freedom against tyranny; it does not repudiate, as if it were a catastrophe, the glory of a legitimate revolution. It does not find itself constrained to banish the victors, after having proclaimed them heroes. It does not dread rebellious proclamations, or calls to arms, or gatherings, or the memory of military defec-tions, or the revolt of guards against a tyrant. This government does not replace the anniversary of the great masterpiece of the people, who spilled their blood to win for themselves liberation and happiness, with royal and dynastic holidays!"

"Well, my dear friend," said the old man, "let me tell you frankly that your complaints do not seem very reasonable to me. How might you expect that royalty and aristocracy could like the memory of a rebellion and a popular revolution? And how could a celebration be beautiful without the spontaneous cooperation of the people? Here it is the republic that organizes our anniversary and our festivals! The people order them! They are made for the people, and it is the people who carry them out with all their enthusiasm and all their power. It is our own carnival, our amateur theater, one of our great proverbs acted out as one great family!"

"Alas!" said Eugene. "We were hoping . . ."

"You were hoping, poor Eugene! Well, keep hoping, for we ourselves hoped for a long time, until, finally, the long period of time and the uselessness of our hopes reduced public opinion and our entire people to despair."

"But are you sure you understand, Milord," the old man continued, addressing me, "why all the citizens wish and are able to be actors in our political dramas, and why our festivals are so magnificent?"

"Certainly. I understand it quite well."

"No, no," cried Dinaïse and Corilla, who were coming back to us, laughing. "He does not understand! He does not understand!"

"Do you truly think, young ladies, that I do not understand? We shall see about that! No one told me that everything having to do with festivals, the anniversary, for example, is set out by law. That law is based on the project presented to the public by the Committee of Public Festivals, a committee that studied all the festivals of ancient and modern peoples. The law was then submitted for the approval of the people. In other words, the People as a whole organized and set up the festival. Consequently, it is not surprising that the People choose to carry out that which they voluntarily approved. No one told me this, but I am sure of it."

"Bravo! Bravo!" said everyone together.

"Nor did anyone tell me that, because the law designates the number of singers, dancers, and musicians at the festival, it also sets up the educational system in such a way that, from ages five to twenty-one, all children practice so that they will be able to dance and play an instrument at the festival. No one told me this, but I am sure it is true!" The applause was even stronger.

"I even understand perfectly well that the people wish and are able to attend their festivals without dust or mud, police or informers, shielded from the sun or rain, seated comfortably so that everyone can see and hear equally well. I also understand perfectly that all the festivals are organized like dramatic plays, and that every one of these plays has a moral and political purpose. That purpose is not the personal pleasure and servile flattery of a king, but is the advantage, glory, and happiness of the people. And if I admire beyond all words the magnificence of your festivals, I admire no less the order, forethought, wisdom. . . . I do not know what else to say about your republic!"

"How far you have come," said Corilla, "on the path of republican passion and feeling!"

"It is true," said Valmor. "Eugene's democracy is going to be a pale shadow compared to Milord's democratic fervor! What a miracle! Dinaros, Eugene, and I can congratulate ourselves on having engineered this miraculous metamorphosis!"

"And you are forgetting," said Eugene, "four other persons who have been far more instrumental than we four have been in this prodigious conversion: the republic, the community, and . . ."

"And who are the other two?" cried Valmor.

"Do you not know who they are?" Eugene replied. "Name them! Name them!"

"Do you not know who they are? Dinaïse and me!" cried Corilla.

"No."

"Yes."

And poor Eugene, forced into a corner by Corilla and Dinaïse, said that it was more difficult to resist the mischievousness of two young women than to repel the attacks of two strong champions.

"You are laughing?" said the grandfather. "Do you not know, my children, that these two young women could teach you a great deal, and that none of you, perhaps, could write as electrifying a proclamation of rebellion as Corilla's; nor could any of you write verses as burning with patriotic passion as Dinaïse's verses!" We read those two pieces, as well as a very beautiful proclamation by Dinaros. We laughed so loudly, booing Dinaros's proclamation while applauding the other two, that the neighbors on our right, who were also in their garden, started to laugh with us.

Valmor explained to us that all Icarians were invited to write similar pieces for the three festival days. An immense number of them had been passed around. Many were quite remarkable. The ten best in each genre would be chosen, printed, and distributed in a short time on the recommendation of a committee charged with examining them all. The conversation continued about the other festivals or great public plays, which were always celebrated in one of the two arenas. Valmor told us that sometimes all the male and female workers were there, grouped by professions, with different banners for each; or all the horses, carts, or dogs. He told us that they even bring in ten feet of water sometimes, and that you can see a multitude of vessels, steamboats, small crafts, and swimmers who, by their great number, their turns, and the variety of forms, colors, and flags, present a most magnificent entertainment, while in winter skating is a most gracious and amusing spectacle as well.

"You can see," said Dinaros, "to what an extent the republic surpasses the monarchy in beautiful and noble festivals, just as the republic goes way beyond the monarchy in its social and political organization. The republic is also far superior in both public and private games and amusements. There is nothing in the ancient or modern world that we have not studied, known, and used to our benefit, saving the good and rejecting the bad elements. Moreover, we like pleasure, and we feel that it is wise to use all the sensual faculties that benevolent nature has given us and to delight in all the treasures she has provided around us and for us, as long as reason, that invaluable gift of benevolent nature, always presides over all our pleasures. And so you will see in our country, as elsewhere, all genres of theater, all games, and all amusements that have no harmful elements. The republic provides the citizens with all the necessary places and equipment. The republic does not even forbid luxuries or superfluities, for you cannot call an amusement superfluous if it has no drawbacks. We have wisely set up three fundamental rules. The first is that all our amusements must be sanctioned by the law or by the people. The second is that we may not seek the pleasurable until we have provided ourselves with that which is necessary and useful. The third is that we do not allow any pleasures other than those that every Icarian can enjoy equally.

"Therefore, we built our workshops before our public buildings. We furnished our bedrooms before adorning our parlors. We manufactured cotton before silk and velvet. We have had saddle horses for riding for only twenty years, and we have had horses for children to ride for only five years. Ten years from now, every family will have a billiard table on its terrace, which will serve as a dining table as well. Right now, every street has only one billiard room shared by thirty-two families. All of our porticos will soon be transformed into gardens, or at least will be adorned with greenery, plants, and garlands, which will make them delightful to walk through. Just like that king of Persia who promised a reward to anyone who might invent a new pleasure, we invite all our citizens to perfect or increase our amusements. Whereas despotism sought new amusements only for the despot, the republic seeks new pleasures only for the people. Whereas the aristocracy—in England, for example—monopolizes everything, outlaws all amusements on Sundays, makes pleasurable activities available during the week only to the leisured class and to the rich, and leaves the English people no other amusement than that of becoming drunk in their public houses in order to forget their abject poverty, the Icarian people, pampered by the republic like a child by its mother, enjoy all pleasures every day. The Icarian people are happier than all the peoples of the earth and all the aristocrats of the world."

"Ah! Yes, happy Icaria," said Eugene, sighing. And his sigh made all of us burst into laughter. The passionate patriot, almost annoyed by our gaiety, engulfed us in the most thundering patriotic torrent, while the good old grandfather merely held his hand and cheered him on.

36 Colonies

I had seen more than ten thousand colonials at the festival, almost all of whom were black, tan, or copper colored. In addition, I had heard many details about the manners and customs of a few uncivilized peoples bordering Icaria, as well as information about the astonishing rapidity of growth of the Icarian colonies. I begged Dinaros to explain in depth their colonial system.

"For a long time," he told us, "we had no need of colonies. But foreseeing that we might be overpopulated one day, we prepared well in advance a colonial establishment on a fertile and almost deserted piece of land inhabited by small native populations of still uncivilized persons, among whom we wished to begin a vast civilizing project. To help us reach this double goal more effectively, we consulted with our neighboring allies. We proposed founding a common colony where each nation would send the same number of families who would form only one people in a single community and whose children could marry only by mixing races and blood together. To prepare the execution of this project more successfully, we asked for and obtained handsome foreign children whom we raised with our own in order to send them at a later date to the colony. At the same time, in conjunction with our allies, we sought all means of pleasing the natives and binding them to us. We sent them old people and children who could neither worry them nor provoke their anger, who brought them all kinds of presents, who settled down in their country and who learned their language and their customs. In this way, we succeeded in attracting to our country some native adults and even some children. We overwhelmed them with caresses, we did everything we could to win them over, we taught them our language, and we sent them back with everything that could gain the confidence and affection of their compatriots. We were not deterred by difficulties and obstacles. This system, followed with patience and consistency, was so successful that the natives came to worship us almost as if we were benevolent gods, begging us to come and establish ourselves in their midst in order to shower more benefits on them.

"It follows that when we decided it was the appropriate time to begin the colony, we had no need of any form of violence. Once we were established, we increased our missionaries in their country and their travelers in ours. We gave them the example of work without demanding any work from them. We instilled within them imperceptibly the desire to work by having them witness its marvelous results. Today, after fewer than thirty years, we have created a magnificent colony as flourishing as Icaria itself. We have civilized seven or eight small native populations who now compete with us; and we have launched civilization to such an extent that it is now unstoppable! It is true that we have spent a great deal; we have paid the natives so that they will allow us to make them happy, but with what great rewards! Our good deeds have conquered peacefully a new Icaria for us and have won over savages to civilization, while preparing the ground for the conquest of the pagan universe for humanity."

"And we Europeans and Christians," cried Eugene, "we who brag about our civilization, we buy slaves; that is, we encourage brigands to steal men, women, and children. After that, we torture them to force them to work, and it is from their sweat and blood that we extract sugar and coffee! We exterminate savage or half-civilized peoples to gain material treasures! Repeating all the horrors of the great barbarian invasion and the Spanish conquest of the Americas, we massacre, we pillage, and we burn in order to preserve a colony and consolidate our power! We carry bloody heads attached to the saddles of our horses, as if we were trying to teach ourselves to become ferocious!" And poor Eugene, red with anger and shame, hid his head in his hands.

37 Religion *(continuation of chapter 20)*

I had often encouraged Valmor to give me the information on religious beliefs in Icaria that during our first talks on religion he deferred to another day. He always avoided my questions. He has finally satisfied my curiosity, and the conversation, which extended to France and England, was extremely interesting. Because Eugene recorded this conversation in his journal and took a more active role in the debate, I will reproduce his account.

Extract from Eugene's Journal

RELIGION

William's request to Valmor to explain Icaria's religious system led to the following discussion:

"I already told you," Valmor said to William, "that two years after the revolution, when it had already brought about many salutary results, Icar had the National Assembly convene a great council composed of priests elected by all other priests, professors elected by all other professors, and the most famous philosophers, moralists, scholars, and writers in order to discuss all questions pertaining to divinity and religion. The council, composed in this way of the most erudite, wise, and judicious men, gathered in addition all individual views that citizens cared to submit to it. All views were examined and discussed for four years. All questions were decided by a vast majority and often unanimously. Well, imagine that the council is assembled, that it is discussing and deciding everything in a long session, and that you are present at its deliberations. Imagine you can see them and hear them over there. Look and listen carefully, but do not interrupt! Afterward you will make your observations. Now listen!

" 'Is there a God, that is, a first cause of which all we see is the effect?' They are going to vote by standing or remaining seated. Look! The whole assembly rises! They propose the opposite. Look carefully again. The whole council remains seated.

" 'Is this God known?'

" 'No!' unanimously.

" 'Is His form known?'

" 'No!' unanimously. 'Thousands of peoples represent Him in a thousand different forms.'

" 'Was man made in His image?' 'We would like to believe that, but we know nothing about it.'

" 'Does the council believe the revelation that Moses says was made to him by a God with a human face?'

" 'No!' unanimously."

"What?" cried William.

"What can I say? The entire council does not believe it. Moreover, you will read its justification.

" 'Does the council believe that the Bible is a human work?'

" 'Yes.' "

"What?" he cried again.

"You have seen it yourself. The entire council has risen. You will read its justification.

" 'Does the council believe what the Bible says?'

" 'No. There are no stories of fairies, witches, and ghosts, no tales of a thousand and one nights, no mythological fables that are not almost as believable as these.'

" 'Does the council believe that Jesus Christ is a God?'

" 'The thousands of religions that fill the earth are all human institutions imagined and created to dominate and govern peoples. All the founders of the principal religions, Confucius in China, Lama in Tartary, Sinto in Japan, Brahma and Buddha in India, Zoroaster in Persia, Osiris and Isis in Egypt, Jupiter and his court in Phoenicia and in Greece, Minos in Crete, Moses in Judea, Pythagoras in Italy, Numa in Rome, Odin in the North, Mohammed in Arabia, Manco-Capac in Peru, and all the others in all the other countries are men of genius, but only men, legislators, civilizers, and governors of their nations.

" 'Jesus Christ, misunderstood and condemned by his fellows, rejected for more than three hundred years by philosophers—that is, by the erudite and enlightened world—is obviously only a man as well, but a man who deserves to be ranked first among human beings for his devotion to the happiness of the human race and for his proclamation of the principles of EQUALITY, FRATERNITY, and COMMUNITY.'

" 'How was the world, and man in particular, formed?'

" 'We know nothing about it.'

" 'Should we adopt the Bible as the preeminent book?'

" 'No. In a time of ignorance and barbarism, it might have been useful because all other books were even worse; but today the only good you can extract from it is a few moral principles. All the rest has become erroneous, absurd, and even indecent, immoral, useless, and harmful. The Bible teaches, for example, that it is the sun that revolves around the earth, when it has been discovered since and proven that it is the earth that revolves around the sun! Moses and Jesus Christ were right in their time, but they never intended their work to be eternal. To wish to make out of the Bible immutable rules for all times and for all peoples is the most shocking nonsense and the most monstrous absurdity.'

" 'Does the council believe in a heaven?'

" 'Oppressed, unfortunate peoples need to believe in one, but we generally have no other misfortunes than illness and moral suffering. We are pleased for those unfortunate people whom the hope of a better life can help to bear their sorrows.'

" 'Does the council believe in hell?'

" 'Victims of tyranny need to believe that tyrants will be punished there, and that belief is useful in consoling them a little, provided that it does not put them to sleep and does not prevent them from punishing the tyrants themselves. Fear of hell might be useful to stop the oppressors, but oppressors do not believe in hell. It is precisely those tyrants who want the oppressed to believe in hell in order to prevent them from thinking about their own emancipation. In Icaria, we have neither tyrants nor criminals nor wicked people, and we do not believe in a hell, which is of no use to us.'

" 'Does the council believe in saints, miracles, the pope, and his infallibility?' "

"Ho!" cried William. "You do not need to tell me the answer. But in truth," he added, "your religion is not a religion! You have no religion!"

"What do you mean by religion?" Valmor replied. "To have a religion, is it necessary to believe in a god with human form, who has the habits and passions of men? Just because you believe in the god of Moses, a jealous, demanding, angry, vindictive, and bloody god, do the thousands of peoples who believe in other gods have no religion according to you? If you had not interrupted me, you would have seen your question decided upon by the council, for the council asked itself: 'Is a religion (that is, a systematic religion accompanied by a specific set of observances) useful to Icarians?' And the council unanimously replied, 'No.' What do you think of that? The council, made up of priests, professors, the elite of the country, and, you could say, the entire people, replied 'No!' "

(Eugene) "And the council was right, in my opinion. Look William, let us reason it out! Because the council did not believe either in the divinity of Jesus Christ or in the divine origin of the Bible, or in the revelation made to Moses, or in a god with a human face who rewards, punishes, and welcomes prayers, would you want the council to have pretended to believe in these things, to have adopted this imaginary religion, to have ordered the people to believe it, and to have brought up children in this belief, which it had declared erroneous and false? Would it have been possible to order the Icarian people to do this, when the people, educated and enlightened, were the council itself—in a word, when the people did not believe this? Would it not have been almost impossible to raise children in this belief when the fathers themselves did not believe it, and our goal was to give our children an education that would make them people who would always be directed by reason and truth? Would deceiving the children not have been like imitating idolaters, pagans, Muslims, and aristocrats, and turning our backs on the revolution and on progress?

"Supposing that it might be to our advantage, in some respect, to inspire in our children a belief that we felt to be unreasonable and false. Even so, the disadvantages would surpass the advantages because error, lies, and superstition make people into beasts and infantilize them, whereas Icarians want their children to become adults. For example, how would the fear of hell benefit Icarians, with their system of community? Is this community not the most perfect summation of philosophy and the purest morality in action? Is it not the most complete realization of the principle of fraternity? Does it not contain in itself all virtues? Does it not reach with certainty the goal that all religions purport to have without ever attaining it: the happiness of the human species? In a word, this community preached by Jesus Christ, is it not in itself a religion, and the most perfect of religions? Once again, William, what use could a happy people have for any other religion? Such people have no reason to commit crimes and never commit any; nor have they any use for a priest's punishments, or fear of the justice of hell, or a penal code, or criminal trials, or prisons."

"And what if you remind us," Valmor said to him, "that the community does not prevent illnesses and certain misfortunes for which religion would be a consolation? I will answer you that the community considerably reduces the number of these illnesses and misfortunes. Through education, it gives the people more strength to bear them. Reason generally suffices. Moreover, it is precisely in these cases that our laws tolerate prayer with hope of a happier life, and that we have temples and priests who act as counselors and consolers."

"So your priests are nothing more than priests of Reason," replied William.

"That only makes them all the more reasonable," Valmor countered.

"You are atheistic, your laws and you yourself!"

"What a horrifying word!" said Valmor. "In earlier times, William would have had us burned at the stake. However, let us come to some understanding and not be like those demented people who begin by fighting each other, and who, discussing the matter after having wounded each other, are greatly surprised to discover that they were in agreement in the first place. What do you mean by *atheist*? If by that word you mean those who do not believe in a god with a human countenance like Jupiter or like the God of Moses, then you will find a great many atheists here. If they frighten you, you should probably run away because you can see many atheists here ready to devour you. But if by *atheists* you mean those people who do not believe in any kind of a god whatsoever, you will find none among us. If you make this distinction, you may decide that our laws either are or are not atheistic. We, on the other hand, feel that there has never been a set of more religious laws than ours, because they all are based on community, and because they have as their single concern our happiness."

"I agree with you completely," I (Eugene) replied, "and I am very sorry that my country has not taken advantage of its many revolutions to establish the religion of community and happiness."

"Oh!" replied William. "It is well known that you French, as pleasant and witty as you are, are nonbelieving, impious atheists who, on Sundays, rush off to your amusements and flee from church. I was shocked to see that even your kings violate the sacred law of the Sabbath to permit people to enjoy all manner of amusements in their palaces. Satan has reserved many places for you in his empire!"

"Be brave, good Milord, keep it up! Damn us devoutly and as a good Christian should because we are idiotic enough to be philosophical and jolly; because we are idiotic enough not to worship the pious Charles IX, who, in accord with the pope and his priests, had one hundred thousand Reformed Christians assassinated. Nor do we worship the devout Charles X, who, in cahoots with his Jesuits and his priests, had thousands of Parisians shot down! Go on, go on! Join some of your fellow countrymen who call us French dogs, not realizing that they are the instruments of their oppressors! You accuse my fellow countrymen of being atheists, so I say that you English are also nonbelievers. As you throw down the gauntlet, I will answer your challenge in order to defend myself and attack you in turn.

"First of all, as for you personally, permit me, my dear friend Milord, to ask you a little question. I am not going to ask you whether, when you are in London or on your estate, you make sure to go to hear a sermon, to refrain from any sort of recreation, to be bored, and to yawn all Sunday long in order to please God. Do tell me, however, if, when you are in Paris or elsewhere, you still go to the Protestant temple and refrain from all pleasures on Sundays."

"No, certainly not!"

"Well, there is my ungodly person!"

"How's that?"

"There is my nonbeliever and my atheist, I repeat, and I will prove it to you. But first, I ask the audience's permission to tell a little personal anecdote." Everyone listened to me with increased attentiveness.

"Poor William has no idea," I said, "that the person he damns with such ease was almost madly devout in his youth. Let me tell you about it." (A movement of surprise from the audience.) "I was already thirteen years of age when a respectable curate, who had taken a liking to me and wanted to make me into a priest, indoctrinated me to such an extent that he persuaded me that God always had one eye open. He saw everything; you could do nothing without his support; you obtained his assistance when you invoked him in all sincerity; and finally, all the deprivations you imposed on yourself in order to please him were acceptable in his sight. I believed this priest with all the purity of my soul. I was the most innocent and fervent among the pious and the believers. Now you will see the consequences of my innocent piety. Listen carefully, William!

"It seemed to me, at every moment and everywhere, that I could see the eye of God, an immense eye that was opened and staring at me" (bursts of laughter). "I was terrified to see this eye high above me in the sky. Even under cover of darkness, I would not have committed the least action that this eye might have condemned. When I went to school, seeing as I was sure I could not write a good composition without God's help, I prayed to him confidently, after first making the sign of the cross so that no one would notice it, by waiting a few seconds in between each of the four touches of the hand" (a new burst of laughter). "However, I would have done it more obviously if I felt it were necessary. When I returned from a walk, famished, if I thought that it would be pleasing to God if I deprived myself of a certain food that I particularly liked, I did it gladly" (more laughter). "If I noticed myself looking with pleasure at a girl, I quickly made the sign of the cross to invoke divine aid against the tempting spirit." (This last detail made them all laugh even more.)

"And how did you get out of it?" asked Valmor.

"A single conversation with a good old man, the father of one of my schoolmates, caused me to have certain thoughts that cured me of my madness (for I was or I would have become mad). First, I prayed to God with all the fervor of my soul. I begged him on my knees; I implored him with joined hands to reveal the truth to me by any kind of sign, by the wink of an eye, for example. I promised him that I would dedicate to him all the days, all the minutes of my life, and that I would throw myself into the flames without hesitation if he ordered me to do so. I even said, I remember: 'Oh my God, all-powerful, infinitely good God, show yourself once more to the whole earth, as it is said that you did to Moses! Show yourself, speak from the heights of the skies, command us! And all men, all without exception, I am sure, will prostrate themselves as I am now and will obey you as I do. The human race, which is rushing toward eternal punishment, will be saved! All-powerful God, good God, just God, mild God, God our Father, speak, show yourself, save your children!!!' "

"And what happened then?" said Valmor.

"The Big Eye did not make the slightest blink, and I ceased believing in God, with my conscience completely clear."

"And if you believed in God today?" said William.

"If I believed, I would prostrate myself this minute before His supreme majesty. I would do everything that might please Him, absolutely everything. I would kill you, dear Milord, Corilla, and Dinaïse, if I thought that your deaths would please Him; or, rather, I would beg you to convert and to be saved. Perhaps I would follow the actions of those saints who exterminated idolaters to prevent them from going to hell, after having thrown a few drops of holy water on their heads so that they would be deserving of eternal happiness. Perhaps I would pray to God, my face against the earth, to enlighten my country and humanity. And those French people whom you accuse of committing a crime because they engage in amusements on Sunday, following the example of their kings; if those people suddenly became believers, you would see them prostrating themselves before their irate master or rushing into churches to appease His anger. Suppose that the entire earth suddenly heard a voice from the sky calling all men. You would see all the nations prostrating themselves at the same moment before their Divine Master. However, my compatriots are no more devout than I am, and they are no more to blame than I am. We would be Muslims or Protestants if we had been born and raised in Constantinople or London, just as you and your compatriots would be Catholics if fate had made you Parisians or Romans. My countrymen laugh at the bigots, whereas those very same bigots excommunicate them.

"And you, pious Milord (for it is time to return to you), you who laughed at my madness a short time ago, you who accuse us of impiousness, I am going to prove to you, as I promised, that you yourself are ungodly. Rather, I have already proved it. See here. Answer this single, simple question. Why do you not observe the Sabbath in Paris as you do in London? Why do you go to the opera in France on a day when you would not even listen to music in England? Come now! Answer me! I am waiting for your answer! Hah! You cannot give me one good reason. The reason is that you do not really believe in observing the Sabbath. You do not believe in a God who created the world in six days and rested from his labors on the seventh, and who ordered a Jew (so that he would repeat it to all other men as soon as he was able) to celebrate the Creator's day of rest and to begin work again on the following Monday, even though the Creator has continued to rest ever since that time. Well then! It follows that you do not believe in the Bible, Revelation, Moses, or Jesus Christ! Yes, Milord, you who are so good, you whom I love so much, whom we all respect, you are a miscreant, an infidel, an ungodly man! You will be damned, poor Milord!" ("Well done! Well done!" cried Valmor and Dinaros, delighted by my vigorous attack.)

"In fact, I imagine that a true believer, who always sees my Big Eye, would be hot, ardent, burning. I imagine he would go mad, like the madmen we see in Charenton and Bedlam. I imagine him becoming a fanatic, like those Indians who choose to be crushed under the wheels of the float that carries the enormous statue of their god Juggernaut. I imagine that fanatic becoming an assassin, a burner, an exterminator of heretics. I even imagine your deputy, Andrew, who, not satisfied with the post office not delivering letters on Sundays, demands a law to prevent hackney cabs, cabriolets, and omnibuses from circulating on that holy day. What I do not understand is your lack of passion, your indifference when it is a question of heaven or hell. I do not understand, Milord, how you can go to the Parisian opera on a Sunday. No, you are not a believer, my dear Milord!

"When you go to the court of the little tiny king of that grain of sand you call Great Britain, you are moved and overwhelmed, are you not, by the sight of his majesty? And when you enter a temple, are you not seized by a holy terror at the sight of the King of Kings, the Sovereign of past, present, and future peoples, the Master of the earth and the universe? Hah! You are an ungodly man and an atheist, my virtuous Milord! When it is a question of a matter of the least interest to you, you come, you go, you spare neither words nor letters nor journeys; but when it is a question of your salvation or damnation for eternity, you remain motionless, steeped in your indifference.

"Look! Through the ceiling, up there, in the middle of the sky, I see the Big Eye of God looking at you and awaiting only your prayers to ensure the happiness of your England. What! You do not prostrate yourself, you do not pray, you do not see the Eye? Well, that is because you do not believe, because you are an impious man, my dear Milord. You pretended you were a believer and a pious person out of malice in order to test us!" (At each of my arguments, all the men burst into laughter, clapping their hands).

"Perhaps he will say to you," said Valmor, "as many priests and aristocrats do: 'We are not stupid enough to believe; but it is necessary for the people to believe, for they are a ferocious beast that may devour us!' "

"Oh, no," I answered. "William loves the people too much to use that kind of language. If he were mad enough to say that, I would reply that people are bestial only because the aristocracy destroys their minds. Witness the Icarian people, who have neither aristocracy nor mind destruction. People are ferocious only because their oppressors are barbaric and turn their anger into rage. Witness the Icarians, who have neither tyrant nor ferocity. The aristocrats—who require a religion in order to keep the people in chains, just as they enact intimidating laws in order to muzzle them—resemble thieves who, after having beaten and robbed the passers-by, would impose a religion upon them, so that they would be resigned and would be satisfied with hoping and praying."

"Well said, well said!" cried Valmor and Dinaros.

"And because you are attacking my compatriots (whom I cannot help loving, even though I detest them!), permit me, Mister Englishman, to examine yours a little, after having already examined your own self. It is true that when they return from visiting France, the English have a contest to see who can fulminate the most against the French, a nation of sinners and miscreants. This does not prevent the pious slanderers from returning in droves each year to this country of shame and scandal to copy its fashions, its habits, its pleasures, and its arts, while hoping to acquire its philosophy of life and its gaiety. It is true that some of your most famous men—O'Connell, for example, whom I have often admired— allow themselves to anathematize all France as irreverent, without thinking that, in Europe's opinion, they are doing more damage to their own reputation of wisdom and judgment than they are to the good name of France. What man on earth has the right to cry out, as a god might do: 'I am infallible; I brand the French nation as impious, and, for that reason, I declare it unworthy of freedom!'

"Moreover, it is true that you English would believe yourselves to be damned if you committed the slightest infraction on Sundays. Your devout citizens would even refuse to tell a foreigner the word for an orange because that would be a worldly act" (bursts of laughter). "A zealous priest would publicly censure a brewer for brewing on Saturday because he would be the accomplice of the beer, which was guilty of working on Sunday" (new bursts of laughter). "Instead of participating in innocent amusements, young girls piously read obscene biblical stories or read in the weekly papers the long series of scandals that the aristocrats have perpetrated during the week." (Everyone looks at one another.)

"Let us count the pious persons in your country. Let us see. First we will subtract those who do not attend the church's religious ceremonies at all. How many young fashionables, elegant women, and aristocrats speak a great deal about religion but never enter a temple and never set eyes upon a Bible? The people who are deprived of any pleasure during the week, on the other hand, rush on Sundays to the cabarets much more than to the temples, for they have no pleasure in life except getting drunk in public houses. And how many members of Parliament, how many men known for their judgment and knowledge, are avowed nonbelievers! Let us also subtract those who go to hear a sermon one Sunday and do not go the next week, who worship God in England and the Devil in Paris. All those half-believers are laughable! I call them infidels and nonbelievers!

"Among those who practice rigorously all the religious observances, let us subtract all the hypocrites. Doesn't England, like France, have those holy men who make religion into their trade and merchandise, and who make special business deals with heaven? Doesn't England even have priests who beat their wives, men like de Laconges who cut the throats of their mistresses, and others like Mingrats who cut the victims of their unholy lust into pieces?

"The remaining ones are those who practice in good faith, and you have no more of them in England than we do in France. Your temples are no more filled than our churches. Even among those, there are many men who have been forced and constrained to go to temple, as well as countless children, old women, cooks and lackeys, ignoramuses and imbeciles who believe only because someone told them to believe, and who would believe all the priests on earth. They think they believe, but they genuflect and pray automatically without conviction and without guidance at important moments! Does my eternally open Big Eye prevent this flock from eating someone else's feed? Does it prevent storekeepers from cheating their customers, servants from stealing from their masters or slandering their mistresses, husbands from beating their wives, and wives from committing more than one form of theft to the detriment of their husbands and children? I am going to go even further. Do you not know a devout ship owner who prays to God to procure for him a good cargo of Negroes that will allow him to earn a great deal of money? Do you not know a devout spouse who prays to God to have her husband go down in a shipwreck? Remember that Neapolitan brigand who recited paternosters and Ave Marias so that God would send a rich milord into the sights of his cannon. Remember that king who, kneeling down before his statue of the Holy Virgin, begged her to allow him to carry out yet one more little assassination. For in truth, when we think about all the abuses of religion, we find that the history of religion is made up of all manner of wild deeds, crimes, and scoundrels who have desecrated humanity!

"And your superb aristocrats, who speak so prudishly about religion, those who practice its rites as well as those who disdain them, do they actually have a religion? It is they who have oppressed that unfortunate Ireland for so long, and who feed off the poverty of the poor people of England! No, William, your aristocrats have no religion; neither does your nation!"

"Oh, my friend," cried William, "does your love for the people not make you unjust toward the English nobility and very severe toward the nation itself?"

"Unjust! I would be very sorry to be unjust, for it is justice above all that I love, for aristocrats as well as for poor workers. I will even confess to you with great pleasure (for it always gives me pleasure to see the good and pain to see the bad) that, in England as well as in France, I know many noble families whose character, good deeds, and generosity I honor. I also know many bourgeois families whose qualities and virtues I admire. I venerate the humanity and charity of several of your religious sects. I admire and respect your nation. I have often defended it against unjust reproaches. In your country, there are many elements that excite my admiration, but that is not because you have religion; it is, on the contrary, despite the fact that you are pious. Pious! What am I talking about? They are bigots and superstitious persons. That hodgepodge of diverse sects, those puerile observances that are considered so important, are they not unworthy of a nation of men?

"However, I still confess, without trying to establish a parallel between the two nations, that the English seem more like men than the French. I would almost say that they are men, surrounded by charming children, and that the French are nice children gathered around a few men of genius. But I persist in affirming, nevertheless, that your nation has no religion whatsoever. Because you have accused me of being unjust, I will add, to be completely fair, that you have no perfect believers other than those who are in Bedlam. To your most charitable pious persons, I would say: 'You are simple in your clothing, lodgings, and food. Good! You are good to your wives, your children, your domestic help, and your fellow religionists. Very good! But you are rich, and there are poor people in your country. You have a superfluity of goods, while millions of your brothers have neither clothing nor bread! If you believe in Jesus Christ, reduce your belongings to the necessities, widen the circle of your alms, give away all your surplus, and then you will have as your reward the ineffable happiness of pleasing God and multiplying to infinity your good deeds as you increase those who follow your example! But, deaf to the voice of Jesus Christ, you save your surplus for yourselves! Well, then, you are not Christians!'

"Moreover, William, the most religious nation is necessarily the most virtuous and the happiest. Despite your religion, or, rather, your bigotry and your Bible, do your courts have fewer crimes to punish than the courts of your neighbors? Do your children have more respect for their parents? Are your women better behaved, your men more virtuous, your people happier? You would not dare assert that, William. And, therefore, speak to us no more of the piety of the English and of the impiety of the French!

"But we should be speaking about the Icarians, and I beg your pardon, gentlemen, for having responded at such length to our friend's provocative remarks. Because he was criticizing the religion of Icaria as well, I should have limited myself to saying the following: 'You, Milord, who have traveled so widely, in what other country have you seen parents who treat their children more tenderly, children who are as respectful and devoted to their parents, girls who are as well behaved, spouses who are as faithful, so paternal a government, such free citizens, so little crime, so much fraternity, so many virtues, and so much happiness, and, finally, priests who are so honorable and so worthy of being honored? In what country have you seen man fulfill so completely the well-meaning intentions of the Creator and make such good use of that inexhaustible treasure of perfection and happiness that Providence has given him: sublime and divine REASON? Under what religion have you seen a people so advanced along the unending road to perfection, with so few reproaches to make to nature and so much thanks to give her for her innumerable gifts? Name for me a single nation as capable of appreciating and admiring the marvels of the creation and the universe, a single nation that knows so well how to worship God in his magnificent works, a people so good at appreciating his justice and goodness, honoring him, and giving him appropriate thanks by imitating that common father of the human race in his LOVE for all his children. Confess it, proclaim it, my dear Milord! The religion of Icaria is the most perfect of all religions!!"

38 France and England

The republic had just received, a few days earlier, a package of English, French, and other newspapers and had just published the statistical analysis of those received in the last six months.

"What a frightening picture!" Valmor's grandfather cried. "Look how many fires and accidents occurred because of the two governments' negligence. Look at the number of bankruptcies, of unemployed workers reduced to begging! Look at the number of trials, duels and suicides, thefts, assassinations and crimes of all sorts, convictions and deaths! Look at the number of riots, conspiracies, and attempted overthrows! Look at the atrocities and massacres in Spain and Algiers! And in the midst of the accounts of so many calamities weighing heavily on the poor peoples and filling our soul with sadness, we find for consolation, recounted in great detail, the festivals, pleasures, and joys of the aristocracy!

"One day I read, in a speech given at the opening of the Houses of Parliament, that the people are happy, and that the government is wise, highly esteemed, loved, and adored. Satisfaction, confidence, and peace reign everywhere. The next day I am astonished to read about horrifying poverty, awful conspiracies, shouts of alarm, and intimidating and terrorizing laws. Outside of Icaria, I see only contradictions and lies, confusion and chaos, oppression and misfortunes. I know full well that this is the inevitable result of your bad social organizations; however, I do not understand your two countries, my dear Eugene and my dear Milord.

"I can understand England a little. I can understand how an ancient group of aristocrats—who have all the fortune and all the power in their hands, who keep the king dependent on them, and who condemn princes, queens, and uncooperative ministers to death—are skillful enough to handle the people and permit them certain freedoms. I understand that this aristocracy would be difficult to uproot, particularly because the country is organized aristocratically at its very foundation. The people have been used to prostrating themselves before their lords for a long time. These people are not bothered and annoyed daily; they have no experience in the use of firearms; and the Popular Party has some measure of victory each year, which gives the population some satisfaction and encourages it to remain patient.

"But France! I see those she called heroes of July or of the barricades arrested, imprisoned, convicted, exiled, and thrown into irons! Hasn't the person who was called 'the People's Choice' been attacked by riots and conspiracies? Don't the electors choose enemies of the revolution? Don't the jurists condemn popular writers?"

"Can you imagine," I said, begging him to excuse my interruption, "that the jurists convicted our Eugene because he said, after the volleys of shots that occurred in June and, two months earlier, in April, that the powers that be had decided to fire into the crowds of rioters? His case was the same as that of Galileo, who was convicted for saying that the earth revolves around the sun!"

"And when I look into it more fully," the old man began again, "I can see France going from feudal royalty to constitutional monarchy, and then to the republic, only to fall back into the empire and then the Restoration. I can see France getting back on her feet in 1830, shaking the whole world with the sound of her civic glory, just as she had shaken the whole world earlier with the sound of her military glory, only to fall back almost immediately into the state from which she had just emerged. For the last forty-seven years, I have seen France giving to other peoples the example of revolutions, provoking them to imitate her, and then abandoning them when her provocations and her example have dragged them into their own conflicts. I see her making heroic efforts and immense sacrifices to win equality and even possessing it for quite a few years, only to let herself be suppressed by the aristocracy. She allowed the aristocracy to give her only one hundred fifty thousand electors out of thirty-three million French people and to rob her of her rights of association and assembly, freedom of the press, and even trial by jury. Finally, she allowed herself to be prostrate once more at the feet of a master. And if that master took it into his head to 'play the lion,' I would not be surprised to see, one day, in one of your newspapers, the president of your deputies, kneeling before him, say to him, like in the fable:

> And you, Sire, heaped much honor upon them
> By eating them!

I am truly sorry, my dear Eugene, that this picture causes you pain, but I do not understand France, or, rather, I understand only too well that she has disgraced herself."

"Yes, you are breaking my heart!" cried Eugene, with tears in his eyes. "You make me blush with shame! Those miserable cowards! How I scorn them, how I despise them, how I would like to. . . ! But what am I saying? What blasphemy! No, no! That is not the true France, my country, my country that I still love and that I will always cherish! Do not stop at the surface or let yourself be fooled by appearances, my venerable friend! There are two Frances, democratic France and aristocratic France. In 1789, in 1792, under the republic, under the consulate, under the empire, under the Restoration, in 1830 and since, you can see those two Frances. One is brave, courageous, thirsty for progress, justice, and freedom, and is a friend to all other peoples. The other is egotistic, hungry for riches and power, frightened, and cruel. The first has made all the revolutions by shedding her blood. The second has made all the counterrevolutions by spending money. The people let their victory be torn from them because they are too confident and too passionate. The aristocrats have been able to conjure away the revolution so often because they always use ruse and perfidy, renegades and traitors, and even foreign bayonets. Let us give esteem and respect, honor and glory to democratic France! And to that aristocratic France . . . Once again, no! For the two Frances are but one nation, divided by despotism that wishes to reign and victimized by the confusion and chaos that produce the vices of its political and social organization. Would not Icaria still resemble France today if it had not had the luck to possess Icar? And would France not resemble Icaria now, if Napoleon or if the prince who emerged from the barricades had possessed the character and will of Icar?"

"But, my dear Eugene," I said to him, "if France is so backward and England so forward, is this not the result of the difference in their national character, one passionate but light and inconstant, the other cold but prudent and persevering?"

"Keep quiet, my dear William, keep quiet! Do not boast of your representative government, which represents only your aristocracy; for your people, submerged in the most frightful poverty, have no real representatives, and the word *people* that you use so often and so pompously is nothing more than a deception and a lie! Do not boast of your freedom for the people, for that freedom does not help them in the slightest to escape their poverty, and your aristocracy knows full well how to steal from the people their rights of freedom of the press, association, and assembly when they begin to become threatening. The aristocracy even has the people slashed by saber and shot by its mercenaries when they dare to have recourse to rioting! Do not boast of being more advanced than we are, for in the areas of philosophy, habits and manners, aristocratic and religious prejudices, and, above all, equality, which is the principal point, your English people are half a century behind our French people. It is true that we are more suppressed. Our aristocracy is more oppressive, and our democracy more oppressed. But why is this the case? It is because our people and our youth have more freedom in their souls, because they are more demanding, because we are in a situation that is essentially revolutionary, because our aristocracy is sitting on a volcano that threatens every day to erupt and swallow it up. If the French people had retained their freedom of the press and their right of association, which the English aristocracy does not fear in the least to grant to its English people, they would already have won back all the rights of which they were deprived. We are enslaved by a free aristocracy, but our enslavement is only temporary. We protest and we resist. Sooner or later, the true principles will triumph as they have triumphed so often, and then we will be half a century ahead of you.

"And if it were true that you were in advance of us, would you not owe that position to France, which has kept you awake since 1789, which pricked your conscience in 1830, and which provided you with your parliamentary reform, your only real progress in the last hundred and fifty years? And if it were true that France has fallen behind, is it fitting that an Englishman reproach her for this when, for forty-seven years, she has made so many heroic efforts and sacrifices to free herself, when the English aristocracy has bribed or supported her enemies for those forty-seven years, and when that same aristocracy supports all nascent despotic governments?

"But, my dear William, let us take care not to blame each other! Let us never confuse our two peoples with their aristocracies and governments! Let us never confuse in our hatred men and institutions! English people and French people, victims one and all of aristocratic domination and of the vices of social organization; let us march in concert and in brotherhood to free ourselves and other peoples! Let us endeavor to imitate Icaria, for our happiness and for that of humanity!"

Eugene's noble emotions gave such pleasure to Icar's old friend that he squeezed his hand several times and ended by embracing him tenderly.

39 Milord's Marriage Plans Set

Today was the outing on the water that we had planned for so long. Approximately thirty-six of us arrived at the banks of the Tair, and we got into a small ship, or, rather, a large boat in which we would be the only passengers; there are boats of all sizes and every family or group can obtain one by reserving it a few days in advance. The smallest boats are propelled by oars, but almost all of the others are driven by steam or other mechanical means. All are charming to behold: painted, decked with banners, and fitted with elegantly decorated awnings.

The weather was superb. The whole river was full of boats and presented to the eye the most animated, varied, and delightful spectacle. We had, however, an even more admirable spectacle, that of the two banks and of the landscape on either side, where art and nature vied for the prize for beautification, for it is the republic that, for the pleasure of its walkers and its voyagers, has the countryside on the banks of rivers and roads landscaped, just as a rich property owner has his park and his garden laid out. But nothing, I think, can compare to the delights of the flowering island where we disembarked after an hour's sail and where we spent the day in games, songs, and laughter. Everything combined to inspire within us thoughts of happiness, so we held a great conference on our loves and our futures.

It was in vain that Valmor—persevering in his victory over himself, taking ineffable joy in his noble devotion, and seeming to take pleasure in strengthening our feelings—had been encouraging Dinaïse and me every day to consent to his project of a triple marriage. We wished to make no definite decision until we had proof that our union would not cause misery either to Valmor or to Miss Henriet. However, two letters that I had received from England the day before helped Valmor to renew his entreaties more energetically. He assured us that he was not so wretched a creature as to run the risk of making a woman unhappy, and that he was certain to find happiness twice over, first in his own marriage and then in witnessing our blissful state. He sought to convince us so fervently that we finally allowed ourselves to be persuaded. When the question was put to a vote, it was unanimously decided, in the midst of transports of joy, that our three marriages would be celebrated on the same day in two months time. Dinaïse made only one stipulation, which was unanimously applauded: that I declare myself a supporter of the community, and that I dedicate my influence and my fortune to spreading it abroad. Before she had finished speaking, I had already replied that with her by my side, I would be the most formidable propagandist. She then added a second stipulation, which met with the same applause: that I bring her back every second year to her mother, her family, and her friends. However, one obstacle remained. The law does not permit a female Icarian to marry a foreigner until he has first obtained a form of naturalization that does not require him to renounce his affiliation to his native land. The law authorizes this naturalization only for a foreigner who has rendered some great service to the republic. Valmor's grandfather assured us that spreading the word in England about the community would be considered as one of the greatest services that a foreigner could render to Icaria. He would undertake to obtain my naturalization.

We were returning full of joy and were already nearing Icara when a sudden accident threw us into a state of fright. One of the little girls, seven years of age, fell into the water. Two of the young boys, one of them ten and the other twelve years old, and even Eugene, were about to rush to her aid when Valmor threw himself into the water, shouting that we should neither move nor have any fear. Dinaros jumped in at almost the same time, after making sure that the boat had been stopped and had been rowed backward, and after telling me to take up the pole and rope and to get ready to hand him either one. Then, at the sound of a little bell installed for the purpose, all the neighboring boats hastened to the various points the body might reach. All this assistance was unnecessary, however, and Valmor and Dinaros did not even have the satisfaction of saving the little girl, whom they were careful not to touch when they saw her reappear in the water and swim without fear or danger. Her mother scolded her gently while embracing her, and people even laughed at the fear that had shown on my face because they were not unaware that the child could swim and that she was in no danger with a diver like Dinaros and a swimmer like Valmor.

40 Women

We were reunited and joyous when Valmor saw Eugene coming through the garden. I quickly said to the women, "Do you want me to tease him to make you laugh? I will get him onto the subject of women, and you will see how he heats up!"

"Yes, yes," cried Corilla and her companions.

"Ah! Here is the gallant Frenchman," I said, laughing.

"And here is the perfidious Englishman," he replied, holding out his hand after greeting everyone graciously.

"And why perfidious?"

"And why gallant?

"What? Are you not gallant?"

"Well, no . . . yes."

"Well, which one are you?"

"Listen! One day an old flirt who had rouged her cheeks was indignant that a young man did not compliment her on the freshness of her complexion. Next, she was annoyed that he did not rush to pick up the glove that she had dropped on purpose. 'How ungallant he is!' she said disdainfully. And so you see, naughty Milord, that what you call French gallantry is not gallantry at all."

"Oh! It was you! And you are like those Icarian gentlemen who think they are lost if they offer the slightest compliment to their wives and dishonored if they speak sweet nothings to them!"

"And that is why you claim that Icarians are ungallant! The Icarians are right! And if these ladies were not here, I would say . . ."

"Say it anyway. These ladies give you leave to do so."

"I would say that when there are women present . . . when we can speak the truth . . ."

"How muddled you become, my poor Eugene, when you try to defend a bad cause!"

"Well, yes, the Icarians are right. They practice true gallantry, not that of lips and words, but that of deeds; not that which suits the inanity of idle whipper-snappers and ludicrous coquettes, but that gallantry that honors both those who practice it and those who inspire it. The Icarians love women, worship them, idolize them."

"How you do go on!"

"They embellish them, they perfect them and strive continuously and in every way to make them happy so that they may in turn get back all the happiness they have given."

"How impassioned you are becoming!"

"I judge men's feelings toward women not on vain flattery and childish adulation, but on what is provided for them: education and improved conditions in the workshop, at home, and everywhere. That is why I affirm, and I will always affirm, that Icarian men are gallant."

"That is your right. As for me, I assert the contrary!"

"Here, we never see husbands amusing themselves together in clubs or elsewhere while their wives are idle at home. We never see a man snatching up the best seat, thus depriving a woman who might need it."

"But in what savage country have you seen such brutishness?"

"Rarely in my country, and often in another country Milord knows well and that is starting to improve. Here, I see that a brother is almost as gallant toward his sister as men are elsewhere toward their mistresses. And I see even more. I see what I have always regretted never seeing anywhere else; I see everyone here applying that principle containing within it all morality: 'Do unto others as you would have others do unto you.' I see every man treat the women in other families as he would like other men to treat his mother or daughter, his wife or sister. As depraved as we are in other countries, there is not a man who is not ready to risk his life to defend the honor not only of his wife and daughter, but of his mother and sister. However, how few of us have respect and consideration for the mothers and sisters of other men! And why should ours be treated better than theirs? In the same vein, we see young men pay excessive attention to young, pretty women but generally neglect older women. Here, young men are just as respectful of and devoted to all old women as they are to their mothers, to all women of their own age group as they are to their sisters. Yes, Mister Fashionable, the Icarian people are the most gallant people on earth" (The ladies applaud.)

"These ladies are too polite to contradict you, particularly in the presence of these gentlemen; but is it not said that Paris is a 'women's paradise'?"

"Yes, that paradise should be in Paris, in France; but today, if Paris is a paradise for a few pretty young favorites of fortune and the aristocracy (and, yes, what a paradise!), is it not a hell for great numbers of unhappy women of the people? Here, on the other hand, Icarian women, all Icarian women, find paradise in their own country. They are cherished and protected in their spring and summer, and doted on and respected in their autumn and winter, forever secure and happy!" (Renewed applause from the women.)

"These ladies will not dare admit it, but do you not find that Icarian gentlemen are a trifle selfish and jealous not to allow their wives to go out without them to shows or in society?"

"Yes, it would be tyrannical if they sought pleasure without their wives; but as they themselves never go out for amusement without their wives, as they have no separate pleasures, as they share all their pleasures with them and find their own happiness in making their wives happy, they are right a thousand times over! The husband who allows his wife the possibility of finding pleasure with another man is neither her protector nor her friend, but an unfaithful wretch and almost her enemy, if he is not mad. Do you understand me?"

"So you approve when Icarians insist that their wives save their most elegant clothing for their meetings with their husbands?"

"Certainly! Here education habituates a wife to be happy when she flirts with no man other than her husband, and I compliment both husbands and wives most sincerely on this behavior, which seems to me the essence of reason. And if I did not fear to humiliate you in front of these ladies, I would say that it is the Icarian women who" (whispered in my ear) "know love and its celestial delights better than any other women."

"Oh! Do not fear to humiliate me! Speak aloud, gallant Frenchman who seems to me as selfish and jealous as Icarian men. As for me, I would rather have my wife follow the English or, rather, the Parisian fashion."

"What? You would permit your wife to be kissed in what are called innocent games?"

"And why not? What harm could there be in my asking you to accompany my wife to the Bois de Boulogne when I am not available? Is that not the height of civilization? Yes, my dear friend, you will be my deputy and her escort. You will waltz at the ball with her and ride at a gallop with her. You will kiss her innocently in innocent games and defend her against the admirers who might annoy her with their flattery. You will save her for me as you would do for yourself and will give great pleasure to her as well as to me, for I wish only her happiness. And what danger can there be for her to be with you, my best friend?"

"What danger? What danger? For her, there would certainly be none, of course, because she would inspire such great respect. But what if the touch of the sun were to ignite everything around it?"

"Well then, you would throw yourself into the water to put out the fire."

"You are trying to make these ladies laugh." (In fact, they were laughing a great deal.) "But all joking aside, answer me! What if the brilliance of the sun . . ."

"You are a flatterer, and I will not let my wife go out anymore with you! But, on the other hand, why not? You can see that your flatteries have made her turn red with anger!"

"I know full well that it is not wise to state all truths, and I know people who take vengeance most rudely on he who tells the truth; but I also know braver souls, and I hope to receive your pardon for my temerity. Moreover, I am a fool to answer all your jokes in bad taste. Your wife would be wiser than you; and if the Englishman had the folly to will it, the Icarian woman would have the wisdom not to permit it."

"To deny? Would I not be the master? Do not the laws of the gallant French themselves categorically order the wife to obey her husband?" (All the women cried out.)

"That is true, just as the laws of the wise English permit the husband to lead his wife, a rope around her neck, to the cattle market and to sell her on the block, as one would a miscreant lamb, for the price of six cents!" ("Oh, how horrid, how dreadful!" echoed voices on all sides.)

"But our law dates back to barbaric times, whereas yours was just enacted in the century of civilization and enlightenment!"

"It is nonetheless a shameful law, made by a despot who wished to impose upon women obedience to marital despotism, in order to set the stage for the husbands' obedience to imperial despotism."

"Would Mister Gallant prefer that the husband obey the wife?"

"No, Mister Joker. In that case, you would appear ridiculous, and I am sure that your wife is too reasonable and knows her own interest too well to want her husband to make a laughing stock of himself; but I would like the law to proclaim, as it does in Icaria, equality between spouses, with the husband's voice merely carrying the most weight; and I would like the law to do everything it does here to ensure that spouses always be in accord and happy together."

"But is your law of obedience not necessary in a country where one of the greatest lords said to the queen herself that there was not a single woman who could not be seduced by gold?"

"And you believe that slanderous remark, repeated by your beautiful 'ladies' who call themselves wiser because they take their prudery to the extreme of blushing if one commits the horrid indecency of pronouncing the most innocuous words in front of them? (It would be indecent to pronounce the words *shirt* or *chicken thigh* in front of an English lady.) Well, tell your lords to bring all their guineas here to try and seduce a single Icarian lady!"

"Yes, but France is not Icaria!"

"Alas, how well I know that! That is what enrages me: seeing our bad social organization making so many French women so miserable! It is for those French women above all that I passionately desire the republic and the community, which would bring all of them as much happiness as the lucky women of Icaria already possess!"

41 Foreign Relations
Project of Communal Association

Every day the foreigners, dining together at their hotel, told each other what they were learning about Icaria and discussed whether the system whose marvelous results they were seeing might be applicable in their respective countries. Unanimous in their admiration, they were far from agreeing about the possibility and the means of applying these principles elsewhere. Contradictory arguments often became so impassioned that they degenerated into disputes. Many said: "Communal ownership of goods, organized as we see it here, is, without a doubt, the most perfect of all social organizations, and someday it will bring happiness to the entire world. No one desires it more strongly than I do, and I would stand up for it today if the others would do the same, but we are not yet virtuous enough, and only our children will have the good fortune to enjoy it."

"I agree," said another. "I would dedicate my fortune and my life to it, but . . ." This nasty *but* kept cropping up.

Eugene, who was breaking lances every day in support of the community, and whose ardor in preaching the gospel had earned him the soubriquet of the *Icaria-maniac*, had the idea of getting together all the foreigners in Icaria in a room where they could discuss and vote on the matter. "You will see," he said to me, "that if we can get them to vote, almost all the *buts* will change to *yeas*, and we might perhaps arrive at a practical result, for it is shameful that the community has created such happiness in Icaria for so long and that the foreigners have done nothing to propagate it in their own countries. . . . Let us be the first to set an example! Let us act!"

We conveyed his idea to a few of the most important foreigners, notably to an old and venerable Scottish missionary called Father Francis, who was renowned for his wisdom. He approved of Eugene's project, and he suggested that we obtain the support of several influential Icarians before our meeting. We spoke about it to Valmor's grandfather that very evening. He embraced us almost joyfully and took the opportunity to inform us about Icaria's relations with foreign peoples.

Foreign Relations

"After having proclaimed the principle of fraternity between Icaria and all other peoples," the old man said to us, "Icar and the republic rejected not a single one of the consequences of this principle. Never did they do anything that would wound a foreign people. Never did they refuse a requested service that they could provide; and the greater the debt owed them, the less they made their superiority felt. But Icar's foremost principle was, in addition, to interfere as little as possible in the affairs of our neighbors, to leave them to themselves, to do nothing to accelerate among them the establishment of the community. He was convinced that Icaria was the country where the experiment would best succeed to the benefit of all nations, and we feared that failed attempts in other countries would compromise the Icarian experiment.

"One of Icar's most insistent recommendations, therefore, was that we occupy ourselves exclusively with our own affairs until the community was perfectly organized at home. Far from pushing our neighbors to hasten their progressive steps, we used our influence to encourage their leaders to moderate their ardor. And our influence was great, for we never had a thought of conquest. We did not even want to incorporate a small people enclosed within our natural borders that asked to become part of us, and it was only after persistent importuning, repeated over a period of several years, and with the spontaneous consent of our other neighbors that we fulfilled its wishes while declaring that we would not admit any other addition.

"We contented ourselves with close alliances, friendly and fraternal relations, trade agreements, good offices of all kinds, and an annual congress to facilitate our mutual dealings, above all those pertaining to our colonies. But today we are strong enough to apply more widely our principal of fraternity, and I have no doubt that all my fellow citizens are ready to facilitate the establishment of community everywhere. It is with this end in mind that we have recently taken several measures to attract foreigners here; and Valmor has just proposed, in his Popular Assembly, to enlarge the hotel set aside to accommodate them. But it is necessary that foreigners help themselves, and I note with great pleasure our young friend Eugene's idea, just as I welcomed with great pleasure Milord's arrival.

"Meet, discuss, discuss some more, and even form associations if you can! Yes, strive to organize a great association of foreigners of all countries in favor of community. If you succeed, I guarantee you the support of Icaria; at least, I will do everything in my power to obtain that support for you.

"Come to an agreement, then, with your companions so that they will want to meet together and consider your projects. I will be responsible for getting a room for your meetings."

Such well-wishing words and such flattering promises from an old friend of Icar, revered in Icara and in all parts of Icaria (for we were aware every day of new proofs of the veneration that Valmor's grandfather inspired), gave so much hope and pleasure to Eugene that we thought he was going to go out of his mind.

42 First Deliberations on the Association Proposal

When our project was communicated by our venerable friend, it was welcomed with so much interest that one of the largest popular meeting rooms was assigned to us and a large number of Icarian notables, both deputies and others, promised to be present at our meeting. This singular session, announced for several days in the national newspaper with the strongest expressions of approval and sympathy, has just taken place.

The president opened the discussion after setting out the purpose of the meeting and indicating the interest that it had generated in the republic. All of the orators expressed their admiration and enthusiasm for the organization of the *Society for Association* in Icaria. Nevertheless, we heard a flood of objections, *ifs* and *buts*, and the conference was dragging on without conclusion or result when Eugene, who had wished to let the others speak first, asked for the floor and pronounced these few words:

"We all know Icaria, and we do not need a long speech to assess the value of its organization. I ask, therefore, that we start by requesting the assembly's opinion on this question: Do you wish to implement Icaria's social organization in your own country? We will proceed from there."

The assembly approved the question with the amendment that only those foreigners who had been here for more than ten days would be eligible to vote. The question was put and voted upon by standing and sitting. We had hoped for a four-fifths majority. Imagine our astonishment when we saw the assembly rise as a single man in favor of the Icarian system. The joy was so great and tumultuous that the president felt it a good idea to suspend the session for a moment. It seemed that the assembly had just decided the fate of the universe. Thus men exaggerate their own importance and their power as soon as they are assembled together!

Eugene, beside himself, was shouting in the middle of a group: "If all my fellow countrymen knew Icaria like we do, and if they were assembled together as we are, I am convinced that the whole of France would reply as we did that she desires community." Each person made the same assertion for his own country.

"If the entire human race were assembled together in this room," cried a voice raised above the others, "that human race would choose to establish the republic and community!"

"And humanity would soon have it!" added another stentorian voice.

A quarter of an hour later the president reopened the session and proposed this question: "Is the system applicable?" and asked if anyone wished to speak against this proposition. We had certainly expected to encounter some opposition on the question of applicability. Nevertheless, we were amazed at the great number of people who stood up to give reasons for their opposition. The debate could not possibly be concluded during this session because the opponents were too numerous; it therefore was postponed until another day, and a commission was chosen and charged with submitting a report.

We had already achieved a great victory by obtaining the solemn declaration that the foreigners assembled in Icaria wished to implement the community in their own countries, and we hoped to convert many of the opponents on the question of applicability. Our hopes were raised even higher when, at the advice and invitation of Valmor's grandfather, Dinaros consented to give for foreigners the next morning a short course on the history of Icaria, or, rather, on the history of the establishment of the community.

END OF PART ONE

Etienne Cabet (1788–1856) was a French utopian socialist, politician, and newspaper editor. *Voyage en Icarie* served to propel his economic, social, and political theories.

Leslie Roberts is translator and coeditor, with historian Michael Chesson, of *Exile in Richmond: The Confederate Journal of Henri Garidel* (2001), which recently won the Founders Award from the Museum of the Confederacy (Virginia). She has published articles on nineteenth- and twentieth-century French and Fran- cophone writers. She is professor of French at the University of Southern Indi- ana in Evansville. She is currently under contract with the Miami Tribe of Oklahoma and the Miami Nation of Indiana to translate the 1690 Illinois/ Algonquian to French manuscript dictionary attributed to Jesuit Father Gravier.

Robert Sutton is a professor of history and the director of the Center for Icar- ian Studies at Western Illinois University. He has served on the board of direc- tors for the Communal Studies Association. He published *Les Icariens: The Utopian Dream in Europe and America* (1994) and collaborated with Michel Cordillot in editing *La sociale en Amérique: Dictionnaire biographique du Mouve- ment Social Francophone aux Etats-Unis (1848–1922)* (2002). He has published many articles on the Icarian communities. His two-volume study *Communal Utopias and the American Experience* is being published in 2003 and 2004.